INVOLUNTARY SERVITUDE

Though he was almost too weak to speak, Sun Wolf asked, "Did you kidnap my men, too?"

Sheera's back stiffened, but she answered steadily, "Only you."

"To free all your men from the Wizard King single-handed?"

"We'll raise a strike force—the ladies of Mandrigyn. We're bringing you back to teach us the arts of war."

"Woman," he told her, "you couldn't pay me enough to go against Altiokis with a troop of skirts commanded by a female maniac like you."

The ugly woman spoke for the first time. "There was anzid in the water you drank. I can arrest the effects of the poison from day to day by spells. And when the city is free, you will be given the true antidote. Otherwise..."

The shock of it cut off his breath like a garrote. Anzid deaths took days—and the victims never ceased screaming!

By Barbara Hambly
Published by Ballantine Books:

THE DARWATH TRILOGY
The Time of the Dark
The Walls of Air
The Armies of Daylight

The Ladies of Mandrigyn

Barbara Hambly

A Del Rey Book

BALLANTINE BOOKS • NEW YORK

A Del Rey Book
Published by Ballantine Books

Copyright © 1984 by Barbara Hambly

All rights reserved under International and Pan-American Copyright Conventions. Published in the United States by Ballantine
Books, a division of Random House, Inc., New York, and simultaneously in Canada by Random House of Canada Limited,
Toronto.

Library of Congress Catalog Card Number: 83-91245

ISBN 0-345-30919-7

Manufactured in the United States of America

First Edition: March 1984

Cover art by Darrell K. Sweet

Map by Shelly Shapiro

To my fellow members of the
West Coast Karate Association
BROAD SQUAD

Anne
Gayle
Helen
Sherrie
Janet
Georgia

With love.

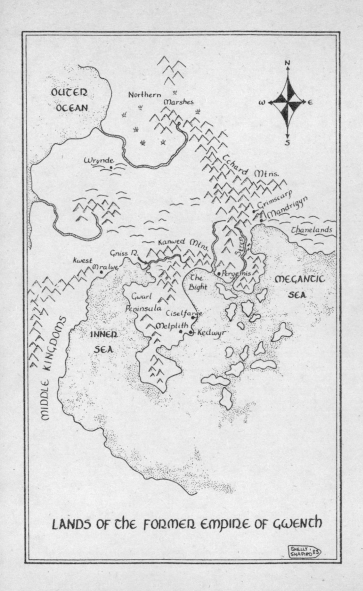

LANDS OF THE FORMER EMPIRE OF GWENTH

CHAPTER

—— 1 ——

"*W*HAT IN THE NAME OF THE COLD HELLS IS THIS?*" SUN* Wolf held the scrap of unfolded paper between stubby fingers that were still slightly stained with blood.

Starhawk, his tall, rawboned second-in-command, glanced up from cleaning the grime of battle off the hilt of her sword and raised dark, level brows inquiringly. Outside, torchlight reddened the windy night. The camp was riotous with the noise of victory; the mercenaries of Wrynde and the troops of the City of Kedwyr were uninhibitedly celebrating the final breaking of the siege of Melplith.

"What's it look like?" she asked reasonably.

"It looks like a poxy proposition." He handed it to her, the amber light of the oil lamp overhead falling over his body, naked to the waist and glittering with a light curly rug of gold hair. Starhawk had been fighting under his command for long enough to know that, if he had actually thought it nothing more than a proposition, he would have put it in the fire without a word.

Sun Wolf, Commander of the Mercenaries, Camp of Kedwyr below the walls of Melplith, from Sheera Galernas of Mandrigyn, greetings. I will be coming to you in your tent tonight with a matter of interest to you. For my sake and that of my cause, please be alone, and speak to no one of this. Sheera.

"Woman's handwriting," Starhawk commented, and ran her thumb consideringly along the gilt edge of the expensive paper.

Sun Wolf looked at her sharply from beneath his curiously

1

tufted brows. "If she wasn't from Mandrigyn, I'd say it was the local madam trying to drum up business."

Starhawk nodded in absent-minded agreement.

Outside the tent, the noise scaled up into a crescendo. Boozy catcalls mixed with cries of encouragement and yells of "Kill him! Kill the bastard!" Between the regular troops of the City of Kedwyr and the City's Outland Militia Levies, a lively hatred existed, perhaps stronger than the feeling that either body of warriors had toward the hapless citizen-soldiers of the besieged town of Melplith. It was a conflict that the Wolf and his mercenaries had stayed well clear of—the Wolf because he made it his policy never to get involved in local politics, and his men because of a blood-chilling directive from their captain on the subject. The noises of drunken murder did not concern him—there wasn't a man in his troop who would have so much as stayed to watch.

"Mandrigyn," Starhawk said thoughtfully. "Altiokis conquered that city last spring, didn't he?"

Sun Wolf nodded and settled himself into a fantastic camp chair made of staghorn bound with gold, looted from some tribal king in the far northeast. Most of the big tent's furnishings had been plundered from somewhere or other. The peacock hangings that separated it into two rooms had once adorned the bedroom of a prince of the K'Chin Desert. The cups of translucent, jade-green lacquer and gold had belonged to a merchant on the Bight Coast. The graceful ebony table, its delicate inlays almost hidden under the bloody armor that had been dumped upon it, had once graced the wine room of a gentlemanly noble of the Middle Kingdoms, before his precious vintages had been swilled by the invading armies of his enemies and he himself had been dispatched beyond such concerns.

"The city went fast," Sun Wolf remarked, picking up a rag and setting to work cleaning his own weapons. "Basically, it was the same situation as we had here in Melplith—factional splits in the parliament, scandal involving the royal family— they have a royal family there, or they did have, anyway— the city weakened by internal fighting before Altiokis marched down the pass. I'm told there were people there who welcomed him as a liberator."

Starhawk shrugged. "No weirder than some of the things the Trinitarian heretics believe," she joked, deadpan, and he grinned. Like most northerners, the Hawk held to the Old Faith against the more sophisticated theologies of the Triple God.

"The Wizard King's Citadel has been on Mandrigyn's back doorstep for a hundred and fifty years," the Wolf continued after a moment. "Last year they signed some kind of treaty with him. I could see it coming even then."

Starhawk shoved her sword back into its sheath and wiped her fingers on a rag. Sun Wolf's talent for collecting and sorting information was uncanny, but it was a skill that served him well. He had a knack for gathering rumors, extrapolating political probabilities from crop prices and currency fluctuations and the most trivial bits of information that made their way north to his broken-down stronghold at the old administrative town of Wrynde. Thus he and his men had been on the spot in the Gwarl Peninsula when the fighting had broken out between the trading rivals of Kedwyr and Melplith. Kedwyr had hired the Wolf and his troop at an astronomical sum.

It didn't always work that way—in her eight years as a mercenary in Sun Wolf's troop, Starhawk had seen one or two spectacular pieces of mistiming—but on the whole it had enabled the Wolf to maintain his troops in better-than-average style, fighting in the summer and sitting out the violence of the winter storms in the relative comfort of the half-ruined town of Wyrnde.

Like all mercenary troops, Sun Wolf's shifted from year to year in size and composition, though they centered around a hard core that had been with him for years. As far as Starhawk knew, Sun Wolf was the only mercenary captain who operated a regular school of combat in the winter months. The school itself was renowned throughout the West and the North for the excellence of its fighters. Every winter, when the rains made war impossible, young men and occasional young women made the perilous journey through the northern wastelands that had once been the agricultural heart of the old Empire of Gwenth to the ruined and isolated little town of Wyrnde, there to ask to be taught the hard arts of war.

There were always wars to fight somewhere. Since the moribund Empire of Gwenth had finally been riven apart by the conflict between the Three Gods and the One, there had always been wars—over the small bits of good land among the immense tracts of bad, over the trade with the East in silk and amber and spices, over religion, or over nothing. Starhawk, whose early training had given her a taste for such things, had once explained the theology behind the Schism to the Wolf. Being a barbarian from the far north, he worshipped the spirits of his ancestors and would cheerfully take money from proponents of either faith. An understanding of the situation had only amused him, as she knew it would. Lately the wars had been over the rising of the Wizard King Altiokis, who was expanding his own empire from the dark Citadel of Grimscarp, engulfing the Thanes who ruled the countryside and such cities as Mandrigyn.

"Will you see this woman from Mandrigyn?" she asked.

"Probably." The noise of the fight outside peaked in a crazy climax of yelling, punctuated by the heavy crack of the whips of the Kedwyr military police. It was the fourth fight they'd heard since returning to the camp after the sacking of the town was done; victory was headier than any booze ever brewed.

Starhawk collected her gear—sword, dagger, mail shirt—preparatory to returning to her own tent. Melplith stood on high ground, above its sheltered bay—one of those arid regions whose chief crops of citrus and olives had naturally turned its inhabitants to trade for their living. Chill winds now blew up from the choppy waters of the bay, making the lampflame flicker in its topaz glass and chilling her flesh through the damp cotton of her dark, embroidered shirt.

"You think it's a job?"

"I think she'll offer me one."

"Will you take it?"

The Wolf glanced over at her briefly. His eyes, in this light, were pale gold, like the wines of the Middle Kingdoms. He was close to forty, and his tawny hair was thinning, but there was no gray either in it or in the ragged mustache that drooped like a clump of yellow-brown winter weeds from the underside of a craggy and much-bent nose. The power and thickness of his chest and shoulders made him seem taller than his six feet when he was standing up; seated and at rest, he reminded her of a big, dusty lion. "Would you go against Altiokis?" he asked her.

She hesitated, not speaking her true answer to that. She had heard stories of the Wizard King since she was a tiny girl—bizarre, distorted tales of his conquests, his sins, and his greed. Horrible tales were told of what happened to those who had opposed him, over the timeless years of his uncanny existence.

Her true answer, the one she did not say aloud, was: *Yes, if you wanted me to.*

What she said was, "Would you?"

He shook his head. "I'm a soldier," he said briefly. "I'm

no wizard. I couldn't go against a wizard, and I wouldn't take my people against one. There are two things that my father always told me, if I wanted to live to grow old—don't fall in love and don't mess with magic."

"Three things," Starhawk corrected, with one of her rare, fleeting grins. "Don't argue with fanatics."

"That comes under magic. Or arguing with drunks, I'm not sure which. I don't understand how there could be one God or three Gods or five or more, but I do know that I had ancestors, drunken, lecherous clowns that they were . . . Hello, sweetpea."

The curtain that divided the tent parted, and Fawn came in, brushing the last dampness from the heavy curls of her mink-brown hair. The pale green gauze of her gown made her eyes seem greener, almost emerald. She was Sun Wolf's latest concubine, eighteen, and heartbreakingly beautiful. "Your bath's ready," she said, coming behind the camp chair where he sat to kiss the thin spot in his hair at the top of his head.

He took her hand where it lay on his shoulder and, with a curiously tender gesture for so large and rough-looking a man, he pressed his lips to the white skin of her wrist. "Thanks," he said. "Hawk, will you wait for a few minutes? If this skirt wants to see me alone, would you take Fawn over to your tent for a while?"

Starhawk nodded. She had seen a series of his girls come and go, all of them beautiful, soft-spoken, pliant, and a little helpless. The camp tonight, after the sacking of the town, was no place for a girl not raised to killing, even if she was the mistress of a man like Sun Wolf.

"So you're receiving ladies alone in your tent now, are you?" Fawn chided teasingly.

With a movement too swift to be either fought or fled, he was out of his chair, catching her up, squeaking, in his arms as he rose. She wailed, "Stop it! No! I'm sorry!" as he bore her off through the curtain into the other room, her squeals scaling up into a desperate crescendo that ended in a monumental and steamy splash.

Without a flicker of an eyelid, Starhawk shouldered her war gear, called out, "I'll be back for you in an hour, Fawn," and departed; only when she was outside did she allow herself a small, amused grin.

She returned in company with Ari, a young man who was Sun Wolf's other lieutenant and who rather resembled an adolescent black bear. They bade the Wolf a grave good evening, collected the damp, subdued, and rather pink-cheeked Fawn, and made their way across the camp. The wind had risen again, cold off the sea with the promise of the winter's deadly storms; drifts of woodsmoke from the camp's fires blew into their eyes. Above them, the fires in the city flared, fanned by the renewed breezes, and a sulfurous glow outlined the black crenelations of the walls. The night tasted raw, wild, and strange, still rank with blood and broken by the wailing of women taken in the sacking of the town.

"Things settling down?" the Hawk asked.

Ari shrugged. "Some. The militia units are already drunk. Gradduck—that tin-pot general who commanded the City Troops—is taking all the credit for breaking the siege."

Starhawk feigned deep thought. "Oh, yes," she remembered at length. "The one the Chief said couldn't lay seige to a pothouse."

"No, no," Ari protested, "it wasn't a pothouse—an out-house..."

Voices yelled Ari's name, calling him to judge an athletic competition that was as indecent as it was ridiculous, and he laughed, waved to the women, and vanished into the darkness. Starhawk and Fawn continued to walk, the wind-torn torchlight banding their faces in lurid colors—the Hawk long-legged and panther-graceful in her man's breeches and doublet, Fawn shy as her namesake amid the brawling noise of the camp, keeping close to Starhawk's side. As they left the noisier precincts around the wine issue, the girl asked, "Is it true he's being asked to go against Altiokis?"

"He won't do it," Starhawk said. "Any more than he'd work for him. He was approached for that, too, years ago. He won't meddle with magic one way or the other, and I can't say that I blame him. Altiokis is news of the worst possible kind."

Fawn shivered in the smoky wind and drew the spiderweb silk of her shawl tighter about her shoulders. "Were they all like that? Wizards, I mean? Is that why they all—died out?"

In the feeble reflection of lamplight from the tents, her green eyes looked huge and transparent. Damp tendrils of hair clung to her cheeks; she brushed them aside, watching Starhawk worriedly. Like most people in the troop, she was a little in awe of that steely and enigmatic woman.

Starhawk ducked under the door flap of her tent, and held it aside for Fawn to pass. "I don't know if that's why the wizards finally died out," she said. "But I do know they weren't all evil like Altiokis. I knew a wizard once when I was a little girl. She was—very good."

Fawn stared at her in surprise that came partly from astonishment that Starhawk had ever been a little girl. In a way, it seemed inconceivable that she had ever been anything but what she was now: a tall, leggy cheetah of a woman, colorless as fine ivory—pale hair, pewter-gray eyes—save where the sun had darkened the fine-grained, flawless skin of her face and throat to burnt gold. Her light, cool voice was remarkably soft for a warrior's, though she was said to have a store of invective that could raise blisters on tanned oxhide. It was more believable of her that she had known a wizard than that she had been a little girl.

"I—I thought they were all gone, long before we were born."

"No," the Hawk said. The lamplight sparkled off the brass buckles that studded her sheepskin doublet as she fetched a skin of wine and two cups. Her tent was small and, like her, neat and spare. She had packed away her gear earlier. The only things remaining on the polished wood folding table were the gold-and-shell winecups and a pack of greasy cards. Starhawk was generally admitted to be a shark of poker—with her face, Fawn reflected, she could hardly be anything else.

"I thought that, too," Starhawk continued, coming back as Fawn seated herself on the edge of the narrow bed. "I didn't know Sister Wellwa was a wizard for—oh, years."

"She was a nun?" Fawn asked, startled.

Starhawk weighed her answer for a moment, as if picking her words carefully. Then she nodded. "The village where I grew up was built around the Convent of St. Cherybi in the West. Sister Wellwa was the oldest nun there—I used to see her every day, sweeping the paths outside with her broom made of sticks. As I said, I didn't know then that she was a wizard."

"How did you find out?" Fawn asked. "Did she tell you?"

"No." Starhawk folded herself into her chair. Like everything else in the tent, it was plain, bare, and easy to pack in a hurry. "The countryside around the village was very wild— I don't know if you're familiar with the West, but it's a land of rock and thin forest, rising toward the sea cliffs. A hard land. Dangerous, too. I'd gone into the woods to gather berries or something silly like that—something I wasn't supposed to do. I was probably escaping from my brothers. And—and there was a nuuwa."

Fawn shivered. She had seen nuuwa, dead, or at a distance.

It was possible, Starhawk thought, watching her, that she had also seen their victims.

"I ran," the Hawk continued unemotionally. "I was very young, I'd never seen one before, and I thought that, since it didn't have any eyes, it couldn't follow me. I must have thought at first that it was just an eyeless man. But it came after me, groaning and slobbering, crashing through the woods. I never looked back, but I could hear it behind me, getting closer as I came out of the woods. I ran through the rocks up the hill toward the Convent, and Sister Wellwa was outside, sweeping the path as she always was. And she—she raised her hand— and it was as if fire exploded from her fingers, a ball of red and blue fire that she flung at the nuuwa's head. Then she caught me up in her arms, and we ran together through the door and shut and bolted it. Later we found places where the nuuwa had tried to chew through the doorframe."

She was silent; if any of the horror of that memory stirred in her heart, it did not show on her fine-boned, enigmatic face. It was Fawn who shuddered and made a small, sickened noise in her throat.

"It was the only time I saw her do magic," Starhawk continued after a moment. "When I asked her about it later, she told me she had only grabbed me and carried me inside."

Across the rim of the untasted cup, Fawn studied the older woman for a moment more. Rumor in the camp had it that the Hawk had once been a nun herself, before she had elected to leave the Convent and follow the Wolf. Though Fawn had never believed it before, something in this story made her wonder if it might be true. There were elements of asceticism and mysticism in Starhawk; Fawn knew that she meditated daily, and the tent was certainly as barren as a nun's cell. Though a cold-blooded and ruthless warrior, the Hawk was never senselessly brutal—but then, few of the handful of women in Wolf's troop were.

It was on the tip of Fawn's tongue to ask her, but Starhawk was not a woman of whom one asked questions without permission. Besides, Fawn could think of no reason why anyone would have left the comforts of the Convent to follow the brutal trail of war.

Instead she asked, "Why did she lie?"

"The Mother only knows. She was a very old lady then— she died a year or so after, and I don't think anyone else in the Convent ever knew what she was."

Fawn's tapering fingers toyed with the cup, the diamonds of her rings winking like teardrops in the dim, golden light. Somewhere quite close, a drunken chorus in another tent began to sing.

"All in the town of Kedwyr,
A hundred years ago or more,
There lived a lass named Sella . . ."

"I have often wondered," Fawn said quietly, "about wizards. Why is Altiokis the only wizard left in the world? Why hasn't he died, in all these years? What happened to all the others?"

Starhawk shrugged. "The Mother only knows," she said again. As ever, her face gave away nothing; if it was a question that had ever crossed her mind, she did not show it. Instead she slapped the deck of cards before Fawn. "Bank?"

Fawn shuffled deftly despite her fashionably long, tinted fingernails. It was one of the first things she had learned when she'd been sold to Sun Wolf two years ago as a terrified virgin of sixteen—mostly in self-defense, since the Wolf and Starhawk were cutthroat card players.

Watching her, Starhawk reflected how out of place the girl looked here. Fawn—whose name had certainly been something else before she'd been kidnapped en route from her father's home in the Middle Kingdoms to a finishing school in Kwest Mralwe—had clearly been brought up in an atmosphere of taste and elegance. The clothes and jewelry she picked for herself spoke of it. Starhawk, though raised in an environment both countrified and austere, had done enough looting in the course of eight years of sieges to understand the difference between new-rich tawdriness and quality. Every line of Fawn spoke of fastidious taste and careful breeding, as much at odds with the nunlike barrenness of Starhawk's living quarters as she was with the rather barbaric opulence of the Chief's.

What had she been? the Hawk wondered. A nobleman's daughter? A merchant's? Those white hands, delicate amid their carefully chosen jewelry, had certainly never handled anything harsher than a man's flesh in all her life. *The loveliest that money could buy*, Starhawk thought, with a wry twinge of bitterness for the girl's sake—*whether she wanted to be bought or not*.

Fawn laid the cards down, undealt. In repose, her face looked suddenly tired. "What's going to become of him, Hawk?" she asked quietly.

Starhawk shrugged, deliberately misunderstanding. "I can't see the Chief being crazy enough to get mixed up in any affair having to do with magic," she began, and Fawn shook her head impatiently.

"It isn't just this," she insisted. "If he goes on as he's doing, he's going to slip up one day. He's the best, they say—but he's also forty. Is he going to go on leading troops into battle and wintering in Wrynde, until one day he's a little slow dodging some enemy's axe? If it isn't Altiokis, how long will it be before it's something else?"

Starhawk looked away from those suddenly luminous eyes. Rather gruffly, she said, "Oh, he'll probably conquer a city, make a fortune, and die stinking rich at the age of ninety. The old bastard's welfare isn't worth your losing sleep over."

Fawn laughed shakily at the picture presented, and they spoke of other things. But on the whole, as she dealt the cards, Starhawk wished that the girl had not touched that way upon her own buried forebodings.

Sun Wolf felt, rather than heard, the woman's soft tread outside his tent; he was watching the entrance when the flap was moved aside. The woman came in with the wild sea smell of the night.

With the lamps at his back, their light catching in his thinning, dust-colored hair and framing his face in gold, he did look like a sun wolf, the big, deadly, tawny hunter of the eastern steppes. The woman put back the hood from her hair.

"Sheera Galernas?" he asked quietly.

"Captain Sun Wolf?"

He gestured her to take the other chair. She was younger than he had thought, at most twenty-five. Her black hair curled thickly around a face that tapered from wide, delicate cheekbones to a pointed chin. Her lips, full almost to the corners of her mouth, were sensual and dark as the lees of wine. Her deep-set eyes seemed wine-colored, too, their lids stained violet from sleepless nights. She was tall for a woman and, as far as he could determine under the muffling folds of her cloak, well set up.

For a moment neither spoke. Then she said, "You're different from what I had thought."

"I can't apologize for that." He'd put on a shirt and breeches and a brown velvet doublet. The hair on the backs of his arms caught the light as he folded his strong, heavy hands.

She stirred in her chair, wary, watching him. He found himself wondering what it would be like to bed her and if the experiment would be worth the trouble it could cost. "I have a proposition for you," she said at last, meeting his eyes with a kind of anger, defying him to look at her face instead of her body.

"Most ladies who come to my tent do."

Her skin deepened to clay-red along the cheekbones and her nostrils flared a little, like a horse scenting battle. But she only said, "What would you say to ten thousand pieces of gold, to bring your troop and do a job for me in Mandrigyn?"

He shrugged. "I'd say no."

She sat up, truly shocked. "For ten thousand gold pieces?" The sum was enormous—five thousand would have bought the entire troop for a summer's campaign and been thought generous. He wondered where she'd come up with it, if in fact she intended to pay him. The size of the sum inclined him to doubt it.

"I wouldn't go against Altiokis for fifty thousand," he said calmly. "And I wouldn't tie up on a word-of-mouth proposition with a skirt from a conquered city for a hundred, wizard or no wizard."

As he'd intended, it prodded her out of her calm. The flush in her face deepened, for she was a woman to whom few men had ever said no. An edge of ugly rage slid into her voice. "Are you afraid?"

"Madam," Sun Wolf said, "if it's a question of having my bowels pulled out through my eye sockets, I'm afraid. There's no amount of money in the world that would make me pick a quarrel with Altiokis."

"Or is it just that you'd prefer to deal with a man?"

She'd spat the words at him in spite, but he gave them due consideration; after a moment, he replied, "As a matter of fact, yes." His hand forestalled her intaken breath. "I know where women stand in Mandrigyn. I know they'd never put one in public office and they'd never send one on a mission like this. And if you're from Madrigyn, you know that."

She subsided, her breath coming fast and thick with anger, but she didn't deny his words.

"So that means it's private," he went on. "Ten thousand gold pieces is one hell of a lot of tin from a private party, especially from a city that's just been taken and likely tapped for indemnity for whatever wasn't carried off in the sack. And since I know women are vengeful and sneaky . . ."

"Rot your eyes, you—" she exploded, and he held up his hand for silence again.

"They have reasons for fighting underhand the way they do, and I understand them, but the fact remains that I don't trust a desperate woman. A woman will do anything."

"You're right," she said quietly, her eyes burning with an eerie intensity into his, her voice deadly calm. "We will do anything. But I don't think you understand what it is to love your city, to be proud of it, ready to lay down your life to defend it, if need be—and not be allowed to participate in its government, not even be allowed by the canons of good manners to talk politics. Holy Gods, we're not even permitted to walk about the streets unveiled! To see the town torn apart by factionalism and conquered, with all the men who did fight for it led away in chains while the wicked, the venal, and the greedy sit in the seats of power . . .

"Do you know why no man came to you tonight?

"For decades—centuries—Altiokis has coveted Mandrigyn. He has taken over the lands of the old mountain Thanes and of the clans to the southeast of us; he sits like a toad across the overland trade roads to the East. But he's landlocked, and Mandrigyn is the key to the Megantic. We made trade concessions to him, turned a blind eye to encroachments along the border, signed treaties. You know that's never enough.

"His agents stirred up trouble and factions in the city, cast doubt on the legitimacy of the rightful Prince, Tarrin of the House of Her, split the parliament—and when we were exhausted with fighting one another, he and his armies marched down Iron Pass. Tarrin led the whole force of the men of Mandrigyn to meet them in battle, in the deeps of the Tchard Mountains. The next day, Altiokis and his armies came into the city."

Her eyes focused suddenly, an amber gleam deep in their brown depths. "I know Tarrin is still alive."

"How do you know?"

"Tarrin is my lover."

"I've had more women in my life," Sun Wolf said tiredly, "than I've had pairs of boots, and I couldn't for the life of me tell you where one of them is now."

"You'd know best about that," she sneered. "The men were all made slaves in the mines beneath the Tchard Mountains—

Altiokis has miles of mines; no one knows how deep, or how many armies of slaves work there. The—girls—from the city sometimes go up there to—do business—with the overseers. One of them saw Tarrin there." The expression of her face changed, suffused, suddenly, with tender eagerness and the burning anger of revenge. "He's alive."

"We'll skip over how this girl knew him," Sun Wolf said. He was gratified to see that tender expression turn to one of fury. "I'll ask you this. You want me and my men to rescue him from Altiokis' mines?"

Almost trembling with anger, Sheera took a grip on herself and said, "Yes. Not Tarrin only, but all of the men of Mandrigyn."

"So they can go back down the mountain, retake the city, and live happily forever after."

"Yes." She was leaning forward, her eyes blazing, her cloak fallen aside to reveal the dark purple satin of her gown, pearled over like dew with opal beads. "No man came to you because there was no man to come. The only males left in Mandrigyn are old cripples, little boys, and slaves—and the cake-mouthed, poxy cowards who would sell their children to feed Altiokis' dogs, if the price were a little power. We raised the money among us—we, the ladies of Mandrigyn. We'll pay you anything, anything you want. It's the only hope for our city."

Her voice rose, strong as martial music, and Sun Wolf leaned back in his chair and studied her thoughtfully. He took in the richness of the gown she wore and the softness of those unworked hands. Supposing the city were taken without sack— which would be to Altiokis' advantage if he wanted to continue using it as a port. Sun Wolf was familiar with the soft-handed burghers who paid other men to do their fighting, but he had never given much thought to the strength or motivations of their wives. Maybe it was possible that they'd raised the sum, he thought. Golden earrings, household funds, monies embezzled from husbands too cowardly or too prudent to go to war. Possible, but not probable.

"Ten thousand gold pieces is the ransom of a king," he began.

"It is the ransom of a city's freedom!" she bit back at him.

Starhawk was right, he thought. *There are other fanatics besides religious ones.*

"But it isn't just the cost of men's lives," he returned quietly. "I wouldn't lead them against Altiokis and they wouldn't go.

It's autumn already. The storms will break in a matter of days. It's a long march to Mandrigyn overland through the mountains."

"I have a ship," she began.

"You're not getting me on the ocean at this time of year. I have better things to do with my body than use it for crab food. We'll be a few days mopping up here, and by then the storms will have started. I'm not waging a winter war. Not against Altiokis—not in the Tchard Mountains."

"There's a woman on board my ship who can command the weather," Sheera persisted. "The skies will remain clear until we're safe in port."

"A wizard?" He grunted. "Don't make me laugh. There are no wizards anymore, bar Altiokis himself—and I wouldn't take up with you if you had one. I won't mix myself in a wizards' war.

"And," he went on, his voice hardening, "I'm not interested in any case. I won't take ten thousand gold pieces to buy my men coffins, and that's what it would come to, going against Altiokis, winter or summer, mountains or flatland. Your girl-friend may have seen Tarrin alive, lady, but I'll wager your ten thousand gold pieces against a plug copper that his brain and his soul weren't his own. And a plug copper's all my own life would be worth if I were fool enough to take your poxy money."

She was on her feet then, her face mottled with rage. "What do you want?" she demanded in a low voice. "Anything. Me— or any woman in the city or all of us. Dream-sugar? We can get you a bushel of it if you want it. Slaves? The town crawls with them. Diamonds? Twenty thousand gold pieces . . ."

"You couldn't raise twenty thousand gold pieces, woman. I don't know how you raised ten," Sun Wolf snapped. "And I don't touch dream-sugar. You? I'd sooner bed a poisonous snake."

That touched her on the raw, for she was a woman whom men had begged for since she was twelve. But the rage in her was something more—condensed, like the core of a flame— and it was this that had caused Sun Wolf to speak what sounded like an insult but was, in fact, the literal truth. She was a dangerous woman, passionate, intelligent, and ruthless; a woman who could wait months or years for revenge. Sun Wolf did not rise from his chair, but he gauged the distance between them and calculated how swiftly she might move if she struck.

Then a draft of wild smoky night breathed suddenly through the tent, and Sheera swung around as Starhawk paused in the doorway. For a moment, the women stood facing each other, the one in her dark gown sewn with shadowy opals, with her wild and perilous beauty, the other windburned and plain as bread, her man's doublet accentuating the wide shoulders and narrow hips, the angular face with its cropped hair. Starhawk's rolled-back sleeves showed forearms muscled like a man's, all crimped with pink war scars.

They sized each other up in silence. Then Sheera thrust past Starhawk, through the tent flap, to vanish into the blood-scented night.

The Hawk looked after her in silence for a moment, then turned back to her chief, who still sat in his camp chair, his hands folded before him and his fox-yellow eyes brooding. He sighed, and the tension seemed to ebb from his muscles as much as it ever did on campaign. The door curtain moved again, and Fawn entered, her dark hair fretted to tangles, falling in a soft web over her slender back.

Sun Wolf stood up and shook his head in answer to his lieutentant's unasked question. "May the spirits of his ancestors," he said quietly, "help the poor bastard who falls afoul of her."

CHAPTER
—— 2 ——

Sunlight lay like a thick amber resin on the surface of the council table, catching in a burning line on the brass of its inlay work, like the glare at the edge of the sea. For all the twinge of autumn that spiced the air outside, it was over-warm up here, and the Council of Kedwyr, laced firmly into their sober coats of padded and reinforced black wool, were sweating gently in the magnified sunlight that fell through the great oriel windows. Sun Wolf sat at the foot of the table between the Captain of the Outland Levies and the Commander of the City Guards, his hands folded, the glaring sun catching like spurts of fire on the brass buckles of his doublet, and waited for the President of the Council to try and wriggle out of his contract.

Both the Outland Captain Gobaris and the City Commander Breg had warned him. They themselves fought for Kedwyr largely as a duty fixed by tradition, and their pay was notoriously elastic.

The President of the Council opened the proceedings with a well-rehearsed paean of praise for the Wolf's services, touching briefly upon his regrets at having had to go to war against such a small neighbor as Melplith at all. He went on to speak of the hardships they had all endured, and Sun Wolf, scanning those pink, sweaty faces and hamlike jowls bulging out over the high-wrapped white neckclothes, remembered the rotten rations and wondered how much these men had made off them. The President, a tall, handsome man with the air of a middle-aged athlete run to fat, came to his conclusion, turned to the ferret-faced clerk at his side, and said, "Now, as to the matter.

of payment. I believe the sum promised to Captain Sun Wolf was thirty-five hundred gold pieces or its equivalent?"

The man nodded in agreement, glancing down at the un-rolled parchment of the contract that he held in his little white hand.

"In the currency of the Realm of Kedwyr . . ." the President began, and Sun Wolf interrupted him, his deep rumbling voice deceptively lazy.

"The word 'equivalent' isn't in my copy of the contract."

He reached into the pouch on his belt and pulled out a much-folded wad of parchment. As he deliberately spread it out on the surface of the table before him, he could see the uneasy glance that passed among the councilmen. They had not thought that he could read.

The President's wide smile widened. "Well, of course, it is understood that—"

"I didn't understand it," Sun Wolf said, still in that mild tone of voice. "If I had meant 'gold or local,' I'd have specified it. The contract says 'gold'—and by international contractual law, gold is defined by assay weight, not coinage count."

In the appalled silence that followed, Captain Gobaris of the Outland Levies leaned his chin on his palm in such a way that his fingers concealed the grin that was struggling over his round, heavy face.

The President gave his famous, glittering smile. "It's a plea-sure to deal with a man of education, Captain Sun Wolf," he said, looking as if he would derive even greater pleasure from seeing Sun Wolf on board a ship that was headed straight for the rocks that fringed Kedwyr's cliffs. "But as a man of edu-cation, you must realize that, because of the disrupted con-ditions on the Peninsula, assay-weight gold coinage is in critically short supply. The balance of imports and exports must be re-established before our stockpiles of gold are sufficient to meet your demands."

"My demands," Sun Wolf reminded him gently, "were made six months ago, before the trade was disrupted."

"Indeed they were, and you may be sure that under ordinary circumstances our treasuries would have been more than suf-ficient to give you your rightful dues in absolute-weight coin-age. But emergency contingencies arose which there was no way to foresee. The warehouse fires on the silk wharves and the failure of the lemon crops on which so much of our export depends caused shortages in the treasury which had to be covered from funds originally earmarked for the war."

Sun Wolf glanced up. The ceiling of the council hall was newly gilded—he'd watched the workmen doing it, one afternoon when he'd been kept kicking his heels here for an hour and a half trying to see the President about the rations the Council members had been selling them.

Gilding was not cheap.

"Nevertheless," the President went on, leaning forward a little and lowering his voice to a confiding tone, which the Outland Captain had told Sun Wolf meant he was about to tighten up the screws, "we should be able to meet the agreed-upon amount in gold coinage in four weeks, when the amber convoys come in from the mountains. If you are willing to wait, all can be arranged to your satisfaction."

Except that my men and I will not be stuck on the hostile Peninsula for the winter, the Wolf thought dryly. If they were paid promptly and left at the end of this week, they might make it over the Gniss River, which separated the Peninsula from the rolling wastelands beyond, before it became impassable with winter floods. If they waited four weeks, the river would be thirty feet higher than it was now in the gorges, and the Silver Hills beyond clogged with snow and blistered by winds. If they waited four weeks to be paid, many of the men might never make it back to winter quarters in Wrynde at all.

He folded his hands and regarded the President in silence. The moment elongated itself uncomfortably into a minute, then two. The next offer would be for local currency, of course—stipulated at a far higher rate than he could get in Wrynde. Silver coinage tended to fluctuate in value, and right now the silver content wasn't going to be high. But he let the silence run on, knowing the effect of it on men already a little nervous about that corps of storm troops camped by the walls of Melplith.

It was General Gradduck, the head of all the Kedwyr forces who had taken most of the credit for breaking the siege, who finally spoke. "But if you are willing to accept local currency . . ." he began, and left the bait dangling.

They expected the Wolf to start grudgingly stipulating silver content on coinage—impossible to guarantee unless he wanted to have every coin assayed individually. Instead he said, "You mean you'd like to renegotiate the contract?"

"Well—" the President said, irritated.

"Contractually, you're obligated for gold," Sun Wolf said. "But if you are willing to renegotiate, I certainly am. I believe, in matters regarding international trade, the custom in the Peninsula is to impanel a jury of impartial representatives of the other states hereabouts, to determine equivalent local currency values for thirty-five hundred in gold."

The President did not quite turn pale at the thought of representatives from the other Peninsular states setting the amount of money he'd have to pay this mercenary and his men. The other states, already alarmed by Kedwyr's attack on its rival Melplith, would love to be given the opportunity to disrupt Kedwyr's economy in that fashion—not to mention doing Sun Wolf a favor that could be tendered as part of the payment the next time they needed a mercenary troop.

He was clearly sorry he had mentioned it.

A pinch-faced little councilman down at the end of the table quavered, "Of all the nerve!"

The President forced one last smile. "Of course, Captain, such negotiations could be badly drawn out."

Sun Wolf nodded equably. "I realize the drain that's already been put on you by our presence here. I'm sure my men could be put up in some other city in the vicinity, such as Ciselfarge."

It had been a toss-up whether Kedwyr would invade Melplith or Ciselfarge in this latest power struggle for the amber and silk trades, and Sun Wolf knew it. If the President hadn't just returned from swearing lasting peace and brotherhood with Ciselfarge's prince, the remark could have been construed as an open threat.

Grimly, the President said, "I am sure that such a delay will not be necessary."

The bar of sunlight slid along the table, glared for a time in Sun Wolf's eyes, then shifted its gleam to the wall above his head. Servants came in to light the lamps before the negotiations were done. Once or twice, Sun Wolf went down to the square outside the Town Hall to speak to the men he'd brought into the town with him, ostensibly to make sure they weren't drinking themselves insensible in the taverns around the square, but in fact to let them know he was still alive. The men, like most of the Wolf's men, didn't drink nearly as much as they seemed to—this trip counted as campaign, not recreation.

The third time the Wolf came down the wide staircase, it was with the fat Captain Gobaris of the Outland Levies and the thin, bitter, handsome Commander Breg of the Kedwyr City Guards. The Outland Captain was chuckling juicily over the discomfiture of the Council at Sun Wolf's hands. "I thought we'd lose our President to the apoplexy, for sure, when you specified the currency had to be delivered tomorrow."

"If I'd given him the week he'd asked for, he'd have had time to get another run of it from the City Mint," the Wolf said reasonably. "There'd be half the silver content of the current coins, and he'd pay me off in that."

The Guards Commander glanced sideways at him with black, gloomy eyes. "I suspect it's what he did last year, when the city contracts were signed," he said. "We contracted for five years at sixty stallins a year, and that was when stallins were forty to a gold piece. Within two months they were down to sixty-five."

"Oh, there's not much I wouldn't put past that slick bastard." Gobaris chuckled as they stepped through the great doors. Before them, the town square lay in a checkwork of moonlight and shadow, bordered with the embroidered gold of a hundred lamps from the taverns that rimmed it. Music drifted on the wind, with the smell of the sea.

No, Sun Wolf thought, signaling to his men. *And that's why I didn't come to this town alone.*

They left their places in the open tavern fronts and drifted toward him across the square. Gobaris scratched the big hard ball of his belly, and sniffed at the wild air. "Winter rains are holding off," he judged. "They're late this year."

"Odd," the commander said. "The clouds have been piling up on the sea horizon, day after day."

Obliquely, it crossed Sun Wolf's mind that the woman Sheera had spoken of having someone on board her ship who could command the weather. *A wizard?* he wondered. *Impossible.* Then his men were around him, grinning, and he raised his thumbs in a signal of success. There were ironic cheers, laughter, and bantering chaff, and Sheera slipped from the Wolf's mind as Gobaris said, "Well, that's over, and a better job of butchery on a more deserving group of men I've never seen. Come on, Commander," he added, jabbing his morose colleague in the ribs with an elbow. "Is there anyplace in this town a man can get some wine to wash out the taste of them?"

They ended up making a circuit of the square, Sun Wolf, Gobaris, and Commander Breg, with all of Sun Wolf's body-guard and as many of the Outland Levies as had remained in the town. Amid joking, laughter, and horseplay with the girls of the local sisterhood who had turned out in their tawdry finery, Sun Wolf managed to get a good deal of information about Kedwyr and its allies from Commander Breg and a general picture of the latest state of Peninsula politics.

A cool, little hand slid over his shoulder, and a girl joined them on the bench where he sat, her eyes teasing with professional promise. Remarkable eyes, he thought; deep gold, like peach brandy, lighting up a face that was young and exquisitely beautiful. Her hair was the soft, fallow gold of a ripe apricot, escaping its artful pins and lying over slim, bare shoulders in a shining mane. He thought, momentarily, of Fawn, back at the camp—this girl couldn't be much older than eighteen years.

The tastes of wine and victory were mingled in his mouth. He said to the men he'd brought with him, "I'll be back." With their good-natured ribaldry shouting in his ears, he rose and followed the girl down an alley to her rose-scented room.

It was later than he had anticipated when he returned to the square. A white sickle moon had cleared the overhanging housetops that closed in the alley; it glittered sharply on the messy water that trickled down the gutter in the center of the street. The noise from the square had entirely faded, music and laughter dying away into four-bit love and finally sleep. His men, Sun Wolf thought to himself with a wry grin, weren't going to be pleased at having waited so long, and he steeled himself for the inevitable comments.

The square was empty.

One glance told him that all the taverns were shut, a circumstance that bunch of rowdy bastards would never have permitted if they'd still been around. Dropping back into the sheltering shadows of the alley, he scanned the empty pavement again—milky where the moon struck it, barred with the angular black frieze of the shadows cast by the roof of the Town Hall. Every window of that great building and of all the buildings round about was dark.

Had the President had them arrested?

Unlikely. The candlelighted room to which the girl had led him wasn't that far from the square; if there'd been an arrest, there would have been a fight, and the noise would have come to him.

Besides, if the Council had given orders for his arrest, they'd have followed him and taken him in the twisting mazes of alleys, away from his men.

A town crier's distant voice announced that it was the second watch of the night and all was well.

Much later than he'd anticipated, he thought and cursed the girl's teasing laughter that had drawn him back to her. But no matter how late he was, his men would never have gone off without him unless so ordered, even if they'd had to wait until sunup.

After a moment's thought, he doubled back toward the harbor gates. It was half in his mind to return to the Town Hall and make a private investigation of the cells that would invariably be underneath it. But as much as his first instinct pulled him toward a direct rescue, long experience with the politics of war told him it would be foolish. If the men had merely been arrested for drunken rowdiness—which the Wolf did not believe for a moment—they were in no danger. If they were in danger, it meant they'd been gathered in for some other reason, and the Wolf stood a far better chance of helping them by slipping out of the city himself and getting back to his position of strength in the camp. If he did not return, it would be morning before Starhawk acted and possibly too late for any of them.

His soft boots made no noise on the cobbles of the streets. In the dark mazes of the poor quarter, there was little sound— no hint of pursuit or of anything else. A late-walking water seller's mournful call drifted through the blackness. From a grimy thieves' tavern, built half into a cellar, smoky and mephitic light seeped, and with it came raucous laughter and the high-pitched, shrieking voices of whores. Elsewhere, the bells of the local Convent—Kedwyr had always been a stronghold of the Mother's followers—chimed plaintively for midnight rites.

The harbor gate was a squat, round tower, crouching like a monstrous frog against the starry backdrop of velvet sky. Slipping out that way would mean an extra mile or so of walking, scrambling up the precarious cliff road, but the Wolf assumed that, if the President had men watching for him, they'd be watching by the main land gates.

Certainly there were none awaiting him here. A couple of men and a stocky, plain-looking woman in the uniforms of the City Guards were playing cards in the little turret room beside the closed gates, a bottle of cheap wine on the table between them. Sun Wolf slid cautiously through the shadows toward the heavily barred and awkwardly placed postern door that was cut in the bigger gates—a feature of many city gates, and one that he habitually spied out in any city he visited.

Slipping out by the postern would put him in full view of the guards in the turret for as long as it took to count to sixty, he calculated, gauging distances and times from the dense shadows of the gate arch. If the guards were not alert for someone trying to get out of the city, he could just manage, with luck. For all his size, he had had from childhood an almost abnormal talent for remaining unseen, like a stalking wolf in the woods that could come within feet of its prey. His father, who was his size but as big and blundering as a mountain bear, had cursed him for it as a sneaking pussyfoot, though in the end he had admitted it was a handy talent for a warrior to have.

It served him well now. None of the card players so much as turned a head as he eased the bar from the bolt slots and stole through.

After the torchlight near the gate, the night outside was inky dark. The tide was coming in, rising over the vicious teeth of the rocks below the cliffs to the southwest, the starlight ghostly on the wet backs of the crabs that swarmed at their feet. As he climbed the cliff path, he saw that there were chains embedded in the weedy stones of the cliff's base, winking faintly with the movement of the waves.

He shuddered with distaste. His training for war had been harsh, physically and mentally, both from his father's inclination and from the customs of the northern tribe into which he had been born. He had learned early that an active imagination was a curse to a warrior. It had taken him years to suppress his.

The cliff path was narrow and steep, but not impassable. It had been made for woodcutters and sailors to go up from and down to the beaches when the tide was out. Only an invading troop attacking the habor gate would find it perilous. He was soaked to the skin from the spray when he reached its top, half a mile or so from the walls; the wind was biting through the wet sheepskin of his jerkin. In the winter, the storms would make the place a deathtrap, he thought, looking about him at the flat, formless lands at the top. Windbreaks of trees crisscrossed all the lands between the cliffs and the main road from the city gates, and a low wall of gray stones, half ruined and crumbling, lay like a snake a dozen yards inland of the cliff top, a final bastion for those blinded by wind and darkness. From here the waves had a greedy sound.

He turned his face to the sea again, the wind flaying his cheeks. Above the dark indigo of the sea, he could discern great columns of flat-topped clouds, guarding lightning within them. The storms could hit at any time, he thought, and his mind went back to the rough country of the wastelands beyond the Gniss River. If there was a delay getting those jokers out of the city jail . . .

He cursed his bodyguard as he turned his steps back toward the road that ran from the land gate of the city Melplith. He'd left Little Thurg in charge of them. *You'd think the little bastard would have the sense to keep them out of trouble*, he thought, first bitterly, then speculatively. In point of fact, Little Thurg did generally have the brains to keep out of trouble and, for all his height of barely five feet, he had the authority to keep men under his command out of trouble, too. It was that which had troubled Sun Wolf from the first.

Then, like a soft word spoken in the night, he heard the hum of a bowstring. A pain, like the strike of a snake, bit his leg just above the knee. Almost before he was aware that he'd been winged, Sun Wolf flung himself down and forward, rolling into the low ground at the side of the road, concealed by the blackest shadows of the windbreaks. For a time he lay still, listening. No sounds came to his ears but the humming of the wind over the stones and the slurred voices of the whispering trees overhead.

Shot from behind a windbreak, he thought, and his hand slipped down to touch the shaft that stood out from his flesh. The touch of it startled him, and he looked down. He'd been expecting a war arrow, a killing shaft. But this was short, lightweight, fletched with narrow, gray feathers—the sort of thing children and soft-bred court ladies shot at marsh birds with. The head, which he could feel buried an inch and a half in his leg, was smooth. After the savage barbs he had from time to time hacked out of his own flesh in twenty-five years of war, the thing was a toy.

He pulled it out as he would have pulled a thorn, the dark blood trickling unheeded down his boot. It was senseless. You couldn't kill a man with something like that unless you put it straight through his eye.

Unless it was poisoned.

Slowly he raised his head, scanning the vague and star-lighted landscape. He could see nothing, no movement in the deceptive shadows of the stunted trees. But he knew they were out there waiting for him. And he knew they had him.

They?

If he was going to be trapped, why not in the town? Unless the President was unsure of the loyalty of his city Troops and the Outland Levies? Would Gobaris' men have rioted at Sun Wolf's arrest?

If they'd thought it was the prelude to being done out of their own pay, they would.

Working quickly, he slashed the wound with his knife and sucked and spat as much of the blood as he could, his ears straining for some anomalous sound over the thin keening of the wind. He unbuckled his damp jerkin and used his belt for a tourniquet, then broke off the head of the slender arrow and put it in his pocket in the hopes that, if he did make it as far as the camp, Butcher would be able to tell what the poison was. But already his mind was reviewing the road, as he had studied it time and again during the weeks of the siege, seeing it in terms of cover and ambush. It was well over an hour's walk.

He got to his feet cautiously, though he knew there would be no second arrow, and began to walk. Through the sweeping darkness that surrounded him, he thought he sensed movement, stealthy in the shadows of the windbreaks, but he did not turn to look. He knew perfectly well they would be following.

He felt it very soon, that first sudden numbness and the spreading fire of feverish pain. When the road dipped and turned through a copse of dark trees, he looked back and saw them, a flutter of cloaks crossing open ground. Four or five of them, a broad, scattered ring.

He had begun to shiver, the breath laboring in his lungs. Even as he left the threshing shadows of the grove, the starlight on the plain beyond seemed less bright than it had been, the distance from landmark to landmark far greater than he had remembered. The detached corner of his mind that had always been capable of cold reasoning, even when he was fighting for his life, noted that the poison was fast-acting. The symptoms resembled toadwort, he thought with a curious calm. Better that—if it had to be poison—than the endless purgings and vomitings of mercury, or the screaming hallucinatory agonies of anzid. As a mercenary, he had seen almost as much of

politics as he had of war. Poison deaths were nothing new, and
he had seen the symptoms of them all.

But he was damned if he'd let that sleek, toothy President
win this one uncontested.

He was aware that he'd begun to stagger, the fog in his
brain making the air glitter darkly before his eyes. Tiny stones
in the road seemed to magnify themselves hugely to trip his
feet. He was aware, too, that his pursuers were less careful
than they had been. He could see the shadows of two of them,
where they hid among the trees. Soon they wouldn't even bother
with concealment.

Come on, he told himself grimly. *You've pushed on when
you were freezing to death; this isn't any worse than that. If
you can make it to the next stand of rocks, you can take a
couple of the bastards out with you.*

It wasn't likely that the President would be with them, but
the thought of him gave Sun Wolf the strength to make it up
the long grade of the road, toward the black puddle of shadow
that lay across it where the land leveled out again. He was
aware of all his pursuers now, dark, drifting shapes, ringing
as wolves would ring a wounded caribou. Numb sleep pulled
at him. The shadow of the rocks appeared to be floating away
from him, and it seemed to him then that, if he pushed himself
that far, he wouldn't have the strength to do anything, once he
reached the place.

You will, he told himself foggily. *The smiling bastard probably told them it would be a piece of cake, rot his eyes. I'll
give them cake.*

In the shadow of the rocks, he let his knees buckle and
crumpled to the ground. Under cover of trying to rise and then
collapsing again, he drew his sword, concealing it under him
as he heard those swift, light footfalls make their cautious
approach.

The ground felt wonderful under him, like a soft bed after
hard fighting. Desperately he fought the desire for sleep, trying
to garner the strength that he felt slipping away like water. The
dust of the road filled his nostrils, and the salt tang of the
distant sea, magnified a thousand times, swam like liquor in
his darkening brain. He heard the footsteps, slurring in the dry
autumn grass, and wondered if he'd pass out before they came.

I may go straight to the Cold Hells, he thought bitterly, *but
by the spirit of my first ancestor, I'm not going alone.*

Dimly he was aware of them all around him. The fold of a

cloak crumpled down over his arm, and someone set a light bow in the grass nearby. A hand touched his shoulder and turned him over.

Like a snake striking, he grabbed at the dark form bent over him, catching the nape of the neck with his left hand and driving the sword upward toward the chest with his right. Then he saw the face in the starlight and jerked his motion to a halt as the blade pricked the skin and his victim gave a tiny gasping cry. For a moment, he could only stare up into the face of the amber-eyed girl from the tavern, the soft masses of her pale hair falling like silk over his gripping hand.

Under his fingers, her neck was like a flower's stem. He could feel her breath quivering beneath the point of his sword. *I can't kill her*, he thought despairingly. *Not a girl Fawnie's age and frozen with terror*.

Then darkness and cold took him, and he slid to the ground. His last conscious memory was of someone jerking the sword out of his hand.

CHAPTER
—— 3 ——

"**A**RI SENT YOU AWAY?" STARHAWK LOOKED SHARPLY
from Little Thurg to Ari, who stood quietly at her side.

Thurg nodded, puzzlement stamped into every line of his
round, rather bland-looking countenance. "I thought it funny
myself, sir," he said, and the bright blue eyes shifted over to
Ari. "But I asked you about it then, and you told me . . ."

"I was never there," Ari objected quietly. "I was never in
Kedwyr at all." He looked over at Starhawk, as if for confir-
mation. They had spent the night with half of Sun Wolf's other
lieutenants, playing poker in Penpusher's tent, waiting for word
to come back from their chief. "You know . . ."

Starhawk nodded. "I know," she said and looked back at
Thurg, who was clearly shaken and more than a little frightened.

"You can ask the others, sir," he said, and a pleading note
crept into his voice. "We all saw him, plain as daylight. And
after the Chief had gone off with that woman, I thought he
met and spoke with Ari. May God strike me blind if that isn't
the truth."

Starhawk reflected to herself that being struck blind by God
was an exceedingly mild fate compared with what any man
who had deserted his captain in the middle of an enemy city
was likely to get. The fact that they were in the pay of the
Council of Kedwyr did not make that city friendly territory—
quite the contrary, in fact. *You can dishonor a man's wife, kill
his cattle, loot his goods,* Sun Wolf had often said, *and he will*

28

become your friend quicker than any ruling body that owes you
money for something you've done for them.

She settled back in the folding camp chair that was set under
the marquee outside Sun Wolf's tent and studied the man in
front of her. The sea wind riffled her pale, flyaway hair and
made the awning crack above her head. The wind had turned
in the night, blowing hard and steady toward the east. The
racing scud of the clouds threw an uneasy alternation of brightness and shadow over the dry, wolf-colored hills that surrounded Melplith's stove-in walls on three sides and formed a
backdrop of worried calculations, like a half-heard noise, to
all her thoughts.

Her silence was salt to Thurg's already flayed nerves. "I
swear it was Ari I saw," he insisted. "I don't know how it
came about, but you know I'd never have left the Chief. I've
been with him for years."

She knew that this was true. She also knew that women,
more than once, mistaking her for a man in her armor, had
offered to sell her their young daughters for concubines, and
the knowledge that there was literally nothing that human beings
would not sell for ready cash must have been in her eyes. The
little man in front of her began to sweat, his glance flickering
in hopeless anguish from her face to Ari's. Starhawk's cold-
bloodedness was more feared than Sun Wolf's rages. A man
who had taken a bribe to betray Sun Wolf could expect from
her no mercy and certainly nothing even remotely quick.

She glanced up at Ari, who stood behind her chair. He
looked doubtful, as well he might; Thurg had always proved
himself trustworthy and had, as he had said, been with Sun
Wolf's troop for years. She herself was puzzled, as much by
the utter unlikeliness of Thurg's story as by the possibility of
betrayal. In his place, she would have thought up a far better
story, and she had enough respect for his brains to think that
he would have, also.

"Where did Ari speak to you?" she asked at last.

"In the square, sir," Thurg said, swallowing and glancing
from her face to Ari's and back again. "He—he came out of
the alleyway the Chief had gone down with that girl and—and
walked over to where we were sitting in the tavern. It was
getting late. I'd already talked to the innkeeper once about
keeping the place open."

"He came over to you—or called you to him?"

"He came over, sir. He said, 'You can head on back to

camp, troops. The Chief and I will be along later.' And he gave us this big wink. They all laughed and made jokes, but I asked didn't he want a couple of us to stay, just in case? And he said, 'You think we can't handle City Troops? You've seen 'em fight!' And we—we came away. I thought if Ari was with the Chief . . ." He let his voice trail off, struggling within himself. Then he flung his hands out. "It sounds like your grandfather's whiskers, but it's true! Ask any of 'em!" Desperation corrugated his sunburned little face. "You've got to believe me!"

But he did not look as if he thought that this was at all likely.

They said in the camp that Starhawk had not been born— she'd been sculpted. She considered him for a moment more, then asked, "He came out of the alley, came toward the tavern, and spoke to you?"

"Yes."

"He was facing the tavern lamps?"

"Yes—they were behind me. It was one of those open-front places—I was at a table toward the edge, out on the square, like."

"And you saw him clearly?"

"Yes! I swear it!" He was trembling, sweat trickling down his scar-seamed brown cheeks. Behind him, just outside the rippling shade of the awning, two guards looked away, feeling that electric desperation in the air and not willing to witness the breaking of a man they both respected. Frantic, Thurg said, "If I'd sold the Chief to the Council, you think I'd have come back to the camp?"

Starhawk shrugged. "If you'd thought you could get me to believe you thought you were talking to Ari, maybe. I've seen too many betrayals to know whether you'd have sold him out or not—but I do find it hard to believe you'd have done it this stupidly. You're confined to quarters until we see whether the Council sends out the money they promised."

When the guards had taken Little Thurg away, Ari shook his head and sighed. "Of all the damned stupid stories . . . How could he have done it, Hawk? There was no way he had of knowing that I wasn't with ten other people—which I was!"

She glanced up at him, towering above her, big and bearlike and perplexed, the slow burn of both anger and hurt visible in those clear, hazel-gray eyes. "That's what inclines me to believe he's telling the truth," she said and got to her feet. "Or what he thinks is the truth, anyway. If I'm not back from Kedwyr in three hours, hit the town with everything we've got and send messages to Ciselfarge . . ."

"You're going by yourself?"

"If they're hiding what they've done, I'm in no danger," she said briefly, casting a quick glance at the piebald sky and picking up her sheepskin jacket from the back of her chair. "I can fight my way out alone as well as I could with a small bodyguard—and if the Council doesn't know the Wolf's missing, I'm not going to tell them so by going in with a large one."

But on the highroad from the camp to the city gates, she met a convoy of sturdy little pack donkeys and a troop of the Kedwyr City Guards, bearing the specified payment from the Council. Thin and morose, like a drooping black heron upon his cobby little Peninsular mare, Commander Breg hailed her. She drew her horse alongside his. "No trouble?" she asked, nodding toward the laden donkeys and the dark-clothed guards who led them.

The commander made the single coughing noise that was the closest he ever came to a laugh. The day had turned cold with the streaming wind; he wore a black cloak and surcoat wound over the shining steel back-and-breast mail, and his face, framed in the metal of his helmet, was mottled with vermilion splotches of cold. "Our President came near to an apoplexy and took to his bed with grief over the amount of it," he told her. "But a doctor was summoned—they say he will recover."

Starhawk laughed. "Ari and Penpusher are there waiting to go over it with you."

"Penpusher," the commander said thoughtfully. "Is he that yak in chain mail who threw the defending captain off the tower at the storming of Melplith's gates?"

"Oh, yes," Starhawk agreed. "He's only like that in battle. As a treasurer, he's untouchable."

"As a warrior," the commander said, "he's someone I would not much like to try and touch, either." A spurt of wind tore at his cloak, fraying the horses' manes into tangled clouds and hooning eerily through the broken lines of windbreak and stone. He glanced past Starhawk's shoulder at the gray rim of the sea, visible beyond the distant cliffs. The sky there was densely piled with bruised-looking clouds. Over the whining of the wind, the waves could occasionally be heard, hammerlike against the rocks.

"Will you make it beyond the Gniss," he asked, "before the river floods?"

"If we get started tomorrow." It was her way never to give anyone anything. She would not speak to a comparative stranger of her fears that they would not, in fact, reach the river in time for a safe crossing. It was midmorning; were it not for Sun Wolf's disappearance, they would have been breaking camp already, to depart as soon as the money was counted. With the rapid rise of the Gniss, hours could be important. As the wind knifed through the thick sheepskin of her coat and stung the exposed flesh of her face, she wondered if the commander's words were a chance remark or a veiled warning to take themselves off before it was too late.

"By the way," she asked, curvetting her horse away from the path of the little convoy, "where does Gobaris keep himself when he's in town? Or has he left already?"

The commander shook his head. "He's still there, in the barracks behind the Town Hall square. It's his last day in the town, though—he's getting ready to go back to his farm and that wife he's been telling us about all through the campaign."

"Thanks." Starhawk grinned and raised her hand in farewell. Then she turned her horse's head in the direction of the town and spurred to a canter through the cold, flying winds of the coming storms.

She found Gobaris, round, pink, and slothful, packing his few belongings and the mail that no longer quite fitted him, in the section of barracks reserved by the Council for the Outland Levies during their service to the town. Few of them were left; this section of the barracks, allotted to the men of the levies, was mostly empty, the straw raked from the bunks and heaped on the stone floor ready to be hosed out, the cold drafts whistling through the leak-stained rafters. The walls were covered with mute and obscene testimony of the rivalry between the Outland Levies and the City Troops.

"I don't know which is worse," she murmured, clicking her tongue thoughtfully, "the lack of imagination or the inability to spell a simple four-letter word that they use all the time."

"Lack of imagination," Gobaris said promptly, straightening up in a two-stage motion to favor the effect of the coming dampness on his lower back. "If one more man had tried to tell me the story about the City Trooper and the baby goat, I'd have strangled the life out of him before he'd got past 'Once upon a time.' What can I do for you, Hawk?"

She spun him a tale of a missing soldier, watching his puffy, unshaven face closely, and saw nothing in the wide blue eyes but annoyance and concern that the man should be found before the rest of the troop left without him. He let his packing lie and took her down to the city hall, shouting down the regular guards there and opening without demur any door she asked to see the other side of. At the end, she shook her head in assumed disgust and sighed. "Well, that rules out trouble, anyway. He'll be either sodden drunk or snugged up with some woman." It took all her long self-discipline and all the inexpressive calm of years of barracks poker to hide the sick qualm of dread that rose in her and accept with equanimity the Outland Captain's invitation to share a quart of ale at the nearest tavern.

She was reviewing in her memory the other possible ways to enter the jail by stealth and search for other cells there when Gobaris asked, "Did your chief get back to the camp all right, then?"

She frowned, resting her hands around the mug on the rather grimy surface of the tavern table. "Why would he not?"

Gobaris sighed, shook his head, and rubbed at the pink, bristly rolls of his jaw. "I didn't like it myself, for all that Ari's a stout enough fighter. If the President had wanted to make trouble, he could have trapped the two of them in the town. It was dangerous, is all."

Starhawk leaned back in her chair and considered the fat man in the cold white light that came in through the open tavern front from the square. "You mean Ari was the only man he had with him?" she asked, playing for time.

"Only one I saw." He threw back his head, revealing a grayish crescent of dirty collar above the edge of his pink livery doublet, and drank deeply, then wiped his lips with an odd daintiness on the cuff of his sleeve. "He might have had others up the alley, mind, but none whom I saw."

"Which alley?" she asked in a voice of mild curiosity, turning her head to scan the half-empty square. No booths or other tavern fronts opened into that great expanse of checked white and black stone today—a rainsquall had already dappled the pavement, and the fleeting patches of white and blue of the sky were more and more obscured by threatening gray.

"That one there." He pointed. From this angle, it was little more than a shaded slot behind the keyhole turrets of an elaborately timbered inn front. "We were at that alehouse there, the Cock in Leather Breeches, waiting for your chief to get back. Then Ari came out of the alley, walked slap up to the bodyguard, and sent 'em off back to camp. I thought it wasn't like the Wolf to be that careless, but nobody asked me my opinion."

"You knew it was Ari."

Gobaris looked surprised. "Of course it was Ari," he said. "He was standing within a yard of me, wasn't he? Facing the lamps of the inn."

Ari was waiting for Starhawk at Sun Wolf's tent when she came back from the city. The camp was alive with the movement of departure, warriors calling curses and jokes back and forth to one another as they loaded pack beasts with their possessions and loot from the sacking of Melplith. Starhawk, being not by nature a looter, had very little to pack; she could have been ready to depart in half an hour, tent and all. Someone—probably Fawn—had begun to dismantle Sun Wolf's possessions, and the big tent was a chaos of tumbled hangings, their iridescence shot with gold stitching, of disordered camp furniture and cushions, and of mail and weapons. In the midst of it, on the inlaid ebony table where their armor had rested last night, sat a priceless rose porcelain pitcher in which slips of iris had been rudely potted. Beside it was a small leather sack.

Starhawk picked up the sack and weighed it curiously in her hand. She glanced inside, then across at Ari. The bag contained gold pieces.

"Every grain of gold he contracted for was delivered," Ari said somberly.

The Hawk stripped off her rain-wet coat and threw it over the back of the staghorn chair. "I'm not surprised," she said. "Gobaris says he saw you, too. Though if it were a setup . . ."

Ari shook his head. "I had the tents of all the men on that detail searched. Little Thurg wasn't the only one, either . . ." He leaned out the tent door and called, "Thurg!" to someone outside. The doorway darkened and Big Thurg came in, making the small room minuscule by his bulk.

Big Thurg was the largest man in the Wolf's troop, reducing Sun Wolf, Ari, and Penpusher to frailty by comparison. The absurd thing about him was that, although he and Little Thurg came from opposite ends of the country and were presumably no relation to each other, in face and build they were virtually twins, giving the general impression that Little Thurg had somehow been made up from the scraps left over from the creation of his immense counterpart.

"It's true, sir," he said, guessing her question, looking down at her, and scratching his head. "We all saw him—me, Long Mat, Snarky, everyone."

"A double?" Starhawk asked.

"But why?" Ari threw out his hands in a gesture of angry frustration. "They paid us!"

Outside, someone led a laden mule past, the sound of the creaking pack straps a whispered reminder that time was very short. Big Thurg folded enormous hands before his belt buckle, his bright eyes grave with fear. "I think it's witchery."

Neither Starhawk nor Ari spoke. Starhawk's cold face remained impassive, but a line appeared between the thick fur of Ari's brows.

Big Thurg went on. "I've heard tell of it in stories. How a wizard can take on the form of a man, to lie with a woman the night, and her thinking all the time it's her husband; or else put on a woman's shape and call on a nurse to ask for a child. When the true mother shows up, the kid's long gone. A wizard could have seen you anywhere about the camp, sir, to know who you were."

"But there aren't any wizards anymore," Ari said, and Starhawk could hear the fear in his voice. Even among the mercenaries, Ari was accounted a brave man, for all his youth—brave with the courage of one who had no need for bravado. But there were very few men indeed who did not shudder at the thought of dabbling in wizardry. She and Ari both knew for a fact that there was only one wizard alive in the world—Altiokis.

Starhawk said, "Thank you, Thurg. You can go. We'll have the guards let Little Thurg go, with our apologies." The big man saluted and left. When she and Ari were alone, she said quietly, "The Chief got an offer the other night to go against Altiokis at Mandrigyn."

Ari swore, softly, vividly, hopelessly. Then he said. "No. Oh, no, Hawk." Around them, the camp was a noisy confusion, but the steady pattering of the rain against the leather tent walls and in the puddles beyond the door came through, like a whispered threat. It would be a long, beastly journey north; there could be no more waiting. Ari looked at her, and in his eyes

Starhawk saw the grief of one who had already heard of a death.

She continued in her usual calm voice. "It would explain why the President sent us our pay. He knows nothing of it. The woman who came and spoke to the Wolf here was from one of Altiokis' cities."

For a time Ari did not speak, only stood with his head bowed, listening to the noises of the camp and the rain and her soft-spoken words of doom. The fading afternoon light laid a gleam like pewter on the creamy brown of his arm muscles; it winked on the gold stitching of his faded, garish tunic and on the jewels among the braided scalps that decorated his shoulders. His gold earrings flashed against his long, black hair as he turned his head. "So what are we going to do?"

Starhawk paused and considered her several courses of action. There was only one of them that she knew she could follow. Knowing this, she did not inquire of herself the reasons why. "I think," she said at last, "that the best thing would be for you to get the troop back to Wrynde. If Altiokis had wanted the Chief dead, he would have killed him here. Instead, it looks as if he spirited him away somewhere." A dozen tales of the Wizard King's incredible, capricious cruelty contradicted her, but she did not give Ari time to say so. She knew that, if she accepted that explanation, she might just as well give Sun Wolf up for dead now. She went on. "I don't know why he took him and I don't know where, but the Citadel of Grimscarp in the East is a good guess. I know the Wolf, Ari. When he's trapped by a situation, he plays for time."

Ari raised his head finally, staring at her in horrified disbelief. "You're not going there?"

She looked back at him impassively. "It's either assume he's there and alive and can be rescued—or decide that he's dead and give him up now." Seeing his stricken look at the coldness of her logic, she added gently, "I don't think either of us is ready to do that yet."

He turned from her and paced the tent in silence. On the other side of the peacock hangings, Fawn could be heard moving quietly about, preparing for departure. Sun Wolf's armor and battle gear still hung on their stand at one end of the room, a mute echo of his presence; the feathers on the helmet's widespread wings were translucent in the pallid light from the door.

Finally Ari said, "He could be elsewhere."

She shrugged. "In that case, it's short odds that he can get

himself out of trouble. If Altiokis has him—which I believe
he does—he'll need help. I'm willing to risk the trip." She
hooked her hands through her sword belt and watched Ari,
waiting.

"You'll go overland?" he asked at last.

"Through the Kanwed Mountains, yes. I'll take a donkey—
a horse would be more trouble than it was worth, between
wolves and robbers, and it wouldn't add anything to my time.
I can always buy one when I reach the uplands." Her mind
was leaping ahead, calculating the campaign details that could
be dealt with—road conditions, provisions, perils—to free
herself from the fear that she knew would numb her heart.

There's nothing you can do right now to help him, she told
herself coldly, *except what you are doing. Feeling fear or worry
for him will not help either him or you.* But the fear smoldered
in her nevertheless, like a buried fire in the heart of a mountain
of ice.

Ari asked, "Whom will you take with you?"

She raised her brows, her voice still calm and matter-of-
fact. "Who do you think could be trusted with the news that
we might be messing with Altiokis? I personally can't think of
anyone."

As he crossed the room back to her, she could see the worry
lines already settling into his face—the lines that would be
there all winter, maybe all his life. Morale in the troop was
going to be hard enough to maintain in the face of the Wolf's
disappearance, without dealing with the added panic that the
Wizard King's name would cause, and they both knew it.

She went on. "A lone traveler is less conspicuous than a
small troop, especially in the wintertime. I'll be all right."

The echo of a hundred nursery tales of Altiokis was in Ari's
voice as he asked, "How will you get into the Citadel?"

She shrugged again. "I'll figure out that part when I get
there."

Ari was the only one to see her off that night. She had
delayed her departure until after dark, partly to avoid spies,
partly to avoid comment in the troop itself. Her close friends
in the troop—Penpusher, Butcher the camp doctor, Firecat,
and Dogbreath—she had told only that she was going to help
the Chief and that they'd both be back at Wrynde in the spring.
Altiokis was not spoken of. After packing most of her things
to be sent back to Wrynde, she had spent the afternoon in

meditation, preparing her mind and heart for the journey in the silence of the Invisible Circle, as they had taught her in the Convent of St. Cherybi.

Ari was quiet as he walked with her down the road toward the dark hills. By the light of his torch, she thought, he looked older than he had this morning. He was in for a hellish winter, she knew, and wondered momentarily if she ought not, after all, to remain with the troop, for she was the senior of the two lieutenants and the one who had more experience in dealing with the town council of Wrynde.

But she let the thought pass. Her mind was already set on her quest, with the calm single-mindedness with which she went into battle. In a sense, she had already severed herself from Ari and the troop; and in any case, she was not sure that her own road would not be the harder of the two.

"Take care of yourself," Ari said. In the sulfurous glare of the torch, the coat of black bearskin he wore gave him more than ever the look of a young beast. The hills stood before them, tall against the sky; above the sea to their backs, the clouds rose in vast pillars of darkness, the winter storms still holding uncannily at bay.

"You, also." She took the donkey's headstall in her left hand, then turned and put her right hand on Ari's shoulder and kissed him lightly on the cheek. "I don't know who's in for a worse time of it."

"Starhawk," Ari said quietly. The wind fluttered at his long hair; in the shadows she could see the sudden jump of his tensed jaw muscles. "What am I going to do," he asked her, "if someone shows up sometime this winter, without you, claiming to be the Chief? How will I know it's really him?"

Starhawk was silent. They were both remembering Little Thurg, speaking to Ari's double in the square of Kedwyr.

Sweet Mother, she thought, *how will I know it's the Chief when I find him?*

For a moment, a shiver ran through her, almost like panic; the fear of magic, of wizards, of the uncanny, threatened to overcome her. Then the face of Sister Wellwa returned to her, withered in its frame of black veils; she saw the hunched back and tiny hands and herself, as a curious child, helping to sort dried herbs in the old nun's cell and wondering why, of all the nuns in the Convent of St. Cherybi, Wellwa alone, the oldest and most wrinkled, possessed . . .

"A mirror," she said.

Ari blinked at her, startled. "A what?"

"Put a mirror somewhere, in an angle of the room where you can see it. A mirror will reflect a true form, without illusion."

"You're sure?"

"I think so," she said doubtfully. "Or else you can take him out to the marshes on a night when there are demons about. As far as I know, Sun Wolf is the only man I've ever met who could see demons."

They had both seen him do it, in the dripping marshes to the north of Wrynde, and had watched him following those loathsome, giggling voices with his eyes through the ice-bitten trees.

"It may be that a wizard can see demons, too, by means of magic," Ari said. "It was said they could see through illusion."

"Maybe," she agreed. "But the mirror will show you a fraud." It occurred to her for the first time to wonder why Sister Wellwa had kept that fragment of reflective glass positioned in the corner of her cell. Whom had she expected to see in it, entering the room disguised as someone else she knew?

"Maybe," Ari echoed softly. "And what then?"

They looked into each other's eyes, warm hazel into cold gray, and she shook her head. "I don't know," she whispered. "I don't know."

She turned away from him and took the road into the darkness of the hills. Behind her and to her left lay the dim scattering of lights visible through the broken walls of Melplith and the collection of red sparks that was the mercenary camp. By dawn tomorrow, the camp would be broken and gone. Kedwyr's Council had smashed its rival's pretensions, and the overland trade in furs and onyx would return to Kedwyr, high tariffs or no high tariffs. Melplith would sink back to being a poky little market town like those farther back in the hills, and what had anybody gained? A lot of people were dead, including one of Gobaris' brothers; a lot of mercenaries were richer; a lot of women had been raped, men maimed, children starved. The wide lands north of the Gniss River were still a burned-over wasteland in which nuuwa and wolves wandered; demons still haunted the cold marshes in whistling, biting clusters; abominations bred in the southern deserts, while the cities of the Peninsula fought over money and those of the Middle Kingdoms fought over religion.

The raw dampness of the wind stung Starhawk's face and

whipped at her half-numbed cheeks with the ends of her hair. She'd meant to crop it before leaving, as she did before the summer campaigns every year, but had forgotten.

She wondered why Altiokis had wanted the Chief. Sun Wolf had obviously sent Mandrigyn's emissary packing—and had himself vanished without a trace the following night.

Revenge? She shuddered inwardly at the tales of Altiokis' revenges. *Or for other reasons? Will Ari, during the course of the winter, find himself faced with a man who claims to be Sun Wolf?*

On the hillside to her left, the slurring rush of the wind through the bracken was cut by another sound, a shifting that was not part of the pattern of harmless noise.

Starhawk never paused in her step, though the burro she led turned its long ears backward uneasily. In this country, it would take a skilled tracker to follow in silence, even on a windy night. The ditches on either side of the hard-packed dirt of the highroad were filled with a mix of gravel and summer brushwood, and the sound of a body forcing passage anywhere near the road was ridiculously loud to the Hawk's trained ears. When the track wound deeper into the foothills, the ditches petered out, but the scrub grew thicker. As she walked on, the Hawk could identify and pinpoint the sound of her pursuer, thirty feet behind her and closing.

Human. A wolf would be quieter; a nuuwa—if there were such things this close to settled territory—wouldn't have the brains to stalk at all. The thought of Altiokis' spies drifted unpleasantly through her mind.

To hell with it, she told herself and faked a stumble, cursing. The scrunching in the brush stopped.

Limping ostentatiously, Starhawk hobbled to the side of the track and sat down in the dense shadows of the brushwood. Under cover of fiddling with her bootlaces, she tied the burro's lead to a branch. Then she slithered backward into the brush, snaked her way down the shallow, overgrown ditch, and climbed up onto the scrubby hillside beyond.

The night was clouding over again, but enough starlight remained to give her some idea of the shape of the land. Her pursuer moved cautiously in the scrub; she focused on the direction of the popping of cracked twigs. Keeping low to better her own vision against the lighter sky, she scanned the dark jumble of twisted black trunks and the mottling of grayed leaves.

Nothing. Her shadow was keeping still.

Softly her fingers stole over the loose sandy soil until they found what they sought, a sizable rock washed from the stream bed by last winter's rains. Moving slowly to remain as quiet as she could, she worked it free of the dirt. With a flick of the wrist she sent it spinning into the brush a few yards away.

There was a satisfactory rustling, and part of the pattern of dark and light that lay so dimly before her jerked, again counter to the general restless movement of the wind. The vague glow of the sky caught the pallid reflection of a face.

Very good, the Hawk thought and eased her dagger soundlessly from its sheath.

Then the wind changed and brought to her, incongruous in the sharpness of the juniper, the sweet scent of patchouli.

Starhawk braced herself to dodge in case she was wrong and called out softly, "Fawn!"

There was a startled shift in the pattern. The shape of the girl's body was revealed under the voluminous folds of a mottled plaid cloak—the dull, almost random-looking northern plaid that blended so deceptively into any pattern of earth and trees. Fawn's voice was shaky and scared. "Starhawk?"

Starhawk stood up, clearly startling the daylights out of the girl by her nearness. They stood facing each other for a time on the windswept darkness of the hillside. Because they were both women, there was a great deal that did not need to be said. Starhawk remembered that most of what she had said to Ari had been in Sun Wolf's tent; of course the girl would overhear.

It was Fawn who spoke first. "Don't send me away," she said.

"Don't be foolish," Starhawk said brusquely.

"I promise I won't slow you down."

"You can't promise anything of the kind and you know it," the Hawk retorted. "I'm making the best time to Grimscarp that I can, over some damned dirty country. It's not the same as traveling with the troop from Wrynde to the Peninsula or down to the Middle Kingdoms and back."

Fawn's voice was desperate, low against the whining of the wind. *"Don't leave me."*

Starhawk was silent a moment. Though a warrior herself, she was woman enough to understand the fear in that taut voice. Her own was kinder when she said, "Ari will see that you come to no harm."

"And what then?" Fawn pleaded. "Spend the winter in

Wrynde, wondering who's going to have me if Sun Wolf doesn't come back?"

"It's better than being passed around a bandit troop and ending up with your throat slit in a ditch."

"You run that risk yourself!" And when Starhawk did not answer, but only hooked her hands through the buckle of her sword belt, Fawn went on. "I swear to you, if you won't take me with you to Grimscarp, I'll follow you on my own."

The girl bent down, the winds billowing the great plaid cloak about her slender body, and picked up something Starhawk saw was a pack from among the heather at her feet. She slung it over her shoulder and descended to where the Hawk stood, catching at the branches now and then for balance, holding her dark, heavy skirts out of the brambles. Starhawk held out a hand to her to help her down to the road. The Hawk's grip was like a man's, firm under the delicate elbow. When they reached the road together, Fawn looked up at her, as if trying to read the expression in that craggy, inscrutable face, those transparent eyes.

"Starhawk, I love him," she said. "Don't you understand what it is to love?"

"I understand," Starhawk said in a carefully colorless voice, "that your love for him won't get you to Grimscarp alive. I elected to search for him because I have a little—a very little—experience with wizards and because I believe that he can be found and rescued. It could easily have been any of the men who came. I can hold my own against any of them in battle."

"Is that all it is to you?" Fawn demanded passionately. "Another job? Starhawk, Sun Wolf saved me from—from things so unspeakable it makes me sick to remember them. I had seen my father murdered—" Her voice caught in a way that told Starhawk that the death had been neither quick nor clean. "I'd been dragged hundreds of miles by a band of leering, dirty, cruel men, I'd seen my maid raped and murdered, and I knew that the only reason they didn't do the same to me was because I'd fetch a better price as a virgin. But they talked about it."

Her face seemed to burn white in the filmy starlight, her body trembling with the hideous memories. "I was so terrified at—at being sold to a captain of a mercenary troop that I think I would have killed myself if I hadn't been watched constantly. And then Sun Wolf bought me and he was so good to me, so kind . . ."

The hood of her cloak had blown back, and the stars glinted on the tears that streaked her cheeks. Grief and compassion filled Starhawk's heart—for that distant, frightened child and for the girl before her now. But she said, with deliberate coldness, "None of that means that you'll be able to find him safely."

"I don't want to be safe!" Fawn cried. "I want to find him—or know in my heart that he's dead."

Starhawk glanced away, annoyed. She had never questioned that she should look for the Chief—her loyalty to him was such that she would have undertaken the quest no matter what Ari had said. Her own unquestioned prowess as a warrior had merely been one of the arguments. Her native honesty forced her to recognize Fawn's iron resolution as akin to her own, regardless of what kind of nuisance she'd be on the road.

The older woman sighed bitterly and relaxed. "I don't suppose," she said after a moment, "that there is any way I could prevent you from coming with me, short of tying you up and dragging you back to camp. Besides losing me time, that would only make the two of us look ridiculous." She stared coldly down her nose when Fawn giggled at the thought. "You know, don't you, that you might cause the troop's departure to be delayed if Ari takes it into his head to search the town for you?"

Fawn colored strangely under the starlight. She bent to pick up her pack again and start toward where the burro was still tethered, head-down against the wind. "Ari won't look for me," she said. "For one thing, you know he wouldn't delay the march north. And besides . . ." Her voice faltered with shame. "I took everything valuable of mine. Clothes, jewels—everything that I would take if I were running off with another man. And that's what he'll think I did."

Unexpectedly, Starhawk grinned. Fawn might not be able to reason her way past their arguments, but she certainly had found a matter-of-fact means of discouraging pursuit. "Don't tell me you have all that in that little pack?"

Startled at the sudden lightening of the Hawk's voice, Fawn looked quickly up to meet her eyes, then returned her smile ruefully. "Only the jewels. I thought we could sell them for food on the way. The rest of it I bundled up and dropped over the sea cliffs."

"Very nice." Starhawk smiled approvingly, reflecting that she was evidently not the only person in the troop to hold possessions lightly. "You have a good grasp of essentials. We'll make a trooper of you yet."

CHAPTER

— 4 —

WHEN SUN WOLF WAS A BOY, HE HAD BEEN STRICKEN BY A fever. He had concealed it from his father as long as he could, going hunting with the other men of the tribe in the dark, half-frozen marshes where demons flitted from tree to tree like pale slips of phosphorescent light. He had come home and hidden in the cattle loft. There his mother had found him, sobbing in silent delirium, and had insisted that they call the shaman of the tribe. It all came back to him now, with the memory of parching thirst and restless pain: the low rafters with their red and blue dragons almost hidden under the blackening of smoke; the querulous voice of that dapper, busy little charlatan with the holy bones and dangling locks of ancestral hair; and his father looming like an angry, disapproving shadow beside the reddish, pulsing glow of the hearth. The Wolf remembered his father's growling voice. "If he can't throw it off himself, he'd better die, then. Get your stinking smokes and your dirty bones out of here; I have goats who could work better magic than you." He remembered the shaman's offended sniff—because, of course, his father was right.

And he remembered the awful agony of thirst.

The dream changed. Cool hands touched his face and raised the rim of a cup to his lips. The metal was ice-cold, like the water in the cup. As he drank, he opened swollen eyelids to look into the face of the amber-eyed girl. The fear that widened her eyes told him he was awake.

I tried to kill her, he thought cloudily. *But she tried to kill me—or did she*? His memory was unclear. Mixed with the

perfume of her body, he could smell the salt flavor of the sea; the creak of wood and cordage and the shift of the bed where he lay told him he was aboard a ship. The girl's eyes were full of fear, but her arm beneath his head was soft. She raised the cup to his cracked lips again, and he drained it. He tried to stammer thanks but could not speak—tried to ask her why she had wanted to kill him.

Abruptly, Sun Wolf slid into sleep again.

The dreams were worse, a terrifying nightmare of racking, helpless pain. He had a tangled vision of darkness and wind and rock, of being trapped and left prey to things he could not see, of dangling over a tossing abyss of change and loss and terrible loneliness. In the darkness, demons seemed to ring him—demons that he alone could see, as he had always been able to see them, though to others—his father, the other men of the tribe, even the shaman—they had been only vague voices and a sense of terror. Once he seemed to see, small and clear and distant, the school of Wrynde, shabby and deserted beneath the sluicing rain, with only the old warrior who looked after the place in the troop's absence sweeping the blown leaves from the training floor with a broom of sticks. The smell and feel of the place cried to him, so real that he could almost touch the worn cedar of the pillars and hear the wailing of the wind around the rocks. Then the vision vanished in a shrieking storm of fire, and he was lost in spinning darkness that cut at him like swords, pulling him closer and closer to a vortex of silent pain.

Then that, too, faded, and there was only white emptiness that blended slowly to exhausted waking. He lay like a hollowed shell cast up on a beach, scoured by sun and salt until there was nothing left, cold to the bone and so weary that he ached. He could not find the strength to move, but only stared at the timbers above his head, listening to the creak and roll of the ship and the slap of water against the hull, feeling the sunlight that lay in a small, heatless bar over his face.

They were in full ocean, he judged, and heading fast before the wind.

He remembered the mountains of clouds, standing waiting on the horizon. If the storms hit and the ship went to pieces now, he would never have the strength to swim.

So it would be the crabs, after all.

But that cold, calm portion of his mind, the part that seemed always to be almost detached from his physical body, found

neither strength nor anger in that thought. It didn't matter—
nothing mattered. The sway of the ship moved the chip of
sunlight back and forth across his face, and he found that he
lacked the strength even to wonder where he was—or care.

An hour passed. The sunlight traveled slowly down the
blanket that covered his body and lay like a pale, glittering
shawl over the foot of the bunk. Like the blink of light from
a sword blade, the chased gold rim of the empty cup on the
table beside him gleamed faintly in the moving shadows. Footsteps descended a hatch somewhere nearby, then came down
the hall.

The door opposite his feet opened, and Sheera Galernas
stepped in.

Not the President of Kedwyr, after all, he thought, still with
that eerie sense of unconcern.

She regarded him impassively from the doorway for a moment, then stepped aside. Without a word, four women filed
in behind her, dressed as she was, for traveling in dark, ser-
viceable skirts, quilted bodices, and light boots. For a time
none of them spoke, but they watched him, lined behind Sheera
like acolytes behind a priestess at a rite.

One of them was the amber-eyed girl, he saw, her delicate,
curiously secretive face downcast and afraid and—*what*?
Ashamed? Why *ashamed*? The rose-tinted memory of her room
in Kedwyr slid through his mind, with the warmth of her scented
flesh twined with his. She was clearly a professional, for all
her youth . . . *Why ashamed*? But he was too tired to wonder,
and the thought slipped away.

The woman beside her was as pretty, but in a different
way—certainly not professional, at least not about that. She
was as tiny and fragile as a porcelain doll, her moonlight-blond
hair caught in a loose knot at the back of her head, her sea-
blue eyes marked at the corners with the faint lines of living
and grief. He wondered what she was doing in the company
of a hellcat like Sheera . . . in the company of any of those
others, for that matter.

Neither of the other two women had or would even make
the pretense of beauty. They were both tall, the younger of
them nearly Sun Wolf's own height—a broad-shouldered, hard-
muscled girl who reminded him of the women in his own
troops. She was dressed like a man in leather breeches and an
embroidered shirt, and her shaven skull was brown from exposure to the sun. So was her face, brown as wood and scarred

from weapons, like that of a gladiator. After a moment's thought, Sun Wolf supposed she must be one.

The last woman stood in the shadows, having sought them with an almost unthinking instinct. The shadows did nothing to mask the fact that she was the ugliest woman Sun Wolf had ever laid eyes on—middle-aged, hook-nosed, her mouth distorted by the brown smear of a birthmark that ran like mud down onto her jutting chin. Her eyes, beneath a single black bar of brow, were as green, as cold, and as hard as jade, infused with the bitter strength of a woman who had been reviled from birth.

They looked from him to Sheera, and on Sheera their eyes remained.

Though he was almost too tired to speak, Sun Wolf asked after a time, "You kidnap my men, too?" There was no strength in his voice; he saw them move slightly to listen. There was a gritty note to it, too, like a streak of rust on metal, that he knew had not been there before. An effect of the poison, maybe.

Sheera's back stiffened slightly with the sarcasm, but she replied steadily, "No. Only you."

He nodded. It was a slight gesture, but all he had strength for. "You going to pay me the whole ten thousand?"

"When you're done, yes."

"Hmm." His eyes traveled over the women again, slowly. Part of his mind was struggling against this paralyzing helplessness, screaming to him that he had to find a means to think his way out of this, but the rest of him was too tired to care. "You realize it will take me a little longer to storm the mines single-handedly?"

That stung her, and those full red lips tightened. The porcelain doll, as if quite against her will, grinned.

"It won't be just you," Sheera said, her voice low and intense. "We're bringing you back to Mandrigyn with us as a teacher—a teacher of the arts of war. We can raise our own strike force, release the prisoners in the mines, and free the city."

Sun Wolf regarded her for a moment from beneath half-lowered lids, reflecting to himself that here was a fanatic if ever he saw one—crazy, dangerous, and powerful. "And just whom for starters," he inquired wearily, "are you planning on having in your strike force, if all the men of the city are working in the mines?"

"Us," she said. "The ladies of Mandrigyn."

He sighed and closed his eyes. "Don't be stupid."

"What's stupid about it?" she lashed at him. "Evidently your precious men can't be bothered to risk themselves, even for ready cash. We aren't going to sit down and let Altiokis appoint the worst scoundrels in the city as his governors, to bleed us with taxes and carry off whom he pleases to forced labor in his mines and his armies. It's our city! And even in Mandrigyn, where it's as much as a woman's social life is worth to go abroad in the streets unveiled and unchaperoned, there are women gladiators like Denga Rey here. In other places women can be members of city guards and of military companies. You have women in your forces yourself. Fighting women, warriors. I saw one of them in your tent that night."

Against the sting of her voice, he saw Starhawk and Sheera again, cool and wary as a couple of cats with the torch smoke blowing about them. Wearily, he said, "That wasn't a woman, that was my second-in-command, one of the finest warriors I've ever met."

"She was a woman," Sheera repeated. "And she isn't the only woman in your forces. They said in the city that you've trained women to fight before this."

"I've trained warriors," the Wolf said without opening his eyes, the exhaustion of even the effort to speak weighting him like a sickness. "If some of 'em come equipped to suckle babies later on, it's no concern of mine, so long as they don't get themselves pregnant while they're training. I'm not going to train up a whole corps of them from scratch."

"You will," Sheera said quietly. "You have no choice."

"Woman," he told her, while that lucid and detached portion of his mind reminded him that arguing with a fanatic was about as profitable as arguing with a drunk and far more dangerous, "what I said about Altiokis still goes. I'm not going to risk getting involved in any kind of resistance in a town he's just taken, and I sure as hell won't do it to train a troop of skirts commanded by a female maniac like yourself. And ten thousand poxy gold pieces, or twenty thousand, or whatever the hell else you'll offer me isn't about to change my mind."

"How about your life?" the woman asked, her voice uninflected, almost disinterested. "Is that reward enough?"

He sighed. "My life isn't worth a plug copper at this point. If you want to chuck me overside, there's surely no way I can stop you from doing it."

It was a foolish thing to have said, and he knew it, for

Sheera was not a woman to be pushed and she was clearly supreme on this ship, as shown by the fact that she'd gotten its captain to put out to sea at this time of the year at all. It struck him again how absolutely alone he was here and how helpless.

He had expected her to fly into a rage, as she had done in his tent. But she only folded her arms and tipped her head a little to one side, the glossy curls of her hair catching in the stiff embroidery of her collar. Conversationally, she said, "There was anzid in the water you drank."

The shock of it cut his breath like a garrote. He opened his eyes, fear like a cold sickness chilling the marrow of his bones. "I didn't drink anything," he said, his mouth dry as the taste of dust. He had seen deaths from anzid. The worst of them had taken two days, and the victim had never ceased screaming.

The ugly woman spoke for the first time, her low voice mellow as the notes of a rosewood flute. "You woke up thirsty from the arrow poison, after dreams of fever," she said. "Amber Eyes gave you water to drink." The long slender hand moved toward the empty cup beside the bed. "There was anzid in the water."

Horror crawled like a tarantula along his flesh. Sheera's face was like a stone; Amber Eyes turned away, cheeks blazing with shame, unable to meet his gaze.

"You're lying," he whispered, knowing that she was not.

"You think so? Yirth has been a midwife, a Healer, and an abortionist long enough to know everything there is to know about poisons—it isn't likely she'd have made a mistake. If you hesitate to join us out of fear of Altiokis, I can tell you now that nothing the Wizard King might do to you if our plan fails would be as bad as that death. You have nothing further to lose by obeying us now."

Weak as he was, he had begun to shake; he wondered how long it took for the symptoms of anzid to be felt. How long had it been since he had been given the poison? It flashed through his mind to take Sheera by that round, golden throat of hers and strangle the life out of her. But weakness held him prisoner; in any case, it would not save his life. And besides that, there was not even sense in cursing her.

When he had been silent for a time, the woman Yirth spoke again, her cold, green eyes looking out from the concealing shadows, clinical and detached. "I am not the wizard that my master was, before Altiokis had her murdered," she said. "But it still lies within my powers to arrest the effects of a poison from day to day by means of spells. When we reach Mandrigyn, I shall place a bounding-spell upon you, that the poison shall not lay hold of you so long as you pass a part of each night within the walls of the city. The true antidote," she continued, with a hint of malice in that low, pure voice, "shall be given to you with your gold when you depart, after the city is freed."

The shaking had become uncontrollable. Fighting to keep panic from his voice, he whispered, "You are a wizard yourself, then. The woman who controls the winds."

"Of course," Sheera said scornfully. "Do you think we'd have dared consider an assault on Altiokis' Citadel without a wizard?"

"I don't think there's anything you're crazy enough not to dare!"

It was on his lips to curse her and die—but not that death. He lay back against the thin pillows, his eyes closing, and the trembling that had seized him passed off. He felt as bleached and twisted as a half-dried rag; even the fear seemed to trickle out of him. In the silence, he could hear the separate draw and whisper of each woman's breath and the faint splash and murmur of water against the hull.

The silence seemed to settle around his heart and brain, white, empty, and somehow strangely calming. He knew he would die, then, hideously, one way or the other. Having accepted that, his mind began to grope fumblingly for ways of playing for time, of getting himself out of this, of fighting his way back to life. *Not*, he told himself with weary savagery, *that I really think there's a chance of it. Old habits die hard.*

And by the spirits of my ancestors freezing down in the cold waters of Hell, I'm going to die a great deal harder.

He drew a tired breath and let it drain from his lips. Something stirred within him, goaded back to feeble and unwilling life, and he opened his eyes and studied the women before him, stripping them with his eyes, judging them as he would have judged them had they turned up, en masse, at the school of Wrynde, wondering if there was muscle as well as curving flesh under Sheera's night-blue gown and which of them was a good enough shot to hit a man with a birding arrow at fifty yards.

"Damn your eyes." He sighed and looked at Sheera again. "So who am I supposed to be?"

She blinked at him, startled by the sudden capitulation. "What?"

"Who am I supposed to be?" he repeated. Tiredness slurred his voice; he tried to garner his waning energy and felt it slip like fine sand through his fingers. His voice had grown weaker. As if some spell of distance had been broken, the women gathered around him, Amber Eyes and the porcelain doll going so far as to sit on the edge of his bunk. Sheera would not let herself so unbend; she stood over him, her arms still folded, her curving brows drawn heavily down over the straight, strong nose.

"If Altiokis has dragged all the men away in chains," he continued quietly, "you can't just have a strange man turn up in your household. Am I your long-lost brother? A gigolo you picked up in Kedwyr? A bodyguard?"

The porcelain doll shook her head. "We'll have to pass you off as a slave," she said, her voice low and husky, like a young boy's. "They're the only men whose coming into the city at this time of the year can well be accounted for. There won't be any merchants or travelers in winter."

She met the angry glitter in his eyes with cool reasonableness. "You know it's true."

"And in spite of the fact that you find it demeaning to be a woman's slave," Sheera added maliciously, "you haven't really got any say in the matter, now, have you, Captain?" She glanced at the others. "Gilden Shorad is right," she said. "A slave can pass pretty much unquestioned. I can get the ship's smith to put a collar on you before we reach port."

"What about Derroug Dru?" Amber Eyes asked doubtfully. "Altiokis' new governor of the town," she explained to Sun Wolf. "He's been known to confiscate slaves."

"What would he want with another slave?" Denga Rey the gladiator demanded, hooking her square, brown hands into the buckle of her sword belt.

Gilden Shorad frowned. "What would Sheera want with one, for that matter?" she asked, half to herself. Close to, Sun Wolf observed that she was older than he had at first thought— Starhawk's age, twenty-seven or so. Older than any of the others except the witch Yirth, who, unlike them, had remained in the shadows by the door, watching them with those cool, jade eyes.

"He can't simply turn up as a slave without any explanation

for why you bought him," the tiny woman clarified, tucking aside a strand of her ivory hair with deft little fingers.

"Would you need a groom?" Amber Eyes asked.

"My own groom would be suspicious if we got another one suddenly," Sheera vetoed.

She looked so perplexed that Sun Wolf couldn't resist turning the knife. "Not as easy as just hiring your killing done, is it? You married?"

A flush stained her strong cheekbones. "My husband is dead."

He gave her a stripping glance and grunted. "Just as well. Kids?"

The flush deepened with her anger. "My daughter is six, my son, four."

"Too young to need an arms master, then."

Denga Rey added maliciously, "You don't want anyone in that town to see you with a sword in your hand anyway, soldier. Old Derroug Dru suspects anybody who can so much as cut his meat at table without slitting his fingers. Besides, he's got it in for big, buff fellows like you."

"Wonderful," the Wolf said without enthusiasm. "Leaving aside where this strike force of yours is going to practice, and where you're going to get money for weapons..."

"We have money!" Sheera retorted, harried.

"I'll be damned surprised if you'll be able to find weapons for sale in a town that Altiokis has just added to his domains. How big is your town place? What did your late lamented do for a living?"

By the bullion stitching on her gloves, the poor bastard couldn't have been worth less than five thousand a year, he decided.

"He was a merchant," she said, her breast heaving with the quickening of her anger. "Exports—this is one of his ships. And what business is it of yours—"

"It is my business, if I'm going to be risking what little is left of my life to teach you females to fight," he snapped. "I want to make damned sure you don't get gathered in and sent to the mines yourselves before I'm able to take my money and your poxy antidote and get the hell out of that scummy marsh you call a town. Is your place big enough to have gardens? An orangery, maybe?"

"We have an orangery," Sheera said sullenly. "It's across the grounds from the main house. It's been shut up for years—

boarded up. It was the first thing I thought of when I decided that we had to bring you to Mandrigyn. We could use it to practice in."

He nodded. There were very few places where orange trees could be left outdoors year-round, yet groves of them were the fashion in all but the coldest of cities. Orangeries tended to be large, barnlike buildings—inefficient for the purpose of wintering fruit trees for the most part, but just passable as training floors.

"Gardeners?" he asked.

"There were two of them, freedmen," she said and added, a little defiantly, "They marched with Tarrin's army to Iron Pass. Even though they had not been born in Mandrigyn, they thought enough of their city's freedom to—"

"Stupid thing to do," he cut her off and saw her eyes flash with rage. "There a place to live in this orangery of yours?"

In a voice stifled with anger, she said, "There is."

"Good." Tiredness was coming over him again, final and irresistible, as if argument and thought and struggle against what he knew would be his fate had drained him of the little strength he had. The wan sunlight, the faces of the women around him and their soft voices, seemed to be drifting farther and farther away, and he fought to hold them in focus. "You—what's your name? Denga Rey—I'll need you for my second-in-command. You fight during the winter?"

"In Mandrigyn?" she scoffed. "If it isn't pouring sideways rain and hail, the ground's not fit for anything but boat races. The last fights were three weeks ago."

"I hope you were trounced to within an inch of your life," he said dispassionately.

"Not a chance, soldier." She put her hands on her strong hips, a glint of mockery in those dark eyes. "What I wonder is, who's going to look after all those little trees so it looks as if there's really a gardener doing the job? If Sheera buys one special, somebody's going to get suspicious."

Sun Wolf looked up at her bleakly. "I am," he said. "I'm a warrior by trade, but gardening is my hobby." His eyes returned to Sheera. "And I damned well better draw pay for it, too."

For the first time, she smiled, the warm, bright smile of the hellcat girl she hadn't been in years. He could see then why men had fought for her hand—as they must have done, to make her so poxy arrogant. "I'll add it in," she said, "to your ten thousand gold pieces."

Sun Wolf sighed and closed his eyes, wondering if it would be wise to tell her what she could do with her ten thousand gold pieces. But when he opened them again, he found that it was dark, the afternoon long over, and the women gone.

CHAPTER

—— 5 ——

*T*HEY SAILED INTO MANDRIGYN HARBOR IN THE VANGUARD OF the storms, as if the boat drew the rain in its wake.

Throughout the forenoon, Sun Wolf had stood in the waist of the ship, watching the clouds that had followed them like a black and seething wall through the gray mazes of the islands draw steadily closer, and wondering whether, if the ship went to pieces on the rocky headlands that guarded the harbor itself, he'd be able to swim clear before he was pulped by the breakers. For a time, he indulged in hopes that it would be so and that, other than himself, the ship would go down with all hands and Sheera and her wildcats would never be heard from again. This thought cheered him until he remembered that, if the sea didn't kill him, the anzid would.

As they passed through the narrow channel between the turret-guarded horns of the harbor, he turned his eyes from the dark, solitary shape of Yirth, standing, as she had stood on and off for the past three days, on the stern castle of the ship; he looked across the choppy gray waters of the harbor to where Mandrigyn lay spread like a jeweled collar upon its thousand islands.

Mandrigyn was the queen city of the Megantic Sea, the crossroads of trade; even in the bitter slate colors of the winter day, it glittered like a spilled jewel box, turquoise, gold, and crystal. Sun Wolf looked upon Mandrigyn and shivered.

Above the town rose the dark masses of the Tchard Mountains, the huge shape of Grimscarp veiled in a livid rack of purplish clouds, as if the Wizard King sought to conceal his fortress from prying eyes. Closer to, he could identify the trashy gaggle of markets and bawdy theaters as East Shore—the suburb that Gilden Shorad had told him lay outside the city's jurisdiction on the eastern bank of the Rack River. The colors of raw wood and cheap paint stood out like little chips of brightness against the rolling masses of empty, furze-brown hills that lay beyond; the Thanelands, where the ancient landholders still held their ancestral sway.

A gust of rain struck him, cold and stinging through the drab canvas of his shirt. As he hunched his shoulders against it like a wet animal, he felt the unfamiliar hardness of metal against his flesh, the traditional slave collar, a slip-chain like a steel noose that the ship's aged handyman had affixed around his neck.

He glanced back over his shoulder, hatred in his eyes, but Yirth had vanished from the poop deck. Sailors, at least half of them women or young boys, were scrambling up and down the rigging, making the vessel ready to be guided into the quays.

There was little activity in the harbor, most shipping having ceased a week ago in anticipation of the storms. Of the sailors and stevedores whom Sun Wolf could see about the docks, most were older men, young boys, or women. The city, he thought, had been hard hit indeed. As the rain-laden gusts of wind drove the ship toward the wharves, he could hear a ragged cheer go up from the vast gaggle of unveiled and brightly clad women who loitered on the pillared promenade of the long seafront terrace that overlooked the harbor. Friends of Denga Rey's, he guessed, noting the couple of nasty-looking female gladiators who swaggered in their midst.

Well, why not? Business is probably damned slow these days.

At some distance from that rowdy mob he picked out other welcoming committees. There was a tall girl and a taller woman whose ivory-blond hair, whipped by the wind from beneath their desperately clutched indigo veils, proclaimed them as kin of Gilden Shorad's. With them was a lady as tiny, and as fashionably dressed, as Gilden—*family*, he thought, no error.

Farther back, among the pillars of the windswept promenade, a couple of liveried servants held an oiled-silk canopy over the head of a tiny woman in amethyst moire, veiled in trailing clouds of lilac silk and glittering with gold and diamonds. *With that kind of ostentation*, he thought, *she has to be a friend of Sheera's.*

No one, evidently, had come to meet Yirth.

A voice at his elbow said quietly, "We made it into harbor just in time."

He turned to see Sheera beside him, covered, as befitted a lady, from crown to soles, her hands encased in gold-stitched kid, her hair a mass of curls and jewels that supported the long screens of her plum-colored veils. She held a fur-lined cloak of waterproof silk tightly around her; Sun Wolf, wearing only the shabby, secondhand shirt and breeches of a slave, studied her for a moment, fingering the chain around his neck, then glanced back at the vicious sea visible beyond the headlands. Even in the shelter of the harbor, the waters churned and threw vast columns of bone-white spray where they struck the stone piers; no ship could make it through the channel now. "If you ask me, we cut that a little too close for comfort," he growled.

Sheera's lips tightened under the blowing gauze. "No one asked you," she replied thinly. "You have Yirth to thank that we're alive at all. She's been existing on drugs and stamina for the last three days to hold off the storms until we could make port."

"I have Yirth to thank," Sun Wolf said grimly, "that I'm on this pox-rotted vessel to begin with."

There was a momentary silence, Sheera gazing up into his eyes with a dangerous tautness to her face. By the look of it, she hadn't gotten much more sleep in the last several days than Yirth had. Sun Wolf returned her gaze calmly, almost mockingly, daring her to fly into one of her rages.

When she spoke, her voice was almost a whisper. "Just remember," she said, "that I could speak to Yirth and let you scream yourself to death."

Equally softly, he replied, "Then you'd have to find someone else to train your ladies, wouldn't you?"

Sheera's next words were forestalled by the arrival of Gilden, veiled diaphanously and preceding a whole line of porters bearing enough luggage for a year in the wilds. She said quietly to Sheera, "Yirth's in her cabin. She'll wait until the crowds have thinned off a bit, then slip away unnoticed. The ship's coming in this way ahead of the storm will have attracted enough notice as it is; we don't want any of Derroug's spies reporting to Altiokis that Yirth was on board."

Sheera nodded. "All right," she agreed, and Gilden moved off, slipping back effortlessly into the role of an indefatigably frivolous, middle-class globe-trotter amid the welter of her luggage.

They had come in among the quays now, the crew making the ship fast to the long stone wharf. The wet air crackled with orders, curses, and shouts. Farther up the rail, Denga Rey and Amber Eyes were leaning over to wave and call to their cronies on the dock. The fitful, blowing gusts of rain beaded the gladiator's shaven scalp and the courtesan's soft, apricot-colored mane of unveiled hair; both Gilden and Sheera, as was proper for women of their station and class, ignored them totally.

The gangplank was let down. A couple of sailors, a woman and a boy, brought up Sheera's trunk. After a single burning, haughty stare from Sheera, Sun Wolf lifted it to his shoulder and carried it down the cleated ramp at her heels.

The wharves of Mandrigyn, as the Wolf had seen from the deck of the ship, were connected at their landward end by a columned promenade, undoubtedly a strolling place in the heat of the summer for the fashionable of the town. In the winter, with its elaborate topiary laid naked by the winds and its marble pillars and statues stained and darkened by flickering rain, it was drafty and depressing. At a score of intervals along its length, it was broken by brightly tiled footbridges that crossed the mouths of Mandrigyn's famous canals; looking down through the nearest bridge's half-hexagon archway, the Wolf could see a sort of sheltered lagoon there, where half a dozen gondolas rocked on their moorings. Beyond these rainbow-colored, minnowlike boats, the canal wound away into the watery city between the high walls of the houses, the waters shivering where they were brushed by squalls of rain. Everything seemed dark with wetness and clammy with moss. Against this background, the tiny lady who emerged from beneath her oiled-silk canopy to greet Sheera seemed incongruously gaudy.

"Sheera, I was terrified you wouldn't make it into the harbor!" she cried in a high, rather light voice and extended tiny hands, gloved in diamond-speckled confections of white and lavender lace.

Sheera took her hands in greeting, and they exchanged a formal kiss of welcome amid a whirl of wind-torn silk veils. "To tell you the truth, I was afraid of that myself." she admitted, with a smile that was the closest Sun Wolf had seen her get to warm friendliness in all their short acquaintance. Sheera was evidently fond of this woman—and, by her next remark, very much in her confidence.

"Did you find one?" the tiny lady asked, looking up into Sheera's face with a curiously intent expression, as if for the moment, Sheera and Sheera alone existed for her. "Did you succeed?"

"Well," Sheera said, and her glance flickered to Sun Wolf, standing stoically, the trunk balanced on his shoulder, a little way off. "There has been a change in plans."

The woman frowned indignantly, as if at an affront. "What? How?" The wind caught in her lilac-colored veils, blowing them back to reveal a delicate-complected, fine-boned face, set off by beautiful brown eyes under long, perfectly straight lashes. For all that she was as overdressed as a saint in a Trinitarian cathedral, she was a well-made little thing, Sun Wolf judged, both dainty and full-breasted. No girl, but a woman of Sheera's age.

Sheera introduced them quietly. "Drypettis Dru, sister to the governor of Mandrigyn. Captain Sun Wolf, chief of the mercenaries of Wrynde."

Drypettis' eyes, originally dark with indignation at being presented to a slave, widened with shock, then flickered quickly back to Sheera. "You brought their commander *here*?"

From the direction of the ship, the whole gaudy crowd of what looked like prostitutes and gladiators came boiling past them, laughing and joking among themselves. At the sight of Sun Wolf, they let fly a volley of appreciative whistles, groans, and commentary so outspoken that Drypettis Dru stiffened with shocked indignation, and blood came stinging up under the thin skin of her cheeks.

"Really, Sheera," she whispered tightly, "if we must have people like that in the organization, can't you speak to them about being a little more—more seemly in public?"

"We're lucky to have them in our organization, Dru," Sheera said soothingly. "They can go anywhere and know everything—and we will need them all the more now."

The limpid brown eyes darted back to Sheera. "You mean you were asked for more money than you could offer?"

"No," Sheera said quietly. "I can't explain here. I've told Gilden to spread the word. There's a meeting tonight at midnight in the old orangery in my gardens. I'll explain to everyone then."

"But . . ."

Sheera lifted a finger to her for silence. From the direction of the nearest lagoon, a couple of elderly servants were approaching, bowing with profuse apologies to Sheera for being late. She made a formal curtsy to Drypettis and took her leave, walking toward the gondola moored at the foot of a flight of moss-slippery stone stairs without glancing back to see if Sun Wolf were following. After a moment, he did follow, but he felt Drypettis' eyes on his back all the way.

While one servitor was making Sheera comfortable under a canopy in the waist of the gondola, Sun Wolf handed the trunk down the narrow steps to the other one. Before descending, he looked back along the quay, deserted now, with the masts of the ships tossing restlessly against the scudding rack of the sky. He saw the woman Yirth, like a shadow, come walking slowly down the gangplank and pause at its bottom, leaning upon the bronze bollard there as if she were close to stumbling with exhaustion. Then, after a moment, she straightened up, pulled her plain frieze cloak more tightly about her, and walked away into the darkening city alone.

From his loft above the orangery, Sun Wolf could hear the women arriving. He heard the first one come in silence, her footfalls a faint, tapping echo in the wooden spaces of the huge room. He heard the soft whisper of talk when the second one joined her. From the loft's high window, he could see their catlike shapes slip through the postern gate at the bottom of the garden that gave onto the Leam Canal and glide silently from the stables, where, Sheera had told him, there was an old smugglers' tunnel to the cellar of a building on the Leam Lagoon. He watched them scuttle through the shadows of the wet, weedy garden, past the silhouetted lacework of the bathhouse pavilion, and with unpracticed stealth, into the orangery itself.

He had to admit that Sheera had not erred in her choice of location. The orangery was the farthest building from the house, forming the southern end of the quadrangle of its outbuildings. A strip of drying yard, the property wall, and the muddy, greenish canal called Mothersditch separated it from the nearest other building, the great laundries of St. Quillan, which closed up at the third hour of the night. There was little chance they would be overheard if they practiced here.

He lay in the darkness on his narrow cot, listened to the high-pitched, muted babble in the room below, and thought about women.

Women. Human beings who are not men.

Who had said that to him once? Starhawk—last winter, or

the winter before, when she was explaining something about that highly individual fighting style of hers . . . It was something he had not thought of at the time. Now it came back to him, with the memory of those gray, enigmatic eyes.

Human beings who are not men.

Even as a child, he had understood that the demons that haunted the empty marshlands around his village were entities like himself, intelligent after their fashion, but not human. Push them, and they did not react like men.

He had met men who feared women and he understood that fear. Not a physical fear—indeed, it was this type of man who was often guilty of the worst excesses during the sacking of a city. This fear was something deeper. And yet the other side of that coin was the yearning to touch, to possess, the desire for the soft and alien flesh.

There was no logic to it. But training this troop wasn't going to be like training a troop of inexperienced boys, or of men, none of whom weighed over a hundred and thirty pounds.

The day's rain had broken after sundown. A watery gleam of moonlight painted the slanted wall above his head. With the cold wind, voices from the garden blew in—Sheera's, speaking to those wealthier women who had come, as if to a party, in their gondolas to the front door of her great, marble-faced townhouse. Women's voices, like music in the wet night.

Was it training, he wondered, that made women distrustful of one another? The fact that so much was denied them? Maybe, especially in a city like Mandrigyn, where the women were close-kept and forbidden to do those things that would free them from the tutelage of men. He'd seen that before—the hothouse atmosphere of gossip and petty jealousies, of wrongs remembered down through the years and unearthed, fresh and stinking, on the occasions of quarrels. Would women be different if they were brought up differently?

Would men?

His father's bitter, mocking laughter echoed briefly through his mind.

Then he became aware that someone was standing by the foot of his bed.

He had not seen her arrive, nor heard the petal-fall of her feet on the floorboards. Only now he saw her face, floating like a misshapen skull above the dark blob of the birthmark, framed in the silver-shot masses of her hair. He was aware that she had been standing there for some time.

"What the . . ." he began, rising, and she held up her hand.

"I have only come to lay on you the bounding-spells to hold the poison in your veins harmless, so long as you remain in Mandrigyn," she said. "As I am not a true wizard, not come to the fullness of my power, I cannot work spells at a distance by the mind alone." Like a skeleton hand, her white fingers moved in the air, and she added, "It is done."

"You did it all right on the ship," he grumbled sullenly.

One end of that black line of eyebrow moved. "You think so? It is one of the earliest things wizards know—how to come and go unnoticed, even by someone who might be looking straight at them." She gathered her cloak about her, a rustling in the darkness, preparing to go. "They are downstairs now. Will you join them?"

"Why should I?" he asked, settling his shoulders back against the wall at the bed's head. "I'm only the hired help."

The rosewood voice was expressionless. "Perhaps to see what you will have to contend with? Or to let them see it?"

After a moment, he got to his feet, the movement of his shoulders easing a little the unaccustomed pressure of the chain. As he came closer to her, he saw how ravaged Yirth's face was by exhaustion. The black smudges beneath her eyes, the harsh lines of strain, did nothing for her looks. The last days of the voyage were worn into her face and spirit as coal dust wore itself into a miner's hands—to be lightened by time, maybe, but never to be eradicated.

He paused, looking into those cold, green eyes. "Does Sheera know this?" he asked. "If, as you say, you aren't a true wizard—if you haven't come to the fullness of your power—it's insanity for you to go against a wizard who's been exercising his powers for a hundred and fifty years—who's outlived every other wizard in the world and seems to be deathless. Does Sheera know you're not even in his class?"

"She does." Yirth's voice was cool and bitter in the darkness of the room. "It is because of Altiokis that I have not—and will never—come to the fullness of my power as a wizard. My master Chilisirdin gave me the knowledge and the training that those who are born with a mage's powers must have. It is that training which allows me to wring the winds to my commanding, to hold you prisoned, to see through the illusions and the traps with which Altiokis guards the mines. But Chilisirdin was murdered—murdered before she could give to me the secret of the Great Trial. And without that, I will never have the Power."

Sun Wolf's eyes narrowed. "The what?" he asked. In the language of the West, the word connoted a judicial ordeal as well as tribulation; in the northern dialect, the word was sometimes used to mean death as well.

The misshapen nostrils flared in scorn. "You are a man who prides himself on his ignorance of these things," she remarked. "Like love, you can never be sure when they will cross your life, will or nil. Of what the Great Trial consisted I never knew—only that it killed those who were not born with the powers of a mage. Its secret was handed down from master to pupil through generations. I have sought for many years to find even one of that last generation of wizards, or one of their students, who might know what it was—who might have learned how one did this thing that melds the power born into those few children with the long learning they must acquire from a master wizard. But Altiokis has murdered them all, or driven them into hiding so deep that they dare not reveal to any what they are—or what they could have been. That is why I threw in my lot with Sheera. Altiokis has robbed us all—all of us who would have been mages and who are now condemned to this half-life of thwarted longings. It is for me to take revenge upon him, or to die in the trying."

"That's your choice," the Wolf said quietly. "What I object to is your hauling me with you—me and all those stupid women downstairs who think they're going to be trained to be warriors."

The voices rose to them, a light distant babbling, like the pleasant sounds of a spring brook in the darkness. Yirth's eyes flashed like a cat's. "They also have their revenge to take," she replied. "And as for you, you would die for the sake of the two pennies they will put upon your eyes, to pay the death gods to ferry you to Hell."

"Yes," he agreed tightly. "But that's my choice—of time and manner and whom I take with me when I go."

She sniffed. "You have no choice, my friend. You were made what you are by the father who spawned you—as I was made when I was born with the talent for wizardry in my heart and this mark like a piece of thrown offal on my face. You had no more choice in the matter than you had about about the color of your eyes."

She gathered the dark veil about her once again, to cover her ugliness, and in silence descended the stairs.

After a moment, Sun Wolf followed her.

A few candles had been lighted on the table near the staircase, but their feeble light penetrated no more than a dozen feet into the vast wooden vault of the orangery. All that could be seen in that huge darkness was the multiplied reflection in hundreds of watching eyes. Like the wind dying on the summer night, the sound of talking hushed as Sun Wolf stepped into the dim halo of light, a big, feral, golden man, with Yirth like a fell black shadow at his heels.

He had not expected to see so many women. Startled, he cast a swift glance at Yirth, who returned an enigmatic stare. "Where the hell did they come from?" he whispered.

She brushed the thick, silver-shot mane back over her shoulders. "Gilden Shorad," she replied softly. "She and her partner Wilarne M'Tree are the foremost hairdressers in Mandrigyn. There isn't a woman in the city they cannot speak to at will, from noblewomen like Sheera and Drypettis Dru down to common whores."

Sun Wolf looked out at them again—there must have been close to three hundred women there, sitting on the worn and dusty pine of the floor or on the edges of the big earth tubs that contained the orange trees. Smooth, beardless faces turned toward him; he was aware of watching eyes, bright hair, and small feet tucked up underneath the colors of the long skirts. Whether it was from their numbers alone, or whether the hypocaust under the floor had been fired, the huge, barnlike room was warm, and the smell of old dirt and citrus was mingled with the smells of women and of perfume. The rustle of their gowns and of the lace on the wrists of the rich ones was like a summer forest.

Then silence.

Into that silence, Sheera spoke.

"We got back from Kedwyr today," she said without preamble, and her clear, rather deep voice penetrated easily into the fusty brown shadows of the room. "All of you know why we went. You put your money into the venture and your hearts— did without things, some of you, to contribute; or put yourselves in danger; or did things that you'd rather not have done to get the money. You know the value of what you gave—I certainly do."

She stood up, the gold of her brocade gown turned her into

a glittering flame, the stiff lace of her collar tangling with the fire-jewels in her hair. From where he stood behind her, Sun Wolf could see the faces of the women, rapt to silence, their eyes drinking in her words.

"All of you know the plan," she continued, leaning her rump against the edge of the table, her gem-bright hands relaxed among the folds of her skirts. "To hire mercenaries, storm the mines, free the men, and liberate the city from Altiokis and the pack of vultures he's put in charge. I want you to know right away that I couldn't hire anyone.

"Maybe I shouldn't have been surprised," she went on. "Winter's coming. Nobody wants to fight a winter war. Every man's first loyalty is to himself, and nobody wanted to risk Altiokis' wrath, not even for gold. I understand that."

Her voice rose a little, gaining strength and power. "But for them it's only money. For us it's our lives. There isn't a woman here who doesn't have a man—lover, husband, father—who either died at Iron Pass or was enslaved there. And that was every decent man in the city; every man who had the courage to march in Tarrin's army in the first place, every man who understood what would happen if Altiokis added Mandrigyn to his empire. We've seen it in other cities—at Racken Scrag, and at Kilpithie. We've seen him put the corrupt, the greedy, and the unscrupulous into power—the men who'll toad-eat to him for the privilege of making their own money out of us. We've seen him put such a man in charge here."

Their eyes went to Drypettis Dru, who had come in with Sheera and taken her seat as close to the table as she could, almost literally sitting at her leader's feet. Throughout the speech, she had been silent, gazing up at Sheera with the passionate gleam of fanaticism in her brown eyes, her little hands clenched desperately in her lap; but as the women looked at her, she sat up a bit.

"You have all heard the evil reports of Derroug," Sheera said in a quieter tone. "I think there are some of you who have—had experience with his—habits." Her dark eyes flashed somberly. "You will know that his own sister has turned against him and has been like my right hand in organizing our cause."

"Not turned against him," Drypettis corrected in her rather high, breathless voice. "My brother's actions have always been deplorable and repugnant to me. He has disgraced our house, which was the highest in the city. For that I shall never forgive him. Nor for his lewdness toward you, nor—"

"Nor shall any of us forgive him, Drypettis," Sheera said, cutting short what threatened to turn into a discursive catalog of the governor's sins. "We have all seen the evil effects of Altiokis' rule starting here in Mandrigyn. If it is to be stopped, we must stop it now.

"*We* must stop it," she repeated, and her voice pressed heavily on the words. "We are fighting for more than just ourselves. We all have children. We all have families—or had them." A murmur stirred like wind through the room. "Since we can't hire men, we have to learn to do what we can ourselves."

She looked about her, into that shadowy, eye-glittering silence. The candlelight caught in the stiff fabric of her golden gown, making her flash like an upraised sword blade.

"We've all done it," she said. "Since Iron Pass, you've all stepped in to take over your husbands' affairs, in one way or another. Erntwyff, you go out every day with the fishing fleet. Most of the fleet is now manned by fishermen's wives, isn't it? Eo, you've taken over the forge . . ."

"Had to," said a big, cowlike woman, whose whips of ivory-fair hair marked her as a relation of Gilden Shorad's. "Woulda starved, else."

"And you've taken Gilden's daughter Tisa for your apprentice, too, haven't you? Sister Quincis, they tell me they've even been appointing women as provisional priests in the Cathedral, something they haven't done in hundreds of years. Fillibi, you're running your husband's store—and running it damned well, too . . . And nobody cares whether any of you wears a veil or not, or has a chaperon. Business is business.

"Well, our business is defending the city and freeing the men. We've all proved women can work as well as men. I think they can fight as well as men, too.

"I think all of you know," she continued, her voice growing grave, "that if you put a woman with her back to the wall, fighting, not for herself, but for her man, her children, and her home, she's braver than a man, tougher than a man—hell, she's tougher than a cornered rat. And, ladies, that's where we are."

If she asked for volunteers, they'd turn out to a woman, the Wolf thought. *She has a king's magic; that magic of trust.*

Damned arrogant bitch.

Sheera's voice was low; a pin could have been heard dropping in the breathing silence of the orangery. "No," she said,

"I couldn't hire men to do it. But I hired one man—to come here and teach us to do it ourselves. *If* we're willing to fight. There's a difference between just giving money, no matter how much money, and picking up a sword yourself. And I tell you, ladies—now is the time to see that difference."

They could not applaud, for the sound would carry, but the silence was a magic crown on those dark curls. *Point them the way*, Sun Wolf thought cynically, *and they'd march to the mines tonight, the silly bitches, and be dead by morning*. Like too many rulers, Sheera had the quality of making others ready to go out and fight without ever asking themselves what it would cost them.

He gave himself a little shove with his shoulder against the doorframe and walked to where she stood before them in that aura of candle flame, flamelike herself in her golden gown. At this movement, she turned her head, surprised. *Maybe she didn't think I'd speak*, he thought, with a prickle of anger at that certainty of hers. He turned to the devouring sea of eyes.

"What Sheera says is true," he agreed quietly, the gravelly rumble of his voice pitched, as a leader must know how to pitch it, to the size of his troop. "A woman fighting for her children—or occasionally for a man—will fight like a cornered rat. But I've driven rats into corners and killed them with the toe of my boot, and don't think that can't happen to you."

Sheera swung around, the whole of her body glittering with rage. He caught her gaze and silenced her, as if he had laid a hand over her mouth. After a moment, his eyes returned to the women.

"So all right, I agreed to teach you, to make warriors out of you; and by the spirits of my ancestors, I'll do it, if I have to break your necks. But I want you all to understand what it is you're doing.

"War is serious. War is dead serious. You are all smaller, lighter, and slower on the run than men. If you expect to beat men in combat, you had damned well better be twice as good as they are. I can make you twice as good. That's my job. But in the process, you're going to get cut up, you're going to get hurt, you're going to get shouted at and cursed, and you'll crawl home so exhausted you can hardly stand up, because that's the only way to get good, especially if you're little enough for some man to lift and carry away under his arm." His eyes picked the diminutive Gilden Shorad out of the crowd and met a hard, challenging, sea-blue stare.

"So if you don't think you can finish the race, don't waste my time by starting it. Whenever I get a batch of new recruits, I end up shaking out about half of them, anyway. You don't have to be tough to start—I'll make you tough. But you have to stay with it. And you have to be committed to killing people and maybe losing a limb or losing your life. That's war."

His eyes raked them, gleaming like a gold beast's in the dimness: the whores, sweet as all the spices of the East with their curled hair and painted eyes; the brown laborer women, prematurely old, like bundles of dowdy serge; the wives of merchants, now many of them merchants themselves, soft and well cared for in their lace and jewels.

"You decide if you can do it or not," he said quietly. "I want my corps here tomorrow night at this time. That's all."

He turned and met Sheera's eyes. Under her lowered lids he could see the speculation, the curiosity and reevaluation, as if she were wondering what she had brought to Mandrigyn.

CHAPTER

—— 6 ——

"*THIS IS A SWORD*," SUN WOLF SAID. "*YOU HOLD IT BY THIS* end."

He glared at the dozen women who stood in a line before him, all of them wheezing with the exertion of an hour of warming-up and tumbling exercises that had convinced them, as well as their instructor, that they'd never be warriors.

"You." He pointed to Gilden Shorad's partner-in-crime, the tiny, fragile-looking Wilarne M'Tree. She stepped forward, bright, black eyes raised trustingly to his, and he tossed the weapon to her hilt-first. She fielded it, but he saw by the way she caught herself that it was heavier than she'd been ready for.

He held out his hand and snapped his fingers. She threw it back awkwardly. He plucked it out of the air with no visible effort.

"You're going to be working with weighted weapons," he told them, as he'd told the two groups he had worked with last night and would tell another group later on tonight. "That's the only way you can build up the strength in your arms."

One of the women protested, "But I thought we—"

He whirled on her. "You *ask* for permission to speak!" he snapped.

Her face reddened angrily. She was a tall, piquant-faced woman with the red-gold hair of a highlander, her breasts small under their leather binding, her legs rather knock-kneed in her short linen drawers, the marks of past pregnancies printed on

70

the muscleless white flesh of her belly. After a moment, she said in a stifled tone, "Permission to speak, sir."

"Permission granted," he growled.

Permission to speak, he had found, was one of the best ways to break the first rush of hasty words. Most recruits didn't know what they were talking about, anyway.

It worked in this case. Her first outburst checked, the woman spoke in sullenness rather than in outrage. "I thought we were training for a—a surprise attack. A sneak attack."

"You are," Sun Wolf said calmly. "But if something goes wrong, or if you're trapped, you may have to take on a man with a sword—or several men, for that matter. You may have to hold off attackers from the rest of the party or maintain a key position while the others go on. You won't just be fighting for your own life then, you'll be fighting for everybody's."

The woman stepped back, blushing hotly and greatly discomfited. With instinctive tact, the Wolf turned to the other women. "That goes for all of you," he told them gruffly. "And for anything I teach. I was hired because I'm a warrior—I know what you're going to run up against. Believe me, everything I teach you has a purpose, no matter how pointless it seems. I can't take the time to explain it to you. Do you understand?"

Cowed, they nodded.

He bellowed at them, "Don't just stand there bobbing your heads up and down! I can't hear your brains rattle at this distance! Do you understand?"

"Yes, sir," Gilden and Wilarne hastened to reply.

He glared at the group of them. "What?"

All of them chorused this time. "Yes, sir."

He nodded brusquely. "Good." He jerked his thumb at the weapons that lay amid a pile of sacking in one corner of the dimly lighted orangery. "There are your weapons. Along the wall you'll find posts embedded in the floor." He pointed to where he had set the posts himself earlier that day, where they would be easily concealable among the old tree tubs and stacks of clay pots. "I want to see your exercise—backhand, forehand, and down, just those three strokes. First just to get the hang of your sword, then as hard as you can, as if you had a man in front of you, out to slice off your heads."

A few of them looked squeamish at the idea; others started eagerly for the weapons. Sun Wolf roared, "Get back into ranks!"

They did—quickly. The tall woman looked as if she might speak, but thought better of it.

"Nobody breaks ranks until I give the order," he barked at them. "If you were my men, I'd smarten you up with a switch. As it is, all I can do is throw you out on your pretty little arses before you endanger the rest of the troop by failure to obey orders. If I tell you to stand in ranks and then I walk out of the room and take a nap, I'd better find you still in ranks and on your feet when I get back, even if it's the next morning. You understand?"

"Yes, sir," they sang out.

"Now go!" He clapped his hands, and the echoes of it were still ringing in the high rafters as the women scattered to obey.

Behind him, a woman's voice remarked, "You're being nice to them."

He glanced back and met Denga Rey's dark, sardonic eyes. Like him, and like most of the women, the gladiator was stripped for exercise, and her brown body was marked with scars of varying age. The feeble lamplight flashed on the bald arch of her skull.

He grunted. "If you call that 'nice,' you have a different standard of it than I do, woman."

"After the gladiators' school," the warrior returned equably, "you're a lover's caress—and I think we've got the same standard, soldier."

He studied her in silence for a moment. She was younger than he'd first thought, probably not more than twenty-one or twenty-two, a big, dark mare of a girl with belly muscles as ridged and ripply as a crocodile's back. In her alternation of silence and mockery on the voyage, he had sensed her animosity toward him and had wondered what he would do if his only possible second-in-command hated him because she was not first. He knew himself to be an intruder to the organization, whether against his will or not. Sheera was still clearly in command, but he had usurped a spot only slightly below hers; no matter how much they needed him, there was bound to be ill will. He had just been wondering whether it would come down to a physical confrontation between himself and the gladiator when, for reasons of her own, she had apparently decided to accept him; but occasionally he still caught her watching him with a strange gleam in her dark eyes.

"There's no point in taking it out on them because I was

dragooned into this lunacy," he said at last. Then, nodding toward them, he asked, "What do you think of them?"

She grinned. "They're rather sweet," she said. "Six months ago, you'd never have got a sword into their dainty little mitts. But since the men have been gone, they've been learning that they can work—not just these women, or the women in the conspiracy, but all of them. They're running the shops, the farms, and the banking and merchant concerns as well. I think some of them, like our Gilden, even enjoy having a blade in their hands."

He admitted grudgingly, "I will say this for them—they did turn out. That surprised me. Most people will put up all the money you want, from a safe distance."

She shrugged her shoulders, the muscles of them shining like brown hardwood. "They did put up a phenomenal amount of money, you know," she remarked. "For all that little Drypettis gets under my skin, she's a damned good organizer when it comes to the tin side of an operation. She was responsible for that end of it."

"Was she?" His eyes traveled down the line of sweating women, hacking doggedly at their posts, as he searched out Sheera's pint-size disciple.

"Of course. She's still the one who holds the purse strings of the operation. When it was just a question of hiring you and your men, she was Sheera's number two person. It's Dru who's kept that damned brother of hers off our backs, too," she added, flicking a speck of dust from the worn black leather of her breast guard. "She's done one hell of a lot for the organization—but damn, that pinch face of hers sticks in my craw. If Sheera hadn't pointed out to her that what we were doing was a military operation, I don't think she'd ever have spoken to me."

His eyes narrowed as they returned to that straight, rigid back and the long tail of thick brown hair that dangled between those slender shoulders.

Not Denga Rey. It was Drypettis whom he had supplanted.

From what he'd seen of her, she wasn't likely to take kindly to being ousted from her place as Sheera's advisor and relegated to mere trooper—the more so because she was not that good a trooper. He remembered her expression on the wharf when Denga Rey, Amber Eyes, and their rowdy friends had rioted past, whistling at him like a crowd of sailors ogling a girl—

an expression not only of embarrassed rage but also almost of pain at having to associate with such people at all.

Politics makes strange bedfellows and no error, he thought and wondered again how these disparate women had ever come together in the first place.

"And what about you?" he asked Denga Rey as the gladiator stood, scarred arms folded, surveying their joint charges. "How'd a nice girl like you end up in a place like this?"

Her eyes mocked him. "Me? Oh, I'm in this only for the sake of the one I love."

He stared at her in surprise. "You have a man up in the mines?" It was the last thing he would have expected of her.

The curved, black eyebrows shot up; then she burst into a whoop of delighted laughter. "A *man*?" she choked, her eyes dancing. "You think I'd do this for a *man*? Oh, soldier, you kill me." And she swaggered off, chuckling richly to herself.

Sun Wolf shook his head and turned his attention back to the laboring women. The hard maple of the practice posts was barely chipped—none of them seemed to have any idea how to hold or use a sword. He rolled his eyes briefly heavenward, as if seeking advice from his ancestors—not, he reflected, that any of the lunatic berserkers whose seed had spawned him had ever found themselves in the position of teaching a bunch of soft-bred and lily-handed ladies the grim arts of war. Then he went patiently down the line, correcting grips that would surely have cost the wielders their weapons at the first blow, if they didn't break their wrists in the bargain.

Most of the young men who had come to him in Wrynde, singly or in small troops, were not novices. They had handled swords, if only in the more gentlemanly arts of dueling or militia training. Their muscles were hardened from the sports of boys or from work. A fair number of these women—the wealthier ones especially—had very clearly done neither sports nor work since childhood. Their bodies, as he viewed them with a critical eye that brought blushes to the cheeks of those who noticed the direction of his gaze, might be trim enough, but their flesh was slack.

He shook his head again. And they expected to be able to storm the mines! He only hoped to be far along the road to Wrynde when they tried it.

He went back along the line, patiently correcting strokes.

Many of them shied from his touch, having been trained to walk veiled and downcast in the presence of men. The tall woman who had challenged him was red-faced and missish; Gilden Shorad, coldly businesslike; Wilarne M'Tree, grave and trusting. Drypettis jerked violently from his correcting hand, and for a moment he saw in her eyes not only a jealous hatred but terror as well. *A virgin*, he thought. *It figures. And likely to remain that way, for all her prettiness.*

Gently, he held out his hand for the sword and demonstrated the proper way to use it. Those huge, pansy-brown eyes followed the movements of his hand devouringly, without once straying to either his body or his face. Her cheeks were scarlet, as if scalded.

For all that she was a tough little piece, and grittily determined to do well, she was another one, Sun Wolf thought, whom he'd have to watch.

It was only at Sheera's insistence that she had been included in the troop at all.

The first muster of women had yielded over a hundred, of whom he had cut almost half on the spot. Some of them had been dismissed purely for physical reasons—fatness, or that telltale pallor of internal pain that marked old childbirth injuries. Many of them he'd cut because of the obvious signs of drunkenness or drug addiction. Four girls he had rejected simply because they were thirteen years old, though they had sworn, with tears, that they were fifteen and their mothers knew where they were. Three women he had dismissed, as tactfully as he could, because his instincts and a very short observation told him that they were quarrelsome, people who fomented discord either for their own amusement or simply unconsciously, as if they could not help it. The female version of this was less physical than that of the male, but the result was the same. In a secret command, troublemakers were not to be tolerated.

The women who were left were mostly young, the wives of craftsmen and laborers, though there was a fair sprinkling of merchants' wives of varying degrees of wealth. About a dozen were whores, though privately, Sun Wolf did not expect most of them to stay the course. Enormous experience in the field had taught him that most women who sold themselves for a living lacked either discipline or the strength to control their lives—and he suspected this to be true even of those whom he had not rejected out of hand for drinking or drugs. One of the women in the final group that remained was a nun, an elderly woman who'd been the Convent baker for twenty years and had a grip like a blacksmith's. He thought of Starhawk and smiled.

Those who were left he had divided into four groups, with instructions to report on alternate nights, either a few hours after sunset or at midnight. With luck, this arrangement would keep Sheera's townhouse and grounds from being obviously the center of activity, for there were three or four ways into the compound, and others were being devised. Yirth had sworn a death curse upon betrayal from within, and the women had sworn fellowship with one another and loyalty to Sheera.

They were as safe as they could be, given the appalling circumstances, but Sun Wolf looked down the line of those white, sweating, sluglike bodies with no particularly sanguine hopes of success.

The women slipped quietly away from the bathhouse at the bottom of the grounds nearly two hours later, gowned once more as the respectable matrons or maidens they had been before they took up the study of arms. From the dark door of the orangery, Sun Wolf watched them, brief shadows against the dull, reddish glow from the pavilion's windows, seeking passages, posterns, plank bridges over the canals, and the narrow back streets that would lead them to gondolas tied up in secluded courtyard lagoons. Light rainfall pattered on the bare, gray stems of the deserted garden. Beyond the walls, the lapping of the canals formed the murmurous background music to all life in that watery city.

The water clock in the dim room behind him told him that it would shortly be midnight. The women of the next group would appear soon.

The cold dampness bit into the bare flesh of his shoulders and legs, and he turned back into the silent wooden vaults of the organgery itself.

Sheera was there, wrapped in a shawl of flame-colored wool whose fringes brushed her bare feet. She was dressed for training in short drawers and leather guards, and her dark eyes were angry.

"Do you have to run them so hard?" she demanded shortly. "Some of them are so exhausted they can hardly stagger."

"You want to ask 'em whether they'd rather be exhausted now or slaughtered to the last woman later on?"

Her face reddened. "Or are you trying to run them all out,

in the hopes that I'll give up my plans to free the men from the mines?"

"Women, I've learned by this time it's no use hoping you'll give up any plan that you've come up with, no matter how witless it is," he snapped at her, walking over to the room's single brazier of charcoal to rub his hands over the molten glow of the blaze. "If those women can't take it, they'd better get out of the army. We don't know what kind of resistance you'll meet with up in the mines. Since you've made me the instructor, I'm damned well going to prepare those women for anything."

"There's no need to—" she began hotly.

"There is, unless they train more than a couple of hours every other night!" He swung back to face her, the reflection of the fire edging him in a line of gold. "And considering that you couldn't come up with more than fourteen swords . . ."

"We're doing what we can about that!" she retorted. "And about finding somewhere else to practice during the daytime. But the first thing Derroug Dru did when he came to power was collect every weapon in the city—"

"I told you that in the beginning."

"Shut up! And he has spies everywhere within the walls."

"Then meet outside the city."

"Where?" she lashed out viciously.

With silky sweetness he replied, "That's your affair, madam. I'm only your humble slave, remember? But I'm telling you that if those women don't get more training than they're getting, they'll never be soldiers."

"Do you sometimes wonder if Sheera is crazy?" he asked Amber Eyes, much later, as the pale glow of the sinking moon broke through the clouds to filter through the loft window and touch the fallow gold of her hair. It lay like a river of silk over his arm and chest, almost white against the brown of his skin.

She considered the matter for a moment, a grave look coming into those usually dreamy, golden eyes. *Bedroom eyes*, he called them, gentle and a little vulnerable, even when she was wielding a sword. At length she said, "No. At least, no crazier than the rest of us."

He shifted his shoulders against the pillow. "That isn't saying much."

She turned her head, where it lay in the crook of his arm, and studied him for a moment, a tiny frown creasing her brow. The moonlight glimmered on the thread-fine chain of gold that encircled her throat, its shadow like a delicate pen stroke where it crossed the tiny points of her collarbone and vanished into the softer shadows of her hair.

The night of the first meeting in the orangery, when he had come up the stairs, she had been here, waiting, sitting on the edge of the narrow bed, clothed only in that heavy golden mane. Never one to question opportunity, Sun Wolf had taken her—that night and on the two nights since. He occasionally wondered why she had come to him, since she was obviously afraid of him; but aside from the love talk of her trade, she was a silent girl, enigmatic and evasive when he spoke to her.

Tonight was the first time she had treated him like a partner in the same enterprise, rather than a customer.

The orangery below them was silent now, and the garden still but for the incessant whisper of the canal beyond the walls. After a final, inconclusive quarrel with Sheera, Sun Wolf had gone to the bathhouse, dark after the departure of the women, its only light the soft, red pulsation under the copper boilers. By this dim glow, he'd stripped, left his clothes on the baroque, black and gilt marble bench in the antechamber, washed, and then swum for a time in the lightless waters of the hot pool.

It had eased his muscles, if not his feelings.

When Amber Eyes had been too long silent, he said, "She's crazy if she thinks she's going to rescue this Prince Tarrin safe and sound. Oh, I know someone's supposed to have seen him alive, but they always say that of a popular ruler."

"Oh, no." She sat up a little, those gold kitten eyes very earnest in the wan moonlight. "I've seen him. In fact, I delivered a message to him only a few weeks ago, the last time I was up in the mines making maps."

Sun Wolf stared at her. "What?"

"Oh, yes," she said. "We've all seen him—Cobra, Crazyred . . ." She named two of the other courtesans in the troop. "Plus a lot of the girls you cut—the pros, I mean. How else could we let him know what's going on here?"

"You mean," Sun Wolf said slowly, "you've been in communication with the men all along?"

"Of course." Amber Eyes sat up with a swift, compact lightness and shook out the splendid pale gold mane around shoulders that gleamed like alabaster in the shadows. She seemed to forget the lanquid grace of a courtesan and hugged her arms around her knees. "I expect Sheera didn't want to tell you about it," she added frankly, "but that end of the organization was set up—oh, long before we went to fetch you."

The disingenuous phrase made him smile. For all her shy appearance, when she wasn't hiding behind what Sun Wolf thought of as her professional manner, Amber Eyes could be disarmingly outspoken. He'd seen it in her dealings with other women in the troop. It was as if she showed to men—to her customers—only what they thought they wanted to see.

"Did Sheera set that up?" he wanted to know.

She shook her head. "This was before Sheera and Dru got into it. It came about almost by chance, really. Well, you know that the city was very hard hit, with the men gone. We—the pros—didn't feel it emotionally so sharply, except for those who had regular lovers who had marched with Tarrin. But I remember one afternoon I went to Gilden's hairdressing parlor—all of us who can afford the prices go to Gilden and Wilarne—and she said that her own husband had been killed, but that Wilarne didn't know whether Beddick—her husband—was alive or dead. Gilden said that many others were in the same situation. Wilarne was half distracted by grief—not that Beddick was anyone to compose songs about, mind you—and I said I'd see what I could learn. So I went riding in the foothills near one of the southern entrances to the mines that looks out onto Iron Pass and I let my horse get away from me and pretended to sprain my foot—the usual." She smiled with remembered amusement. "The superintendent of that end of the mines was very gallant.

"After that it was easy. The next time I went up, I brought friends. The superintendents of the various sections of the mines and the sergeants of the guards don't get into town often. It's forbidden to them to have women up to the barracks, but who's going to report it? Gilden and I were able to set up a regular information service that way, getting news of who was dead and who was alive—Beddick the Bland for one, and, eventually, Tarrin."

Her face clouded in the veiled moonlight. "That was how Sheera came into it in the first place. She'd heard that there was a way of getting news. She got word to me through Gilden. By that time we had girls going up almost every day and we were starting to pass messages in code. Tarrin, it turned out, was starting to organize the miners already, passing messages from gang to gang as they were taken here and there to different work sites in the mines. The men are taken from one place to another in darkness, so they haven't any clear idea of where they are in the tunnels; if a man wanders away from his gang, he can wander in the deeper tunnels until he dies. The tunnels are gated, too, and locked off from one another. But they were starting to work up maps by the time we got in touch with them. On our end, we'd already begun to make maps of the mine entrances, the guardrooms, and where the main barracks are that guard the tunnels from the mines up into the Citadel of Grimscarp itself."

Sun Wolf frowned. "There are ways from the Citadel down into the mines?"

"That's what the miners say. It's because the Citadel's so inaccessible from the outside—it's very defensible, of course, but because of the way it's placed, on the very edge of the cliff, the road from Racken Scrag—the Wizard King's administrative town at the other end of Iron Pass—has to tunnel through a shoulder of the mountain itself even to get to the gates. Since it was so expensive to bring food up the Scarp, they connected that tunnel directly with the mines; now they haul the food straight up from Racken through the mountain itself. The ways into the Citadel from the mines are said to be heavily guarded by magic and illusion."

"But if you women storm the mines," the Wolf said grimly, "Altiokis can send his troops right down on top of you directly from the Citadel. Isn't that right?"

"Well . . ." Amber Eyes said unhappily. "If we strike quickly enough . . ."

"Wonderful." He sighed and slumped back against the pillows. "More battles have been lost because some fool of a general was basing his plans on 'if this or that.'"

"We do have Yirth, though," the girl said defensively. "She can protect us against the worst of Altiokis' magic and spot his illusions."

"Yirth." He sniffed, his fingers involuntarily touching the metal links of his chain. "That's how she got into this, isn't it?"

"Well, yes." Amber Eyes looked down at her hands, restlessly pleating a corner of the sheet between her fingers. Outside, a wind-tossed branch scratched like a ghoul's fingers at the roof. The lantern on a passing gondola reflected in a watery smear of dark gold against the window's rippled glass.

"It was Sheera who brought Yirth into it," she said at length. "We all knew Yirth, of course—I don't think there's a woman in the city who hasn't gone to her for contraceptives, abortions, love philters, or just because she's the only doctor in the city who's a woman. Sheera was one of the very few who knew she was a wizard. She never had anything to do with the organization when all we did was pass information back and forth.

"But when Sheera came into it—she changed it. Before, it had all been so hopeless. What was the point in communicating with the men in the mines, even if they were men you loved, if there was no hope of their ever getting out? If something went wrong here—if your property was confiscated, or your friends arrested—you couldn't tell them of it, really, because it would only add to their misery. But Sheera was the one who said that where information could be exchanged, plans could be formed. She gave us hope.

"And then Dru figured out a way that we could get money from the treasury, and they started raising funds to hire mercenaries. And . . ." She spread her hands, her fine fingers almost translucent in the ivory moonlight. "Our organization became a part of theirs—and Tarrin's. Tarrin and the men are still getting us information on the mines, sending it through the skags . . ."

"The what?" The word was familiar to him from mercenary slang; he knew it to mean the cheapest sort of women who'd sell themselves to hide tanners and garbagemen for the price of a cup of inferior wine.

"The skags." She widened those soft, mead-colored orbs at him. "You know—the ugly women or the fat ones or the old, flabby ones. The guards think it's hilarious to throw them to a gang of miners. Some of the slaves down there have been in the mines so long they're almost beasts themselves." The delicate lips tightened into momentary hardness, and an anger that he had never seen before flashed in those kitten eyes. "They'll drag one of these women down and toss her into a slave barracks, say, 'Have at her, boys,' and then leave."

She was silent for a moment, looking out into the distance, drawing the edge of the sheet over and over through her fingers. Outwardly her face was calm, but her rage against the men who had the power to do this—and perhaps against all men— was like a heat that he could feel through her silken skin where it touched his shoulder. And who was he to argue? he wondered bitterly. The memory of things that he himself, or men he had known, had considered funny while half drunk and sacking a city silenced him before her anger.

Then she shrugged and put the anger aside. "But it's the skags who communicate from gang to gang of the men. Mostly Tarrin's orders keep them from being abused. The superintendents keep mixing the newcomers, the men of Mandrigyn, in with older miners—there are thousands of them down there—to prevent the men from plotting among themselves. But they only spread the plot. And the rest of us—the ones most of these men wouldn't let their wives talk to before the war—have gotten maps of the mines and wax impressions of the keys to the gates—you know Gilden's sister Eo is a smith? She copies the keys—and details of where the armories are."

He settled his back against the wall and regarded her almost wonderingly in the shadows. Outside, the moonlight was dimming, and the smell of rain blew in through the window like a cold perfume. Limned by the faint light, the girl's face looked young, almost childlike; he remembered her by candlelight in the rose-scented room in Kedwyr, laughing that soft, throaty, professional laugh as she drew him into the conspiracy's trap. He realized that it was a compliment to him that she showed him her other face—frank, open, without artifice, the face she showed her women friends. Undoubtedly, it was the face she showed her lover. He found himself wondering if she had a lover, as opposed to a "regular"; or if he, like Gilden's nameless husband, like Beddick M'Tree, like so many others, had followed Tarrin of the House of Her on that last campaign up to the Iron Pass.

The warm weight of her settled against his shoulder, a gesture of intimacy that was less sexual than friendly, like a cat deciding to settle on his knee. "We've been talking too much," she said, and her professional voice was back, soft and teasing.

"One more question," he said. "Why are you here?"

She smiled.

He intercepted her reaching hand. "You're afraid of me, aren't you?"

He felt her body shift in the circle of his arm; when she answered, her voice was that of a girl of nineteen, scarred by what she was, but frank and without artifice. "I was," she said. Moonlight tipped her lashes in silver as she looked up at him. "But I didn't think it was fair for you not to know how things stood with the organization. Dru and Sheera said that the less you knew, the less you could tell anyone. But as for your question . . ." Her lips brushed his in the darkness. "I have my secrets, too."

He drew her to him. As he moved, the links of the chain around his neck jangled faintly in the silence of the dark loft.

CHAPTER

—— 7 ——

THE PROBLEMS OF WEAPONS AND OF A SECONDARY PLACE TO practice by daylight, away from Derroug Dru's spies, were solved, not by Sheera's ingenuity, but by fate, guided presumably by Sun Wolf's deceased and uproariously amused ancestors.

The Thanelands that lay to the east of Mandrigyn had long been under the governorship of Altiokis; indeed, the haughty and old-fashioned Thanes of the clans that held them had been the first to swear allegiance to the Wizard King. But Altiokis' realm had spread to the richer cities of the coastlands and had drawn upon the slave-worked veins of gold and silver in the mountains for its wealth. The Thanelands were left, as they had always been, as a useless and sparsely populated backwater. The roads winding into those gray hills from the jumble of taverns and dives of East Shore led nowhere. After the sheep that grazed on the scraggly grass and heather had been folded in for the winter, the Thanelands lay utterly empty.

So it was an easy matter for the women to slip across the Rack River in the predawn darkness of a rainy morning and be away from all sight of the city by sunup, to run in the wilderness of whin and peat bogs unobserved.

Freezing wind blew another squall of rain over Sun Wolf's bare back. In the low ground between the drenched, gray hills, the water lay like hammered silver, just above the freezing point; on the high ground, the rocks made the easiest going, for the wet, bare, winter-tough brambles could scratch even the most liberally mud-armored flesh.

Ahead of him, the main pack of the running women bobbed through the colorless light of the wan afternoon. They were clearly flagging.

Those who hadn't braided their hair up wore it in slick, sodden cloaks down over their backs. Just ahead of him, a slender woman raised her arms to gather up a soaked blond coil that reached almost down to her shapely backside, her pace slackening as she did so. Sun Wolf, overtaking her in the slashing rain, bellowed, "You going to mess with your poxy hair in battle, sweetheart?"

She turned a startled, flowerlike face upon him, now haggard with fatigue; others, as guilty as she, looked also. He raised his voice into a cutting roar, meant to be heard over the din of battle. "Next person who touches her hair, I'm going to cut it off!"

They all buckled to and ran harder, arms swinging, knees pumping, leather-bound breasts bouncing, drawers sticking wetly to their bodies in the rain. They had all come to the conclusion, in the course of the last week, that there was not a great deal that Sun Wolf would not do.

And that, he thought grimly as he increased his own pace and forged easily ahead through the pack, was as it should be.

Very few of the women ran well. Tisa did—Gilden Shorad's leggy fifteen-year-old daughter. So did whatever her name was— a rangy, homely mare of a fisherman's wife—Erntwyff Fish. So did Denga Rey. The rest of them had been soft-raised, and even the hardiest had neither the wind nor the endurance for sustained fighting.

A few of them, Sun Wolf was amused to note, still suffered agonies of self-consciousness about being near naked in the presence of a man.

He passed Sheera, laboring exhaustedly in the rear third of the field. Her black hair was plastered to her cheeks where it had come out of its braids; she was muddy, wet, gasping, and still enough to stir a man's blood in his veins. He hoped viciously that she was enjoying training as a warrior.

On the whole, Sun Wolf was surprised at how many had lasted that first week.

A week's hard training had cut their numbers down to fifty, and it spoke well for their determination that any had remained at all. All of them—maidens, matrons, and those who were neither—had been subjected to the most taxingly rigorous physical training that Sun Wolf could devise: tumbling to train the reflexes and identify the cowards; weights and throwing to strengthen the arms; hand-to-hand fighting, wrestling, or dueling with blunted weapons; running on the hills. These were preliminaries to the more vicious arts of infighting and sneaky death to come.

Women who the Wolf would have sworn would make champions with the best had dropped out; half-pints like Wilarne M'Tree and maladroits like Drypettis Dru were still with them. He could see those two from where he ran, laboring along a dozen yards behind the rest of the pack.

Sun Wolf was rapidly coming to the conclusion that he did not and never would understand women.

Starhawk . . .

He had always thought of Starhawk as different from other women, even from the other warrior women of his own troop. It was only now, when he was surrounded by women, that elements of her personality fell into place for him, and he saw her as both less and more enigmatic, a woman who had rejected the subjugation these women had been trained in—had rejected it long before her path had crossed his own.

Briefly the memory of their first meeting flitted through his mind; how cold the spring sunlight had been in the garden of the Convent of St. Cherybi, and how strong the smell of the new-turned earth. He saw her again as the tall girl she had been, ascetic, distant, and cold as marble in the dark robes of a nun. He'd forgotten why he'd even been at the Convent— probably extorting provisions from the Mother there—but he remembered that moment when their eyes met and he knew that this woman was a warrior in her heart.

He had never believed that he would miss her as much as he did. Amber Eyes was sweet-natured and supremely beddable, exactly the kind of girl he liked—or had liked, anyway—but it was Starhawk for whom he reached, as a man in danger would reach for his sword. He had never quite gotten over not having her there at his side.

His front runners were cresting the final hill above the copse of woods where they had gathered that morning. They'd covered about two and a half miles—not bad for a first run, for women untrained to it, he thought as he slacked his pace and let himself fall back through the pack once more. He yelled a curse at Gilden, who was flagging, her face the bright fuschia hue that extremely fair women turned in exhaustion; she staggered into a futile but gratifying attempt at a burst of speed.

He cursed them as he would have cursed his men, calling them cowards, babies, sluts. As he fell back farther in the group, to run beside the grimly stumbling Sister Quincis, he yelled, "I've seen Trinitarian heretics run faster than that!"

They broke over the crest of the hill in a spilling wave. Below them, the land lay barren and grayish brown under the sluicing rain, the long snake of silver water in the bottom of the vale reflecting the colorless sky. The brush around it was black, dead with winter. Sun Wolf slowed his pace still further to round in the last of the stragglers. Denga Rey, her hard brown muscles shining with moisture, had already reached the mere below.

He yelled after them, "Run, you lazy bitches!" and collected a look from Drypettis that could have been bottled and sold to remove the veneer from furniture. He was almost standing still as Wilarne M'Tree staggered past. He hurried her on her way with a swat on her little round rump.

By the time he reached the growing group around the water, two or three of them had recovered enough breath to begin throwing up.

"You do that in the woods under the leaves where it's not going to be seen by an enemy scout!" he roared at the green-faced and retching Eo. "You want Altiokis' spies to follow the stink of you to your hideout? I mean it!" he added as she started to double over again and, seizing her by the back of the neck, he shoved her toward the trees. Others had begun to stumble in that direction already.

To Sheera, for whom it was too late, he ordered, "Clean that up."

Without a word, for she was far past speech, she gathered up leaves to obey him.

"And the rest of you start walking," he ordered curtly. "You'll get chilled if you stand around, and I'm not going to have the lot of you sniveling and fainting on me at practice tonight."

"Very nice!" A voice, deep and harsh as a crow's, laughed from the sheltering darkness of the nearby woods. "I had been told that any excuse for a red-blooded male in Mandrigyn had been sent to the mines. I am pleased to see that the reports were exaggerated."

Sun Wolf swung around. White-faced, Sheera got to her feet. A tall bay horse stepped from the tangled brambles of the thickets. The woman on its back sat sidesaddle, her body straight as a spear. In the shadows of a green oilskin hood, hazel-gray eyes flashed mockingly. The cloak covered most of her, except for the hem of her gown and her gloves, and these were of such barbaric richness as to leave little doubt about her station. The bay's bridle had cheekpieces of brass, worked into the shape of flowers.

"Marigolds," Sheera said quietly. "The emblem of the Thanes of Wrinshardin."

The old woman turned her head with a slow, ironic smile. "Yes," she purred. "Yes, I am Lady Wrinshardin. The Thane's mother, not his wife. And you are, unless I am much mistaken, the legendary Sheera Galernas, in whose honor my son once wrote such puerile verse."

Sheera's chin came up. The thick curls of her black hair plastered wetly to her cheeks, and the rain gleamed on her bare arms and shoulders, which had already turned bright red with cold and gooseflesh. "If your son is the present Thane of Wrinshardin who courted me when I was fifteen," she replied coolly, "I am pleased to see that your taste in poetry so closely parallels my own."

There was a momentary silence. Then that mocking smile widened, and Lady Wrinshardin said, "Well. At the time, I presumed that, like most town-bred hussies, you had turned down the chance of wedding decent blood out of considerations of money and the boredom of country life. I am pleased to see that you acted rather from good sense." The sharp, faded old eyes casually raked the scene before her, taking in the exhausted, bedraggled woman and the big man with the chain about his neck who had not the eyes of a slave.

"I don't suppose I have ever seen a man chase this many women since my husband died," she remarked in her harsh, drawling voice. "And even he never did so fifty at a time. Is running about the hills naked in the wintertime a new fad in the town, or could it be that there is a purpose behind this?"

"Not anything anyone's likely to hear of."

Lady Wrinshardin turned her head slowly at the sound of Denga Rey's voice, as if she had just noticed the big gladiator. The wrinkled eyelids drooped. "Do I detect a threat in that rather cryptic utterance?" she inquired disinterestedly.

The horse flung up its head with a squeal of fear. From the wet underbrush of the woods, a ring of women materialized behind and around Lady Wrinshardin, some of them a little pale, but all as grim-faced as bandits.

One eyebrow slowly ascended that corrugated forehead. "Goodness," she murmured to herself. Then, with a quick tweak of the reins, she wheeled the horse and spurred through the line, heading for open country.

"Stop her!" Sheera barked.

Hands grabbed at the bridle, the horse rearing and lashing out at the women who crowded so close around it. Denga Rey caught the bit, dragging its head down while the animal twisted violently to get free. "Enough!" Lady Wrinshardin said sharply, keeping her seat on that pirouetting saddle with the aplomb of a grandmother riding her rocking chair. "You've proved your courage; there's no need to be redundant about it to the point of damaging his mouth."

The dark woman released her pressure on the bit, but did not step back. Tisa clung grimly to the rein on the other side, her hair in her eyes, looking absurdly young. The haughty noblewoman gazed about at the women hemming her in, and the mocking, amused smile returned to her wrinkled face.

Abruptly she extended her hand to Tisa. "You may help me down, child."

Startled, the girl held out her clasped hands to make a step. With a single lithe movement, Lady Wrinshardin stepped to the ground and crossed the wet grass to where Sheera stood. She had the haughty and self-centered carriage of a queen.

"Your troops are well trained," she remarked.

Sheera shook her head. "Only well disciplined." Alone of the women, she did not appear to be awed by that elegant matriarch. Even Drypettis, whose family—as she hastened to remind anyone who was interested—was among the highest in the city, was cowed. After a moment, Sheera added, "In time, they will be well trained."

The eyes flickered to Sun Wolf speculatively, then back to Sheera again. "You were wise not to wed my son," the lady said, putting back the oilskin hood to reveal a tight-coiled braid of white hair pinned close about her head. "He has no more courage than a cur dog that suffers itself to be put out into the rain and fed only the guts of its kills. He is like his father, who also feared Altiokis. Have you met Altiokis?"

Sheera looked startled at the question, as if meeting the Wizard King were tantamount to meeting one's remoter ancestors, Sun Wolf thought—or meeting the Mother or the Triple God in person.

The lady's thin lip curled. "He is vulgar," she pronounced.

"How such a creature could have lived these many years..."
Under their creased lids, her eyes flickered, studying Sheera,
and her square-cut lips settled into their fanning wrinkles with
a look of determination. Sun Wolf was uncomfortably reminded
of an old aunt of his who had kept all of his family and most
of the tribe in terror for years.

"Come with me to the top of the hill, child," she said at
last. The two women moved off through the wet, winter-faded
grass; then Lady Wrinshardin paused and glanced back, as if
as an afterthought, at the Wolf. "You come, too."

· He hesitated, then obeyed her—as everyone else must also
obey her—following them up the steep slope where granite
outcrops thrust through the shallow soil, as if the body of the
earth were impatient with that thin and unproductive garment.
Greenish-brown hills circled them under the blowing dun rags
of the hoary sky.

"My great-grandfather swore allegiance to the Thane of
Grimscarp a hundred and fifty years ago," Lady Wrinshardin
said after they had climbed in silence for a few moments, with
the tor still rising above their heads, vast as an ocean swell.
"Few remember him or the empire that he set out to build, he
and his son. In those days, many rulers had court wizards. The
greater kings, the lords of the Middle Kingdoms in the southwest, could afford the best. But those who served the Thanes
were either the young, unfledged ones, out to make their rep-
utations, or the ones who hadn't the ability to be or do anything
more. They were all of a piece, pretty much—my great-grandfather had one, the Thanes of Schlaeg had one... and the
Thanes of Grimscarp, the most powerful of the Tchard Mountain Thanes, had one.

"His name was Altiokis.

"This much I had from my grandfather, who was a boy
when the Thane of Grimscarp started setting up an alliance of
all the Thanes of all the great old clans, the ancient warrior
clans here, in the Tchard Mountains, and down along the Bight
Coast, where they hadn't been pushed out by a bunch of jumped-
up tradesmen and weavers who lived behind city walls and
never put their noses out of doors to tell which way the wind
was blowing. This was in the days before the nuuwa began to
multiply until they roamed the mountains and these hills like
foul wolves, the days before those human-dog-things, those
abominations they call ugies, had ever been heard of. The old
Thane of Grim wanted to get up a coalition of the Thanes and

the merchant cities and he was succeeding quite nicely, they say.

"But something happened to him. Grandfather couldn't remember clearly whether it was sudden or gradual; he said the old Thane's grip seemed to slip. A week, two weeks, then he was dead. His son, a boy of eighteen, ruled the new coalition, with Altiokis at his side. None of us was ever quite sure when the boy dropped out of sight."

The steepness of the hill had slowed their steps, the old woman and the young one leaning into the slope. Glancing back, the Wolf could see the other women moving about down below, their flesh bright against the smoky colors of the ground. Tisa and her aunt, Gilden's sister, the big, bovine Eo, were holding the horse still and stroking its soft nose; Drypettis, as usual, was sitting apart from the others, talking to herself; her eyes were jealously following Sheera.

The freshening wind cracked in Lady Wrinshardin's cloak like an unfurling sail. The wry old voice went on. "Altiokis' first conquest was Kilpithie—a fair-sized city on the other side of the mountains; they wove quite good woolen cloth there. He used its inhabitants as slaves to build his new Citadel at the top of the Grim Scarp, where he'd raised that stone hut of his in a single night. They said that he used to go up there to meditate. From there he raised his armies and founded his empire."

"With the armies of the clans?" Sheera asked quietly.

They had paused for breath, but the climb had warmed her again, and she stood without shivering, the wind that combed the hillcrests tangling her black hair across her face.

"At first," the lady said grimly. "Once he began to mine gold from the Scarp and from the mountains all about it, he could afford to hire mercenaries. They always said there was another evil that marched in his armies, too—but maybe it was only the sort of men he hired. He pollutes all he touches. Strange beasts multiply in his realm. You know ugies? Ape-things—the Tchard Mountains are stiff with them, though they were never seen before. Nuuwa—"

"Altiokis surely didn't invent nuuwa," Sun Wolf put in. He shook his wet hair back, freeing it of the chain around his neck; he was aware of the old lady's sharp eyes gauging him, judging the relationship between the chain and Sheera against the sureness and command in his voice. He went on. "You get nuuwa turning up in records of one place or another for as far back as the records go. They're mentioned in some of the oldest songs of my tribe, ten, twelve, fifteen generations ago. Every now and again, you'll just get them, blundering around the wilderness, killing and eating anything they see."

The fine-chiseled nostrils flared a little, as if Lady Wrinshardin were unwilling to concede any evil for which Altiokis were not reponsible. "They say that nuuwa march in his armies."

"I've heard that," the Wolf said. "But if you know anything about nuuwa, you'd know it's impossible. For one thing, there just aren't that many of them. They—they simply appear, but their appearances are few and far between."

"Not so few these days," she said stubbornly. She pulled her oilskin cloak more tightly about her narrow shoulders and continued up the hill.

"And anyway," the Wolf argued as he and Sheera fell into step with her once more, "they're too stupid to march anywhere. Hell, all they are is walking mouths . . ."

"But it cannot be denied," the lady continued, "that Altiokis spreads evil to what he touches. The Thanes served him once out of regard for their vows to the Thane of Grim. Now they do so from fear of him and his armies."

They stopped at the crest of the hill, while the winds stormed over and around them like the sea between narrow rocks. Below them on the other side, the Thanelands rolled on, silent and haunting in their winter drabness, possessed of a weird spare beauty of their own. The dead heather and grass of the hills of slate-gray granite gleamed silver with wetness. Twisted trees clung to the skyline like bent crones and shook flailing fists at the heavens.

Far off, in a cuplike depression between three hills, a single, half-ruined tower pointed like a broken bone end toward the windy void above.

"What you're doing is foolish, you know," the lady said.

Sheera's nostrils flared, but she said nothing. *Quite a tribute*, the Wolf thought, *to the old broad's strength of character, if she can keep Sheera quiet*.

"I suppose there's some scheme afoot in the city to free Tarrin and the menfolk and retake Mandrigyn. As if, having beaten them once, Altiokis could not do so again."

"He beat them because they were divided by factions," Sheera said quietly. "I know. My husband was the first man in Derroug Dru's party and had more to do than most with Altiokis' victory. Many of the men who supported Altiokis'

cause—the poorer ones, whose favor he did not need to buy—
were sent to the mines as well. And my girls, the whores who
go up to the mines, tell me that there is another army of miners,
from all corners of Altiokis' realm, who would fight for the
man who freed them."

"Your sweetheart Tarrin."

Color blazed into Sheera's face, her red lips opening to
retort.

"Oh, yes, my girl, we've heard all about your Golden Prince,
for all that his family were parvenus who made their money
off a salt monopoly and from draining the swamps to build
East Shore. Better blood than your precious husband's, anyway." She sniffed.

"My husband—" Sheera began hotly.

Lady Wrinshardin cut her off. "You really think this pack
of white-limbed schoolgirls can be taught to overcome Altiokis'
mercenaries?"

Sheera's lips tightened, but she said nothing.

The lady glanced down into the vale behind them, as haughty
as if she reviewed her own troops. Her hands, in their crimson
and gold gloves, stroked the oilskin of her cloak.

"I'll tell you this, then. If you succeed in what you aim,
don't return to the city. The tunnels of the mine connect with
the Citadel itself. Cut off the serpent's head—don't go back
to hide behind her walls and wait for it to get you."

Eyes widening with alarm, Sheera whispered, "That's impossible. Those ways are guarded by magic. Altiokis himself
is deathless . . ."

"He wasn't birthless," Lady Wrinshardin snapped. "He was
born a man and, like a man, he can be killed. Attack the Citadel,
and you'll have the Thanes on your side—myself, Drathweard
of Schlaeg, and all the little fry as well. Wait for him to put
the city under siege again, and he'll fall on you with everything
he's got."

She jerked her chin toward the rolling valleys and distant
tower. "That's the old Cairn Tower. The Thanes of Cairn ran
afoul of the fifteenth Thane of Wrinshardin, God rest what
passed in them for souls. The place hasn't been inhabited since.
It is a good run," she added with a malicious glitter in her eyes,
"from here."

And turning, she moved back down the hill, straight and
arrogant as a queen of these wild lands. Sheera and Sun Wolf

marked the location of the tower with their eyes and followed
her down.

While she was mounting her horse beside the mere again,
the lady said, as if as an afterthought, "They used to say that
weapons were stored there. I doubt you'll find any of the old
caches, but you are welcome to whatever you come across."

She settled herself in the saddle and collected the reins with
a spare economy of movement that spoke of a life lived in the
saddle. "Come out of that web-footed marsh to visit me, if you
will," she added. "We need to further our acquaintance."

So saying, she wheeled her horse and, ignoring the other
women as if they had not existed, rode through them and away
over the moors.

After that they met mornings and evenings, rotating the
groups—by daylight in the ruins of the old Cairn Tower, by
lamplight in the boarded-up orangery. Sun Wolf announced
that running to and from the peasant hut where they frequently
hid their cloaks would provide the conditioning necessary for
wind and muscles, and thereafter seldom took the women on
a general run. Within a week he could tell which ones ran to
and from the tower and which walked.

The ones who walked—there were not many—were cut.

And all the while, he could feel them coming together as a
force under his hand. He was beginning to know them and to
understand the changes he saw in them, not only in their bodies
but in their minds as well. With their veils and chaperons, they
had—timidly at first, then more boldly—discarded the instinctive notion that they were incapable of wielding weapons, even
in their own defense. Since his conversation with Amber Eyes,
Sun Wolf had often wondered what went on in the minds of
those pliant, quiet ones, the ones who had been raised to tell
men only what they wanted to hear. These women looked him
in the face when they spoke to him now, even the shyest. He
wondered whether that was the effect of weapons training or
whether it was because, when they weren't learning how to
fight, they were running the financial life of the city.

He had to admit to himself that, after a discouraging start,
they were turning out to be a fairly good batch of warriors.

The weapons they found cached in the Cairn Tower were
old, and their make cruder and heavier than was general among
the expert metalworkers of Mandrigyn. Gilden's sister Eo and
young Tisa set up a forge at the tower to lighten them as much

as they could without losing the weight necessary to parry and deliver killing strokes. Denga Rey, watching the practice at the tower one day, suggested that the half-pints of the troop use halberds instead.

"A five-foot halberd can be used in battle like a sword," she said, watching Wilarne laboring to wield her weapon against a leggy black courtesan named Cobra. The roofless hall of the old fortress made a smooth-floored, oval arena some forty feet in length, and the women were scattered across it, wrestling, fighting with weapons, practicing the deadlier throws and breaks of sneak attacks. For once it was not raining, and, except in the low places, the floor was dry. The Wolf had worked them here on days when mud coated them so thickly that it was only by size and the way they moved that they could be distinguished.

From where he and the gladiator stood on what must have been the old feasting dais, they could look out across the sunken floor of the room to the steps and the empty triple arch of the doorway and to the moors beyond. There must have been a courtyard of some kind there once—now there was only a flattened depression in the ground and little heaps of stones covered with lichens and weeds. And below him, between him and the door, the women were busy.

He wondered what the Hawk would make of them.

Denga Rey continued. "Most of the little ones are using swords that are as light as possible for effective weapons— and they are still having troubles. In a pitched fight, a man could outreach them."

Sun Wolf nodded. With luck, they would surprise the guards at the mines and free and arm the men from the guards' armories without the need for a pitched battle. But long experience had taught him never to rely on luck.

The only problem with having the smaller women use halberds in battle came from Drypettis, who took it as a personal affront that the Wolf would make allowance₃ for her size. In a tight voice, she told him, "We can succeed on your own terms, Captain. There is no need to condescend."

He glanced down at her, startled. At times she sounded like an absurd echo of Sheera, without Sheera's shrewdness or her sense of purpose. Patiently, he said, "There's only one set of terms to measure success in war, Drypettis."

That tight little fold at the corners of her mouth deepened.

"So you have told us—repeatedly," she retorted with distaste. "And in the crudest possible fashion."

Behind her, Gilden and Wilarne exchanged a glance; the other small women—Sister Quincis and red-haired Tamis Weaver—looked uneasy.

"Have I?" the Wolf rumbled quietly. "I don't think so.

"Success in war," he went on, "is measured by whether or not you do what you aim to—not by whether you yourself live or die. The success of a war is not measured in the same terms as the success of a fight. Succeeding in a war is getting what you want, whether you yourself live or die. Now, it's sometimes nicer to be alive afterward and enjoy what you've fought for—provided what you've fought for is enjoyable. But if you want it badly enough—want others to have it—even that isn't necessary. And it sure as hell doesn't matter how nobly or how crudely you pursue your goal, or who makes allowances or who condescends to you in the process. If you know what you want, and you want it badly enough to do *whatever you have to*, then do it. If you don't—forget it."

The silence in that single corner of the half-ruined tower was palpable, the shrill grunts and barked commands in the hall beyond them seeming to grow as faint and distant as the keening of the wind across the moors beyond the walls. It was the first time that he had spoken of war to them, and he felt all the eyes of this small group of tiny women on him.

"It's the halfway that eats you," he said softly. "The trying to do what you're not certain that you want to do; the wanting to do what you haven't the go-to-hell courage—or selfishness—to carry through. If what you think you want can only be got with injustice and getting your hands dirty and trampling over friends and strangers—then understand what it will do to others, what it will do to you, and either fish or cut bait. If what you think you want can only be got with your own death or your own lifelong utter misery—understand that, too.

"I fight for money. If I don't win, I don't get paid. That makes everything real clear for me. You—you're fighting for other things. Maybe for an idea. Maybe for what you think you ought to believe in, because people you consider better than you believe in it, or say they do. Maybe to save someone who fed and clothed and loved you, the father of your children—maybe out of love and maybe out of gratitude. Maybe you're fighting because somebody else's will had drawn you into this, and you'd rather die yourself than tell her you have other goals than hers. I don't know that. But I think you'd better know it—and know it real clearly, before any of you faces an armed enemy."

They were silent around him, these half-pints, these small and delicate women. Wilarne's eyes fell in confusion, and he saw rose flush up under her wind-bitten cheeks.

But it was Drypettis who spoke. "Honor demands—"

"To hell with honor," the Wolf said shortly, understanding that she had not heard one word he had said. "Women don't have honor."

She went white with anger. "Maybe the women you habitually consort with do not—"

"Captain!" Denga Rey's voice cut across the scuffling, sharp and uneasy. "Someone coming!"

Every sense suddenly snapped alert. He said briefly, "Hide." All around them, at the sound of the gladiator's words, the women had been fading from sight, seeking the darkness of the arches that had once supported a gallery around the hall, now a ruin of scrub and shadow; they were concealing themselves in the hundred bolt holes afforded by ruined passages and half-collapsed turrets whose stones were feathered with dry moss and fern. Gilden and Wilarne clambered up inside the monstrous flue of the hall's old chimney as if trained from childhood as climbing boys.

Only Drypettis stood where she was, rigid with anger. "You can't..." she began, almost stifling with rage.

Sun Wolf seized her arm impatiently and half threw her toward a droop-eyed hollow of a broken doorway. "Hide, rot your eyes!" he roared at her and ran to where only Sheera and Denga Rey stood, visible on either side of the triple arch of the raised door.

From here, the valley in which the Cairn Tower was situated could be seen in one sweep of trampled brown grass and standing water. Desolately empty, it lay hemmed in by the stone-crested hills and the gray weight of cloud cover, a solitude unbroken save by a few barren and wind-crippled trees. Then, in that solitude, something moved, a figure running toward the tower.

"It's Tisa," Sheera said, surprise and fear in her voice. "She was on watch at Ghnir Crag, keeping an eye on the direction of town."

Denga Rey said, "There's something else moving down there, too. Look, in the brush along the side of the crag."

The girl plunged, stumbling, up the ruined steps and into Sun Wolf's arms. She was panting, unable to catch her breath—not the measured wind of a racer, but the panic gasps of one who had fled for her life.

"What is it?" Sun Wolf asked, and she raised her face to stare into his with widened ayes.

"Nuuwa," she choked. "Coming here—lots of them, Captain."

"More than twenty?"

She nodded; her flesh was trembling under his hands at what she had so narrowly escaped. "I couldn't count, but I think there were more than twenty. Coming from all sides . . ."

"Pox rot the filthy things. Turn out!" he bellowed, his voice like thunder in the weed-grown walls. "We're under attack! Nuuwa—lots of 'em!"

The shadows blossomed women. Just under half the strength of the troop was there that day, eighteen women counting Sheera.

"Twenty nuuwa!" Denga Rey was saying. "What the hell are that many nuuwa doing in the Thaneland? That's ridiculous! You never see more than a few at a time, and never . . ."

But as she was cursing she was gathering up her weapons. Women were running all around, leaping up the crazy walls under Sheera's shouted commands. Some of them had bows and arrows; others had the heavy, old-fashioned swords. All of them had daggers.

But if you are close enough to use a dagger on a nuuwa, Sun Wolf thought, *it is far too late.*

He could see them now, moving out in the hills. Slumped bodies were creeping along the road, or emerging from the brushy slopes between the hills with a deceptively quick, shambling lope. He felt his hair prickle at the numbers of them. By the First Ancestor of the World, how many were there?

"Somebody make a fire," he ordered, and went scrambling up the slumped remains of a gallery stair to the broken platform above the door. The view from the top turned him sick with dread.

The nuuwa had broken cover from the hills all around and were converging on the tower. Eyeless heads wagged loosely on lolling necks; shoulders were bent so that the creatures' big, claw-nailed hands flopped, twitching, around their knees. The hollows of those eaten-out eye sockets swayed back and forth, as if they still sighted through the scarred-over, fallen flesh. If it were not for the way the nuuwa moved—dead straight, with no consideration for the rise and fall of the ground—they might almost have been mistaken for true men.

Sun Wolf counted almost forty.

From here, he could look down upon all of the Cairn Tower. What remained of the curtain wall that had once surrounded the place lay in a sloppy ring around the oval tower itself. Wall and tower were not concentric—the tower stood at one end, so that its triple-arched doorway, empty of any defensive barrier, looked straight out into the valley. Below him, he could see the women fanning out along the broken top of the curtain wall, the bare flesh of their shoulders and the colors of their hair very bright against the winter drabness of lichenous stone and yellowed weeds and heather. No need to conceal themselves, for nuuwa did not track their prey by sight. No need for strategy, for the nuuwa understood none.

All they understood—all they sought—was flesh.

From the wall, he heard the whining *thwunk* of bowstrings and saw two of the advancing creatures stumble. One of them lumbered to its feet again and came on, the arrow sticking through its neck like a hatpin through a doll; the other staggered a few steps, spouting blood from a punctured jugular, then fell, its grotesquely grown teeth snapping in horrible chewing motions as it tried to wallow its way along. Another of the creatures tripped over it in its advance, then got up and shambled on. Nuuwa—in common with all other predators—would not touch the flesh of nuuwa. The ground was prickled with arrows. Most of the women had terrible aim.

Smoke stung his eyes. Below him in the court, he could see that Gilden had got a fire going—Tisa was gathering up branches, sticks, anything that could be used as torches. Sheera and Denga Rey both had fire in their hands as they stood in the open arches of the door. Nuuwa had just enough instinct to fear the heat of fire. From his vantage point, the Wolf could see that in some fashion they knew that there was no wall at the doorway. Half a dozen were shambling toward the two women who stood in that gap.

He came down from the platform at a run.

Wet mud and pits of last week's thin snowfall scummed the crazy steps. The entire curtain wall must have the same vile footing, he thought. Then he heard it, beyond the higher ruins of the tower. From along the wall, now out of his sight, came the slithering crash of dislodged stone and falling bodies, the hooting grunts of the nuuwa, and the soft, smacking *thunk* of steel biting naked flesh.

He had a torch in one hand and a sword in the other as he sprang up the steps to the empty gateway instants before the nuuwa came lolloping, gape-mouthed, to meet the women. Sheera made the mistake of slashing at the widest target—the breast—and the creature she cut fell on her with a vast, streaming wound yawning in its chest, eyeless face contorted, mouth reaching to bite. The Wolf had decapitated the first creature within range; he spun in the next split second and hacked off both huge hands that gripped Sheera's arm, allowing her to spring back out of range and slash downward on the thing's neck. It was all he had time for—nuuwa were pressing up toward them, heedless of the cut of the steel; spouting blood drenched them, hot on the flesh and running down slippery underfoot. Beside him, he was vaguely aware of Denga Rey, fighting with the businesslike brutality of a professional with sword and torch.

He felt something gash and tear at his ankle, then saw that a fallen nuuwa had sunk its teeth into his calf. He slashed downward, severing the head as it tore at his flesh. Clawed hands seized his sword arm, and he cut at the eyeless face with his torch, setting the matted hair and filthy, falling beard aflame. The creature released him and began shrieking in a rattling, hoarse gasp, blundering against its fellows and pawing at the blaze. Denga Rey, freed for an instant, kicked it viciously back, and it went rolling down the steps, face flaming, howling in death agonies as others stumbled over it to close in on the defenders.

Through the confusion of that hideous fight and the searing agony of the head still clinging doggedly to his calf, Sun Wolf could hear the distant chaos of cries, hoarse grunts, and shrill shouts. He heard a scream, keening and horrible, rising to a fever pitch of rending pain and terror, and knew that one of the women had been overcome and was being killed. But like so many things in the heat of battle, he noted it without much interest, detached, grimly fighting to avoid a like fate himself. Another scream sounded closer, together with a slithering crash of bodies falling from the wall. From the corner of his eye, he saw locked forms writhing on the icy clay of the hall floor, a tangle of threshing limbs and fountaining blood. Eo the blacksmith sprang forward with one of those huge two-handed broadswords upraised as if it were as light as a willow switch.

He saw no more; filthy hands and snapping, slobbering mouths pressed close around him. For a moment, he felt as if he were being engulfed in that horrible mob, driven back into the shadow of the empty gateway and wondering where the drop of the steps was.

Then steel zinged near him; as he decapitated one of the things grabbing and biting at him, Denga Rey's sword sliced the spine of another, and it fell, rolling and spasming, at his feet. Those were the last of the immediate attackers. He swung around and saw that the steps were piled knee-deep in twitching bodies, from which a thick current of brilliant red ran down to pool among the rocks. Behind him, the tower was silent, save for a single voice raised in a despairing wail of grief.

The nuuwa were all dead.

He looked down to where the severed head still locked on his calf with a death grip. Fighting a surge of nausea, he bent down and beat at the joint of the jawbone with the weighted pommel of his sword until the jaw broke and he was able to pull the thing off by its verminous hair. Hands shaking, he knelt on the slimy steps and held out his hand for Denga Rey's torch, since his own had been lost in the fight. Reversing it, he drove the flaming end into the wound. Smoke and the stink of burning meat assailed his nostrils; the pain went through his body like a stroke of lightning. Distantly, he was aware of the sound of Sheera's being sick in a corner of the hall.

He flung the torch away and collapsed on his hands and knees, fighting nausea and darkness. It wasn't the first time he had had to do this, from nuuwa or from other wounds, but it never got any easier.

Footsteps pattered on the clay floor. He heard the murmur of voices and opened his eyes to see Amber Eyes binding up Denga Rey's bloody arm with someone's torn, gold-embroidered scarf.

Both women hastened to his side, and Amber Eyes knelt to bandage his wounds. Her hands were sticky with gore. When he had breath to speak, Sun Wolf asked them, "You bitten anywhere?"

"Few slashes," the gladiator said shortly.

"Burn 'em."

"They're not deep."

"I said burn 'em. We aren't talking about sword cuts in the arena; nuuwa are filthier than mad dogs. I'll do it for you if you're afraid."

That got her. She damned his eyes, without malice, knowing he was right. Under her swarthy tan, even she looked pale and sick.

After a quick, brutal cauterization, he helped her to her feet, both of them leaning a little on Amber Eyes for support. They were joined in a moment by a very pallid Sheera, her hair in wet black strings before her eyes. Like theirs, her limbs were plastered in gore. Sun Wolf shook himself clear of Denga Rey and limped to put a gentle hand on her shoulder.

"You all right?"

She was quivering all over, like a bowstring after its arrow was spent. He sensed that it was touch and go whether she would fall on his shoulder in hysterics; but after a moment she drew a deep breath and said huskily, "I'll be all right."

"Good girl." He slapped her comfortingly on the buttock and was rewarded with the kind of glare generally reserved for the humbler sort of insects in their last moments before a servant was called to swat them. He grinned to himself. She'd obviously got over the first shock.

There were no other women in the empty hall. Slowly, limping with the pain of their wounds, the four of them staggered to the narrow postern that let them into the ruined circle of the curtain wall. Like the steps, the ground there was littered with the bodies of dead nuuwa with severed heads and hands and feet. Dark blood dripped down the stones and soaked into the winter-hard ground. At the far end of the court, the women stood in a silent group, staring in nauseated fascination at a tall, rawboned woman named Kraken, who was kneeling, her face buried in her hands, over the dismembered and half-eaten body of sharp, little, red-haired Tamis Weaver. Kraken was rocking back and forth and wailing, a desolate moaning sound, like a hurt animal.

After a moment Gilden and Wilarne moved in, bitten and painted with the blood of their dead enemies, and gently helped Kraken to her feet and led her away. She moved like a blind woman, half doubled over with grief.

Sun Wolf looked around at those who were left. He saw women with scared faces, gray with shock and nausea, the ends of their tangled hair pointy with blood. Some of them had been bitten, clawed, chewed—there'd be more work, burning the wounds, the agonizing aftermath of war. The place stank with that peculiar battleground smell, the vile reek of blood and vomit and excrement, of death and terror. Some of them, like

Erntwyff Fish, looked angry still; others, like Sister Quincis and Eo, seemed burned out, as if only cold ash remained of the fire that had carried them alive through battle. Others looked merely puzzled, staring about in confusion, as if they had no idea how they had come to be wounded, exhausted, cold, and sick in this slaughterhouse place. More than one was crying, with shock and grief and relief.

But none of them looked, or would ever again look, quite as they had.

The Wolf sighed. "Well, ladies," he said quietly, "now you've seen battle."

CHAPTER
——— 8 ———

*T*HE RAIN THAT SLASHED AGAINST THE BOLTED SHUTTERS OF the Brazen Monkey made a far-off, roaring sound, like the distant sea. With her boots extended toward the enormous blaze that was the only illumination in the shadowy common room, Starhawk scanned the few travelers still on the roads in this weather and decided that she and Fawn would take turns sleeping tonight.

Inns in this part of the mountains were notorious in any event, but during the dry season, when the caravans from Mandrigyn, Pergemis, and the Middle Kingdoms filled even this vast common room to capacity, there was some degree of safety. Most merchants were decent enough fellows, and no traveler would suffer to see another robbed, if only from the knowledge that it could happen to him next. During the rains it was different.

Opposite her, on the other worn and narrow plank bench, an unshaven little man with a loose mouth and a looser eye kept glancing over at Fawn, who stood at the far end of the long room, haggling with the innkeeper. Two others were hunched over pewter mugs of beer and the remains of a haunch of venison at one of the tables, oblivious to their surroundings. The Hawk wasn't prepared to bet on any of their help, if there were trouble.

In a businesslike fashion, she began reviewing exits from the common room and escape routes from the inn.

Down at the other end of the room, Fawn was still nodding, the occasional sweetness of her low voice punctuating the innkeeper's ingratiating whine. They'd been haggling about the price of rooms, food, and supplies for the last fifteen minutes, a protracted process that Fawn was capable of continuing for upward of an hour without ever losing her air of grave interest. The heat of the room was drying her great plaid cloak; in the smoky amber of the firelight, Starhawk could see the steam rising from it, like faint breath on a snowy night.

From Kedwyr, they'd journeyed through the olive and lemon groves of the brown hills to the poorer inland cities of Nishboth and Plegg. Those cities had long ago knuckled under to Kedwyr's dominance and had shrunk to little better than market towns, with their decaying mansions of stone lace and the crumbling ruins of their mosaic cathedrals dreaming of better days. After two days on the road, the rains had hit, freezing winds roaring in from the sea and torrents of black water pouring from the skies, flooding the roads and turning innocuous streams in the barren foothills behind Plegg into boiling, white millraces.

They had climbed toward Gaunt Pass and the wide road that twisted through the gray spires of the Kanwed Mountains from the East to the Middle Kingdoms. Snow had caught them three days from the pass itself, and for days they had plowed and floundered their way through that icy world of winds and stone, discouraged, exhausted, making sometimes as little as five miles a day. From the pass, they had taken the road along the rim of the mountain mass, with the tree-cloaked shoulders of the main peaks towering thousands of feet above them, invisible in the gray turmoil of clouds.

Through it all, Fawn had never complained and had done her loyal best to keep up with Starhawk's surer pace. For all that she had spent the last two years in the soft living of a concubine, she was tough, and the Hawk had to admit that the girl was less trouble than she had at first feared. In Plegg, where they'd sold her jewels, she'd gotten a far better price than Starhawk had expected that sleepy, half-deserted town could have paid; and she'd shown an unexpected flair for bargaining for food, lodging, and fodder for the donkey along the way. Starhawk didn't see how she did it—but then, like most mercenaries, the Hawk had always paid three times the local rate for everything and had never been aware of the difference.

She had asked Fawn about it one night, when they'd been camped in a rock cave above Gaunt Pass, with a fire lighted at the entrance to frighten away wolves. Blushing, Fawn had admitted, "My father was a merchant. He always wanted me to learn the deportment of a lady, to better myself through an elegant marriage, but I knew too much about the cost of things ever to appear really well bred."

The Hawk had stared at her in astonishment. "But you're the most ladylike person I've ever met," she protested.

Fawn had laughed. "It's all the result of the most agonizing work. I'm really a storekeeper at heart. My father always said so."

Fawn came back across the room now, the fire picking smoky streaks of red from the close-braided bands of her dark hair. The greasy little rogue in the inglenook looked up at her, and even the two blockheads at the table raised their noses from their beer mugs as she passed.

"You want to bet you get an offer of free room?" Starhawk asked as Fawn seated herself on the worn, blackened oak of the bench at her side.

"I've already had one, thanks," the girl replied in a low voice and glanced across at the greasy man, who met her eyes and gave her a broken-toothed leer. She looked away, her cheeks even redder than the firelight could have made them. "I've paid for supper, bed, breakfast, bait for the donkey, and some supplies to go on with."

Starhawk nodded. "He have any idea how far to the next inn?"

"Fifteen miles, he says. The Peacock. After that there's nothing until Foonspay, twenty-five miles beyond, and that's a fair-sized village."

The Hawk did some rapid mental calculations. "Tomorrow night in the open, anyway," she said. "Maybe the night after, depending on the road. If this rain turns to snow again, it's going to be hell's own mess."

Movement caught her eye. The greasy little man had shuffled over to the bar, where he stood talking in a low voice to the innkeeper. Starhawk's eyes narrowed.

"Did you ask for the supplies tonight rather than in the morning?"

Fawn nodded. "He said yes, later."

She sniffed. "We'll make damned sure of it, then. I'm going out to the stables to collect the packs. I don't want there to be any reason we couldn't get out of here in the middle of the night if we wanted to."

Fawn looked unhappy, but Starhawk's wariness was legendary in the troop and had more than once saved the lives of scouting parties under her command. She left the common room as quietly as possible, crossing the soup of mud, snow, and driving rain in the yard only after she was fairly certain of the whereabouts of the innkeeper and the slattern who did his cooking. The Brazen Monkey boasted no stableman. Inspecting the interior of the big stone stables built into the cliff that rose from the muck of the inn yard, the Hawk thought the place rather too well stocked and kept for the little traffic they must have had in the last few weeks before these late rains.

She collected all the supplies and equipment except the actual packsaddle itself, slinging them by straps over her arms and shoulders, and waited in the darkness of the big arched doorway until she saw both the innkeeper's shadow and the woman's cross the lamplight of the half-open door. They'd be going to the common room, with supper for Fawn and herself. Picking her footing carefully, she slipped back into the inn by way of the shadows along the wall and up the twisting stairs to their room.

Seeing the damp and bug-infested mattresses on the two narrow cots, she was just as glad she'd brought up their own bedding. The room itself was freezing cold, and the roof leaked in two places. Nevertheless, she wrestled the bolt of the shutters back and looked out into the streaming darkness of the night. A foot or so below the sill of the window, the thatch of the kitchen roof was swimming like a hay meadow in a flood, steam rising from it with the heat below. Satisfied, she closed the shutters again, but did not bolt them; she checked the door bolt, shoved the supplies well under the beds, and went downstairs.

The greasy little man was leaning against the table, talking to an unhappy-looking Fawn. Starhawk crossed the room to them, looked him up and down calmly, and asked, "You invite this cheesebrain to supper, Fawnie?"

The man started to sputter some kind of explanation. Starhawk looked him in the eyes, calculating, fixing his features in her mind to know again. His eyes shifted. Then he ducked his head and hastily left the room, the rain blowing in from the outside door as it opened and shut again behind him.

Starhawk slid onto the bench opposite Fawn and applied herself to venison stew and black bread.

Fawn sighed. "Thank you. I couldn't seem to get rid of him..."

"What did he want?" the Hawk asked, around a mug of beer.

"He came over and offered to tell me about the road ahead. And I—I thought he sounded as if he knew what he was talking about, but I couldn't be sure."

"More likely he's trying to find out which way we're going and where we'll be by dark tomorrow night. How much did that robber want for the kennel he's stuck us in?"

As Starhawk hoped, Fawn cheered up at that. She'd talked the innkeeper down to half the asking price; recounting it brought a sparkle to her soft eyes. They spoke of other inns and inn- keepers, of bargaining and prices, swapping stories of some of the more outrageous payments that Sun Wolf or other mer- cenaries they'd known had either asked or been offered. Neither spoke of their destination or of what they would do when they reached the impenetrable walls of Altiokis' Citadel; by tacit consent, each kept her own hope and her own fear to herself.

In time, another man came down from upstairs, a wizened, spade-bearded little cricket in black who looked like a decayed gentleman from one of the more down-at-heels cities of the Peninsula with his starched neck ruff and darned, soot-gray hose. He settled himself beside the two blockheads in the pad- ded coats who were drinking ale and talking in quiet voices; eventually they all went upstairs to bed.

Starhawk became uncomfortably aware of how her voice and Fawn's echoed in the empty common room and how dark were the shadows that clotted under its smoke-blackened raf- ters. Outside, the wind groaned louder over the rocks. Its sound would cover that of anyone's approach.

She was glad enough to leave the hall. By the light of a feeble tallow dip, she and Fawn climbed the narrow corkscrew of stairs to the cold room under the rafters.

"Well, these beds will have a use, after all," she commented wryly as she dropped the door bolt into its slot. Fawn laughed and pulled one end of the heavy log frame away from the wall. "Not like that—here. We'll lift. No sense telling that old cut- throat downstairs what we're doing."

It was a struggle to barricade the door quietly. Halfway through their task, a sound arrested the Hawk's attention; she held up her hand, listening. The inn walls were thick, but it sounded as if others in the place had the same idea.

Fawn unrolled her bedding along the wall where the bed had been, carefully arranging it to avoid the major leaks in the roof. "Do you really think they'll try to rob us in the night?" Her voice had gotten very quiet; her eyes, in the flickering light of the already failing dip, had lost the ebullience they'd shown downstairs. Her face looked shadowed and tired. Starhawk reflected that for all her bright courage, Fawn did not travel well. She looked worn down and anxious.

"I almost hope so," the Hawk replied quietly. She blew on the flame, and the room was plunged into inky darkness. "I'd far rather deal with it here than on the road tomorrow."

Silence settled over the inn.

Between her travels, wars, and the long watches of ambush, the Hawk had developed a fairly clear estimate of time. At the end of about three hours, she reached over and shook Fawn awake, talked to her in the darkness for a few minutes to make sure that she *was* awake, then lay back and dropped at once into the light, wary, animal sleep of guard dogs and professional soldiers. She surfaced briefly when the rain lightened an hour and a half later; she heard the drumming of it fade to a soft, restless pattering in the dark, like tiny feet running endlessly across the leaky thatch, and, below that sound, the soft murmur of Fawn's voice, whispering the words of an old ballad to herself to keep awake and pass the time. Then she slept again.

She wakened quickly, silently, and without moving, at the urgent touch of Fawn's hand on her shoulder. She tapped the knuckles lightly to show herself awake and listened intently for the sounds that had alerted the girl to danger.

After a moment, she heard it: the creak of a footstep on the crazy boards of the hall. It was followed by the sticky squeak of wet leather and the clink of a buckle. But more than any single clue, she could sense, almost feel, the weight and warmth and breath gathered in the darkness outside their door.

Starhawk sat up, reached to where her sword lay beside her on the dirty floor, and drew its well-oiled length without a sound. With luck, she thought, Fawn would remember to have her dagger ready; she wasn't going to warn anyone that they were awake by asking aloud.

A single crack of light appeared in the darkness, a thin chink from the yellowish glow of a tallow dip. In the utter darkness, even that dim gleam was bright as summer sun. Then she heard the scraping of a fine-honed dagger being slid through the door crack under the bolt, pushing it gently up. There was a soft, distinct *plunk* as it dropped backward out of its slot. Then came another long and listening silence.

Fawn and the Hawk were both on their feet. Fawn moved back toward the window, as they had previously agreed; Starhawk stepped noiselessly toward the barricaded door. The slit of light widened, and bulky shadows became visible beyond. There was a jarring vibration, followed by a soft-voiced curse, rotting their eyes for a pair of impudent sluts. A heavy shoulder slammed against the wood, and the barricading bed grated and tipped back as the huge shape of a man slid sideways through the narrow gap.

The door opened inward and to the right. The intruder had to enter left shoulder first. Killing him was as easy as sticking a frog. He gasped as the sword slid in, and his knees buckled; there was the stink and splatter of blood, and Starhawk sprang back as others slammed and pushed the door in, cursing furiously, falling over the body and the bed, and dropping the light in the confusion. The Hawk went in silently, hacking and thrusting; voices shouted and cursed. Steel bit her leg. She thought there were three still living, blundering around in the darkness like blind pigs in a pit.

Then she heard Fawn scream, and a man's heavy rasp of breathing where she guessed the girl would be. A body tangled with hers, hands grappling her legs and pulling her off balance. A hoarse voice yelled, "Over here! I got one!" She cut downward at the source of the voice, then swung in a wide circle with her sword and felt its tip snag something that gasped and swore; the man pulled her down, clutching and grappling, too close now for the sword to be of use. She dropped it, hacking with her dagger; then light streamed in over them, and more men came thundering in from the hall.

The light showed the raised knife of the man who clutched her thighs, and Starhawk cut backhand as he turned his head toward the newcomers, opening both windpipe and jugular and spraying herself in a hot fountain of blood. The first man through the door tripped over the corpse there, then the bed; the second man clambered straight up over all three, his huge bulk blotting the light, and threw himself like an immense lion on the only bandit left standing. He knocked the man's blade aside with a backhand blow that would have stunned a horse, caught him by the throat, and slammed his head back against the stone wall behind with a hideous crunch. Then he swung around, his square, heavy-jawed face pink and sweating in the faint gleam of brightness from the hall, as if seeking new prey. Past him, Starhawk saw Fawn standing flattened against the wall by the shuttered window, her face white and her disheveled clothing smeared with dark blood. There was a dagger in her hand and a gutted robber still twitching and sobbing at her feet.

The big newcomer relaxed and turned to the jostling scramble of his companion in the doorway. "Don't drop the light, ye gaum-snatched chucklehead," he said. "We're behind the fair." One step took him to Fawn. "Are you hurt, lass?"

The man who'd tripped unraveled himself from the trampled remains of the collapsed bed and stumbled again over the dead bandit in his hurry to reach Starhawk, who was still sitting, covered with blood and floor-grime, beneath her slaughtered assailant. He knelt beside her, an even bigger man than the first one, with the same lock of brown hair falling over grave, blue-gray eyes. "Are ye hurt?"

Starhawk shook her head. "I'm fine," she said. "But thank you."

Much to her surprise, he lifted her to her feet as if she'd been a doll. "We'd have been sooner," he said ruefully, "but for some shrinking violet's wanting to barricade our door . . ."

"Violet yourself," the other man retorted, in the burring accent of the Bight Coast. "If we'd been the first ones they attacked, you'd have been glad enough for the warning and delay—if the sound of their shoving over the bed had waked you at all."

The bigger man swung about, like a bullock goaded by flies. "And what makes you think any bandit in the mountains is something you and I together couldn't handle without even troubling to wake up?"

"You sang a different tune night before last, when the wolves raided—"

"Ram! Orris!" a creaky voice chirped from the doorway. The two behemoths fell silent. The scrawny little gentleman in the starched ruff whom Starhawk had seen briefly down in the common room came scrambling agilely over the mess in the doorway, holding aloft a lantern in one hand. The other hand was weighted down by a short sword, enormous in the bony grip. "You must excuse my nephews," he said to the women, with a courtly salaam appallingly incongruous with the gruesome setting. "Back home I use them for a plow team, and thus their manners with regard to ladies have been sadly neglected."

He straightened up. Bright, black eyes twinkled into Starhawk's, and she grinned at him in return.

"Naagh . . ." Ram and Orris pulled back hamlike fists threateningly at this slur on their company manners.

The little man disregarded them with sublime unconcern. "My name is Anyog Spicer, gentleman, scholar, and poet. There is water in the room next to us, since I'm sure ablutions are in order . . ."

"First I'm going to find that damned innkeeper, rot his eyes," Starhawk snapped, "and make sure he doesn't have any other bravos hiding out around here." She looked up and saw that Fawn's face had gone suddenly from white to green. She turned to the immense man who still hovered at her side. "Take Fawn down to your room, if you would," she said. "I'll get some wine when I'm in the kitchen."

"We've wine," the big man—Ram or Orris—said. "And better nor what this place stocks. I'll come with you, lassie. Orris, take care of Miss Fawn. And see you don't make a muff of it," he added as he and Starhawk started for the door.

Orris—the handsomer of the two brothers and, Starhawk guessed, the younger by several years—raised sharply back-slanted dark eyebrows. "*Me* make muff of it?" he asked as he gently took Fawn's arm and removed the dagger that she still held in her nerveless hand. "And who fell over his own big feet blasting into the room like a bull through a gate, pray? Of all the gaum-snatched things . . ."

"Be a fair desperate gaum would take the time to find your wits to snatch 'em . . ."

Starhawk, who sensed that the brothers would probably argue through battle and world's end, caught Ram's quilted sleeve and pulled him determinedly toward the door.

There were no more bandits at the inn. They found the innkeeper, disheveled and groaning, in the room behind the kitchen, amid a tangle of sheets in which he said he had been tied after being overpowered. But while he was explaining all this at length to Ram, Starhawk had a look at the torn cloth and found no tight-bunched creases, such as were made by knots. The woman said sullenly that she had locked herself in the larder from fear of them. Both looked white and shaken enough for it to have been true, but Starhawk began to suspect that by killing the bandits, she had demolished the couple's livelihood. She smiled to herself with grim satisfaction as she and Ram mounted the stairs once more.

"You're no stranger to rough work, seemingly," Ram said, his voice rather awed.

Starhawk shrugged. "I've been a mercenary for eight years," she said. "These were amateurs."

"How can you tell?" He cocked his head and gazed down at her curiously. "They looked to me as if they were born with shivs in their fists."

"A professional would have put a guard on your door. And what in the hell does 'gaum-snatched' mean? That's one I never heard before."

He chuckled, a deep rumble in his throat. "Oh, it's what they say to mean your wits have gone begging. Gaums are— what you call?—dragonflies; at least that's what we call 'em where I come from. There are old wives who say they'll steal away a man's wits and let him wander about the country until he drowns himself walkin' into a marsh."

Starhawk nodded as they turned the corner at the top of the stair and saw light streaming out of one of the rooms halfway down the hall. "In the north, they say demons will lead a man to his death that way—or chase him crying to him from the air. But I never heard it was dragonflies."

They came to the slaughterhouse room. By the light of the lamp she'd appropriated from the kitchen, Starhawk saw that the greasy little man who'd spoken to Fawn was the one Orris had brained. It was a good guess, then, that the innkeeper had indeed been in league with them. Ram jerked his head toward the door as they passed it. "What about them?"

"We'll let our host clean up," Starhawk said callously. "It's his inn—and his friends."

Orris and Uncle Anyog had moved the women's possessions to their own room while Ram and the Hawk were reconnoitering. Beds had been made up on the sagging mattresses. Fawn was asleep, her hair lying about her in dark and careless glory on the seedy pillow. By the look of his boots, Uncle Anyog had been investigating the stables. He reported nothing missing or lamed.

"Meant to do that after we'd been settled," Starhawk said, collecting spare breeches, shirt, and doublet from her pack and preparing to go into the next room to wash and change. "Maybe they didn't mean to take you three on at all. If you asked after the two of us, the innkeeper could always tell you we'd departed early."

"Hardly that," Orris pointed out. "Else we'd overtake you on the road, wouldn't we?"

"Depends on which direction you were going in."

In the vacant room, she took a very fast, very cold damp-cloth bath to get the dried blood out of her flesh and hair, cleaned the superficial gash on her leg with wine and bound it up, and changed her clothes. When she returned to the brothers' room, Uncle Anyog was curled up asleep on the floor in a corner; Ram and Orris were still talking quietly, arguing over how good a bargain they'd really gotten on some opals they'd bought from the mines in the North. Starhawk settled herself down with a rag, a pan of water, and a bottle of oil, to clean her weapons and leather before moving on. The night was far spent and she knew she would sleep no more.

Orris finished pointing out to his brother some facts about the fluctuation in the price of furs and how opals could be held for a rise in prices—neither argument made any sense to Star-hawk—and turned to her to ask, "Starhawk? If you don't mind my asking—which direction were you bound in, you and Miss Fawn? It's a rotten time to be on the roads at all, I know. Where were you headed?"

"East," the Hawk said evasively.

"Where east?" Orris persisted, not taking the hint.

She abandoned tact. "Does it matter?"

"In a way of speaking, it does," the young man said earnestly, leaning forward with his hands on his cocked-up knees. "You see, we're bound for Pergemis, with a pack train of fox and beaver pelts and opals and onyx from the North. We've met trouble on the road before this—the man we took with us was killed five nights ago by wolves. If there's more trouble with bandits along the way, we stand to lose all the summer's profits. Now, I make no doubt you're a fighter, which we could do with; and neither of us is so bad at it himself, which Miss Fawn could do with. If you were bound toward the south . . ."

Starhawk hesitated a moment, then shook her head. "We aren't," she said. Pergemis lay where the Bight washed up against the feet of the massive tablelands that surrounded the Kanwed Mountains, far to the southwest of Grimscarp. She continued, "But our road lies with yours as far as Foonspay. That will get us out of the mountains and out of the worst of the snow country. If you have no objection, we'll join you that far."

"Done," Orris said, pleased; then the light died from his honest, slab-sided face, and his eyes narrowed. "You're not ever bound for Racken Scrag, are you, lass? It's a bad business, all through that country, mixing with the Wizard King."

"So I've heard," Starhawk replied noncommittally.

When she said no more, but returned to cleaning the blood from the handle of her dagger, Orris grew fidgety and went on. "Two girls traveling about alone . . ."

"Would probably be in a lot of danger," she agreed. "But it happens I've killed quite a few men in my time . . ." She tested the dagger blade with her thumb. "And since I could probably give you five years, I'd hardly qualify as a lass."

"Yes, lass, but . . ."

At this point, Ram kicked him—no gentle effort—and the two brothers relapsed into jovial bickering, leaving Starhawk to her silent thoughts.

In the days that followed, she had cause to be thankful for their partnership, for all that the brothers periodically drove her crazy with their fits of chivalry. Orris never ceased trying to find out the women's destination and objectives, not from any malice but, what was worse, out of the best of intentions to dissuade them from doing anything foolish or dangerous. Starhawk admitted to herself that their journey was both foolish and dangerous, but that fact did not make it any less necessary, if they were going to find and aid Sun Wolf and learn what, if any, designs Altiokis had toward the rest of the troop. Orris' automatic assumption that, having met them only a day or so ago and being completely in ignorance of the reasons for their quest, he was nevertheless better qualified than they to judge its rightness and its possibilities of success alternately amused Starhawk and irritated her almost past bearing.

Likewise, the brothers' good-natured arguments and insults could be carried far past the point of being entertaining. When they weren't poking fun at each other's appearance, brains, or social manners, they joined verbally to belabor Uncle Anyog for his habit of reciting poetry as he walked, for his small size, or for his flights of rhetorical eloquence, all of which Anyog took in good part. Around the campfires in the evenings, the brothers listened, as enthralled as Fawn and the Hawk were, to the little man's tales of heroes and dragons and to the silver magic of his songs. Years in the war camps had given Starhawk an enormous tolerance for the brothers' brand of bovine wit, but she found herself more than once wishing that she could trade either or both of them for a half hour of absolute silence.

But, she reasoned, hers was not to choose her companions. Noisy, busy blockheads like the brothers and the hyperloquacious Anyog were far preferable to travelling through the mountains in winter alone.

The Peacock Inn, when they reached it, was deserted, with snow drifting through the windows of its shattered common room. In the stable, Starhawk discovered the bones of a horse, chewed, broken, and crusted with frost, but clearly fresh; the splintered shutters and doors of the ground floor had scarcely been weathered. With thick powder snow squeaking under her boots, she waded back across the yard. In the common room, she found Fawn and Uncle Anyog, huddled together, looking uneasily about them and breathing like dragons in the fading daylight. Orris and Ram came down the slippery drifts of the staircase.

"Nothing abovestairs," Orris reported briefly. "The door at the top's been scratched and pounded, but no signs that it was forced. Whatever's done this, it's gone now; but we'd probably be safer spending the night up there."

"Will the mules go up the steps?" Starhawk asked. She told them what she'd found in the stables. There were six mules, besides her own little donkey.

Orris started to object and lay out a schedule for double watches on the stable, but Ram said, "Nay, we'd best have 'em up with us. If any ill fell to 'em, we'd be fair put to it between here and Foonspay, never mind leaving behind the pelts and things."

It was a stupid and ridiculous way to spend an evening, Starhawk thought, shoving and coaxing seven wholly recalcitrant creatures up into the chambers usually reserved for their social superiors. Uncle Anyog helped her, with vivid and startlingly elaborate curses—the elderly scholar was more agile than he looked—while Orris and Ram set to with shovels to clear a place around the hearth for cooking, and Fawn gathered straw bedding in the stables and kindling in the yard.

As night settled over the frozen wastes of the mountains and they barricaded themselves into the upper storey of the inn, Starhawk found herself feeling moody and restless, prey to an uneasy sense of danger. The brothers' boisterousness did nothing to improve her temper, nor did the grave lecture Orris gave her on the necessity for them all to keep together. As usual, she said nothing of either her apprehension or her irritation. Only Ram glanced up when she left early for her watch. Fawn and Orris were too deeply immersed in a lively discussion of the spice trade to notice her departure.

The silence of the dark hallway was like water after a long fever. She checked the mules where they were stabled in the best front bedroom, then followed the feeble glow of the tallow dip to the head of the stairs, where Uncle Anyog sat before the locked door.

His bright eyes sparkled as he saw her. "Ah, in good time, my warrior dove. Trust a professional to be on time for her watch. Are my oxen bedded down?"

"You think Orris would shut his eyes when he has an audience to listen to his schemes for financing a venture to the East?"

Though she spoke with her usual calm, the old man must have caught some spark of bitterness in her words, for he smiled up at her wryly. "Our pecuniary and busy-handed child." He sighed. "All the way from Kwest Mralwe, through the woods of Swyrmlaedden, where the nightingales sing, through the golden velvet hills of Harm, and across the snow-shawled feet of the Mountains of Ambersith, he favored me with the minutest details of the latest fluctuations of the currency of the Middle Kingdoms." He sighed again with regret. "That's our Orris. But he is very good at what he is, you know."

"Oh, I know." Starhawk folded her long legs under her and sat beside him, her back braced against the stained plaster of the wall. "To make a great deal of money, a person has to think about money a great deal of the time. I suppose that's why, in all the years I've been paid so handsomely, I'm never much ahead. No mercenary is."

The salt-and-pepper beard split in a wide smile. "But you are far ahead of them in the memory of joy, my dove," he said. "And those memories are not affected by currency fluctuations. I was an itinerant scholar all over the world, from the azure lagoons of Mandrigyn to the windy cliffs of the West, until I became too old and they made me be an itinerant teacher, instead—and I've been paid fortunes by universities of Kwest Mrawle and Kedwyr and half the Middle Kingdoms. Now here I am, returning in my old age to be a pensioner in my sister's house in Pergemis, to stay with a girl whose only knowledge ever lay in how to add, subtract, and raise big, wayfaring sons." He shook his head with a regret that was only partially self-mockery. "There is no justice in the world, my dove."

"Stale news, professor." The Hawk sighed.

"I fear you're right." Uncle Anyog extended one booted toe to nudge the stout wood of the door. "You saw the marks on the other side?"

She nodded. Neither Ram nor Orris had identified them.

She herself had seen their like only once before, as a small child. "Nuuwa?"

He nodded, the stiff white petals of his ruff bobbing, catching an edge of the light like an absurd flower. "More than one, I should say. Quite a large band, if they were capable of breaking into the inn."

Starhawk's face was grave. "I've never heard of them running in bands."

"Haven't you?" Anyog leaned forward to prick up the tallow dip that sat in a tin cup between them on the floor. His shadow, huge and distorted, bent over him, like the darkness of some horrible destiny. "They get thicker as you go east—didn't you know? And they've been seen in bands since early last summer in all the lands around the Tchard Mountains."

She glanced sideways at him, wondering how much he knew or guessed of her destination. Down below in the inn, she could hear the soft scrabbling noises of foxes and weasels quarreling over the garbage of dinner. For some reason, the sound made her shudder.

"Why is that?" she asked, when the silence had begun to prickle along her skin. "You're a scholar, Anyog. What are nuuwa? Is it true that they used to be men? That something—some sickness—causes them to lose their eyes, to change and distort as they do? I hear bits and pieces about them, but no one seems to know anything for certain. The Wolf says that they used to appear only rarely and singly. Now you tell me that they're coming out of the East in big bands."

"The Wolf?" The little man raised one tufted eyebrow inquiringly.

"The man I'm—Fawn and I—are seeking," Starhawk explained unwillingly.

"A man, is it?" the scholar mused, and Starhawk unaccountably felt her cheeks grow warm.

She went on hastily. "In some places I know, they say that a man has only to walk out in the night air to become a nuuwa; I think your nephews' tale about gaums—dragonflies—may have something to do with it. Not true dragonflies, but perhaps something that looks or moves like them. But no one knows. And I'm beginning to find that fact in itself a little suspicious."

He looked sharply across at her, his dark eyes suddenly wary. Starhawk met his gaze calmly, wondering why she had the momentary impression that he was afraid of her. Then he looked away and folded his fine little hands around his bony knees. "A wizard might know," he said, "were there any left."

The memory came back to her of the eyeless, mewing thing that had beaten and chewed at the Convent gates; she remembered Sister Wellwa, flinging fire from her knotted hands, and a sliver of mirror angled in the corner of a room. She recalled Little Thurg's speaking to a man who was not what he seemed.

"Anyog," she said slowly, "in all of your travels—have you ever heard of other wizards besides Altiokis?"

The silence stretched, and the flickering gleam of the tallow dip outlined the scholar's profile in an edge of gold as he continued to look steadily away from her into the darkness. At length he said, "No. None whom I have ever found."

"Are there any yet alive?"

He laughed, a soft, cracked little chuckle in the dark. "Oh, there are. There are said to be, anyway. But those who are born with the Power have more sense than to say so these days. If they learn any magic at all, they're careful to make their staffs into little wands that can be hidden up their sleeves, if they're men, or concealed as broom handles. There's even a legend about a wizard who hired herself out as governess to a rich man's children and who kept her staff hidden as the handle of her parasol."

"Because of Altiokis?" Starhawk asked quietly.

The old man sighed. "Because of Altiokis." He turned back to her, the dim, uncertain glimmer making his face suddenly older, more tired, scored with wrinkles like the spoor of years of grief. "And in any case, there are fewer and fewer wizards who have crossed into the fullness of their power. They have the little powers, what they can be taught by nature or by their masters, if they have them—or so I've heard. But few these days dare to attempt the Great Trial—even such few as are left who remember what it was."

He got to his feet, dusting the seat of his breeches, his scrawny body silhouetted against the dim light from the room where Ram and Orris were arguing over the time it took to sail from Mandrigyn to Pergemis in the summer trading.

"And what was it?" Starhawk asked curiously, looking up at Anyog as he flicked straight the draggled lace at his cuffs.

"Ah. Who knows? Even to admit knowledge of its existence

puts a man under suspicion from Altiokis' spies, whether he knows anything about wizardry itself or not."

He strolled off down the hall, wiry and awkward as some strange daddy longlegs, whistling an air from some complex counterpoint sonata in the dark.

CHAPTER
—— 9 ——

"*I* DON'T LIKE IT." STARHAWK FROWNED AS SHE STUDIED THE town below her.

Beside her, Ram folded his great arms against him for warmth. In his wadded layers of purple quilting, he looked immense, his blunt, homely face reddened by the cold. "It all seems quiet," he objected doubtfully.

Starhawk's gray gaze slid sideways at him. "Very quiet," she agreed. "But not one of those chimneys is smoking." She pointed, and a stray flake of mealy snow, shaken from the pine boughs overhead, settled into the fleece of her cuff. "This snow fell two nights ago, and nothing's tracked it since—not in the street, nor from any of those houses to the sheds behind."

Ram frowned, squinting. "You're right, lass. Your eyes are keener than mine, but 'twas stupid of me not to look. There are tracks round about the walls, aren't there?"

"Oh, yes," Starhawk said softly. "There are tracks." She turned back, scrambling down from the promontory that overlooked the little valley in which lay the village of Foonspay. Her feet slid in the slick powder of the snow; even though she stepped in her own tracks, the going was rough. Ram lost his balance twice, falling amid great clouds of billowing powder; nevertheless, he offered her his arm for support with dogged gallantry at every swell of the ground.

Snow had fallen the night they had spent at the Peacock Inn, then rain and more snow. The road, such as it was, had become crusted and treacherous, and they had lost most of a day floundering through it, exhausted by the mere effort of taking a step. Around them, the woods had lain in silence, a silence that prickled along Starhawk's nerves. She had found herself listening, seeking some sound—any sound. But no squirrel had dislodged snow from the green-black branches of the somber pines overhead; no rabbit had squeaked in the teeth of a fox. For two nights, not even wolves had howled; in her scouting to both sides of the buried road, Starhawk had seen no track of any bird or beast.

There was something abroad in the woods, something before which even the wolves ran silent.

The others felt it, too. Up ahead, she could see the six mules and the donkey as dark blobs on the marble whiteness of the snow, the vivid blue of Orris' quilted jacket, Anyog's rusty black, and Fawn's green and brown plaid—a tight little cluster of colors, huddled together in fear. They all jumped when she and Ram emerged through the trees.

"The town's deserted," she said as she came near.

"The buildings are standing, but the Mother only knows what's prowling around them. Let's get into the open. Then I'll take Ram and go ahead to scout the place."

The brothers nodded their agreement, but she saw the doubt in their faces—Orris because, deep down in his heart, he believed that he should be giving the orders, in spite of the fact that he knew Starhawk to be his superior in matters of defense, Ram because he knew it, too, and considered it an unseemly thing for a woman to be.

She supposed, as she led the way cautiously down the gentle slope of the road, that most women would have been pleased and flattered by the big man's protectiveness. She merely found it irritating, as if he assumed her to be unable to protect herself—and all the worse because it was both unconscious and well meaning. Sun Wolf, she reflected, glancing over her shoulder at the unnaturally silent woods, would help her out of trouble, but assumed that she could hold up her end of the fight just fine.

She scanned the sky, which was darker than the time of day could account for, then looked over her shoulder again—a habit she'd picked up these days. Ahead of them, the stone walls and snow-laden roofs of the town grew larger, and she ran her eye over them, searching for some sign, some mark. Her back hackled with nervousness. The shutters of several buildings had been broken and scratched, the marks yellow against the gray of weathering. She stumbled, her feet sliding and breaking through the crusts of the snow, and she gripped the headstall of the mule she led for balance. Behind her, the others were doing the same. The world was silent but for the hiss of Orris' cursing and the crunching of hooves and boots in the snow. The dark buildings seemed to stare at them with shadowy eyes through the mauve-tinted twilight.

Orris' voice sounded hideously loud. "You want to scout that great house there in the center of town? The door's shut and the shutters are intact. There'll be room for us there and for the beasts as well."

"Looks good," Starhawk agreed. "Ram—"

The mule beside her jerked its head free of her hold and reared up with a piercing squeal. Starhawk swung around, scanning the silent crescent of trees at their backs.

It came lumbering from the woods with that queerly staggering gait, the eyeless head lolling on the weaving neck. Starhawk yelled, "Nuuwa!" even as Orris cried out, pointing— pointing as three more shambling forms dragged themselves from the crusted brush of the surrounding woods. Starhawk swore, though she had known from what Anyog had said at the Peacock that there might be several of them, and flung Anyog the lead rein of the mule. "Make for the big house!" she called to the others. "And for God's sake . . ."

Then she saw something else, a floundering in the brush all around the edges of the woods, and she heard Anyog whisper, "Holy Three!"

Fawn screamed.

Starhawk had never seen that many nuuwa together. There were twenty at least, floundering through the snow at a jagged lope, their misshapen arms swinging for balance. She plunged after the rest of the party, moving as fast as she dared, her boots breaking through the buried crusts of the snow, panic heating her veins like cheap brandy. Her memories threw up at her the child she had been, fleeing screaming toward the Convent walls with the groaning, mouthing thing slobbering at her heels—merging with the creatures that pursued her now. There was a hideous slowness to the flight, like running in a dream. The nuuwa fell and rose and fell again, lunging toward them with a terrible inexorability. As in a dream, she could see every detail of them with preternatural vividness—the deformed, discolored teeth in the gaping mouths, the rotted eye sockets seared over with dirty scar tissue, the running sores that blotched the flabby flesh.

Ahead of her, Fawn fell for the tenth time; Ram dragged her to her feet and fell himself. Starhawk, stopping to let them remain ahead of her, cursed them for a pair of paddle-footed oafs and calculated that, if they slowed the flight much more, none of them would make it to safety.

The walls bulked up like cliffs; she could see the scattered bones of humans and animals half covered with snow in the streets. She guessed that the nearest nuuwa, the ones lumbering directly behind her, were some hundred feet to the rear, their groaning yammer and the slurpy bubble of their breath seeming to fill her ears. She thought of turning and fighting. Once she stopped, she'd draw them, and the others would go on . . .

Rot that, she thought indignantly. *I'm not a piece of meat to be thrown to wolves . . .*

Great Mother, but I know what is!

She yelled, "Anyog, stop! Stop!"

Not only the old man but the whole train checked, the mules plunging and screaming on their leads. Fawn slipped again and fell to her knees in the deep snow. Starhawk yelled, "The rest of you go on! Anyog, bring back one of those mules! *Now!*"

"What is it you're after doing . . ." Orris began.

Arguing, Great Mother! Starhawk thought with what horrified indignation was left her. "Rot your eyes, *get running!*" she screamed at them.

"But . . ."

"MOVE!"

Anyog was already beside her, hauling one of the screaming, pitching animals by its lead. For a moment, it was touch and go whether Orris would get them all killed by continuing the discussion, but the closing ring of nuuwa around him seemed to decide him. He threw his whole weight against the headstalls of the mules he led. Ram dragged Fawn to her feet, fighting their way along like a pair of wallowing drunks.

Gasping, his face under its little spade beard as white as his bedraggled ruff, Anyog managed to get the mule within Starhawk's range. The nearest nuuwa were thirty feet away, howling as they slithered in the snow, drool foaming from their lips. The Hawk stabbed her sword point-down in the snow, whipped the dagger from her belt, and grabbed the mule's headstall. Anyog realized what she was doing and added his own weight to bring the thrashing head down. The mule reared, and the steel bit deep into the great vein of the neck.

She'd shoved the gory dagger back into its sheath and pulled her sword free before the beast even fell. It rolled to the ground, heaving in its death agony, crimson spouting everywhere, searingly bright against the snow. She and Anyog plunged back in the direction of the town, Anyog going like a gazelle for two steps before he outraced his own balance and went down in a sprawling heap of bones.

Starhawk saw him fall from the corner of her eye; at the same time she saw the first nuuwa fall slavering on the screaming mule. The stink of the fresh blood drew the creatures; they were already tearing hunks of the live and steaming flesh from the mule where it lay. Anyog scrambled to his feet, neither calling out to her nor asking her to stop, and floundered after her. They were past the time when one could wait for the other. That would only mean that they would die together.

She heard the nuuwa mewing and wheezing behind her and the scrunch of those staggering feet in the snow. She caught them in her peripheral vision—one near enough to overtake her before she reached the black cliff of the building, two others farther back. She braced her feet and whirled, her sword a flashing arc in the wan twilight.

The nuuwa fell back from the slicing blade, blood and guts dripping down from the slit in its abdomen. Then it flung itself on her again, mouthing and grabbing and tripping over its own entrails, as another came lumbering up from the side. Others were close, she thought as she dispatched the first one. An instant's delay would have them all on her. Two fell upon her simultaneously. As she severed the head of the one in front, the weight of the second struck her back, the stink of it overwhelming her as the huge teeth ripped at the leather of her coat. She twisted, hacking, fighting the frenzy of panic at the slobbering thing that rode her. Distantly, she could hear Anyog's despairing screams. The clawing weight on her back bore her down, unreachable by her sword blade. The hissing, foaming mouth grated on the back of her skull. With a final writhe, she slithered free of her coat, springing clear and running frantically between the houses.

The gray bulk of the largest house in town loomed before her, broken by a black mouth of door with a mill of terrified mules around it. Scrunching footfalls seemed to fill her ears, staggering behind her with whistling gasps of breath. The steps of the house tripped her feet. Orris' voice bawled curses at the mules, and from the corner of her eye, she glimpsed her nearest pursuer—not a nuuwa at all, but Anyog, with one of the foul things clutching at him, clinging and dragging.

It felled him on the steps, almost at Starhawk's feet, the greedy, filthy mouth tearing gouts of flesh from his side. Starhawk sprang down toward them, her sword blazing in the gray murk of dusk, cleaving down like an axe on those writhing bodies. The rest of the nuuwa were six or eight paces behind; she dragged the old man up and flung him to the blurred purple bulk that she knew was Ram. Snapping jaws peeled three inches of leather from her boot-heel as she made it through the door. The slamming of it was like thunder in the empty building.

The nuuwa screamed outside.

They laid Anyog down beside the fire that Fawn managed to kindle in the great hearth of the downstairs hall. As Starhawk had suspected, the place had been the principal inn of Foonspay, and there were signs that much of the population of the village had lived here for several days, crowded together, for protection. While she worked over Anyog with what makeshift dressings she could gather, with needles and thread, boiling water, and cheap, strong wine, she wondered how many of them had been killed before they'd managed to get away, and if they'd made it to safety elsewhere, or had been killed on the road.

Ram and Orris took brands from the raised brick hearth to light their way as they explored the pitch-darkness of the inn corridors while Fawn went to find a place for the mules. Dimly, the hooting grunts of the nuuwa could be heard beyond the thick walls and heavy shutters. Within, all was deathly silent.

It had been said once that wizards were Healers—that their power could cleanse the hidden seeds of gangrene, close the bleeding for the flesh to heal. As she worked, bloodied to the elbows, Starhawk knew that it would take such power to save the old man's life. Against the darkness of his beard, Anyog's face was as colorless as wax, pinched and sunken. Long experience had given her intimate knowledge of the death marks, and she saw them here.

How long she worked she did not know, nor how long, afterward, she sat at the old man's side, watching the colors of the fire play over the colorless flesh of his face. She had no idea where the others were, nor, she thought to herself, did it particularly matter. They had their own concerns, merely in staying alive; it wasn't for her to trouble them with stale news. They must all have known, when they carried the old man in, that he would die.

In time, the thin, cold fingers under hers twitched, and Anyog's creaky voice whispered, "My warrior dove?"

"I'm here," the Hawk said, her voice carefully neutral in the still, firelighted dimness of the room. To hearten him, she said, "We'll turn you over to your sister yet."

There was a thin whisper of laughter, instantly followed by an even thinner gasp of pain. Then he murmured, "And you, my dove?"

She shrugged. "We're going on."

"Going on." The words were no more than the hissing of his breath. "To Grimscarp?"

For a long moment she was silent, sitting with her back to the chipped brickwork of the raised hearth, looking down at the shrunken form that lay among the huddle of stained blankets before her. Then she nodded and said simply, "Yes."

"Ah," he whispered. "What other destination would you hide with such care from our ox team? But they are right," he murmured. "They are right. Do not go there, child. Altiokis destroys that which is bright and pure. He will destroy you and the beautiful Fawnie, for no other reason than that you are what you are."

"Nevertheless, we must go," she said softly.

Anyog shook his head, his dark eyes opening, fever-bright in the firelight. "Don't you understand?" he whispered. "Only another wizard can enter his Citadel, unless to come in as his captive or his slave. Only a wizard can hope to work against him. Without magic of your own, you are helpless before him; he will trap you with illusion and trick you to your own destruction. His power is old; it is deep; it is not the magic of humankind. An evil magic," he murmured, the lids sliding shut once again over the glassy eyes, the flesh around them stained dark and mottled with the sinking of his flesh. "Not to be defied."

Something rustled in the darkness. Starhawk looked up sharply, the cool tension of battle leaping to her heart, but she saw nothing in the impenetrable shadows that loomed in every corner of the vast room. As lightly as a mother who wished not to disturb the sleep of her child, she slipped her hands from beneath Anyog's and stood up, her sword springing almost of itself to her grip, the reflex of long years of war. Yet when she reached the stone archway that led into the hall, she found nothing and heard no sound in the passage beyond.

When she returned to his side, Anyog was asleep, the little

white hands that had never done work harder than the making
of music or the writing of poems lying as motionless as two
bunches of crushed sticks upon the sunken chest. She satisfied
herself that a thread of breath still leaked through those white
lips, then sat where she had been and gradually let the silence
surround her in a kind of despairing peace. She knew that
Anyog was right—without the help of a wizard, she could not
hope to enter the Citadel or to rescue the Wolf from the Wizard
King's toils. In a way, she supposed that she and Fawn had
both known it from the first, though neither of them had been
willing to admit it; neither had been willing to give Sun Wolf
up.

From that silence, she sought the deeper stillness and peace
of meditation, focusing her mind upon the Invisible Circle,
upon the music that no one could hear. Many of the nuns had
looked into fire to begin it; Starhawk was too good a warrior
to night-blind herself that way, but she had learned, in her long
years as a mercenary, that she could find the starting place in
her mind alone.

The fire crackled and whispered in the grate, its unimag-
inable variations of color playing like silk over the edges of
brick and wood and flesh. Starhawk became slowly aware of
the air that stirred through the winding corridors of the dark
inn, of the stress and weight of the beams where they joined
overhead, and of the moldering thatch above, cloaked by the
frost-silver of the moon. Her awareness spread out, like water
over a flood plain—of the mules, sleeping in the darkness of
what had become their stable, of Fawn weeping there, of the
weighty tread of the brothers as they explored the inn, of the
nuuwa prowling and yammering outside; and of the stars in
the distant night.

She was aware when the still air of the room was touched
by magic.

It came to her as faint as a thread of half-heard music, but
clear, like the scent of a single rose in a darkened room. She
had not thought that magic would feel like that. It was nothing
like the blaze of thrown fire or the deadly webs of illusion
woven by the Wizard King and spoken of in four generations
of terrified whispers. It was a very simple thing, like the aura
of brightness that had sometimes seemed to cling about old
Sister Wellwa—akin to meditation, but moving, rather than
still.

She heard the faint, trembling voice of Uncle Anyog, whispering spells of healing in the darkness.

In time, she came out of her meditation. Anyog's muttering voice ran on a bit, then stilled. Without the shift in her consciousness, in her awareness, she might have thought only that he raved with fever, and perhaps he had counted on this. He lay motionless, his open eyes reflecting the embers of the fire like candles in a darkened room. She moved toward him and rested her hand upon his.

"You are a wizard," she said softly, "aren't you?"

A hoarse rattle, like a sob, escaped his throat. "Me? Never." The dry fingers twitched beneath hers, lacking the strength to grip. "At one time I thought—I thought . . . But I was afraid. Afraid of Altiokis—afraid of the Great Trial itself. I ran away— left my master—pretended to love other things more. Music— poems—going in fear lest any suspect. Garnering little potbound slips of power, consumed by the dreams of what I might have had."

The fever-bright eyes stared up into hers, brilliant and restless. Overhead, the boards creaked with the brothers' heavy stride. Somewhere in the darkness, a mule whuffled over its fodder. "My warrior dove," he whispered, "what is it that you seek of the Wizard King? What is this dream that I see in your eyes, this dream you will follow to your own destruction in his Citadel?"

Starhawk shook her head stubbornly. "It is not a dream," she replied, her voice low. "He is my chief—Altiokis has him prisoner."

"Ah." The breath ran thinly from the blue lips. "Altiokis. My child, he does not lightly loose what he has taken. Even could you find a wizard—a true wizard—to aid you, you would not live long enough to die at your captain's side."

"Perhaps not," Starhawk said quietly and was silent for a time, staring into the sunken glow of the hearth; the flames were gone, and only the deep, rippling heat of the coals was left, stronger than the fire, but unseen. At length she asked, "And did giving up your dream bring you happiness with your safety, Anyog?"

The withered face worked briefly with pain, then grew still She thought that he slept, but after a long silence, his lips moved. His voice was thin and halting. "This man whom you seek," he murmured. "You must love him better than life."

Starhawk looked away. The words went through her mind

like the grinding of a sword blade in her flesh, shocking and sudden, and she understood that Anyog had spoken the truth. It was a truth that she had hidden from the other warriors of Sun Wolf's troop, from Sun Wolf himself, and from her own consciousness; yet she felt no surprise in knowing that it was true. For years she had told herself that it was the loyalty a warrior owed to a chosen captain, and that, at least, had spared her jealousy toward the Wolf's numerous concubines. From her girlhood, she had known herself plain, and the Wolf had his pick of beautiful girls.

But she was not the only one who loved him better than life.

She closed her teeth hard upon that bitterness and stared dry-eyed into the darkness. Once the thing had been brought into the open, she could not unknow it, but she understood why she had worked to deceive herself almost from the first. Anything was better than the chasm of this despair.

Ram's voice echoed in the inn kitchen, through the half-open door that led into the common room where Starhawk sat. He was saying something to Orris—something about wedging the windows there tighter shut—and Starhawk sighed. Whether her feelings toward Sun Wolf were a soldier's loyalty or a woman's love, whether he ever knew it or was even still alive to care, didn't alter the more immediate fact that she was trapped in an inn with the nuuwa yammering and chewing at the brickwork outside. *First things first*, she told herself wryly, getting to her feet. *There'll be time to mess with love—and magic—if you're alive this time tomorrow*.

She found the brothers conferring in the shadows beside the vast, cold kitchen hearth, the light of Orris' torch throwing reflections like the gleaming eyes of dragons on the copper bottoms of the pans and on the drinking water in the stone basin nearby. The nuuwa could be heard from outside, scratching and mouthing at the window frames, their grunting moans occasionally broken by long, piercing wails. "How is he?" Orris asked.

Starhawk shook her head. "Tougher than he looks," she replied. "I'd have bet he'd be dead by now—and lost my money. All secure here?"

They both looked deeply surprised. Orris recovered himself first and gave his opinion that the shutters wou'd hold. "We've driven wedges in some of the downstairs ones," he added. "God knows there are axes and wedges aplenty in the wood room, though little enough wood. But as to how we're going to get out of this hole . . ."

"We'll manage," Starhawk said. "If worst comes to worst, we can pack Uncle Anyog on one of the mules and leave the rest of them as bait."

"But the pelts!" Orris protested, horrified. "And the stores! All this summer's trading . . ."

"Mother will kill us," Ram added.

"She'll have to stand at the end of a long line," Starhawk reminded him, jerking her thumb toward the shuttered windows. "Where's Fawnie?"

She found Fawn in the parlor they'd converted to a stable, huddled in the shadows among the unloaded packs of furs, her face buried in her hands. The strangled sounds of her weeping were what had drawn Starhawk, for the room was lightless and the long corridor from the common room almost so. The Hawk stood hidden by the black arch of the doorway, listening to that horribly muffled sound, her instinct to go and comfort the girl's fears forestalled by the new awareness that Anyog's words had brought into consciousness within her mind.

She loved Sun Wolf. Loved him not as a warrior loved a leader, but as a woman loved a man; and she could conceive of loving no man but him.

Her childhood had taught her that love meant the subjection of the will to the will of another. She had seen her mother invariably bow to her father's wishes, for all the love that had been between them. She remembered those girls who had competed in subservience to become her brothers' humble wives, baking their bread, cleaning their houses, giving up the brightness of their youth to bear and care for their sons. She had seen Fawn—and all those other soft, pliant girls before her—girls who had been Sun Wolf's slaves, whether bought with money or not.

There had been times when the Wolf had asked her to do things she did not like. But his requests had never been without a reason, and his reasons had always been honest. From being his student, she had become his friend, perhaps the closest friend he had. For all his easy camaraderie with his men, there was a part of himself that he kept hidden from them, the part of him that argued theology on long winter evenings, or arranged and rearranged rocks in a garden until they fitted his sense of stillness and perfection. To her he had shown that part of himself—to her only.

Yet this girl was his woman.

My rival, Starhawk thought, with a tang of bitter distaste. *Is that what we'll come to, I and this woman with whom I've shared a dozen campfires over the mountains? My companion in danger, who split watches with me and bargained with the innkeepers? Are we going to end up hair-pulling, like a couple of village girls fighting over the affections of one of the local louts?*

The thought was ugly to her, like the base and soiling memories of her older brothers' sweethearts and their cheap subterfuges to gain dances with them at the fairs.

And, for that matter, what has Fawn taken from me? Nothing that I ever would have had. I broke my vows for Sun Wolf and broke my body to learn from him the hard skills of war. I'll never regret doing either of those things—but from the first, he never wanted me for his woman.

Isn't it enough to be counted as his friend?

The woman in her remembered how Fawn had rested her small hands so lightly on the broad shoulders and kissed the thin place at the top of his hair. No, it wasn't enough.

Yet she saw also, with curious clarity, that Fawn had all the things that she herself lacked—gentleness, the capacity to receive love without distrusting the motives of its giver, the yielding softness that complemented the Wolf's overwhelming strength, and the magic garment of her beauty that made her precious in his eyes.

It would be easier, she reflected, *if Fawnie were a spoiled, grasping little bitch. Then, at least, I would know what to feel.* But then, of course, the Wolf would not have chosen her for his own. And she would certainly not have sold all that she had and left safety and comfort to seek him among the dangers of Altiokis' Citadel.

Fawn was eighteen, wretched, and very frightened; it was this, rather than any consideration of Sun Wolf one way or the other, that finally drew the Hawk to her side, to comfort her in awkward and unaccustomed arms.

In spite of her exhaustion, Starhawk slept badly that night after her watch. Anyog's words returned to her, again and again: *You must love him better than life . . . Only another wizard can enter his Citadel . . . Only a wizard . . . His power is old; it is deep . . . An evil magic, not to be defied . . .*

Never fall in love and never mess with magic . . .

In her dreams, she found herself stumbling through tortuous, shadow-haunted hallways, where the trunks of trees forced apart the stones of the crumbling walls and weeds trailed in the water that pooled across the slimy floors. She was seeking for someone, someone who could help her, and it was desperately important that she find him before it was too late. But she had never sought anyone's help before this; her battles she had always fought alone—she did not know the words to call out. In the darkness, she heard Sister Wellwa's neat little footfalls retreating from her, saw the pale gleam of Anyog's starched, white ruff. And behind her from the vine-choked turnings of the corridors, other sounds came to her—blundering bodies and harsh, snuffling breath. She struggled to break the grip of the dream, but she was too tired; the slobbering, mewing sounds in the dark seemed to come closer.

With a great effort, she opened her eyes and saw Fawn sitting on the raised hearth, bending over to catch the words that Uncle Anyog was whispering. The redness of the sunken fire outlined her face in an edge of ruby; her lips looked taut and set. The air of the room was stuffy. Through the muzziness of half sleep, Starhawk heard Ram and Orris making their rounds elsewhere in the inn—soft, blundering noises, bickering voices. Uncle Anyog fell silent, and Fawn reached down to wipe the sweat that beaded his sunken cheeks.

Then she got to her feet and gathered her plaid cloak around her over the white shift that was all that she wore. Her unbound hair glinted with slivers of amber and carnelian in the dying light. Starhawk asked her cloudily, "Where are you going?"

"Just to get some water," Fawn said, putting her hand to the kitchen door.

There was a basin there, Starhawk remembered, her tired mind moving slowly. She'd seen it when she'd spoken to Ram and Orris, standing next to the monstrous darkness of the overhanging chimney . . . the chimney . . .

Her shout of "No!" was drowned in Fawn's scream as the door opened.

She thought, later, that she must have been on her feet and moving even as Fawn cried out. She caught up the blanket as a shield; that and the thick folds of the cloak that Fawn still clutched around her body were enough to entangle the first nuuwa and save Fawn from its ripping rush. The second and third blundered over the struggling, howling monster on the threshold. Starhawk decapitated one even as it plunged at her, then whirled to hack at the other as it ripped a mouthful of flesh from Fawn's arm. The head went bouncing and rolling, the bloody mouth still chewing, the hands clutching at the girl as if it could devour her still.

Starhawk kicked shut the kitchen door and slammed the bolt, catching a vague glimpse of other movement, struggling and flopping, in the vicinity of the hearth.

When she turned back, Ram and Orris were already cutting loose the thing that gripped Fawn. By the light of Ram's torch, it could be seen to be covered with soot that made a blackish muck, mingled with its spouting blood. Fawn was unconscious. For a sickening instant, Starhawk thought that she was dead.

The Wolf will never forgive me . . .

My rival . . .

Was I deliberately slow?

Great Mother, no wonder he says it's unprofessional to love! It makes hash of your fighting instinct!

"They're coming down the chimney," she said. Ram was just standing up. It could not have been more than sixty seconds from the time Fawn had opened the kitchen door. "They'll be all over the roof."

With a quickness astonishing in so huge a man, Ram was at the nearest window, peering through a knot in the shutter at the thin moonlight outside. From within the kitchen, there was a crashing and a vast yammer of sounds; the great bolts of the door sagged suddenly under the heaving weight of bodies.

"Can we break for it?" he demanded, turning back. The dot of moonlight lay like a little coin on his flat-boned, unshaven cheek.

"Are you mad?" Orris demanded hoarsely. "They'll be off the roof and on our backs—"

"Not if we torch the inn."

"Look, you gaum-snatched cully, they'll have left some to guard the doors—"

"No," the Hawk said. She'd rushed to the other side of the room to open the shutter there a crack. The chink of air showed the white snow of the street empty between the blackness of the buildings. "They don't even have the brains to work in concert, as wolves do. Having found a way into the inn, they'll all take it. Listen, they don't even know enough for them all to throw themselves against the door at once or to use the table in there for a ram."

Orris got to his feet, with Fawn limp and white in his arms, except for the spreading smear of crimson on her shift. "By the Three, creatures more witless than my brothers!" he cried. "I never thought to find them."

"You'll find as many of them as you can do with, if you don't stir those moss-grown clubs you've been calling feet all these years," Ram snapped, making a run for the mules' parlor. Starhawk was seizing torches and throwing together bedding, one ear turned always to listen to the growing din in the kitchen. She raked what was left in the woodbox against the kitchen door and picked up a torch from the blaze on the hearth.

"What about Anyog?" Orris demanded, and knelt at the old man's side. "We can't make a litter, nor even a travois..."

"Pack him like killed meat, then," the Hawk retorted, having been taken off battlefields that way herself. "He'll die, anyway, if he's left here." Already she could see the hinges of the kitchen door moving under the thrashing weight. Orris stared at her, gape-mouthed with horror. "Rot you, do as I say!" she shouted, as she would at a trooper in battle. "We haven't time to waste!"

Orris scrambled to obey her. *If Anyog is a wizard,* she thought, *Altiokis or no Altiokis, he'll put forth what power he has to stay alive. That's all we can hope for now.*

But just as she was a professional soldier, the brothers were professional merchants and could pack five mules and a donkey with the lightning speed acquired in hundreds of emergency disencampments. In moments, it seemed, the mules were squealing and kicking in the hall, with Orris cursing them and lashing at them with a switch. Ram came running back to Starhawk's side, an axe and wedges from the wood room like toys in his great hands. From the tail of her eye, Starhawk had a glimpse of the long, muffled bundle that was Uncle Anyog tied over the back of one mule and of Fawn, somehow on her feet and wrapped in the old man's rusty black coat, stumbling to open the great outside doors.

Icy air streamed in on them. The ululations of the creatures in the kitchen had grown to fever pitch. The doors were sagging as she and Ram made the rounds of the other parlors. Flame licked upward over the rafters and blazed in the mules' straw that they'd scattered across the floor. The kitchen door was breaking as she flung her torch at it, then raced back through the furnace of the common room to where Ram waited for her, framed against the snowy night beyond.

Half a dozen wedges sealed the doors. As they sprang down the steps to where Orris waited with the mules, the Hawk glanced back to see, silhouetted against the roof flames, the black shapes of the nuuwa, shrieking and screaming like the souls of the damned in the Trinitarian hells.

Nothing challenged them as they made their way from the town. As they wound their way up the road into the mountains beyond, they could see the light behind them for a long time.

CHAPTER

— 10 —

"Mother's crying."

Sun Wolf glanced up at this new, soft voice intruding into the solitude of the rain-wet garden. Sheera's daughter, Trella, who was sitting beside him with the trowel and handrake in her small grip, said automatically, "She isn't either."

The tiny boy who had brought this news picked his way through the damp, turned ground to where the Wolf and the little girl sat on a huge rock; he seemed infinitely careful about not getting mud on his black slippers and hose. Trella, who was six and had been assisting Sun Wolf in his duties as gardener since he had come to Sheera's townhouse, had no such considerations. Her black wool skirts were kilted up almost to her thighs, and two little legs in wrinkled black stockings stuck out over the edge of the rock like sticks.

The boy said nothing, only stared at them both with Sheera's beautiful, pansy-brown eyes.

"Mother never cries nowadays. And Nurse says you're not supposed to suck your thumb like a baby," Trella added, as a clinching argument.

He removed thumb from mouth, but held onto it with his other hand, as if he were afraid it would fall off or dry out if not protected. "She cried when Father died;" he said defensively. "And Nurse says you're not supposed to sit on rocks and plays with the slaves."

"I'm not playing with him, I'm helping him work," Trella said with dignity. "Aren't I?"

"Indeed you are," Sun Wolf replied gravely, but there was

137

a glitter of amusement in his beer-colored eyes as he regarded Sheera's children.

He seldom saw Graal Galernas, age four; though the boy was physically a miniature Sheera, he was soft, rather timid, and stood very much upon his dignity as the head of the House of Galernas. Trella presumably favored their deceased father; she was a sandy-haired, hazel-eyed, snub-nosed child who stood in awe of no one but her beautiful mother. Sun Wolf had met the two when they'd sneaked away from their nurse to play in the orangery, as was evidently their wont. It was a custom Sheera had never mentioned, and he wondered if she knew. Graal had bored quickly of gardening, but Trella had helped him build the succession houses along the south orangery wall, in the course of which project she had provided him with a surprising and varied assortment of information about Sheera herself.

Now Graal said, "She did too cry when Father died."

Trella shrugged. "She was crying before that. She cried when the messengers came to the house about the battle and she was crying when she got back from Lady Yirth's later that day. And I heard her crying down in the kitchen when she was mulling some wine for Father."

"She never did that," her brother contradicted, still hanging onto his thumb. "We've got servants to mull wine." He was shivering, despite the silver-laced velvet of his tiny doublet; though it had stopped raining some hours ago, the day was cold and the air damp. In the barren drabness of the empty garden, he looked like a dropped jewel against the dirt.

"Well, she did too," Trella retorted. "I was playing in the pantry and I heard her. And then she went up to her room and cried and cried and she was still up there when Father got stomach cramps and died, so there."

Tears flooded the boy's soft eyes, and his thumb returned to his mouth. Around it he mumbled wretchedly, "Nurse says you're not supposed to play in the pantry."

"That was months and months and months ago, and if you tattle, I'll put a snail in your bed." Just to be prepared, she hopped down from the rock and began to hunt for the promised snail. Graal backed hastily away and fled crying toward the house.

Sun Wolf sat, his knees drawn up, on the river-smoothed stone and watched the child go. Then he glanced back at the little girl, still grubbing purposefully about in the loose, turned earth of the rock garden bed he'd been preparing. "He loved your father, didn't he?"

She straightened up, flushed and sullen. "He's just a baby." That, evidently, settled father and brother both.

If they knew so much, the Wolf wondered whether they knew about their mother and Tarrin as well.

He himself would no more have told a child that her father was a collaborator or her mother a slut than he would have whipped a puppy for something it did not do, and for pretty much the same reasons. He looked upon children as young animals, and neither Graal nor Trella seemed to mind this offhand treatment. But his own childhood had taught him that there was very little that men and women would not do to their children.

He wondered what it was that Sheera had gotten from Yirth to put in her husband's mulled wine.

Wind stirred the bare branches of the hedges above the hollow where they worked; silver droplets of rain shook loose over them. Sun Wolf paid the drops no heed—he'd been wet and cold a good portion of his life and thought nothing of it— and Trella, who had been consciously imitating him for some weeks, ignored them as well. The smell of the earth mingled with the damp, musty silence as he arranged and rearranged the smooth, bare bones of the rocks, seeking the indefinable harmony of shape, and it wasn't until much later that Trella broke the silence.

"She isn't crying," she declared. After a moment she added, "And anyway, it's just because that man's here to see her."

"That man," Sun Wolf knew, was Derroug Dru, Altiokis' governor of Mandrigyn.

Sure enough, a short while later he saw the dapper little figure of the governor emerge from the orangery and stroll along the path with a servant to hold a gilt-tasseled umbrella over his head. The family resemblance to Drypettis was marked; both were tiny, but where Drypettis was slender, Governor Derroug Dru was a skinny, crooked little runt, the haughty set of whose head and shoulders dwindled rapidly to weak and spindly legs. One leg was nothing more than a twisted bone cased in silken hose whose discreet padding accentuated, rather than hid, its deformity; he walked with a cane, and Sun Wolf had seen how all of his entourage slowed their steps to match his, not out of courtesy, but out of fear. His thinning brown hair was suspicously bright around the temples, and his eyes,

brown and dissipated, were carefully painted to hide the worst
marks of excess. Right now, he had only the one servant with
him, but the Wolf knew he usually traveled with a whole shoal
of hangers-on and several bodyguards. He was not a man popular in Mandrigyn.

Amber Eyes had told the Wolf that before Altiokis had
taken the town, she and her friends used to draw straws, the
short straw having to take Derroug. Since he had become governor, his vices had become more open.

Sun Wolf bent his head, smoothing the damp earth around
the stones. He heard the tap of the cane and the slightly dragging
stride pause on the flagstoned path; he felt the man's eyes on
him, hating him for his height. Then Derroug passed on. It
was beneath the dignity of the governor of Mandrigyn to notice
a slave seriously.

At his elbow, Trella's voice whispered, "I hate him!"

He glanced from the little girl to the elegant figure ascending
the terrace steps, a splash of white fur and lilac silks against
the mottled grays and moss-stained reds of the back of the
house and the startling white of the marble of pavement and
pilaster. Sheera never spoke of the govenor, but he had come
to see her several times since the Wolf had been there, and
never when Drypettis was present. Sun Wolf guessed that the
little woman ran interference between her brother and her
friend—which, totally aside from her former position in the
conspiracy, might explain Sheera's attachment to her.

It had begun to rain again. The children's nurse came bustling along the path to scold Trella for being out without a
maidservant, for not wearing her veils, for getting her hands
dirty, and for consorting with a rough and dirty man. "Speaking
to a man alone . . . a fine little trull people will take you for!"
she clucked, and Trella hung her head.

Sun Wolf wiped his hands on his patched breeches and said
dryly, "I've been accused of a lot of things in my time, woman,
but this is the first anyone's ever thought I'd try to corrupt a
six-year-old." He did not like the nurse.

She elevated her well-shaped little nose to a slightly more
lofty angle than usual and retorted, "It is the principle. A girl
cannot learn too young what is beyond the lines of propriety.
It appalls me to see what is happening in the town these days—
women going barefaced and sitting right out at the counters of
public shops like prostitutes in their windows . . . and consorting
with prostitutes, too, I shouldn't wonder! That hussy who was

here earlier actually had paint on her face! What my old lord would have said . . ."

She retreated down the path, holding the unwilling child close to her skirts, clucking and fluttering to herself about the city's fall from virtue.

Sun Wolf shook his head and gathered up his tools. The rain was the fine, blowing, fitful sort that heralded a heavier storm come nightfall; it plastered his long hair down over his shoulders and soaked quickly through the coarse canvas of his shirt. Still, he stood for a time, studying the rocks where he'd settled them—the smooth granite boulder buried half heeled over, so that the long fissure in its side was visible and it formed a sort of cave underneath, protected by the four smaller stones. The lines of it were right, making a sort of music against the starkness of the liver-colored earth, but he thought that he would have liked to have Starhawk's opinion.

In a way it troubled him, how often that thought had crossed his mind.

He had always known she was a good lieutenant. Not only her skill in taking on and defeating much larger men but also the inhuman cold-bloodedness that she habitually showed the troops put them in awe of her, and that was as it should be. As a leader, he had valued her wary painstakingness and her lucidness in defining problems and solutions. As a man set apart by his position as chief, he had valued her company.

It wasn't until now that he realized how much he simply valued her. On campaign, days or weeks might go by without his seeing her, but he had known she was always there. Now sometimes he would waken in the night and realize that if something went wrong—which he had no doubt that it would—he would never see her again. He had half expected to die in Mandrigyn, but he had never before thought of death in those terms.

It was a dangerous thought, and he pushed it from his mind as he entered the vast brown shadows of the orangery. It was, he thought, what his father had meant when he spoke of going soft—a blurring on the hard edge of a warrior's heart. And why, damn it all? Starhawk wasn't even pretty.

Not what most fools would call pretty, anyway.

Rain beat on the portion of the orangery roof that was not covered by the loft. The great room echoed softly with its dull roaring. In the now-familiar darkness, the few trees that had not been moved out into the succession houses were grouped like sleeping trolls in a corner, concealing the practice hacking-posts. The table still stood at the end of the room near the door that led to his narrow stairs. On an overturned tub, her head in her hands, staring blindly at the gray boards of the wall, sat Sheera, the heavy wool of her crimson gown falling like a river of blood about her feet.

Her son had been right. She had clearly been crying.

Her eyes, when she raised them as he passed, were red-rimmed and swollen, but he saw her force hardness into them and calm into her face. She said, "How soon can the women be ready to attack the mines?"

"With or without a wizard to help?" he countered.

The tiredness in her face turned to anger, like a flash of lighted blasting powder, and she opened her mouth to snap something at him.

"A real wizard, not the local poison monger."

The red lips closed, and the hard lines that he had lately seen so often carved themselves from the flared nostrils to the taut corners of her mouth. "How long?"

"A month—six weeks."

"That's too long."

He shrugged. "You're the commander—Commander."

He turned to go, and she surged to her feet and seized his arm, thrusting him around to face her again. "What's wrong with going in now?"

"Nothing," he said. "As long as you don't care that all of your friends who've been loyal enough to you—and to their patriotic and pox-rotted cause—to half kill themselves and put their families in danger by learning how to soldier are going to die because you lead them into battle half prepared."

Her hand dropped from his arm as if his flesh had turned to a serpent's scales. But he saw in her anger a lurking fear as well, the desperation of a woman fighting fate and circumstance with dwindling reserves of strength.

"Don't you understand?" she asked, her voice trembling with weariness and rage. "Every day we wait, *he* gets stronger; and every day we wait, the chances double that Tarrin will be hurt or put to death in the mines. They already suspect him of organizing trouble there; he has been whipped and racked for it, then thrown back onto the chain to do his full share of the work with his limbs half dislocated. One day word of it will get back to Altiokis. But without him, the men's resistance would crumble—he is all their hope, and the brightness of his courage all that stands between their minds and the numbing despair of slavery.

"I know," she whispered. "He is a born leader, a born king; and he has a king's magic, to draw the hearts of his followers unquestioningly. I loved him from the moment we met; from the instant we laid eyes on each other, we knew we would be lovers."

"And does that keep you from playing along with the courtship of Derroug Dru?" the Wolf demanded snidely.

"Courtship?" She spat the word at him scornfully. "Pah! Is that what you think he wants? Marriage or even an honorable love? You don't know the man. Because I was the wife of his chief supporter, the most important and richest man of his faction in the town, he held off. But he would always follow me with his eyes. Now he comes around like a dog when the bitch is in season..."

Sun Wolf leaned his broad shoulders against one of the rude cedar pillars that held up the roof, "Then I guess poisoning your husband was a little hasty on your part, wasn't it?"

Her eyes flashed at him like a beast's in the gloom of the vast hall. "Hasty?" she snarled at him. "Hasty, when that pig had pretended to go over to Tarrin's faction, during the feuding before Altiokis' attack; when he encouraged every man loyal to Tarrin, every man loyal to his city, to join Tarrin's army, already knowing what would happen to them at Iron Pass? There was nothing he did not deserve for what he did that day."

She was striding back and forth, the faint sheen from the windows rippling like light on an animal's pelt, her face white against the bloody color of her gown and the blackness of her hair. "What he did that day has cut across my life, cut across the life of every person in this city. It has left us uprooted, robbed us of the ones we love, and put us in continual peril of our lives. What did he deserve, if not that?"

"I don't know," Sun Wolf said quietly. "Considering that's exactly what you did to me, without so much as a second thought, I can't give a very fair answer to that question." He left her and mounted the dark, enclosed stairway to his loft, the rain beating like thunder around him and over his head.

CHAPTER
—— 11 ——

*I*T WAS RAINING IN PERGEMIS. THE HARD, LEADEN DOWNPOUR beat a fierce tattoo on the peaked slate roofs of that crowded city with a sound almost like the drumming of hail. The cobblestones of the sloping street, three storeys below the window where Starhawk sat, were running like a river; white streams frothed from the gutters of the roofs. Beyond the close-angled stone walls, the distant sea was the same cold, deep gray as the sky.

Starhawk, leaning her forehead against the glass, felt it like damp ice against her skin. Somewhere in the tall, narrow house she could hear Fawn's voice, light and bantering, the tone she used to speak to the children. Then her footfalls came dancing down the stairs.

She is on her feet again, the Hawk thought. *It is time to travel on.*

The thought pulled at her, like a load resumed before the back was fully rested. She wondered how many days they had lost. Twenty? Thirty? What might have befallen the Wolf in those days?

Nothing that she could have remedied, she thought. And she could not have left Fawn.

By the time they had reached the crossroads, where the southward way to the Bight Coast parted from the highland road that led to Racken Scrag and eventually to Grimscarp, the mauled flesh of Fawn's arm and throat had begun to fester. Starhawk had done what she could for it. Anyog, whose hurts by chance or magic remained clean, was far too ill to help her. There had been no question of a parting of the ways.

By the time they had reached Pergemis, Fawn had been raving, moaning in an agony of pain and calling weakly for Sun Wolf. In the blurred nightmare of days and nights that had followed, in spite of all that the lady Pel Farstep could do, the girl had wandered in desperate delirium, sobbing for him to save her.

During those first four or five days in the house of the widowed mother of Ram and Orris, Starhawk had known very little beyond unremitting tiredness and fear and remembered clearly meeting no one but Pel herself. The mother of the ox team was ridiculously like her brother Anyog—small, wiry, with hair as crisp and white-streaked as his beard. She had taken immediate charge of Fawn and Starhawk both, nursing the sick girl tirelessly in the intervals of running one of the most thriving mercantile establishments in the town. Starhawk's memories of that time were a blur of stinking poultices that burned her hands, herbed steam and the coolness of lavender water, exhaustion such as she had never known in war, and a bitter, guilty wretchedness that returned like the hurt of an old wound every time she saw Fawn's white, drawn face. The other members of the household had been only voices and occasional faces peering in at the door.

Her only clear recollection of the events of that time had been of the night they had cut half a handful of suppurating flesh from Fawn's wound. She had sat up with Fawn afterward, the girl's faint, sleeping breath the only sound in the dark house. She had meditated, found no peace in it, and was sitting in the cushioned chair beside the bed, staring into the darkness beyond the single candle, when Anyog had come in, panting with the exertion of having dragged himself there from his own room on the other side of the house. He had shaken off her anxious efforts to make him sit; up until recently he had been worse off than Fawn and still looked like a corpse in its winding sheet, wrapped in his draggled bed robe.

He had only clung to her for support, gasping, "Swear to me you will tell no one. Swear it on your life." And when she had sworn, he had sat on the edge of the bed and clumsily, with the air of one long out of practice, worked spells of healing with hands that shook from weakness.

Pel Farstep had remarked to Starhawk after this that her

brother's sleep seemed troubled. In his nightmares, he could be heard to whisper the name of the Wizard King.

In addition to Pel, the family consisted of her three sons—Imber was the oldest, splitting the headship of the Farstep merchant interests with her—Imber's wife Gillie, and their horrifyingly enterprising offspring, Idjit and Keltie. Idjit was three, alarmingly suave and nimble-tongued for a boy of his years and masterfully adept at getting his younger sister to do his mischief for him. In the spring, Gillie expected a third child. "We're praying for another lassie," Imber confided to Starhawk one evening as she played at finger swords with Idjit before the kitchen hearth, "given the peck of trouble this lad's been."

The household further boasted a maid, a manservant, and three clerks who slept in the attics under the streaming slates of the roof, plus two cats and three of the little black ships' dogs seen in such numbers about the city. Pel ruled the whole concern with brisk love and a rod of iron.

It was a house, Starhawk thought, in which she could have been happy, had things been otherwise.

There would be no glory here, she mused, gazing out into the dove-colored afternoon rain; none of the cold, bright truth of battle, where all things had the shine of triumph, edged in the inky shadow of death. There was none of the strenuous beauty of the warrior's way here and no one here who would understand it. But life in more muted colors could be comfortable, too. And she would not be lonely.

Loneliness was nothing new to Starhawk. There were times when she felt that she had always been lonely, except when she was with Sun Wolf.

These days of rest had given her time to be alone and time to meditate, and the deep calm of it had cleared her thoughts. Having admitted her love to herself, she did not know whether she could return to being what she had been; but without the Wolf's presence, she knew that it would not much matter to her where she was or what she did. There was the possibility—the probability after so much time—that he was dead and that her long quest would find only darkness and grief at its end.

Yet she could not conceive of abandoning that quest.

It was nearing lamplighting time. The room was on the south side of the house, facing the sea, and brightness lingered on there when, in the rest of the house, Gillie and the maid Pearl began to set out the fat, white, beeswax candles and the lamps of multicolored glass. The hangings of the bed—the best guest bed that she had shared with Fawn for the last week, since Fawn's recovery—were a rich shade of red in daylight, but in this half-light they looked almost black, and the colors of the frieze of stenciled flowers on the pale plaster of walls had grown vague and indistinguishable in the shadows. Opposite her, above the heavy carved dresser, a big mural showed some local saint walking on the waters of the sea to preach to the mermaids, with fish and octopi meticulously depicted playing about his toes.

Sitting in the window seat, Starhawk pulled the thick folds of her green wool robe closer about her. Her hair was damp from washing and still smelled of herbed soap. She and Ram had taken Idjit and baby Keltie down walking on the stone quays after lunch, as the gulls wheeled overhead piping warnings of the coming storm. The expedition had been a success. Idjit had induced Keltie to fetch him crabs from one of the tide pools at the far end of the horn of land that lay beyond the edge of the docks, and Starhawk had had to slop to the rescue, with Ram hovering anxiously about, warning her not to be hurt. *A most satisfying day for all concerned*, she thought and grinned.

For a woman who had spent her entire life in the company of adults—either nuns or warriors—she was appalled at how idiotically fond she was of children.

It would not be easy, she knew, to leave this pleasant house, particularly in light of what she and Fawn must face.

Yet the days here had been fraught with guilty restlessness; nights she had lain awake, listening to the girl's soft breath beside her, wondering if the days she spent taking care of Fawn were bought out of Sun Wolf's life.

But she could not abandon her among strangers. And this knowledge had made Starhawk philosophical. There had been entire days in which she had been truly able to rest and peaceful evenings in the great kitchen or in the family room, listening to Gillie play her bone flute and talking of travel and far places with Ram. When Fawn was able to come haltingly down the stairs, she joined them. Starhawk was amused to see that she had won Orris' busy heart with her quick understanding of money and trade.

For Starhawk, at such times, it was as if she had refound her older brothers. After Pel and Fawn and Gillie had taken themselves off to bed, she had spent evening after evening drinking and dicing with the three big oxen, telling stories, or listening to them speak of the northeastward roads.

"You aren't the only ones who've spoken of the nuuwa running in bands these days," Imber said, tucking his long-stemmed pipe into the corner of his mouth and gazing across the table at Starhawk with eyes that were as blue, but much quicker and shrewder, than those of either of his brothers. "After these gomerils left for the North, we had word of it, before the weather closed the sea lanes. I had fears they'd come to grief in the mountains."

Orris frowned. "You mean, others have seen bands as big?"

"Eh—twice and three times that size." Imber leaned forward to his carved chair and pushed his glass toward Ram, who had charge of the pitcher of mulled wine. "Fleg Barnhithe told me some sheepman from the Thanelands said there'd been a band there numbered near forty . . ."

"Forty!" the others cried, aghast.

"They're breeding up in the mountains somewhere." Imber sighed, shaking his head. "It's made fair hash of the overland roads. Them and other things, other kinds of monsters . . ."

Starhawk frowned, remembering her words with Anyog in the half darkness of the corridor of the deserted Peacock Inn. "Breeding?" she said softly. "Now, I've heard tell they're men— or were once men."

"That's impossible," Orris stated, a little too quickly. "Blinding's a punishment that's practiced everywhere, and those who are blinded don't even lose their reason, much less turn into—into those. And anyway, a blinded man doesn't follow the way they do. Nor has any man that kind of—of insane strength."

But his eyes flickered as he spoke, and there was a touch of fear in his voice; if the nuuwa had once been men, the hideous corollary was that any man stood in danger of becoming a nuuwa.

"I've seen men close to that kind of strength in battle," Starhawk objected. She folded her long, bony hands on the waxed oak of the table top. "I've met men you'd have to kill to stop—men driven by necessity for survival out of all bounds of human strength."

"But if it was a thing that—that happened, as if it were a sickness, wouldn't it happen to women, too? I don't think anyone's ever seen a woman of 'em."

"But that goes double for them breeding," Ram pointed out,

filling the glasses with the wine like molten gold in the gleaming lamplight. "Anyroad, they'd never reproduce—they'd eat their own young, as they do everything else they come on."

"The Mother doesn't mold them out of little clay bits," Starhawk said.

Orris laughed. "You'll never convince our Ram of it."

"Nah, just because he didn't have no schooling, bar what the wardens of the jail could give him . . ." Imber teased, his eyes sparkling with mischief.

"Better nor what the kennelman gave you," Ram retorted with a broad grin, and the discussion degenerated into the rough-and-tumble kidding that Starhawk had grown used to in that boisterous house.

But the memory of that evening came back to her now as she thought of taking the road again. She shivered and drew up her knees under the soft folds of the robe, resting her chin on her crossed wrists. Neither she nor Fawn had spoken to any of them of their destination; not for the first time, she was thankful for the brothers' collective denseness that prevented them from guessing what Anyog had known. She had no desire to deal with the overwhelming rush of protectiveness that even the suspicion would have brought out in them.

From somewhere below, she caught Fawn's voice, like a drift of passing perfume; ". . . if that's the case, then keeping a fortified post in the North open year-round would pay, wouldn't it?"

Pel's brisk tones replied, "Yes, but the returns on the trade in onyx alone . . ."

It must have been years, the Hawk thought, since Fawn had been in company with the kind of people she had grown up with, years since she had heard that clever, practical language of finance and trade. Starhawk smiled a little to herself, remembering Fawn's shamefaced admission that she was a merchant at heart. Her father—whose bones had been lying these two years, bleached where the robbers had scattered them—had tried to make a great lady of her; Sun Wolf had made a skilled and practiced mistress of her; it was only now, after trial and struggle and desperate adventure, that Fawn was free to fly her own colors. In spite of what she knew to be their rivalry for the same man, Starhawk was proud of her.

Heavy footfalls creaked in the hallway. Ram's, she identified them, and realized that the room had grown dark. She got to her feet and lighted a spill from the embers of the glowing hearth. She was touching the light to the wick of a brass lamp in the shape of a joyous dolphin when the footsteps paused, and Ram's hesitant knock sounded at the door.

"Starhawk?" He pushed it shyly open. He, too, was sleek and damp from his bath, the sleeves of his reddish-bronze tunic turned back from enormous forearms, the thin, gold neck chain he wore like a streak of flame in the lamplight.

She smiled at him. "The infants all bathed?"

He laughed. "Aye, for all that Keltie wailed and screamed until I'd let her bathe with Idjit and me. It was a fine, wet time we had in the kitchen, let me tell you. It's like high tide on the floor, and the steam like the fogs in spring."

Starhawk chuckled at the thought, noticing, as she smiled up at him, how the rose-amber of the light put streaks of deep gold in his brown hair and tiny reflections in his eyes. She saw the graveness of his face and her laughter faded.

"Starhawk," he said quietly, "you spoke this afternoon of moving on. Going away to seek this man of Fawnie's. Must you?"

. . . this man of Fawnie's. She looked away, down at her own hands, spangled with the topaz reflections of the lamp's facets. *Trust Ram*, she thought, *to go protective on me . . .* "I'll have to go sooner or later," she replied. "It's better now."

"Must it be—sooner or later?"

She said nothing. The oil hissed faintly against the cold metal of the lamp; the smell of the scented whale oil, rich and faintly flowery, came hot to her nostrils, along with the bland smells of soap and wool. She did not meet his eyes.

"If the man's been missing this long, he's likely dead," Ram persisted softly. "Starhawk, I know you have vows of loyalty to him as your chief and I respect that, I truly do. But—could you not stay with us?"

The drumming of the rain on the slates crept into her silence, and the memory of the bleak cold of the roads. She felt the bitter, weary knowledge that she would have to find a wizard somewhere, if she wanted to have any chance at the tower of Grimscarp at all, and that the going would be harder now, with maybe only that final grief at the end.

If it's this hard for me, she thought, *what will it be for F wn, alone?*

Doggedly, she shook her head, but could not speak.

"In the spring . . ." he began.

"In the spring, it will be too late." She raised her head and saw his face suddenly taut with emotion, the big square chin thrust out and the flat lips pressed hard together.

"It's too late now," he said. "Starhawk—must you make me write it all down, and me no good hand with words? I love you. I want to marry you and for you to stay here with me." And with awkward passion, he folded her in his great arms and kissed her.

Between her shock that any man would ever say those words to her and the rough strength of his grasp, for a moment she made no move either to yield or to repulse. The two affairs she had had while in Sun Wolf's troop had been short-lived, almost perfunctory, a clumsy seeking for something she knew from the start that she would never find. But this was different. He was offering her not the warmth of a night, but a life in this place at his side. That, as much as the shape and strength of a man's body in her arms, drew her.

He must have felt her waver, unresponsive and uncertain, for his arms slacked from around her, and he drew back. There was misery in his face. "Could you not?"

Shakily and for the first time, she looked at him not as a traveler like herself nor as an amateur warrior to her professionalism, but as a man to her womanliness. It had been comforting to rest her head on that huge barrel of a chest and to feel the massive arms strong around her, a comfort like nothing else she had known. She found herself thinking, *He is very much like the Chief* . . . and turned away, flooded with a helpless sense of shame, bitterness, and regret.

Silently she damned Anyog for doing this to her, for making her aware of herself as a woman and of his nephew, that good, deserving ox, only in terms of the man she truly wanted and could never hope to have.

She heard the rustle of his clothing and stepped away from his hand before he could touch her again. "Don't," she murmured tiredly and looked up, to see the hurt in his eyes.

"Could you not give up the way of the warrior, then?" he asked softly, and the guilt that burned her was all the sharper for the fact that she had never spoken to him of another love. The very genuine liking she had for him made it all the worse.

But she loved him no more than she loved Ari; and she could not conceive of herself marrying a lumpish, earnest merchant and having to deal with his clumsy efforts to protect her and to rule her life.

"It wouldn't be fair to you," she said.

"To take me a warlady to wife?" A faint smile glimmered in his eyes. "But you'd no longer be a warrior then, would you? I'd be the mock of my brothers, maybe, but then you could protect me and lay about them for me, you see."

And when she said nothing, the flicker of mischief died from his face.

"Eh, well," he said after a time. "I'm sorry I spoke, Hawk. Don't feel you need leave this house before you wish, just to get clear of my ardor. I'll not speak again."

She lowered her eyes, but could find nothing to say. She knew she should speak, and tell him that, though she did not love him, she liked him hugely, better than either of his brothers; tell him that were she not struggling with a love as hopeless as it was desperate, she would like nothing better than to join his loud and brawling family . . . But she could not. There was no one, in fact, whom she could speak to of it—there was only one person whom she trusted with her feelings enough to tell, and he was the one person who must never know.

. . . this man of Fawnie's.

She changed her clothes and went downstairs to supper. She had little idea of what she ate or of the few things she replied to those who spoke to her. Ram was there, pale and quiet under the gibes of his brothers. Though she was past noticing much, Starhawk was aware that Fawn, too, had very little to say. Pel Farstep's sharp, black eyes flicked from face to face, but the shrewd little merchant made no mention of their silence and was seen to kick her youngest son under the table when he bawled a question to Ram, asking, was he in love, that he couldn't eat?

They always said that love affects women this way, Starhawk thought, fleeing the convivial clamor in the supper room as soon as she decently could. *Great Mother, I've eaten hearty dinners after sacking towns and slitting the throats of innocent civilians. Why should saying "No" to one lumpish burgher whom I don't even love make whatever it was that Gillie spent her time and sweat in the kitchen for taste like flour paste and ash? The Chief would kill me.*

No, she thought. *The Chief would understand.*

She paused before the mirror in her room and stood for a long time, candle in hand, studying the pale, fragile-boned face reflected there.

She saw nothing that anyone by any stretch of courtesy would call pretty. For all the delicacy of the cheekbones and the whiteness of the fair skin, it was a face cursed with a chin both too long and too square, with lips too thin, and with a nose that was marked with that telltale, bumpy crookedness that was the family resemblance of fighters. Fine, pale hair caught the candle's light, which darkened it to the color of corn silk—in sunlight it was nearly white, tow and flyaway as a child's. It had grown out some in her journeying, hanging wispy against the hollows of her cheeks. Sunlight, too, would have lightened her eyes almost to silver; in this light, they were smoke-colored, almost as dark as the charcoal-gray ring that circled her pupils. Her lashes were straight and colorless. There was a scar on her cheek, too, like a rudely drawn line of pink chalk. In her bath, she had noted again how the line of it picked up again at her collarbone and extended for a handspan down across pectoral muscle and breast.

She remembered a time when she had been proud of her scars.

Who but Ram, she wondered, would offer to take a warlady to wife? Certainly not a man who had his choice of fragile young beauties like Fawn.

The door opened behind her. The liquid deeps of the mirror showed her another candle, and its sheen rippled over a gown of brown velvet, tagged with the pale ecru lace such as the ladies of the Bight Islands made, with a delicate face lost in shadow above.

She turned from the mirror. "How do you feel?" she asked.

Fawn shrugged and set the candle down. "Renewed," she replied quietly. "As if—oh, as if spring had come, after a nightmare winter." She crossed to the small table that stood beside the window and picked up her hairbrush, as was her nightly wont. But she set it down again, as she had set down untasted forkfuls of flour paste and ash at tonight's supper. In the silky, amber gleam of candle and lamp, her fingers were trembling.

"Ready to take the road again?" the Hawk asked, her voice ringing tinnily in her own ears. *This man of Fawnie's*, Ram had said. But that, she told herself, was nothing that she had to burden Fawn with. It was no doing of hers that she had been stolen away from her family and had taken Sun Wolf's fancy. The Wolf was lost and in grave danger, and Fawn had put her life at risk to find him.

Fawn was silent for a long moment, staring down at the brush, her face turned away. In a muffled voice, she finally said, "No." She looked up with wretched defiance in her green eyes. "I'm not going on."

Even Ram's unexpected proposal of marriage had not struck Starhawk with such shock. For a moment, she could only stare, and her first feeling was one of indignation that this girl would abandon her quest for her lover. "What?" was all she could say.

Fawn's voice was shaking. "I'm going to stay here," she said haltingly, "and—and marry Orris."

"What?" And then, seeing the girl's eyes flood with tears of shame and wretchedness, Starhawk crossed the room in two quick strides and caught her in a swift hug, reassuring her while her own mind reeled in divided confusion. "Fawnie, I—"

Fawn began sobbing in earnest. "Starhawk, don't be angry with me. Please don't be angry with me. Sun Wolf was so good to me, so kind—he saved me from I don't know what kind of slavery and misery. But—but Anyog was right. I was there at the inn when he said we would never enter the Citadel without the help of a wizard—I was listening in the hall. And he's right, Hawk. We can't go against Altiokis by ourselves. And there are no wizards anymore. He's the last one left, the only one . . ."

Not if I can put the screws to Anyog in some way, he's not, Starhawk thought grimly. But she only said, "We'll find one." Her honesty drove her to recognize Fawn's love for the Wolf to be as valid as her own, even as it had driven her to allow the girl to accompany her in the first place.

"No," Fawn whispered. "Hawk, even if we could—it isn't only that." She drew back, looking earnestly up at the older woman with those wide, absinthe-green eyes. "Starhawk, it isn't enough. I want a home; I want children of my own. Even if we find him, even if he's not dead, I don't want to live as a mercenary's woman. I love Sun Wolf—I think I'll always love him. But I won't go on being a glorified camp follower. I can't."

Her trembling fingers gestured at the dim room, with its curtained bed and softly shining lamps, its stiff-robed, ridiculous saint preaching to the mermaids in the sea, with their weedy hair flowing down over their breasts. "This is the sort of house that I grew up in, Hawk. This is the life I know. I belong here. And believe me," she added with a wry smile, "marrying into a firm of spice merchants is a better thing, in the long run, than being mistress to the richest mercenary in creation."

Flabbergasted, Starhawk could not speak, but only look in puzzlement at that beautiful, secretive face and wonder that anyone who actually had Sun Wolf's love could give it up for a bustling, pompous busybody like Orris Farstep.

Fawn disengaged herself quietly from Starhawk's grasp and walked to the window. The lace at her throat almost covered the bandages that remained over the wounds that the nuuwa had left; like Starhawk, she would carry scars to the end of her days. Her voice was soft as she went on. "I spoke to Pel about it this afternoon. I know Orris is fond of me. And I—I want this, Hawk. I want a home and a family and a place; I want to know that my man isn't going to get himself killed in a war next week or discard me for someone else next year. I love this place and I love these people. Do you understand?"

"Yes," the Hawk said, her voice so low that she was almost not sure that it could be heard over the clamoring sounds in her own heart and mind. "Yes, I understand."

Fawn's back was a shape of darkness against the deep well of the window's shadow; the candle threw a little wisp of light along the edge of the lace and on the halo of her hair. "What will you do?" she asked.

Starhawk shrugged. "Go on alone."

She took her leave of them next day. Pel, Orris, Gillie, and the children went with her to see her off at the city's land gate, wrapped in oilskins to keep off the rain. Anyog, though he was able now to get about, had remained at home, as had Ram and Fawn, each for a different, personal reason.

All the way through the steep-slanted cobbled streets of the town, Orris had kept up a worried stream of caution and advice regarding the roads through the Stren Water Valley that would take her northeast to Racken Scrag, about the bandits who were said to haunt them, and concerning the dangers of Altiokis' lands. "It isn't only the bandits stealing your horses you'll have to worry about, lass," he fretted—Pel had given Starhawk a riding mare and a pack mule. "That Altiokis, he's hiring mercenaries, and the countryside's stiff with them. They're dangerous fellows . . ."

The Hawk sighed patiently, glancing sideways at Orris from beneath her streaming hood. "I know all about mercenaries that I need to."

"Yes, but—"

"Leave the poor woman alone," Pel ordered briskly. "By God, how she put up with you all the way from Foonspay I'll never know." Her smile flashed white in the gypsy brown of her face. Her hood was of the fashionable calash type—under its boned arch, the piled braids of her widow's coif gleamed faintly in the rainy daylight. She quickened her step to where Starhawk walked in front of the little cavalcade of led horses and took the Hawk's hand in her own little square one.

In a softer voice, she said, "But we're all glad that you have been here, child. Your staying made all the difference to Fawn. In the pinch, it may even be that it saved her life to know that she had not been abandoned in a strange place."

Starhawk said nothing. She felt uncomfortable about Fawn, almost guilty. But her impassive face showed nothing of the turmoil within her as she looked around at the bright-painted walls of this rain-drenched, fish-smelling town. Pel seemed to accept her silence for what it was and moved along briskly beside her, keeping her heavy black skirts lifted above the runnels that trickled among the cobblestones.

Orris persisted. "But mercenaries—they're a bad breed, Starhawk, begging your pardon for saying so. And they say the Dark Eagle whom Altiokis has put in charge of all his mercenaries is the worst..."

"The Dark Eagle?" Starhawk raised her dark, level brows.

"Aye. He's a wicked man, they say..."

"Oh, bosh," Pel retorted. "Our girl's probably served with him; haven't you, child?"

"As a matter of fact, I have," she admitted, and Orris looked shocked.

From the saddle of the riding mare, Idjit announced, "I be goin' with the Hawk."

"Say, 'I *am* going with the Hawk,'" corrected Gillie, who was leading the mare. "And in any case, you aren't, laddie."

"Then I maun't say't," the boy retorted in the broad Bight Coast dialect that his mother was laboring diligently to erase from his speech. Keltie, perched amid the packs on the mule, watched her brother with worship in her round, blue eyes.

Their mother looked annoyed with this challenge, but Starhawk only said, "That's all right, Gillie. Even if I could take a child along—which I can't—I wouldn't have one with me who talked like a fisherman."

At this rebuke from his hero, Idjit subsided, and Pel hid a

grin. They had reached the squat towers of the city gate. Amid the crowds of incoming countryfolk and local farmers, they said good-by, Starhawk lifting the children down and mounting in Idjit's place, leaning from the saddle to clasp their hands. She missed them already—and more than these who had come to see her off, she missed Ram and Anyog and Fawn. But there was nothing that she could have said to them in parting. What could she say to a man she was leaving to seek another, or to the woman who had abandoned that quest? And though in the end she had not had the heart to speak to Anyog of her desperate need for even a cowardly and unfledged wizard's aid, she knew that Anyog knew it. She did not blame him for his fear, but she knew that he blamed himself.

"The Stren Water Valley will be in flood this time of year," Orris advised. "Best go up it by the foothills."

The mare shied, more offended than afraid, as a market woman chivied a herd of geese through the gate; in the shelter of the gatehouse eaves, a boy was selling roast chestnuts out of a brazier full of coals, his thin, monotonous song rising above the general din. Light and steady, rain drummed on the shining slates and on Starhawk's black oilskin cloak. The sound of rain and the smell of fish and the sea would always be twined in her mind with these people—with the two children hanging onto Gillie Farstep's hands, with the monumental Orris, fussing at her to watch what inns she put up at, and with Pel Farstep, like a little brown sparrow, reaching up to take her hands in farewell.

"Keep yourself safe, child," she said gently. "And remember, wherever you are, there is a home here for you if you need one."

Starhawk bent from the saddle and kissed the brown cheek. Then she turned the horse's head; the mule stretched out its neck to the full extent of the lead before it followed. She left the Farsteps in the crowded shadows of the noisy gate and did not look back.

You have parted from so many people, she told herself, to still that treacherous ache in her heart. *In time, you got over all but one and you'll get over these*.

She made herself wonder if the Dark Eagle would take her on as a mercenary; that would get her into the Citadel, without the need to search for a wizard to aid her. From things Ram and his brothers had said, most people didn't believe in the existence of wizards anymore—only in Altiokis, inhuman,

deathless, undefeatable, coiled in the darkness of the Tchard
Mountains like a poisonous snake beneath the kitchen floor.

The wet wind lifted her cloak. Shreds of white cloud blew,
unveiling the distant foothills of those mountains and the rolling
uplands, stony and deserted, that guarded all approaches to
them on this side. How long would it be, she wondered, before
Altiokis turned his energies toward the Bight Coast, as he had
turned them toward Mandrigyn and the straits of the Megantic?

Once she would have watched the proceedings with interest,
as Sun Wolf did, gauging the proper time to apply for work
amid the chaos. She had burned and looted many cities—this
was the first time, she realized, she had dwelt in one in peace.
Pel, Ram, and Orris were the burghers she and her men had
helped kill; Idjit and Keltie were the children who had been
sold into slavery to pay them.

She shook her head, forcing those thoughts into the background of her mind. *One thing at a time*, she told herself, *and
the thing now is to figure out what I'm going to do when I
reach the Citadel walls*. The Dark Eagle would know of her
unshakable loyalty to the Wolf—he'd seen them work together
when they'd all been fighting in the East. Even if she came up
with a story of disaffected loyalties, the timing, with the Wolf,
being a prisoner in the Citadel, would give the game away.

She had to find a wizard—one who was not too terrified
of Altiokis to admit his powers, preferably one who had passed
this Trial that Anyog had spoken of. But there was all the
Mother's green earth to search in and all the days that she had
lost in Pergemis pressing on her, reminding her how little time
it took for a man to die.

Damn Fawnie, anyway, she thought, exasperated, and then
felt a twinge of guilt. She did not rationally expect that the girl
would have known at the outset that she would not be going
on from Pergemis; and in any case, Pel Farstep might very
well have been right. It would be easy to die, lying friendless
among strangers. Yet knowing Fawn for her rival, Starhawk
could never have abandoned her to her death.

Hooves clattered on the hard surface of the highroad. Starhawk swung around in the saddle, the freshening wind blowing
the hood back from her hair. It was a single rider, wrapped
like herself in a black oilskin poncho, the folds of it whipping
like the horse's black, tangled mane and tail in the moist chill
of the air. They drew up beside her, horse and rider steaming
with breath.

Starhawk said, "Are you out of your lint-picking mind?"

"I suspect so." Uncle Anyog was panting, clinging to the pommel of the saddle for balance, his face white against the darkness of his salt-and-pepper beard. "But I couldn't let you go on, my warrior dove. Not alone."

She regarded him from beneath lowered lids. "You going to start calling me 'lass,' as Ram does?"

He grinned. She reined her mare around and started up the road for the foothills and the way to the Tchard Mountains, Anyog jogging at her side.

"For that matter, did Ram put you up to this?" she asked suddenly.

"It would do my wits greater credit if I said he'd threatened me with a horrible death if I didn't go to your aid." The old man sighed. "But alas, in old age one learns to take credit for one's own follies. None of them knows a thing, my child. I left Pel a note."

"It must have covered three pages," she remarked.

Anyog was recovering his breath a little. She could see, under the oilskin, that he was dressed as he always was—as a gentleman—in his drab and sober black, the starched white lace of his ruff like petals around his face. "In the finest iambic pentameter," he amplified. "My dove, I know why you refused our Ram's hamlike but gold-filled hand—and I suspect I know why you left the Convent." Her head swiveled sharply around, her gray eyes narrowing. "Oh, yes—I have seen you meditate and I know you didn't learn that as a mercenary . . . But why did you become a Sister to begin with?"

She drew rein, meeting that bright, black scrutiny with cold reserve. "I never turn down an offer of help," she said. "And now that you have offered, I won't send you back, because I need you. But that doesn't mean I won't gag you and pack you up to Grimscarp, the way we packed you into Pergemis, if you ask after things that are none of your affair."

She clucked to the mare and moved off.

"But it is my affair, my dove," the little man said, wholly unperturbed. "For I think we are more alike than you know. You became a Sister, I suspect, for the same reasons that you later became a warrior—because you would not tolerate the slow breaking of your spirit to the yoke of a house and a child and some man's whims, and any life seemed preferable to that—because you need a life of the brighter colors, because you prefer lightning-edged darkness to an eternal twilight. My child," he said softly, urging his bay mare up beside hers on the narrow road, "I could no more have remained a pensioner in my estimable sister's house than I could become a warrior like yourself.

"I have lived with my fear a long time," he continued, drawing the oilskin closer about his body as the wind turned chill once again. "Not until now had I realized how it had come to rule me."

CHAPTER
—— 12 ——

S UN WOLF PAUSED IN HIS PACING, HEARING THE SOUND OF soft, approaching footfalls in the darkness. *From the stairs*, he thought. His sigh was deep and bored, and he shifted his weight as a man would do on a long stint of guard. The pattering steps halted. Around him, the vast, chilly darkness was lambent with breath.

Somewhere a board creaked. Then weight struck his shoulders and the back of his knee—light, muscled weight, like a cat's, vicious and controlled. At the first breath of impact, he twisted, slithering free of the smooth arms that sought his neck. In the darkness, he reached back and expertly tweaked the short little nose that snorted with exertion so close to his ear.

He felt his assailant step away. With an oily hiss of hot metal, someone uncovered a dark-lantern. Behind him, Gilden stood panting, regarding him with injured chagrin.

All around the room, their hair tight-braided and their smooth arms traced in the shadows with the faint, clear lines of muscle definition, the ladies of Mandrigyn watched him, a sea of aggrieved eyes.

"You're pulling with your shoulders," he told Gilden, looking down into those long-lashed, sea-blue eyes. "Your center of balance is lower than a man's—that's why you women have hell's own time throwing each other. It's one of your advantages against a man. Throw from the hips—like this—lever me down. Somebody your size, trying to use brute force against someone my size, is more than stupid—she's suicidal."

Gilden colored, but said, "Yes, sir. Thank you, sir."

"And I heard you coming."

She said something else then, sotto voce and obviously picked up from Crazyred's vocabulary.

He glanced at the assembled ladies. "Next?"

Behind him, he heard Gilden's swift hiss of intaken breath, a voiceless protest. When he turned and raised one shaggy brow at her, she asked, "Couldn't I try again?"

"No," he said gently, "because you had only one chance, and now you're dead. Go sit down."

She returned without a word to her place on the edge of one of the upturned tree tubs between Wilarne and her daughter, Tisa. Sun Wolf, for the tenth time so far that evening, walked over to the little potting room that opened off the main orangery, so that he would neither see nor hear—supposedly—where his next assailant would begin her attack. The single dark-lantern that illuminated the vast room threw his shadow, huge and grotesque and swaying, across the gray boards of the wall; he heard Denga Rey fuss with the lantern slide and curse when she scorched her fingers. As he closed the door behind him, he heard the soft rise of talk. Gilden, glib as always, had informed him that this was to cover any noise that the next attacker might make in taking her place, but Sun Wolf suspected that it was simply because the women liked to talk.

It was something he'd found was true even of Starhawk, though there wasn't a man in the troop who'd believe that. So far as he knew, he was the only one she talked to freely, not with the inconsequential small talk of war and the camp, but of things that really concerned her, the past and the future, gardening, theology, the nature of fear. In an odd way, he had felt curiously honored when he had realized that this was true, for Starhawk's facade was one of the coldest and most distant that he had ever seen. Most of the men were a little afraid of her.

He himself had been appalled by the realization that he loved her.

For one thing, one of the most fatal mistakes any commander could make was to fall in love with one of his captains, whether man or woman. It always became known, and he had never seen a time when trouble had not come of it.

For another thing, Starhawk was heart and bones a warrior; logical, emotionless, and ruthless with anything that came in the way of her chosen course. The affairs she had had with other members of the troop had been terminated the minute the men had interfered with her training. Sun Wolf was not entirely certain what her reaction would be if he should return to Wrynde and tell her, "I love you, Starhawk."

And yet, he found himself very much looking forward to returning to Wrynde and finding her there, grave, homely, sarcastically demanding if he'd been kidnapped by all those women for stud.

There was a respectful tap at the door. He came out and signaled Denga Rey to kill the lamp again. Then he began to walk, with a slow pace like a sentry's, the length of that empty darkness, listening for his next student in this lesson in how to take out and kill a man.

It was Eo, not quite as heavy and not nearly as clumsy as she had been. She acquitted herself well, timing her footsteps against his and remembering to throw from the hip, not the shoulders. He hit the floor hard and tapped her arm as the bone of her wrist clamped his windpipe shut. She released him instantly, and the light went up to show her bending anxiously over him, afraid she had done him real harm. He sat up, rubbing his throat and grinning; it was very much like the blacksmith to knock a man senseless and beg his pardon contritely when he came to.

That was something he had found quite common to the women, this concern for one another's bruises. Curse and revile himself blue in the face as he might, he could seldom get even the smallest aggression toward one another out of them. Their technique was good. Most of them understood the leverage their small size needed and, between running and strenuous, night-and-morning training, they were developing the reflexes necessary to put them even with larger and heavier opponents. But he was forever seeing someone at sword practice get in a really telling wallop on her opponent, then immediately lower her weapon and make sure the other woman wasn't hurt before going on. It drove Sun Wolf nearly crazy; if he hadn't seen them fight against the nuuwa, he would have tried—unsuccessfully, he presumed—to wash his hands of the whole affair.

He had found out many things about women in the last few weeks.

He had learned that women, among themselves, could carry on conversations whose bawdiness would have set any mercenary of the Wolf's acquaintance squirming. He'd learned this the evening he'd gone to soak himself in the hot tub, partitioned from the main bathhouse, after training, when the women were in the main part of the baths and had assumed he'd gone up to bed. It had been a startling and eye-opening experience for a man raised on the popular masculine myth of feminine delicacy. "*I* wouldn't even tell jokes like that," he'd said later to Amber Eyes, and she had dissolved into disconcerting giggles.

Another alarming thing about the women was their prankishness. The ringleaders in everything from ambushing him as he emerged, pink and dripping, after his bath to sending him anonymous and horrific love letters were Gilden Shorad and Wilarne M'Tree, outwardly as gracious and poised a pair of matrons as ever a man made his bow to in the street.

But the main thing that he had found was their strength— dogged, ruthless, and, if necessary, crueler than any man's. It had an animal quality to it, forged by years of repression; for all their beauty and sweetness, these were fifty people who would do whatever it was necessary to do, and the single-mindedness of it sometimes frightened him.

He thought of it now, sitting at last alone in the potting room, warming his hands over a brazier of coals, listening to the women depart. The rain had resumed, pattering noisily on the roof overhead, murmuring in the waters of the canals. Most mornings, the lower islands of the city were flooded, the great squares before its floating miracles of churches and town hall transformed to wastes of water crossed with crude duckboards. The damp cold ate at his bones. The women were wrapped like treacle-cured hams in leather and oiled silk, their voices a soft music in the semidark.

The next class would be starting soon. Through the slits of the shuttered window of the potting room, he watched their shadows flicker against the lights of the house and smiled a little at the thought of them. They'd come a long way—from veiled, timid creatures blushing at the presence of a man— even the ones who had children and had presumably conceived them somehow—to cool and deadly fighters. If what Gilden and others told him was true, they'd become hardheaded, matter-of-fact businessmen and shopkeepers as well.

The men of Mandrigyn, he thought wryly, were in for one hell of a surprise when they finally got home.

The potting room was dark, but for the poppy-red glow of the brazier; shadowy shapes of trowels, rakes, and sprouted bulbs lurked gold-edged in the shadows. The smells of the place were familiar to him—humus, compost, cedar mast, the wetter, rockier scent of gravel, and the faintly dusty smell of the half hod of sea coal in the corner. From the door, he caught Sheera's voice, low and tense, speaking to someone outside, then Drypettis' high, piercing tones. He heard Tarrin's name spoken—that lost Prince and golden hope, slaving to organize the mines—and then Drypettis' voice again.

"But he is worthy of you, Sheera," she said. "Of all of them, he is the only man in the city worthy of your love—the greatest and the best. I have always thought it."

"He is the only man in the city whom I have ever loved," Sheera replied.

"That's what infuriates me; that you and he should be en-slaved and humiliated—he by the mines and the lash, you by the base uses of the barracks. That you should stoop to using a—a violent clodhopper who can keep neither his eyes nor his hands off those who are fighting for their city . . ."

"I assigned Amber Eyes to him," Sheera corrected diplomatically. "She didn't object."

"He could have had the decency to have left her alone!"

Sheera laughed. "Oh, really, Dru! Think how insulted she would have been!"

He could almost see the sensitive lips pinch up. "I'm sure that was his only consideration," Drypettis retorted with heavy sarcasm, and a moment later he heard the soft boom of the closed door. Then Sheera's footfalls approached, slow and tired, and she stood framed in the darkness of the potting room doorway.

Sun Wolf hooked a stool from under the workbench and pushed it toward her with his foot. She looked worn and stretched, as she always did these days when one of the girls from the mines brought her news of Tarrin. She ignored the proffered seat.

"If she hates me that much," the Wolf said, holding his hands to the luminous coals, "why does she stay? She's free to quit the troop and she'd be no loss."

Sheera's mouth tightened, and an angry glint flickered in her eyes. Stripped for training, she held an old blanket wrapped about her shoulders, its thick folds muffling the strong shape of her body. "I suppose that you, as a mercenary, would judge everyone by your own standards," she retorted. "It's inconceivable to you that, no matter what someone's personal feelings about her leadership are, she could remain out of loyalty to a higher goal. Like me—like all of us." She jerked her head back toward where the half-seen shapes of Denga Rey and Amber Eyes could be distinguished, talking quietly at the far end of the room. "Drypettis is a citizen of Mandrigyn. She wants to see her city proud and free—"

"The fact that she's the governor's sister couldn't have anything to do with her staying, could it?" Sun Wolf rasped.

Sheera sniffed scornfully. "Derroug could find a hundred better spies."

"Whom you trust?"

"Who are more acceptable to your tastes, anyway," Sheera snapped back at him. "She may be a hideous snob; she may be unreasonably obstinate; she may be rigid and vain and prudish beyond words; but I've known her all my life, since we were girls in school together. She wouldn't betray us."

"She could betray us by being too self-involved to know what she's doing." He moved his shoulders, rubbed the aching muscles of his neck, and encountered, as he did a dozen times a day, the steel of the slip-chain that lay around his throat like a noose.

"Whatever else she is, she isn't stupid."

"She's a weak link."

"Not in this case."

He swung back toward her. "In any case," he snapped. "You all have weaknesses of one kind or another. It's a commander's business to know what they are and take them into account. A single unstable member could wreck the whole enterprise, and I say that woman is about as unstable as any I've ever seen."

"It would be an insult to throw her out of the troop at this point without cause," Sheera retorted hotly. "When it was only a matter of organization, she was virtually second in command . . ."

"Or is it that you just like having a faithful disciple?"

"As much as you hate not having one." She was angry now, carnelian reflections of the fire leaping in her eyes. "She's been loyal to me, not only as a conspirator but as a friend."

"As commander—"

Her voice gritted. "May I remind you, Captain, that *I* am the commander of this force."

The silence between them was as audible as the twang of an overstrained rope. In the ruddy light, her eyes seemed to burn with the reflected fires of the brazier. But whatever words would have next passed between them were forestalled by the opening of the orangery doors and the joking voices of Crazyred and Erntwyff Fish. "So he says, 'What cheap bastard gave you only a copper?' And she says, 'What do you mean? They *all* gave me a copper.'"

The women were coming in for the second class. After a long moment, Sheera turned on her heel, her blanket swirling like a cloak with her steps, and went to speak to them, leaving Sun Wolf standing silent in the potting room, looking out at her through the frame of the dark door.

The next morning he left the house at dawn to seek the witch Yirth in the city.

He had the impression of having seen Yirth several times since they had spoken in his loft on the night of that first meeting, but he would have been hard pressed to say precisely where or when. She was a woman adept at making herself unnoticed. *No small feat*, he thought rather crudely, *for someone that ugly*, forgetting that, for all his size, he, too, had a talent for staying out of sight. He had hesitated to seek her out, knowing that it was in truth her hand, not Sheera's, that held the choke rein on his life. Moreover, he was not entirely certain that he would be able to find her.

As soon as curfew lifted, he went out, leaving Amber Eyes curled unstirring in his bed, and took one of the secret exits of the women out of the grounds. The night's rain had ceased, and the canals lay as opaque as silver mirrors among the moss-streaked walls; the dripping of the rooftrees upon the narrow footpaths and catwalks that bordered the water fell hollow into the stillness of the morning, like the intermittent footsteps of drunken sprites.

He had taken care not to go about in the city too often; Altiokis used mercenary troops as part of the city garrison, and there was always a chance that he would be recognized by one of them. But more than that, there was something in any captured town that made the Wolf uneasy—a sense of being spied upon, a sense that, if he called for help when in trouble, no one would come. The battle at Iron Pass had indeed, as Sheera had said, stripped the city of all that was healthy and decent, and the men whom he met in the streets were mostly cripples, addicts—for Mandrigyn was one of the key ports in the dream-sugar traffic from Kilpithie—or else had a furtive air of shame and deceit about them that made them obviously unsuitable. Even the slaves he saw in the town were a bad crop, the stronger ones having been confiscated as part of the indemnity after the

battle and sent with their masters to labor in the mines. Sun
Wolf's health and his size made him conspicuous—and matters
were not helped by the several women who had sent unequi-
vocally worded notes to Sheera, requesting a loan of his—
unspecified—services.

He crossed through the spiderweb windings of twisting streets
and over plank bridges that spanned canals he could have jumped,
had there been room on those jammed islets for a running start.
On catwalks that paralleled the canals or circled the courtyard
lagoons along the second or third storey of the houses that
fronted them, crones and young girls were already appearing,
to shake out bedding in the damp air and call gossip back and
forth across the narrow waters. In the black latticework of
alleys, ankle-deep in icy water on the lower islands, he saw
the lights going up in kitchens and heard the rattle of ironware
and the scrape of metal on stone as ashes were raked. Crossing
a small square before the black and silent fortress of a three-
spired church, he smelled from somewhere the waft and glory
of bread baking, like a ghost's guiding glimpse of the heaven
of the saints.

In the silvery light of morning, the city market was a riot
of colors: the rain-darkened crimson of the servants of the rich
and the wet blue of country smocks; the somber viridians of
spinach and kale and the crisp greens of lettuces; the scarlets
and golds of fruits; and the prodigal, cloisonné brightness of
pyramids of melons, all shining like polished porcelain under
their beading of rain. The smells of sharp herbs and fishy mud
smote him, mixed with those of clinging soil and the smoky
tang of wet wool; he heard girls' voices as sweet as the hothouse
strawberries they cried and old countrymen's half-unintelligible
patois. Raised as he had been in the barbaric North, Sun Wolf
had been a grown man before he had ever seen a city marketplace; and even after all these years, the impact of kaleidoscopic
delight was the same.

From a countrywoman in a stall where game birds hung like
great feathered mops, he asked the direction of the woman
Yirth; and though she gave him a suspicious look from dark
old eyes, she told him where Yirth could be found.

The house stood on the Little Island, tall, faded, and old.
Like most of the houses there, it was of the old-fashioned style,
half timbered and lavishly decorated with carving, every pillar,
doorpost, and window lattice encrusted with an extravagant
lacework of saints, demons, and beasts, wreathed about with

all the flowers of the fields. But the paint and gilding had long since worn off them. Standing before the door, Sun Wolf had the impression of being on the edge of a dark and carven wood, watched from beneath the trellised leaves by deformed and malevolent elves. Yet the house itself was severely clean; the shutters that were hinged to every window of its narrow face were darkly varnished, and the worn brick of the step was washed and scraped. He heard his own knock ring hollowly in the fastnesses of the place; a moment later, he heard the light, soft touch of the wizard's approaching stride.

She stepped aside quickly to let him in. Sun Wolf guessed that few people lingered on that step.

"Did Sheera send you?" she asked.

"No." He saw the flicker of suspicion cross the sea-colored eyes. "I've come on my own."

The single dark bar of brow deepened in the middle, over the hooked nose. Then she said, "Come upstairs." On the lower isles, none but the very poorest used the ground floors of their houses for anything except storage.

Yirth's consulting room was dark, long, and narrow, the tall window at its far end looking out over the greenish light of a canal. Plants curtained it, crowding in pots or hanging like robber gangs all from the same gallows, and the light that penetrated was green and mottled. Around him, the Wolf had a sense of half-hidden things, of clay crocks containing herbs lining the dark shelves, of books whose worn bindings gleamed with wax and gold, and of embryos preserved in brandy and herbs hung in dried and knobby bunches from the low rafters. Unknown musical instruments slept like curious monsters in the corners; maps, charts in forgotten tongues, and arcane diagrams of the stars lined the pale plaster of the walls. The place smelled of soap, herbs, and drugs. He felt the curious, tingling sense of latent magic in the air.

She turned to face him in the tabby shadows. "What did you want?" she asked.

"I want to know what I can give you, or what I can do for you, to have you set me free." It came to him as he spoke that there was, in fact, nothing that he could give her, for he had quite literally no possessions beyond his sword. *A hell of a spot*, he thought, *for the richest mercenary in the West*.

But Yirth only considered him for a moment, her hands folded over the gray web of her shawl. Then she said, "Kill Altiokis."

His hand slammed down on the long table that divided the room, making the glass bottles there jump, and his voice crackled with anger. "Curse it, woman, that wasn't your price on the ship!"

The black brow moved; the eyes did not. "It is the price I claim to set you free now," she responded coolly. "Otherwise, your bargain with Sheera stands. You shall be freed—and paid—when the strike force marches."

"You know as well as I do that's insane."

She said nothing, using her silence against him.

"Damn your eyes, you know that lunatic woman's going to get every skirt in that troop killed!" he stormed at her. "I've worked on those women and I've taught them, and some of them will be damned fine warriors in about two years' time, if they live that long, which they won't if they go into battle with a green captain. But if she's stubborn enough to do it, then all I want is to be out of here—to have nothing further to do with it or with her!"

"I fear you have no choice about that," Yirth replied calmly. She rested her hands on the dark wood of the table; the wan light picked out their knots and sinews, making them hardly human, like the strange, folded shapes of an oak burl. "Men go to war for their own entertainment, or for some other man's— women, only because they must. Altiokis, now—Altiokis is deathless and, being deathless, he is bored. It amuses him to conquer cities. Have you seen what happens to a city under his rule?"

"Not being suicidal," the Wolf rumbled irritably, "I've avoided cities under his rule."

"Not being a merchant, or the father of children, or a tradesman needing to make his living, you can do that, I suppose," Yirth returned. "But Tarrin—Tarrin fought for the men who were, and for the generation of men who would not see their children grow up under Altiokis' rule. He and Sheera seek to free Mandrigyn. But my goal is different. I seek to see the Wizard King destroyed, rooted out, as he rooted out and destroyed the other wizards. We are not insane, Captain—the insane ones are those who let him live and grow."

"You don't even know he can be killed," Sun Wolf said. "He's been a wizard since before you were born. We don't even know if he's a man or a demon or what he is."

"He's a man," she lashed out, coldly bitter.

"Then why hasn't he died?" the Wolf demanded. "All the

magic in the world won't prolong a man's life—not for a hundred and fifty years! Else we'd have an army of superannuated wizards from all the ages in the past crawling down the walls like ants. But demons are deathless . . ."

"He's a man," she insisted. "Swollen and corrupt on his own immortality. His desires are a man's desires—power, lands, money. His caprices are a man's caprices, not a demon's. He has found a way—some way—of prolonging his life, indefinitely for all we know. Unless he is stopped, he will continue to grow, and all that he touches will rot." She turned and strode to the glimmering window, the light catching the pale streaks in her hair, like wood ash in a half-burned fire. "It is his death I seek, whatever the cost."

"Pox rot you, you're not even a wizard yourself!" he yelled at her. "You've never even gone through this bloody Great Trial I keep hearing about; you haven't got the strength to blow out his bedroom candles! You're as big a fool as Sheera is!"

"Bigger," she bit out, whirling to face him, and Sun Wolf could feel the tension smoking from her, like mist from a pond on a freezing night. "Bigger—because Sheera fights with hope, and I have none. I know what Altiokis is—I know just how great is the gap between his powers and mine. But if he can be drawn into battle, there is a chance, however slim. I will use the might of a freed Mandrigyn to destroy him, as he destroyed my master—as he destroyed my future. If I can do so, I shall be satisfied, though it costs me my life. As a wizard in a town under his rule, I know that it will only be a matter of time before he learns of my existence, and my life would be forfeit then, no matter what I did."

"And what about the cost to the others?" he stormed at her. "What about their lives that Altiokis will destroy?"

"I thought you cared only about your own, Captain," she jeered at him. "We all have our motives, as you yourself have said. Without me, they would still fight. Without you, without Sheera, without Tarrin. Without them, I would have found another weapon to wield against the Wizard King. Depend upon it, Captain, you are a part of us, your flesh and your fate sealed to ours. You can no more desert us now than the string can desert the bow. The others do not fully see this; even Sheera understands it only in terms of her own need, as they all do. But late or soon, the Wizard King must be met. And willing or unwilling, knowing or unknowing, you, Sheera, Tarrin, every man in the mines, and every woman in Mandrigyn will play a part of that meeting."

Sun Wolf stared at her for a moment, silent before her deadly bitterness. Then he said again, "You're insane."

But she only looked at him with those eyes like jade and polar ice. She stood like a black-oak statue, framed in the trailing greenery of the window, wrapped in the misty and terrible cloak of her power. She made no move as his storming footfalls retreated down the sounding well of the stair, nor when the door banged as he let himself out into the narrow street.

In black anger, Sun Wolf made his way through the streets of Mandrigyn. He saw now that, even in the unlikely event that he could talk or coerce that hellcat Sheera into releasing him, Yirth would never let her do it. He had heard women called vacillating and fickle, but he saw now that it was only in such matters as were of little moment to them. Given a single target, a single goal, they could not be shaken. It was a race now, he thought, to finish the training of the strike force before someone in the city learned of what was happening.

He traversed the Spired Bridge and turned aside through the Cathedral Square to avoid the dissolving throngs in the market. Morning was still fresh in the sky, the air cold and wet against his face and throat, and the sea birds crying among the heaped pillows of clouds, warning of storms to come. On two sides of the square, bright-colored clusters of silks and furs proclaimed the patrons of the bookbinders' stalls there; on the third side, a small troop of Governor Derroug's household guards stood watch over his curtained litter beside the Cathedral steps. The usual sycophants were there. The Wolf recognized Stirk, the harbor master, looking like a dressed-up corpse at a Trinitarian funeral, and the fat brute who was Derroug's captain of the watch. Above them, the Cathedral rose, its gold and turquoise mosaics glimmering in the pale morning, buttress and dome seeming to be made of gilded light.

As he passed the steps, a voice beyond him called out, "Captain!"

He knew the voice, and his heart squeezed in his breast with fear and fury. He kept walking. If anyone was within earshot, he had best not stop.

Thin and clear as a cat's mew, Drypettis' voice called out again. "Captain!"

A quick glance showed him no one close enough to hear. He turned in his tracks, hearing the approaching footsteps down the church's tessellated ascent and the restive jittering of tangled gold.

Fluttering with veils, like a half-furled pennoncel pinned with gems, the little woman came scurrying importantly up to him. "Captain, I want you to tell Sheera—" she began.

Sun Wolf caught her by the narrow shoulders as if he would shake the life from her. "Don't you ever," he said in a soundless explosion of wrath, "don't you *ever* address me as captain in public again."

The prim-mouthed face went white with rage, though she must have known that she was in the wrong. Under the thread-drawn saffron of her puffed sleeves, he felt the delicate muscle harden like bone. "How dare you!" she snarled at him. With a wrench she freed herself of his grip. "How dare you speak to *me . . .*"

Anger crackled into him—an anger fed by Yirth's mocking despair, by Sheera's stubbornness, and by the dangers that he had long sensed closing around him. Impatiently he snapped, "You're bloody right I'll speak to you, if you're ever stupid enough to . . ."

She shrank from his pointing finger, pale, blazing, spitting like a cornered cat. The rage in her eyes stopped him, startled, even before she cried, "Don't you touch me, you lecherous blackguard!"

The clipped, mincing accents of Derroug Dru demanded, "And what, pray, is this?"

Altiokis' governor had just emerged from the great bronze doors of the Cathedral and was standing at the top of the steps, twisted and elegant against his backdrop of clients. From where he stood, he could look down upon Sun Wolf. "Unhand my sister, boy."

The guards who had been around the litter were already approaching at a run.

CHAPTER
—— 13 ——

THE SLAVES' CELL OF THE JAIL UNDER THE CITY RECORDS Office was damp, filthy, and smelled like a privy; the straw underfoot crawled with black and furtive life. For as many people as there were chained to the walls, the place was oddly quiet. Even those lucky enough to be fettered to the wall by a long chain—long enough to allow them to sit or lie, at any rate—had the sense to keep their mouths shut. Those who, like Sun Wolf, had had their slave collars locked to the six inches or so of short chain could only lean against the dripping bricks in exhausted silence, unable to move, to rest, or to reach the scummy trough of water that ran down the center of the cell.

The Wolf wasn't certain how long he'd been there. Hours, he thought, shifting his cramped knees. Like most soldiers, he could relax in any position; it would be quite some time before the strain began to tell on him. Others were not so fortunate, or perhaps they had been here longer. There was a good-looking boy of twenty or so, with a soft mop of auburn hair that hung over his eyes, who had fallen three times since the Wolf had been there. Each time he'd been brought up choking as the iron slip-collar tightened around the flesh of his throat. He was standing now, but he looked white and sick; his breathing labored, his eyes glazed and desperate, as if he could feel the last of his strength leaking away with every minute that passed. The Wolf wondered what crime the boy had committed, if any.

Across the room, a man was moaning and retching where he lay in the unspeakable straw—the opening symptoms to

full-scale drug withdrawal. Sun Wolf shut his eyes wearily and
wondered how long it would be before someone got word to
Sheera of where he was.

Drypettis would do that much, he told himself. She had
been in the wrong to call him by his title rather than by his
name; but much as she might hate to admit she'd made a
mistake, and much as she hated him for supplanting her as
Sheera's right hand in the conspiracy, she wouldn't endanger
Sheera's cause for the sake of her own pride—at least he hoped
not.

The far-off tramp of feet came to him. Iron rattled. He heard
Derroug's rather shrill voice again, coldly syrupy. The Wolf
remembered the jealous, bitter glare the little man had given
him as the guards had dragged him down here. The footsteps
came clearer now, the clack of the cane emphasizing the uneven
drag of the crippled foot.

Sun Wolf sighed and braced himself. The fetid air was like
warm glue in his lungs. Across the room, the drug addict had
begun to whimper and pick at the insects, both visible and
invisible, that swarmed over his sweating flesh.

There was a smart slap of saluting arms and the grate of a
key in the lock. Sun Wolf opened his eyes as torchlight and a
sigh of cooler air belched through the open door; he saw figures
silhouetted in the doorway at the top of the short flight of steps.
Derroug stood there, one white hand emerging like a stamen
from a flower of lace to rest on the weighted gold knob of his
cane. Sun Wolf remembered the cane, too—the bruise from
it was livid on his jaw.

Beside Derroug was Sheera, topping him by half a head.

"Yes, that's him," she said disinterestedly.

He thought he saw the little man's eyes glitter greedily.

A guard in the blue and gold livery of the city came down
the steps with the keys, followed by another with a torch. They
unlocked his neck chain from the wall, but left his hands manacled behind him, and pushed him forward down the long room,
the torchlight flashing darkly from the scummy puddles on the
floor. At the bottom of the steps, they stopped, and he looked
up at Sheera, haughty and exquisite in heliotrope satin, amethysts sparkling like trapped stars in the black handfuls of her
hair.

She was shaking, like a too tightly tensioned wire before it
snapped.

"You insulted my sister," Derroug purred, still looking down at the taller man, though Sun Wolf had the odd feeling that it was not he who was being spoken to, but Sheera. "For that I could confiscate you and have you cut and put to work cleaning out latrines for the rest of your life, boy."

I'd kill you first, Sun Wolf thought, but he could feel Sheera's eyes on him, desperately willing him to be humble. He swallowed and kept his attention fixed on the pearl-sewn insets of lace around the flounced hem of her gown. "I know that, my lord. I am truly sorry—it was never my intention to do so." He knew if he looked up and met those smug eyes, something of his own desire to ram those little white teeth through the back of that oily head might show.

"But after consulting with your—mistress—" The cool voice laid a double meaning upon the term of ownership, and Sun Wolf glanced up in time to see Derroug run his eyes appraisingly over Sheera's body. "—my sister has agreed to forget the incident. You are, after all, a barbarian, and I am sure that my lady Sheera could ill spare your—services."

He saw Sheera's cheeks darken in the torchlight and Derroug's insinuating smile.

He made himself say, "Thank you, my lord."

"And since you are a barbarian," Derroug continued primly, "I am positive that your education has been so far neglected that you are not aware that it is customary to kneel when a slave addresses the governor of this city."

Sun Wolf, who was perfectly conversant with the laws of servitude, knew that the custom was nothing of the kind—that this little man merely wished to see a bigger one on his knees before the governor. Awkwardly, because his hands were still bound behind him, he knelt and touched his forehead to the stinking clay of the dirty steps. "I am sorry, my lord," he murmured through clenched teeth.

Sheera's voice said, "Get up."

He obeyed her, schooling his face to show nothing of the rage that went through him like the burning of fever, wishing that he had Starhawk's cool impassivity of countenance. He saw Derroug watching him intently, saw the little pointed tip of a pink tongue steal out to lick his lips.

"But I'm afraid, Sheera darling, that you are partly at fault for not having schooled him better. I know these barbarians— the lash is all they understand. But as it happens, I have— something better." The governor's glinting brown eyes slid sideways at her, his gaze traveling slowly over her, like a lingering hand. "Would you object to my dispensing a salutary lesson?"

Sheera shrugged and did not look in Sun Wolf's direction. Her voice was carefully unconcerned. "If you think it would benefit anyone."

"Oh, I'm sure it would." Derroug Dru smiled. "I think it will be of great benefit to you both. Lessons in the consequences of willful disobedience are always worth watching."

As the guards conducted them down the narrow corridors under the Records Office, Sun Wolf felt the sweat making tracks in the grime of his face. A lesson in the consequences of disobedience could mean anything, and Sheera was evidently quite prepared to let him take it. Not, he reflected in that grimly calm corner of his mind, that there was anything she could do about it. Like him, she had the choice of trying to fight her way out of it now and very likely implicating and destroying all the others in the troop in the resulting furor or going along and gambling on her bluff. Among the lurching shadows of the ever-narrowing halls, her back was straight and uncommunicative. The gleam of the torch flame spilled down the satin of her dress as she held it clear of the filthy flagstones; Derroug's hand, straying to touch her hip, was like a flaccid white spider on the shining fabric.

"Our Lord Altiokis has recently sent me—ah—assurances that can be used to punish those who are disobedient or disloyal to me as his governor," he was saying. "In view of the recent upheavals, such measures are quite necessary. There must be no doubt in my mind of the loyalty of our citizens."

"No," Sheera murmured. "Of course not."

Behind her, Sun Wolf could see she was trembling, either with rage or with fear.

A guard opened a door, the second to the last along the narrow hall. Torchlight gleamed on something smooth and relfective in the darkness. As he stepped aside to let Sheera precede him into the room, Derroug asked the sergeant of the guards, "Has one of them been let loose?"

"Yes, my lord," the man muttered and wiped his beaded face under the gold helmet rim.

The little man smiled and followed Sheera into the room. Other guards pushed Sun Wolf down the two little steps after them. The door closed, shutting out the torchlight from the hall.

The only light in the room came from candles that flickered

behind a thick pane of glass set in the wall that faced the door. It showed Sun Wolf a narrow cell, such as commonly contained prisoners important enough to be singly confined, its bricks scarred by the bored scrapings of former inmates. The room was small, some five feet by five; it hid nothing, even from that diffuse gleam. The reflections of the candles showed him Sheera's face, impassive but wary, and the greedy gleam in the governor's eyes as he looked at her.

"Observe," Derroug purred, his hand moving toward the window. "I have been privileged to see Altiokis' cell like this, built in the oldest part of his Citadel; I have been more than privileged that he has—ah—sent me the wherewithal to establish one of my own. It is most effective for—disloyalty."

The room beyond the glass was clearly another solitary cell. It was only a little larger than the first, and utterly bare of furniture. Candles burned in niches close to the ceiling, higher than a man could reach. It contained four or five small lead boxes; one of them had been opened. The cell door, clearly the last door along the hall down which they had passed, was shut, but the Wolf could hear more guards approaching along the corridor. Mixed with their surer tread, he could distinguish the unwilling, shuffling step of a prisoner's feet.

Something moved in the semidark of the room beyond the window. For a moment, he thought it was only a chance reflection in the glass, but he saw Sheera's head jerk to catch the motion as well. In a moment there was another flicker, bright and elusive. There was something there, something like a whirling flake of fire, drifting and eddying near the ceiling with a restless motion that was almost like life.

Sun Wolf frowned, following it with his eyes through the protective window. Whether it was bright in itself or merely reflective of chance flames, he could not tell. It was difficult to track its motions, for it skittered here and there, almost randomly, like a housefly on a hot day or a dragonfly skimming on the warm air over the marshes; it was a single, moving point of bright flame in the murk beyond the glass.

There was a fumbling noise in the corridor. With astonishing quickness, the door visible in the other room opened and slammed shut again behind the man who had been thrust inside—the red-haired young slave who had stood opposite Sun Wolf in the jail. The prisoner stumbled, throwing his unbound hands wide for balance; for an instant he stood in the center

of the room, gaping about him, baby-blue eyes wide and staring
with fear.

The boy swung around with a startled cry.

Like an elongating needle of light, the flake of fire—or
whatever it was—struck, an instantaneous vision of incredible
quickness. The young man staggered, his hands going to cover
one of his eyes as if something had stung it. The next instant,
his screaming could be heard through the stone and glass of
the wall.

What followed was sickening, horrifying even to a mercenary inured to all the terrible fashions in which men slew
one another. The boy bent double, clutching his eye, his screams
rising to a frenzied pitch. He began to run, clawing blindly,
ineffectually, at his face, falling into walls. The Wolf saw the
thread of blood begin to drip from between the grabbing fingers
as the boy's knees buckled. He registered, with clinical awareness, the progress of the pain by the twisting jerks of the boy's
body on the floor and by the rising agony and terror of the
shrieks. Sun Wolf noted how the frantic fingers dug and picked,
how the helpless limbs threshed about, and how the back writhed
into an arch.

It seemed to take forever. The boy was rolling on the floor,
screaming . . . screaming . . .

Sun Wolf could tell—he thought they all could tell—when
the screams changed, when the fire—poison—insect—whatever it was—ate its way through to the brain. Something broke
in the boy's cries; a deafening, animal howl replaced the human
voice. The body jerked, as if every muscle had spasmed together, and began to roll and hop around the cell in a grotesque
and filthy parody of life. Glancing at Sheera, Sun Wolf saw
that she had closed her eyes. Had she been able to, she would
have brought up her hands to cover her ears as well. Beyond
her, Derroug's face wore a tight, satisfied smile; through his
flared nostrils, his breathing dragged, as if he had drunk wine.

Sun Wolf looked back to the window, feeling his own face,
his own hands, bathed in icy sweat. If there were ever a suspicion, ever a question, about the troop, the governor had only
to show the suspect what he himself had just seen. There was
no doubt that person would tell everything—the Wolf knew
that he would.

The screaming continued, a gross, bestial ululation; the body
was still moving, blood-splotched hands fumbling at the stones
on the floor.

Derroug's voice was a soft, almost dreamy murmur. "So you see, my dear," he was saying, "it is best that we ascertain, once and for all, who can—demonstrate—their loyalty to me." And his little white hand stole around her waist. "Send your boy home."

"Apologize to Drypettis?" Sun Wolf paused in the act of pouring; the golden brandy slopped over the rim of the cup and onto his hand. The pine table of the potting room was pooled with red wine and amber spirits; the laden air reeked of them, heavy over the thick aromas of dirt and potting clay. His eyes were red-rimmed, bloodshot, and unnaturally steady. He had been drinking methodically and comprehensively since he had returned home that morning. It was now an hour short of sunset, and Sheera had just returned. His voice was only slightly thickened as he said, "That haughty little snirp should never have called me captain in public and she knows it."

Sheera's mouth looked rather white, her lips pressed tight together, her dark hair still sticking to her cheeks with the dampness of her bath. The Wolf was half tempted to pull up a chair for her and pour her a glass—not that there was much left in any of the bottles by this time. He had never seen a woman who looked as if she needed it more.

But Sheera said, "She says she never called you captain."

He stared at her, wondering if the brandy had affected his perception. "She what?"

"She never called you captain. She told me she called out to you and told you to take a message to me, and you refused and told her you were no one's errand boy . . ."

"That's a lie." He straight-armed the brandy at one shot and let the glass slide from his fingers. Then rage hit him, stronger than any drink, stronger than what he had felt for Derroug while on his knees before the governor in the prison.

"Captain," Sheera said tightly, "Dru spoke to me just before I left the palace. She would never have called you by your title in public. She knows better than that."

"She may know better than that," Sun Wolf said levelly, "but it's possible to forget. All right. But that's what she called me, and that's why—"

The controlled voice cracked suddenly. "You're saying Dru lied to me."

"Yes," the Wolf said, "that's what I'm saying. Rather than admit that she was in the wrong." It crossed his mind fleetingly that he should not be arguing—not drunk as he was, not this afternoon, not after the kind of scene he was fairly certain had taken place with Drypettis immediately after what amounted to rape. He could see the lines of tension digging themselves tighter and tighter into Sheera's face, like the print of ugly memories in her tired flesh, and the sudden, uncontrollable trembling of her bruised lips. But her next words drove any thought from his mind.

"And what would you rather do than admit you're wrong, Captain?"

"Not lie about one of my troops."

"Hah!" She had picked up a small rake, turning it nervously in fingers that shook; now she threw it back to the table with ringing violence. "Your troops! You'd have tossed her out from the start—"

"Damned right I would," he retorted, "and this is why."

"Because she was never to your taste, you mean!"

"Woman, if you think all I've had to do in the last two months has been to put together a harem of assassins for myself—"

"Rot your eyes, what else have you been doing?" she yelled back at him. "From Lady Wrinshardin to Gilden and Wilarne—"

"Let's not forget the ones who were assigned," he roared, pitching his voice to drown hers. "If you're jealous..."

"Don't flatter yourself!" she spat at him. "That's what sickens you, isn't it? You can't stand to teach women the arts of war because those are your preserve, aren't they? The only way you can take it is if you make them your women. They have your permission to be good so long as you're better, and the ones who get to be the best you make damned sure will love you too much ever to beat you!"

"You don't know what the hell you're talking about and you sure aren't warrior enough to know what it means!" he lashed back at her, hurling the brandy bottle at the opposite wall, so that it shattered in an explosion of alcohol and glass. "The best of the women I know is better than any man—"

"Oh, yes," the woman sneered furiously. "I've seen that best one of yours, and she looked at you the way a schoolgirl looks at her first beau! You've never given two cow patties together for anything about this troop! You wouldn't care if we were all destroyed, so long as you aren't threatened by anyone else's excellence!"

"You talk to me about that when you've been a warrior anywhere near as long as I have—or the Hawk has!" he stormed at her. "And no, I don't give two cow pats together for you and your stupid cause. And yes, part of it's because of the ladies whom I don't want to see get their throats cut in your damfool enterprise—"

"Tarrin—"

"I'm damned sick of hearing about pox-rotted Tarrin and your reeking cause!" he roared.

Red with rage, she shouted over his voice, "You can't see any higher than your own comforts—"

He yelled back at her, "That's what I've said from the beginning, rot your poxy eyes! I'd have washed my hands of the whole flaming business, and of you, too—stubborn, bull-headed hellcat that you are! I'm through with you and your damned tantrums!"

"You'll stay and you'll like it!" Sheera raged. "Or you'll die screaming your guts out a day's journey from the wall, and that's the only choice you've got, soldier! You'll do what I tell you or Yirth may not even give you that choice!"

She whirled in a flame-colored slash of skirts and veils and stormed from the little room, slamming the flimsy door behind her. He heard her footsteps stride into the distance, crashing hollowly, and at last heard the thunderous smash of the outer door. Through the window, he saw her stride up into the twilight of the garden toward the house, past the rocks he had settled among the bare roots of juniper, and past the dark pavilion of the bathhouse. She was sobbing, the dry, bitter weeping of rage.

Deliberately, Sun Wolf picked up a wine bottle from the table and hurled it against the opposite wall. He did the same with the next and the next and the next—and all the others that he had consumed in the course of the day, since he had returned from seeing what it was that Derroug had hidden beneath his palace. Then he got up and made his way with a perfectly steady stride to the stables, saddled a horse, and rode out of Mandrigyn by the land gate, just as the sun was setting.

He rode throughout the night and on into morning. The alcohol burned slowly out of his blood without lessening in him the determination to thwart Sheera, once and for all. Anzid was just about the last choice he would have taken, had he been allowed to pick his own death, but horrible death of some sort would come to him for certain if he remained in Mandrigyn.

Today he had seen at least one that was worse than anzid. And in any case, he would die his own man, not Sheera's slave.

He turned the horse's head toward the west, traversing in darkness the half-flooded fields, spiky with sedge and with the bare branches of naked trees. Before midnight, he reached the crossroads where the way ran up to the Iron Pass and the greater bulk of the Tchard Mountains and out over the uplands to pass through the rocks of the Stren Water Valley down to the rich Bight Coast. It had been in his mind to ride north up the pass, knowing that Sheera would never think to seek him on Altiokis' very doorstep. And seek him she would, of that he was certain. She would never endure this last defiance from him. He had vowed that he would not give her the satisfaction of ever finding his body, of ever knowing for certain that he was dead.

Besides, if she found him before the anzid killed him, it might be possible for her to bring him back.

But in the end, he could not take the Citadel road. He turned the mare's head westward where the roads crossed and spurred on through the dripping silence of the dark woods.

He wondered if the Hawk would understand what he was doing.

Ari, he knew, would have apologized to Drypettis with every evidence of sincerity and a mental vow to take it out of that pinch-faced little vixen later. And the Hawk . . . The Hawk would have told them at the outset that she would die and be damned to them—or else have found a way to avoid the entire situation.

What had Sheera meant about the way the Hawk had looked at him? Was it simply Sheera's jealousy or her hate? Or did she, as a woman, see things with a woman's different eyes.

He didn't think so, much as he would have liked to believe that Starhawk had looked at him with something other than that calm, businesslike gaze. In his experience, love had always meant demands—on the time, on the soul, and certainly on the attention. Starhawk had never asked him for anything except instruction in their chosen craft of war and an occasional daffodil bulb for her own garden.

It was Starhawk, in fact, who had defined for him why love was death to the professional, on one of those long winter evenings in Wrynde when Fawn had gone to sleep, her head on his lap, her curls spilling over his thigh. He and the Hawk had sat up talking, half drunk before the white sand of the sunken hearth, listening to the rain drumming on the cypresses

of the gardens outside. It was he who had spoken of love, who
had quoted his father's maxim: *Don't fall in love and don't
mess with magic.* Love was a crack in a man's armor, he had
said. But the Hawk, with her clearer insight, had said that love
simply caused one to cease being single-minded. For a warrior,
to look aside from the main goal of survival could mean death.
He could not love, if his goal was to survive at all costs.

Could a woman who loved speak of love with such clear-
eyed brutality?

Could a woman who didn't?

Dawn came, slow and gray through the wooded hills. Yellow leaves muffled the road in soaked carpets; overhanging
branches splattered and dripped on the Wolf's back. He rode
more slowly now, scouting as he went, taking his bearings on
the crowding hills visible above the bare trees. South of the
road, those hills shouldered close, massive and lumpy, stitched
with narrow ravines and a rising network of ledges, half choked
in scrub and wild grape. Here and there, he heard the frothing
voices of swollen streams, booming among the rocks.

Wind flicked his long hair back over his shoulders and laid
a cold hand on his cheek. He had forgotten how good it felt
to be alone and free, even if only free to die.

It was midafternoon when he let the horse go. He sent it
on its way along the westward road with a slap on the rump,
and it trotted off gamely, leaving tracks that Sheera was sure
to follow. With any luck, she'd trail it quite a distance and
never find his body at all. It would rot that hellcat's soul, he
thought with a grim inward smile, to think that he might, by
some miracle, have eluded her—to think that, somewhere in
the world, he might still be alive and laughing.

He was already beginning to feel the anzid working in his
veins, like the early stirrings of fever. He struck back through
the woods in an oblique course toward the rocks of the higher
hills and the caves that he knew lay in the direction of Mandrigyn. It was a long way, and he went cautiously, covering
his tracks, wading in the freezing scour of the streams, and
finding his way over the rocky ground by instinct when the
daylight faded again into evening.

He had always had sharper senses in the dark than most
men; he had had that ability as a child, he remembered, and
it had been almost uncanny. Even in the cloud-covered darkness
and rising wind, he made out the vague shapes of the trees,
the ghostly birches and leering, gargoyle oaks. His nose told

him it would rain later, destroying his tracks; wind was already tugging at his clothes.

The ground underfoot grew steep and stony, rising sharply and broken by the outcropped bones of the earth. He found that his breath had begun to saw at his lungs and throat, a cold sharpness, as if broken glass were lodged somewhere inside. Still the ground steepened, and the foliage thinned around him; vague rock shapes became visible above, rimmed with a milky half-light that only the utter darkness of the rest of the night let him see at all. Weakness pulled at him and a kind of feverish pain that had no single location; nausea had begun to cramp his stomach like chewing pincers.

The first wave of it hit him in the high, windy darkness of a broken hillside, doubling him over, as if a drench of acid had been spilled through his guts. The shock of it took his breath away and, when the pain faded, left him weak and shaking, feeling sickened and queerly vulnerable. After a time, he got to his feet, hardly daring to move for fear the red agony would return. Even as he staggered on, he felt it lying in wait for him, lurking behind every fiber of his muscles.

It took him another hour to find the kind of place that he sought. He had been looking for a cave deep in the hills, so far from the road that, no matter how loudly he screamed, no searchers would hear. What he found was a ruined building, a sort of chapel whose broken walls were wreathed and hung with curtains of winter-brown vines. In the crypt below it was a pit, some twenty feet deep and circular, ten or fifteen feet across. Thrown pebbles clinked solidly or rustled in weeds; the little light that filtered through the blowing branches above him showed him nothing stirring but wind-tossed heather.

By now he was sweating, his hands trembling, a growing pain in his body punctuated by lightning bolts of cramps. Cautiously, he hung by his hands over the edge, then let himself drop.

It was a mistake. It was as if his entire body had been flayed apart; the slightest shock or jar pierced him like tearing splinters of wood. The sickening intensity of the pain made him vomit, and the retching brought with it new pains, which in turn fed others. Like the first cracking of a sea wall, each new agony lessened his resistance to those mounting behind it, until they ripped his flesh and his mind as a volcano would rip the rock that sealed it. Dimly, he wondered how he could still be conscious, or if the agony would go on like this until he died.

It was only the beginning of an endless night.

Sheera found him in the pit, long after the dawn that barely lightened the blackness of the rainsqualls of the night. Wind tore at her wet riding skirts as she stood looking down from the pit's edge and snagged at the dripping coils of her hair. Though it was his screaming which had drawn her, his voice had cracked and failed. Through the rain that slashed her eyes, she could see him still moving, crawling feverishly through the gross filth that smeared every inch of the pit's floor, groaning brokenly but unable to rest.

In spite of the rain, the place smelled like one of the lower cesspools of Hell. Resolutely, she knotted the rope she had brought with her to the bole of a tree and shinned down. Her lioness rage had carried her through the night hunt, but now, seeing what was left after the anzid had done its work, she felt only a queer mingling of pity and spite and horror. She wondered if Yirth had been aware that the death would take this long.

From fever or pain, he had thrown off most of his clothes, and the rain made runnels through the filth that smeared his blue and icy flesh. He was still crawling doggedly, as if he could somehow outdistance the agony; but as she approached, he was seized with a spasm of retching that had long since ceased to bring up anything but gory bile. She saw that his hands were torn and bloody, clenched in pain so tightly she thought the force of it must break the bones. After the convulsion had ceased, he lay sobbing, racked by the aftermath, the rain trickling through the stringy weeds of his hair. His face was turned aside a little from the unspeakable pools in which he half lay, and the flesh of it looked sunken and pinched, like a dying man's.

There were no sounds in the pit then, except for the dreary, incessant rustle of falling water and his hoarse, wretched sobbing. That, too, she had not expected. She walked a step nearer and stood looking in a kind of horrible fascination at the degraded head, the sodden hair thin and matted with slime, and the broken and trembling hands. Quietly, she said, "You stupid, stubborn bastard." Her own voice sounded shaky to her ears. "I've got a good mind to go off and leave you, after all."

She had not thought he'd heard. But he moved his head a

little, dilated eyes regarding her through a fog of pain from pits of blackened flesh. She could tell he was almost blind, fighting with every tormented muscle of his body to bring her into focus, to speak, and to control the wheezing thread of his scream-shattered voice into something that could be heard and understood.

He managed to whisper, "Leave me, then."

Her own horror at what she had done turned to fury, fed by the weariness of her long night's terrified searching. Through darkness and clouds of weakness, Sun Wolf could see almost nothing, but his senses, raw as if sandpapered, brought him the feel of her rage like a wave of heat. For a moment, he wondered if she would kick him where he lay or lash at him with the riding whip in her hands.

But then he heard her turn away, and the splash of her boots retreated through the puddles that scattered the pit's floor in the rain. For an elastic time he lay fighting the unconsciousness that he knew would only bring him the hideous terror of visions. Then he heard the rattle of her horse's retreating hooves, dying away into the thundering clatter of the rain. He slipped again into the red vortex of delirium.

There was utter loneliness there and terrors that reduced the pain ripping through his distant body to an insignificant ache that would merely result in his eventual death. Worse things pursued and caught him—loss, regret, self-hate, and all the spilling ugliness that festered in the bottommost pits of the mind.

And then, after black wanderings, he was aware of moonlight in a place he had never been before and the far-off surge of the sea. Blinking, he made out the narrowing stone walls of one of those beehive chapels that dotted the rocky coasts of the ocean in the northwest, the darkness around the Mother's altar, and the shape of a warrior kneeling just beyond the uneven circle of moonlight that lay like a tiny carpet in the center of the trampled clay floor.

The warrior's clothing was unfamiliar, the quilted, shiny stuff of the Bight Coast. The scarred boots he knew, and the sword that lay with the edge of its blade across the moonlight, a white and blinding sliver. The bent head, pale and bright as the moonlight, he could have mistaken for no other.

She looked up, and he saw tears glittering on the high cheekbones, like rain fallen on stone. She whispered, "Chief?" and got haltingly to her feet, her eyes struggling to pierce the gloom that separated them. "Chief, where are you? I've been looking for you . . ."

He held out his hand to her and saw it, torn and filthy, as he had seen it lying in the slime of the pit. She hesitated, then took it, her lips like ice against it, her tears scalding the raw flesh.

"Where are you?" she whispered again.

"I'm in Mandrigyn," he said quietly, forcing the scorched remains of his voice to be steady. "I'm dying—don't look for me further."

"Rot that," Starhawk said, her voice shaking. "I haven't come all this way just to—"

"Hawk, listen," he whispered, and she raised her eyes, the blood from his hand streaking her cheek, blotched and smeared with her tears. "Just tell me this—did you love me?"

"Of course," she said impatiently. "Wolf, I'll always love you. I always have loved you."

He sighed, and the weight settled heavier over him, the grief for what could have been. "I'm sorry," he said. "I wasted the time we had—and I'm sorry for what that did to you."

She shook her head, even the slight brushing movement of it tearing at the rawness of his overtaxed body. He shut his teeth hard against the pain, for he could feel himself already fraying, his flesh tugged at by the winds of nothingness.

"The time wasn't wasted," Starhawk said softly. "If you'd thought you loved me as you loved Fawnie and the others, you would have kept me at a distance, as you did them, and that would have been worse. I would rather be one of your men than one of your women."

"I see that," he murmured, for he had seen it, in the twisting visions of the endless night. "But that speaks better of you than it does of me."

"You are what you are." Her voice was so quiet that, over it, he could hear the distant beat of the sea on the rocks and the faint thread of the night wind. Her hands tightened like icy bones around the broken mess of his fingers, and he knew she could feel him going. "I wouldn't have traded it."

"I was what I was," he corrected her. "And I wanted you to know."

"I knew."

He had never before seen her cry, not even when they'd cut arrowheads from her flesh on the battlefields; her tears fell without bitterness or weakness, only coursing with the loneliness that he had himself come to understand. He raised his hand to touch the white silk of her hair. "I love you, Hawk," he whispered. "Not just as one of my men—and not just as one of my women. I'm sorry I did not know it in time."

He felt himself slip from her, drawn back toward that bleak and storming darkness. He knew his body and his soul were breaking, like a ship on a reef; all his garnered strength sieved bleeding through the wreckage of spars. All the buried things, the loves and hopes and desires that he had derided and forgotten because he could not bear to see them denied him by fate, poured burning from their cracked hiding places and challenged him to deny them now.

They were like ancient dreams of fire, as searing as molten gold. He heard his father's derisive jeers through the darkness, though the voice was his own; the old dreams burned like flame, the heat of them greater than the pain of the anzid burning through his flesh. But he gathered the dreams into his hands, though they were made of fire, of molten rage, and of wonder. The scorching of their power seared and peeled the last of his flesh away, and his final vision was of the stark lacework of his bones, clutching those forgotten fires.

Then the vision disappeared from him, as his own apparition had faded from Starhawk's grasp. He opened his eyes to the slanted wood of the loft ceiling, fretted with the wan sunlight that filtered through the bare trees of Sheera's courtyard. He heard the murmur of Sheera's voice from below in the orangery and Yirth's terse and scornful reply.

Yirth, he thought and closed his eyes again, overborne by horror and despair. All his efforts of that long day to hide his trail from Sheera—and she had only to ask Yirth to speak his name and look into standing water. The night he had spent in the pit, the pain, and the unnamable grief had been for nothing.

Weak and spent, there was nothing of his scoured flesh or mind that would answer his bidding; had he had the strength to do so, he would have wept. The women had won. He was still alive and still their slave. Even had he been able to find a way to elude Yirth's magic, he knew he would make no further attempt at escape. He would never have the strength to go through that again.

CHAPTER
—— 14 ——

*H*AD SUN WOLF BEEN ABLE TO, HE WOULD HAVE AVOIDED Yirth's care, but he could not. For two days he lay utterly helpless, drinking what little she gave him to drink, feeling the shadows shrink and rise with the passage of the cloudy days, and listening to the rain drum on the tiles or trickle, gossiping, from the eaves. In the nights, he heard the women assemble below, the thud of feet and the sharp bark of Denga Rey's voice, Sheera's curt commands, and mingling of voices in the gardens, as they came and went from the bathhouse. Once he heard a hesitant tread climb the stairs toward his loft, pause just below the turn that led to his door, and wait there for a long time, before retreating once again.

He slept a great deal. His body and mind both felt gutted. Sometimes the women who came—Amber Eyes, Yirth, occasionally Sheera—would speak to him, but he did not remember replying. There seemed to be no point in it.

On the third day, he was able to eat again, a little, though meat still nauseated him. In the afternoon, he went down to the potting room and repaired the damage that neglect had done to his bulbs and to the young trees in the succession houses. Like a spark slowly flickering to life against damp tinder, he could feel himself coming back to himself, but the weariness that clung to his bones made him wary of even the slightest tax on either his body or the more deeply lacerated ribbons of his soul. When he heard Sheera come into the orangery in the changeable twilight at sundown, he avoided her, fading back into the shadows of the potting room when she entered it and slipping unseen out the door behind her.

After the women had come and gone that night, he went to lie in the hot water and steam of the bathhouse, listening to the wind that thrashed the bare branches overhead, feeling, as he had felt as a child, that curious sense of being alive with the life of the night around him.

He returned to a sleep unmarred by dreams.

Voices in the orangery woke him, a soft, furtive murmuring, and the swift patter of bare feet. During his illness, though she had nursed him by day, Amber Eyes had not spent the night there. He wondered whether she had had another lover all along while Sheera had assigned her to keep him occupied. The room was empty as he rolled soundlessly to his feet and stole toward the stairway door.

He could hear their voices clearly.

". . . silly cuckoos, you should never have tried it alone! If you'd been taken . . ."

It was Sheera's voice, the stammering tension giving the lie to the anger in her words.

"More of us wouldn't have done any good," Gilden's huskier tones argued. "It would have just made more to be caught . . . Holy God, Sheera, you weren't there! I don't know what it was! But . . ."

"Is she still there, then?" Denga Rey demanded sharply.

Gilden must have nodded. After a moment, the gladiator went on roughly. "Then we'll have to go back."

"But they'll know someone's trying to rescue her now." That was Wilarne's voice.

By the spirits of my ancestors, how the hell many of them are in on it, whatever it is? Sun Wolf asked himself.

Exercising every ounce of animal caution he possessed, trusting that whatever noise they were making down in the orangery would divert their minds, if the stairs creaked—though it shouldn't, if their training had done them any good!—he slipped down the stairs, stopping just behind where he knew his body would catch the light.

There were five of them, grouped around the seed of light that glowed above the clay lamp on the table. A thread of gold reflection outlined the sharp curve of Denga Rey's aquiline profile and glistened in her dark eyes. Beside her, Sheera was wrapped in the cherry-red wool of her bed robe, her black hair strewed over her shoulders like sea wrack. The three women before them were dressed—or undressed—for battle.

From his hiding place, Sun Wolf noted the changes in those delicate-boned bodies. The slack flesh had given place to hard muscle. Even Eo, towering above the two little hairdressers, had a taut sleekness to her, for all her remaining bulk. Under dark cloaks, they wore only the leather breast guards of their training outfits, short drawers, and knife belts. Their hair had been braided tightly back; Wilarne's had come half undone in some kind of struggle and lay in an asymmetrical rope over her left shoulder, the ends tipped and sticky with blood.

Sheera's women, he thought, had gone to battle before their commander was ready for it. He wondered why.

Sheera was saying, "When was she arrested? And why?"

Eo fixed her with cold, bitter blue eyes. "Do you really need to ask why?"

Sheera's back stiffened. Gilden said, with her usual diplomacy, "The reason was supposedly insolence in the street. But he spoke to her yesterday outside Eo's forge . . ."

Eo went on bitterly. "Well, he can hardly seriously suspect a fifteen-year-old girl of treason."

"We had to act fast," Wilarne said, dark almond eyes wide with concern. "That's why we weren't in class tonight."

"You'd have done better to come and get help," Denga Rey snapped.

In the darkness of the stairs, Sun Wolf felt sudden anger kindle through him, startling and cold. *Tisa*, he thought. *Gilden's daughter—Eo's niece and apprentice*. A girl whose adolescent gawkishness was fading into a coltish beauty. He wondered if she, too, had been given an opportunity to prove her "loyalty" to Derroug and had been arrested for rebuffing him.

Gilden was saying, "We went in over the wall near the Lupris Canal. We took out two guards, weighted the bodies, and dumped them. But—Sheera, the guards in the palace compound itself! I swear they see in the dark. There was no light, none, but they saw us and came after us. We could hear them. One of them caught Wilarne . . ."

"I don't understand it," Wilarne whispered. Her hands, fine-boned and as little as a child's, clenched together in the memory of the fight and the fear. "He—he didn't seem to feel pain. Others were coming—I hurt him, I know I hurt him, but it didn't stop him, it didn't do anything. I barely got away . . ."

"All right," Sheera said. "I'll send a message to Drypettis, tell her what's happened, and see if she can get us into the palace."

"She'll be watched," Sun Wolf said. "And you couldn't get a message to her tonight."

It was the first time that he had spoken in three days, and they swung around, startled, not even knowing that he had been there watching them. Having spoken to Starhawk from the pit, he was no longer surprised at what remained of his voice, but he saw the frown that folded Sheera's brow at the rasping wheeze of it, the worry in Eo's broad, motherly face, and the flood of joy and relief in the eyes of Gilden and Wilarne. They had, he realized, been truly frightened for him.

Sheera was the first to speak. "Derroug doesn't suspect Dru . . ."

"Maybe not of treason, but he knows she'd do just about anything you bade her. Whether he understands that there's some kind of connection between you and Gilden, I don't know . . . But in any case, we've got to get Tisa out of there before he tries to lay hands on her."

He intercepted a look from Gilden and realized that, for all her briskly matter-of-fact attitude about her daughter, she was not quite the offhand mother she seemed. He also realized that she had not expected him to agree with her. Gruffly, he amplified. "If Derroug tries to force her, she'll fight—and she'll fight like a trained warrior, not a scared girl. Then the cat's really going to be out of the bag. So when did you take out the guards, Gilden?"

Gilden stammered, recovering herself, "About two hours ago," she said. "They were starting their watch—the watches are four hours."

"We'll need a diversion, then." He glanced across at Sheera. "Think you can find Derroug's sleeping quarters again?"

Her face scarlet, she said, "Yes," in a stifled voice.

"Change your clothes, then, and bring your weapons. Denga, you stay here. I'm not surprised the little bastard's guards saw you skirts in the dark if you didn't blacken your flesh."

Gilden, Wilarne, and Eo looked at one another in confusion.

"But never mind, you're lucky you weren't killed, and we'll leave it at that. I don't know if you've made any provision for the plot being blown, Sheera, but it's too late to make one now. You know that if anyone's captured, she'll talk. You were in that cellar, too."

At the memory of the red-haired young slave's screams, Sheera went pale, her face drained of color as quickly as it had suffused.

"Myself, I'd sit tight and try to bluff it out. But if we're not back by morning, Denga, you can assume that you're in command and Derroug knows everything. Take whatever steps you think you need to."

"All right," the gladiator said.

"We'll get Tisa to Lady Wrinshardin's. Derroug know she's your daughter?" This last was addressed to Gilden, who shook her head.

"Good." He stood for a moment, studying his two half-pints, dainty little assassins with blood in their hair. "One more thing. As I said, we'll need a diversion. You two are so good at coming up with pranks—by the time I come back, I want you to think of a real good one."

And the interesting thing was that, when he came downstairs five minutes later, wearing only a short battle kilt, boots, and his weapons, they had thought of one.

"There they go." Turning his face slightly to keep his nose out of the muddy roof tiles, Sun Wolf glanced down into the barracks courtyard of the governor's palace, then across at Sheera, who lay spread-eagled in the shadows of the ornamental parapet at his side. She raised her head a little; the view from the roof of the counting house that backed the barracks court was excellent. Men could be seen pouring out of the barracks, sleepily pulling on their blue and gold livery or rubbing unshaven faces and cursing. In their midst, solicitously supported by the fat captain, minced the veiled forms of Gilden and Wilarne, dressed to the eyebrows in a fashion that would have done Cobra and Crazyred proud.

He heard the faint breath of Sheera's laughter. "Where on earth did Gilden get that feather tippet?" she whispered. "That's the most vulgar thing I've ever seen, but it must have cost somebody fifty crowns!"

Strident and foul, Gilden's voice carried up to them in a startlingly accurate rendering of a by-no-means carefully bred courtesan's tones. "The bastard said something about burning the records—that all his Highness' troops wouldn't do him a speck of good without records."

Sheera whispered, "The Records Office is in the northeast corner of the palace. Derroug's quarters are at the southwest."

"Right." Moving carefully, Sun Wolf slid down the sharp slant of the roof, edged around a lead gargoyle, and lowered himself down to the oak spar of a decorated beam end that thrust itself out into space, a dozen feet above the dark slot of the alley that separated counting house from barracks wall. The gap was negligible, though the landing was narrow—eighteen inches at the top of the parapet. In this corner of the old defense works that had once surrounded this part of the grounds, the stonework looked neglected and treacherous. He jumped, out and down, his body flexing compactly as it hit the top of the crenelations, and he sprang neatly down to the catwalk a few feet below.

He looked back up to the roof. Sheera had the sense to keep moving, smoothly and swiftly, once she broke cover. The windy darkness of the night was such that everything seemed to be moving—it would have been difficult to distinguish the movement as human. Since his ordeal in the pit, Sun Wolf was aware that he could see clearly now in darkness—he thought that his sense of direction, always excellent, had improved as well. In the shadows, he could see Sheera's face, tense and watchful, as she reached the edge of the roof. She lowered herself over, her feet feeling competently for the beam, her blackened arms momentarily silhouetted against the paler plaster of the house.

A cat-leap, and she was beside him. Silently, she scanned the dark bulk of the palace before them, then pointed southwest.

Thanks to the alarm, the barracks were empty. They descended from the wall by the turret stair of the guardhouse itself, ducking through the stable wing that Sheera knew, from her acquaintance with Drypettis, ran the length of the west side of the grounds, merging with the kitchens on the southwest corner. As they dodged along the walls, in the darkness Sun Wolf could sense the restlessness of the horses in their stalls, excited by the winds and by the far-off turmoil from other quarters of the palace. At the first opportunity, he drew Sheera through the postern of the carriage house and thence up a ladder to the lofts that ran continuously over the long rows of boxes. Twice they heard the voices of grooms and sleepy, grouchy stableboys below them, but no one associated the uneasiness of the animals with anything but the wind.

Certainly the guards, running here and there throughout the rest of the palace grounds in search of unspecified anarchists out to burn the Records Office, never thought to look for them among the governor's cattle.

From the loft, they climbed to the roof of the kitchens and over the tall, ridged backbone of the rooftree. Lights milled distantly, clustering around the tall, foursquare shapes of the northern administrative wing. To their left lay the south wall of the palace enclosure, hiding the Grand Canal behind its marble-faced stone; the lights of the great houses on the other side glittered few and faint at this hour, and their reflections thrown by the waters rippled over the stone lacework like moire silk.

Something was moving about in the dark space of the kitchen gardens. *Dogs?* the Wolf wondered. *But in that case, there would be barking.* Still, the noise was animal, not human.

From where he lay flattened on the slanted roof, he could make out the little postern and water stairs, through which Gilden, Wilarne, and Eo had said they'd entered, and the empty catwalk above it.

He heard quick, slipping movement on the tiles, and then warm flesh stretched out beside him. Sheera whispered, "Can we cross the garden without being seen?"

"There's something down there," the Wolf replied, barely above a breath. "Animals, I think—hunting cats or dogs." He edged sideways, keeping his head below the final, crowning ridge of the kitchen roof, a sharp friezework of saints and gargoyles, green with age where they were not crusted into unrecognizable lumps of white by long communion with the palace pigeons. The tiles were warmer under his bare flesh as he slipped around a great cluster of chimney pots and raised his head again.

"There," he murmured. "The covered walkway from the kitchens into the state dining room. You said yourself, the times you've eaten with the governor, the food arrived three-quarters cold."

"To be dropped on gold plates to complete the chilling," Sheera agreed, quietly amused. "Yes, I see. That lighted window above and to the left will be the anteroom to his bedchamber. That one there is the window that lights the end of the hall."

"Good." Booted toes feeling for breaks in the tiles, he eased himself backward down the slant of the roof. Below him, the stable courts were a maze of rooftrees and wells of darkness. Wind flickered over his skin, stirring the long wisps of his hair. The tiles, offensive with moss and droppings, were rough under his groping hands, still only partially healed. At the bottom of the roof, a sort of gutter ran the length of the kitchens, and he slipped along it, moving swiftly, to the peaked end of the building that overlooked the edge of the gardens on the canal side. The wind was stronger here, channeled by the walls; it carried on it the fish smell of the sea and the high salt flavor of the wind. Down below him, the gardens were a restless murmuration of skeletal trees and brown, wiry networks of hedge, an uneasy darkness broken by anomalous shufflings.

Bracing himself on the gutter, the Wolf worked loose a tile. The noise of the wind that streamed like cool water over his body covered the scraping sounds of his task—indeed, they almost covered the sounds of the voices. He heard a man curse and froze, flattening himself on the uneven darkness of the roof and praying that the mix of lampblack and grease that covered his body hadn't scraped off in patches to show the paler flesh beneath.

From below, he heard a guard's thorough, businesslike cursing. A second voice said, "Nothing out here."

"Any sign of Kran?"

Evidently a head was shaken; the Wolf pressed his face to the filthy tiles, wondering how long it would be until one or the other of them looked up.

"Damned funny, him missing a match-up with the guard on the next beat like that . . . If them troublemakers came in from this side . . ."

"When they're out to burn the Records Office? Not qualified likely. Good thing them two sluts got us word of it . . ."

"So why check the stables? Rot that sergeant's eyes . . ."

Then, with a curious, almost atavistic sensation, Sun Wolf knew that it was within his power to prevent the guards from looking up. It was nothing he had ever experienced before, but it tugged at him; an overwhelming knowledge of a technique, a shifting of the mind and attention, that he could not even define to himself. It was as natural as slashing after a parry, as ingrained in him as footwork; yet it was nothing he had done or even conceived of doing before. It was akin to the way he had always been able to avoid people's eyes—but never from a position of complete exposure.

Without moving, without even looking down, he consciously and deliberately prevented either of them from looking up, as if he drew that thought from their minds by some process he had never known of, except in his childhood dreams. Whether it was for this reason, or because the night was cold and windy and the men disgruntled, neither *did* look up.

"Let's get on, mate, I'm poxy freezing. There's nothing here."

"Aye. Rot his eyes, anyway . . ."

A door closed. The Wolf lay for a moment on the windswept tiles, counting the retreat of their footfalls, until he was sure they were gone. Then he hefted the lump of loose tiles in his hand, leaned around the edge of the gable, and threw them down into the dark corner of garden beyond.

The tiles crashed noisily in the dry hedges below. The Wolf ducked back around the corner of the roof as more crashes answered, and whatever had been below—dogs or sentries— bounded to investigate. Hidden from them by the angle of the roof, he slid along the gutter and made his way, swift as a tomcat, up the slope to where Sheera lay. He could see movement flicker around the corner at the far end of the kitchens as he scrambled up beside her; in that short span of bought time, he half rose to climb over the uneven teeth of the roof ridge and down to the top of the walkway.

The walkway top was flat—a stupid thing, in as rainy a town as Mandrigyn. *Probably leaks like a sieve all winter*, he thought, crawling flat on his belly along it. A quick glance showed him Sheera directly behind, her body as grazed and filthy as his own; another quick glance showed him the gardens below, still empty. He addressed a brief request to his ancestors to keep them that way and scanned the available windows.

"Captain!" Sheera whispered.

He glanced back at her. The wind veered suddenly and he smelled smoke.

As a man adept at the starting of fires, he recognized it as new smoke, the first springing of a really commendable blaze. Looking, he saw it rolling in a formidable column from the north end of the palace, streaming in huge, white-edged billows in the wind. Voices were shouting, feet racing; everyone who had been turned out for the original alarm was dashing toward the fire, and everyone who had not was following close behind.

Gilden and Wilarne were nothing if not thorough.

Scrambling to the nearest window sill, Sun Wolf drove his boot through the glass.

It was, as Sheera had said, the end window of a long corridor, dimly lighted with lamps of amber glass and muffled by carpets of blue Islands work and iridescent silk. He ducked through the nearest door into an antechamber, searching for the way into the bedroom; then a noise behind him in the hall made him swing around. He saw Sheera, frozen in the act of following him into the doorway, black and filthy as a demon from one of the dirtier pits of Hell; and before her in the hall, his crippled body clothed in a lavish robe of crimson brocade and miniver and his prim face wearing an expression of profound and startled astonishment, was Derroug Dru himself.

For one instant, they faced each other; from the tenebrous antechamber, Sun Wolf saw the jump of the governor's chest and the leap of breath in his throat as he inhaled to shout for the guards . . .

He never made a sound. Sheera was taller than he and heavier; training day after day to the point of exhaustion had made her lightning-fast. For all his power to bend others to his will, Derroug was a cripple. Sun Wolf saw the dagger in Sheera's hand but doubted that Derroug ever did. She caught the body and was dragging it into the anteroom, even as blood sprayed from the slashed arteries of the throat. The room stank of it, sharp and metallic above the suffocating weight of balsam incense. Her hands glistened in the faint reflection of the corridor lamps.

"Throw something over him," Sun Wolf whispered as she pushed the door to behind her. "That cuts our time—pray Tisa really *is* here and we don't have to go hunt for her."

As Sheera bundled the body into a corner, he was already crossing the anteroom to the bolted door on the other side. He slammed back the bolts and stepped through. "Tisa . . ."

Something hit his shoulders and the back of his knee; cold and slim, an arm locked across his windpipe, and small hands knotted below the corner of his jaw in a strangle. Reflex took over. He rolled his shoulders forward, ducked, and threw. Incredibly light weight went sailing over his head, to slam like a soaked blanket into the deep furs of the floor.

Under the softness of the carpets was hard tile, and a thin little sob was wrenched from her, but Tisa was rolling to her feet as he caught her wrists. She'd kept her head clear of the impact, but tears of terror and pain streamed down her face. Then she saw who he was and turned her face away, ashamed that he should see her weep.

It was no time, the Wolf thought, to be a warrior—especially if one was fifteen and the victim of a powerful and cruel

man. He gathered her into his arms. She was shaking with
silent terror, burying her small, pointed face in the grimy muscle of his hard chest. Sheera stood silent in the doorway, her
hands red to the elbows, watching as he stroked Tisa's disheveled ivory hair and murmured to her as a father might to
a child frightened by a nightmare.

"He's dead," he said softly. "It's all right. We've come to
get you out, and he's dead and won't come after you."

The girl stammered, "Mother . . ."

"Your mum's out burning down the other side of the palace,"
the Wolf said, in the same comforting accents. "She's fine—"

Tisa raised her head, her cheek all smutched with blacking,
green moss stains, and bird droppings. "Are you kidding me?"
she asked, laughter and suspicion fighting through her tears.

The Wolf made wide eyes at her. "No," he said. "Did you
think I was?"

She wiped her eyes and swallowed hard. "I'm not crying,"
she explained, after a moment.

"No," he agreed. "I'm sorry I hurt you, Tisa."

"You didn't hurt me." Her voice was shaky; the breath had
been very soundly knocked out of her, if nothing else.

"Well, you damned near strangled me," he returned gruffly.
"You think you can swim?"

She nodded. She was wearing, he now saw, a kind of loose
white robe, clearly given to her by Derroug. It was slightly too
large for her and sewn over with white sequins and elaborate
swirls of milky, opalescent beads. Against it, he saw her transformed, no longer a coltish girl, but a half-opened bud of
womanhood. Her eyelids were stained dark with fatigue and
terror, her hair pale against the silk, almost as light as Starhawk's in the shimmer of the bedroom lamp. The gown was
cut so as to reveal half her young bosom. Before taking her
post to attack, she'd prosaically pinned the robe with a ruby
stickpin that glowed beneath her collarbone like a huge bead
of blood.

She was as light as a flower in his hands as he lifted her to
her feet. Her eyes lighted on Sheera and widened at the sight
of the blood.

Sun Wolf whispered, "Let's go. They'll be looking for him,
now that the fire's started."

As they slipped back through the anteroom and out the
window, Tisa breathed, "What happened to your voice, Captain? And I thought . . ."

"Not now."

Obediently, she gathered handfuls of her voluminous skirts and followed Sheera down onto the roof of the walkway. Even to his sharper eyes, the gardens below looked deserted. He could see, vague against the deeper dark of the shadowed wall, the shape of the postern gate.

"Wait here till I signal," he said softly. "A whistle like a nightjar. Then keep to the shadows along the wall. If it's locked, we'll have to go up the steps to the parapet and dive."

Sheera gauged the height of the wall. "Thank God it's the Grand Canal. It's the deepest one in the city."

Sun Wolf slithered down the side of the walkway and into the gardens below.

The overcast was growing thicker with the night winds that fanned the blaze on the north end of the palace. The din was audible over the moaning of the wind. *It should keep them all busy for at least another hour*, he calculated and began to move, slowly and cautiously, along the wall toward the inky wells of shadow that lay between him and the gate.

The blackness here was almost absolute; a month ago he would have been able to see nothing. As it was, he was aware of shapes and details with a sense that he was not altogether certain was sight—an effect of the anzid, he guessed, as well as that curious ability to prevent people from looking at him.

That would come in handy, he thought. Come to think of it, he realized he had used it twice before tonight—when he'd evaded Sheera almost unthinkingly in the narrow confines of the potting room, and earlier this evening, when he had first come down the stairs to hear the war council in the orangery. The professional in him toyed with ways of developing that strange talent; but deep within him, a tug of primitive excitement shivered in his bones, as it had done when he had first known that he could see demons and others could not.

The postern was unguarded, but locked. He glanced around the blackness under the gate arch and found the narrow stair to the parapet above. The garden behind him still appeared deserted, but a tension, a premonition of danger, had begun to prickle at the nape of his neck. The brush and hedges seemed to rustle too much, and the wind, laden with smoke and shouting, seemed somehow to carry the scent of evil to his nostrils. He whistled softly, like a nightjar, and saw swift movement near the covered walk, then the flash of Tisa's almost luminous white gown.

They were halfway across the garden when something else moved, from around the corner of the kitchen building.

The things were armored like men, but weaponless. From where he stood at the bottom of the parapet stair, the Wolf could see that they walked steadily, oblivious to the darkness that made the fugitive women's steps so halting and slow. They moved so softly that he wasn't sure Sheera and Tisa were aware of them, but his own sharpened vision showed them clearly to him. There were four, wearing the fouled liveries of Derroug's guards, their eyeless heads swinging as if they also could see in darkness.

They were nuuwa.

Realization hit him, and horrible enlightenment, as if pieces of some huge and ghastly puzzle had fallen into place. Rage and utter loathing swept over him, such as he had never felt toward anyone or anything before. The nuuwa began to lope. Sheera swung around, hearing the steps on the grass, but her eyes were unable to pierce the utter darkness.

Sun Wolf bellowed, "Run for it! Here!"

His sword whined from its sheath. Unquestioning, the women ran, Tisa stripping out of her billowing white robe as it caught on the dead limbs of a thorn hedge. They ran blindly, stumbling, blundering through soft earth and gray tangles of vine and hedge, and the nuuwa plunged soundlessly after. He yelled again, a half-voiceless croaking that was answered by wild commotion in the windows of the palace behind them. Tisa hit the stairs first, with Sheera a few strides behind. The nuuwa were hard on their heels, running sightlessly with the drool glistening on those gaping, deformed mouths.

Sword naked in his hand, Sun Wolf followed the women up the steps, the foremost of the pursuers not three feet behind. At the top of the wall, Tisa dived, plunging down into the dark murk of the canal; Sheera's dark-stained, gleaming body outlined momentarily against the reflected lamps in the villas across the way as she followed. When the Wolf reached the parapet, huge hands dug into his flesh from behind, and he writhed away from the fangs that tore like great wedges of rusty iron into his shoulder. He turned, ripping with his sword, knowing he had only seconds until they were all on him, literally eating him alive. As the blade cleaved the filthy flesh of the nuuwa's body, the misshapen face was inches from his own, the huge mouth still rending at him, flowing with blood, the empty eye sockets scabbed wells of shadow.

Then he was plunging down, and the freezing, salty, unspeakably filthy waters of the canal swallowed him. The nuuwa, nothing daunted, flung themselves over the wall after their prey. Weighted in their armor, too blind and too stupid to swim, they sank like stones.

In her usual silence, Yirth gathered up her medicines and glided from the dim confines of the loft. Sun Wolf lay still for a time, staring up at the slant of the ceiling over his head, as he had stared at it four mornings ago, when he had awakened to know that Sheera had indeed won.

But there was no thought of Sheera now in his mind.

He was thinking now of Lady Wrinshardin, of Derroug Dru, and of Altiokis.

He felt weak from loss of blood, woozy and aching from the pain of Yirth's remedies. Against his cheek on the pillow, his hair was damp, and his flesh chilled where the lampblack and grease had been sponged off it. Sheera, in her velvet bed, and Tisa, safe at the Thane of Wrinshardin's castle, would both be striped like tigers with bruises and scratches from that last crashing flight through the gardens.

He himself scarcely felt the pain. Knowledge still burned in him, and the heat of fury that knowledge had brought; deformed, hideous, the face of the nuuwa returned to his thoughts, no matter what he did to push it aside. The grayish light beyond the window grew broader, and he wondered if he had best get up and go about his business for the benefit of whatever servants of the household might be questioned by Derroug's successors.

Weakness weighted his limbs. He was still lying there when the door of the orangery opened and shut, and he heard the creak of light feet on the steps, the soft, thick slur of satin petticoats, and the stiff rubbing of starched lace.

He turned his head. Sheera stood in the doorway, where she had so seldom come before. Cosmetics covered the scratches on her face; but below the paint, he thought she looked pale and drawn. In that crowded and terrible night, he realized, she had avenged herself on Derroug. But it had been a businesslike, almost unthinking revenge.

"I came to thank you for last night," she said tiredly. "And— to apologize for things that I said. You did not have to do what you did."

"I told you before," Sun Wolf rasped, his new voice still scraping oddly in his ears. "All it would have taken was for our girl to tackle Derroug the way she tackled me for there to have been a lot of questions asked. And as for the other business—you were tired and I was drunk. That should never have happened."

"No," Sheera said. "It shouldn't have." She rubbed her eyes, the clusters of pearl and sardonyx that decorated her ears and hair flickering in the wan light of morning. "I've come to tell you that you're free to leave Mandrigyn. I'm going to speak to Yirth—to have her give you the antidote to the anzid—to let you go. For what you did . . ."

He held out his hand. After a moment's hesitation, she stepped forward, and he drew her to sit on the edge of his bed. Her fingers felt like ice in his.

"Sheera," he said, "that doesn't matter now. When you march to the mines—when you free the men—what are you going to do?"

Taken off guard, she stammered, "I—we—Tarrin and I will lead them back here . . ."

"No," he said. "Lady Wrinshardin was right, Sheera. Yirth is right. Don't wait for Altiokis to come to you. Those ways from the mines up to the Citadel itself—could Amber's girls find them?"

"I suppose," she said hesitantly. "Crazyred says she's seen one of them. But they're guarded by magic, by traps . . ."

"Yirth will have to deal with that," he told her quietly. "She'll have to find some way to get you through them—and she will, or die trying. Sheera, Altiokis has to be destroyed. He's got an evil up there worse than anything I imagined—and he's breeding it, creating it, calling it up out of some other world, I don't know. Lady Wrinshardin guessed it; Yirth knows it. He has to be destroyed, and that evil with him."

Sheera was silent, looking down at her hands where they rested among the folds of her gown. Once she might have triumphed over his admission that she was right and he wrong—but that had been before the pit, and before the garden last night.

Watching her eyes, he realized that, since she had spoken with Lady Wrinshardin, she had known in her heart that they would have to storm the Citadel.

He went on. "Those were nuuwa that pursued us from Derroug's gardens last night. Nuuwa under the control of Altiokis, I would guess—as nuuwa under his control are said to march in his armies. When he's done with them—as he was after the battle of Iron Pass—he turns most of them out, to overrun the conquered lands; or else he gives them over to his governors as watchdogs. I think they deform, they deteriorate, in time— and that's why Altiokis and Derroug have to go on creating new ones."

"Creating?" She raised her head quickly; he could see in her face the hideous comprehension knocking on the doors of her mind, as it had knocked on his last night.

"You remember that room in Derroug's prison? That—that thing that looked like a flake of fire, or a shining dragonfly?"

She glanced away, nauseated by the memory. After a moment, the thick curls of her hair slipped across her red satin shoulder as she nodded. He felt her cold fingers tighten over his.

"That red-haired boy became the creature who tore up my shoulder last night," he told her.

CHAPTER
—— 15 ——

*F*ROM PERGEMIS, THE ROAD WOUND NORTHEAST, FIRST THROUGH
the rich croplands and forests of the Bight Coast, then through
mist-hung, green foothills, where snow lay light upon the ground,
printed with the spoor of fox and beaver. In the summer, it
would have been possible to take a ship from the port, around
the vast hammer of cliff-girt headlands and through the gray
walls of the Islands, to the port city of Mandrigyn below the
walls of Grimscarp itself. But the world lay in the iron grip of
winter. Starhawk and Anyog made their way into the Wizard
King's domains slowly, overland, as best they could.

In the higher foothills, the rains turned to snow, and the
winds drove down upon them from the stony uplands above.
When they could, they put up at settlements—either the new
villages of traders and hunters or the ancient clan holds of the
old Thanes, who had once ruled all these lands and now lived
in haughty obsolescence in the depths of the trackless forests.

Starhawk found the going far slower than she had anticipated, for Anyog, despite his uncomplaining gameness, tired
easily. In this weather, and in this country, an hour or two of
travel would leave the little scholar gray-faced and gasping,
and the time span shortened steadily as they pressed on. She
would have scorned the weakness in one of her own men and
used the lash of her tongue to drive him. But she could not do
so. It was her doing that the old man had undertaken the hardships of a winter journey when he should have been still in
bed, letting his wounds heal. Besides, she admitted to herself,
she'd grown to be extremely fond of the old goat.

Never before had she found that her personal feelings toward someone bred tolerance of his weakness. *Have I grown soft*, she wondered, *those weeks in Pel Farstep's house? Or is this something love does for you—makes you kinder toward others as well?*

Dealing with the irrationalities of love that she found in her own soul frightened her. Her jealousy of poor Fawn had been as senseless as was her stubbornness in pursuing a hopeless quest for a man who was almost certainly already dead and who had never spoken to her of love in the first place. She knew herself to be behaving stupidly, yet the thought of turning around and retracing her steps to Pergemis or Wrynde was intolerable to the point of pain. Meditation cleared and calmed her mind, but gave her no answer—she could find herself within the Invisible Circle, but she could not find another person.

No wonder the Wolf had always steered clear of love. She wondered how she could ever find the courage to tell him that she loved him and what he would say when or if she did.

And with love, she found herself involved in magic as well.

"Why did you never go on to become a wizard?" she asked one evening, watching Anyog as he brought fire spurting to the little heap of sticks and kindling with a gesture of his bony fingers. "Was it fear of Altiokis alone?"

The bright, black eyes twinkled up at her, catching the glittering reflection of the sparks. "Funk—pure and simple." He held out his hands to the blaze. The light seemed to shine through them, so thin they were. The white ruffles at his wrists, like those at his throat, were draggled and gray.

Starhawk eyed him for a moment, where he hunched like a cricket over the little blaze, then half glanced over her shoulder at the dark that always seemed to hang over the uplands to the north.

He read her gesture and grinned wryly. "Not solely of our deathless friend," he explained. "Though I will admit that that consideration loomed largest in my mind when I deserted the master who taught me and took the road for sunnier climes in the south.

"My master was an old man, a hermit who lived in the hills. Even as a little boy, I knew I had the Power—I could find things that were lost or start fires by looking at bits of dried grass. I could see things that other people could not see. This old man was a mystic—crazy, some said—but he taught me . . ."

Anyog paused, staring into the shivering color of the blaze. "Perhaps he taught me more than he knew.

"I tasted it then, you see." He glanced up at her, standing above him, across the leaping light; the fire touched in his face every wrinkle and line of gaiety and dissipation. "Tasted glory—tasted magic—and tasted what that glory would cost. He was a shy old man, terrified of strangers. I had to hunt for him for two weeks before he would even see me. He distrusted everything, everyone—all from fear of Altiokis."

Starhawk was silent, remembering that whitewashed cell in the distant Convent and the mirror set in an angle of its walls. Somewhere in the woods an owl hooted, hunting on soundless wings. The horses stamped at their tethers, pawing at the crusted snow.

The dark eyes were studying her face, wondering if she understood. "It meant giving up all things for only one thing," Anyog said. "Even then I knew I wanted to travel, to learn. I loved the small, bright beauties of the mind. What is life without poetry, without wit, without music? Without the well-turned phrase and the sharpening of your own philosophy upon the philosophies of others? My master lived hidden—he would go for years without seeing another soul. If I became a wizard like him, it would mean the same kind of life for me."

The old man sighed and turned to pick up the iron spits and begin setting them in their place over the fire. "So I chose all those small beauties over the great, single, lonely one. I became a scholar, teacher, dancer, poet—my *Song of the Moon Dog and the Ocean Child* will be sung throughout the Middle Kingdoms long after I am gone—and I pretended I did not regret. Until that night at the inn, when you asked me if my safety had bought me happiness. And I could not say that it had."

He looked away from her and occupied himself in spitting pieces of the rabbit she had shot that afternoon on the long iron cooking spike. Starhawk said nothing, but hunted through the mule's packs for barley bannocks and a pan to melt snow for drinking water. She was remembering the warm safety of Pel Farstep's house and how she had not even thought twice about leaving it to pursue her quest.

"And then," Anyog continued, "I feared the Great Trial. Without passing through that, I could never have come to the fullness of my power in any case."

"What is it?" Starhawk asked, sitting down opposite him. "Could you take it now, before we reached Grimscarp?"

The old man shook his head; she thought the withered muscles of his jaw tightened in apprehension in the flickering firelight. "No," he said. "I never learned enough magic to withstand it, and what I learned . . . It has been long since I used that. The Trial kills the weak, as it kills those who are not mageborn."

She frowned. "But if you passed through it—would it make you deathless, like Altiokis?"

"Altiokis?" The winged brows plunged down suddenly over his nose. For an instant she saw him, not as a half-sick and regretful little old man, but as a wizard, an echo of the Power he had passed by. "Pah. Altiokis never passed the Great Trial. According to my master, he never even knew what it was. My master knew him, you see. Vain, lazy, trifling . . . the worst of them all."

He might have been a classical poet speaking of the latest popular serenade writer. She half smiled. "But you've got to admit he's up there and you're down here, hiding from him. He's got to have acquired that power from somewhere."

Anyog's voice sank, as if he feared that, this close to the Citadel of the Wizard King, the very winds would hear. "He has," he told her quietly.

Her glance sharpened, and she remembered the smoky darkness of the inn at Foonspay and the old man's raving quietly before the sinking fire, with Fawn standing quiet, hidden in the shadows of the corridor. "You spoke of that before," she said.

"Did I? I didn't mean to." He poked the fire, more for something to do than because it needed stirring. The wind brought the voices of wolves from the hills above, sweet and distant upon the hunting trail. "My master knew it—but very few others did. If Altiokis ever found out that it was known, he would guess that my master had taught others. He would find me."

"Where does Altiokis get his power?"

Anyog was silent for a time, staring into the fire, and Starhawk wondered if he would answer her at all. She had just decided that he would not when he said softly, "From the Hole. Holes in the world, they are called—but I think Holes *between* worlds would be more accurate. For it is said that something lives in them—something other than the gaums that eat men's brains."

"Gaums . . ." she began.

"Oh, yes. My nephews call them after dragonflies, but they're things—whatever they are—that come out of the Holes. They are mindless, and they eat the minds of their victims, so that their victims become mindless, too—nuuwa, in fact. The Holes appear—oh, at intervals of hundreds of years, sometimes. My master said they were ruled by the courses of the stars. Sunlight destroys them—they appear at night and vanish with the coming of dawn."

Something moved, dark against the mottled background of broken snow and old pine needles; Anyog looked up with a gasp, as if at an enemy footfall, and Starhawk, following his gaze, saw the brief green flash of a weasel's eyes. The old man subsided, shivering and rubbing his hands.

At length he continued. "The Holes vanish with sunlight— as do the gaums, if they don't find a victim first. But this Hole Altiokis sheltered. He is said to have built a stone hut over it in a single night, and from that time his powers have grown. It animates his flesh, giving him life—but he has changed since then. I don't know." He shook his head wearily, a harried, sick old man once more. "He had only to wait for the great mages of his own generation to die and to kill off those who followed before they came to greatness. As he will kill me."

His voice was shaky with exhaustion and despair; looking at him across the topaz glow of the fire, Starhawk saw how white he looked, how darkly the crazy eyebrows stood out against the pinched flesh. As if he'd been a boy trooper, funked before his first battle, she said hearteningly, "He won't kill you."

They left the magical silence of the foothills, to climb the Stren Water Valley.

Fed by the drowning rains on the uplands above, the Stren Water roared in full spate, spreading its channels throughout the narrow, marshy country that lay between the higher cliffs, cutting off hilltops to islands, and driving those farmers who eked their living from its soil to their winter villages on the slopes above. Starhawk and Anyog made their way along the rocky foothills that bordered the flooded lands, always wet, always cold. Anyog told tales and sang songs; of wizardry and Altiokis, they did not speak.

They made a dozen river crossings a day—sometimes of boggy little channels of the main flood, sometimes of boiling white streams that had permanent channels. At one of these, they lost the packs and almost lost the mule as well. Starhawk suspected that the struggle with the raging waters had broken something within Anyog; after that, he had a white look about the mouth that never left him and he could not travel more than a few miles without a rest.

She had always been a blisteringly efficient commander, using her own supple strength to drive and bully her men to follow. But she found that her fears for Sun Wolf, though unabated, left room for a care for the old man, who she was sure now would never be able to help her, and she broke the journey to give him a day's rest while she hunted mountain sheep in the high rock country to the northwest.

She was coming back from this when she found the tracks of the mercenaries.

It had been a small band—probably not more than fifteen, she guessed, studying the sloppy trail in the fading afternoon light. Their mere presence in the valley told her they were out of work and had been so for at least three months, since the rains had begun, holed up somewhere, living off the land by hunting or pillage—too small a group to be hired for anything but tribal war between the Thanes; and most of the Thanes in these parts hadn't the money to hire, anyway, and wouldn't go to war in the winter if they could.

Starhawk cursed. Her experience with out-of-work mercenaries was that they were always a nuisance and generally robbers to boot; she would have to trail them to make sure where they were headed and what they were up to before she would feel safe returning to camp.

She had shot a sheep in the high rocks, one of the small, shaggy crag jumpers, and was carrying the carcass over her shoulders. She hung it from the limb of a tree to keep it from wolves and hung her coat up with it; she might want her arms free. Then she transferred her sword from her back, where she'd been carrying it on the hunt, to her hip, restrung her bow, and checked her arrows. She had been a mercenary for a long time—she was under no illusions about her own kind.

The trail was fresh; the droppings of the few horses still steamed in the cold evening. She found the place where they'd turned aside from the main trail through the hills at the sight of Anyog's campfire—she could still see the smoke of it herself, rising through the trees from the wooded hollow where she'd left him. As she clambered cautiously down the rocks that skirted the downward trail, she began to hear their voices, too, and their laughter.

She muttered words that did greater credit to her imagination than to her convent training. They wanted horses, of course. She hoped to the Mother that Anyog had more sense than to antagonize them—not that anything would be likely to help him much, if they were drunk—which, by the sound of it, they were.

She'd chosen the campsite carefully—a wooded dell surrounded by thin trees with a minimum of large boulders, difficult to spy into and impossible to sneak up on. She pressed her body to the trunk of the largest available tree and looked down into the dell.

There were about a dozen men, and they were drunk. One or two of them she thought she recognized—mercenaries were always crossing one another's paths, and most of them got to know one another by sight. The leader was a squat, hairy man in a greasy doublet sewn over with iron plates. It was before him that Anyog knelt on hands and knees, his gray head bowed and trickling with blood.

At this distance it was hard to hear what the leader was saying, but it was obvious the robbers had already appropriated the livestock. Starhawk could see the two horses and the mule among the small cavy of broken-down nags at the far edge of the clearing; the camp was strewn with cooking gear, and a couple of snaggle-haired camp followers stood among the half circle of men with her and Anyog's bedrolls. She barely felt her anger in the midst of her calculations. The horses were unguarded at the rear of the cavy, since most of the men were up front, watching the fun with Anyog. The animals would provide better cover if she could get to them.

More laughter burst from the circle of men; a couple of them jostled for a better position. She saw the leader's hand move, and Anyog began to crawl, evidently after something thrown into the muddy pine needles. Bawling with laughter, the mercenary captain reached out his boot and kicked the old man in the side, sending him sprawling. Doggedly, Anyog got back to his hands and knees and continued to crawl.

Starhawk was familiar with the game; paying for the horses, it was called. A player threw coppers at greater and greater distances and made the poor bastard crawl after them while everyone kicked him over. The game was on a par with ducking the mayor of the village, or forcing his wife to clean the captain's boots with her hair—the sort of thing that went on during the sacking of a town. It was hilariously funny if a person was drunk, of course, or had just survived a battle that could have left him feeding the local cats on his spilled guts.

But sober, and watching it played on a man who had done her nothing but kindness, she felt both anger and distaste. It was, she saw, akin to rape; and like rape, it could easily get out of hand and end with the victim dead as well.

She began to edge her way through the trees toward the far side of the cavy. The gathering darkness helped her—it had been blackly overcast all day, with snow falling lightly in the high country where she had hunted; the world smelled of rain and frost. The men, moreover, aside from being drunk, were totally engrossed in their game. Anyog was kicked down again and lay where he had fallen. It was hard to tell in the twilight, but Starhawk thought he was bleeding from the mouth. She decided then that, whether or not they offered him further injury, she would kill them. One of the camp followers, a slut of sixteen or so, walked over to the old man and kicked him to make him get up; Starhawk saw his hands move as he struggled to rise.

The mercenaries closed in around him.

It took her a few extra seconds to cut the reins of the horses from the tether rope; the men were yelling and laughing and never saw her until she was mounted. She fired into their midst, calmly and without rage; her first arrow took the captain straight through the throat, above the iron-plated doublet; her second pinned the camp follower between the breasts.

She was mounted; the height and the weight of the horse gave her an edge over their numbers, though later she suspected that she would have taken on the twelve of them, even had she been afoot. She came plowing in among them from the darkness, the last light flashing from her sword blade as from the sickle of the Death Goddess of ancient days—silent, inhuman, merciless as the Plague Star. She killed two before they even had their weapons drawn, and the horse accounted for a third, rearing as they closed around it and smashing the man's skull with an iron-shod hoof. Another man seized her leg to pull her down and she took his hands off at the wrists. She left him standing, screaming, staring at the spouting stumps, as she turned and beheaded the other camp follower and another man who was grabbing at her from the opposite side. Two men had the bridle, dragging and twisting to pull the horse down; she dug in her heels and drove the animal straight ahead over them, so that they had to release their grip or be trampled. One of them she hacked through the shoulder as she went by, and he crumpled, screaming and kicking in the plowed, wet pine mast.

All this she did calmly, without feeling. She was a technician of death and good at her job; she knew what she wanted to do. The men were running in all directions, drunk and confused. Someone got to the packs; a moment later, an arrow embedded itself in the saddletree a few inches from her leg. She wheeled the horse and rode at the man. Another shaft sang wide beside her, his aim erratic from panic or from cheap gin; then he dropped his bow and ran, and she cut him through the spine as she overtook his flight.

The men who were chasing the fleeing horses she brought down with arrows, as if they were hares. Only the last stood and fought her, sword to sword, when her arrows were spent; and though she was dismounted by this time and he was both larger and heavier than she, she had the advantage of speed.

She pulled her grating sword blade from his ribs, wiped it on his clothes, and turned back to where Anyog lay in the trampled slush. The cold brightness of battle still clung to her; she looked down at the crumpled body and thought, *Another deader*.

Then the grief hit her, like the howling of a wolf at the moon.

She looked around her at the bodies that lay like dark lumps of mud against the slightly lighter blur of the pine needles. The air smelled heavy with blood, like a battlefield; already foxes were creeping from the woods, sniffing at the carrion. In the night, there would be wolves. She saw that at least one of the mercenaries had been a woman, something that she hadn't noticed in the heat of the fight. And none of their deaths would bring Anyog back.

Gently, she knelt beside him and turned him over. His breath caught in a gasp of pain; she saw that he was not, in fact, dead; but he would have to be a powerful wizard indeed to pull himself back from the darkness now. Around her, the trees began to whisper under the falling of rain.

Starhawk worked through the night, rigging a shelter for him and for the fire she built, and making a travois. Beyond the circle of the firelight, she was conscious of continual movement, of faint snarlings and growls, and huge green eyes that flashed with the reflected light. The single horse she had sal-

vaged—one of Pel Farstep's—snorted with fear and jerked at
its tether, but nothing threatened them from the rainy blackness.
The kill was fresh and enough to glut a pack.

The sodden dawn was barely glimmering through the trees
when she moved on. She collected what little food the mercenaries had carried, plus several skins of raw liquor—Blind
White, it was called—and all the arrows she could recover.
As she was tying Anyog to the travois, the dark eyes opened,
glazed with pain, and he whispered, "Dove?"

"I'm here," she said gruffly. "Uncle, I'm sorry. I . . ."

His voice was a thread. "Couldn't let you face . . .
Altiokis . . . alone . . ."

He coughed, bringing up blood. Starhawk stood up and went
to hang the rest of their meager supplies over the various pro-
jections of the saddle, fighting the guilt that came from bitter
enlightenment and the sudden understanding of why Anyog
had joined her in her hopeless quest. She stood for a moment,
leaning her throbbing head against the horse's withers while
the rain streamed down through her pale, dripping hair. Ram
had taken his courage in his hands, as he had said, and spoken
to her; and having spoken, had been turned down. Perhaps it
was Anyog's age that had robbed him of the courage to speak,
or perhaps it was the prior knowledge that his love for her
would not be returned. But it was the old man, not the young,
who had come with her to his death.

Starhawk sighed. She had learned a long time ago that crying
only wasted time. They had a long road to go.

It was almost nightfall before they came to shelter. Because
she could not scout the countryside, Starhawk backtrailed the
mercenaries, hoping that they had spent the previous night in
a place not too exposed to the elements. The rain had lightened
through the afternoon, but the cold was deeper, and she began
to fear snow. The road led them up the hard, rocky tracks into
the higher foothills, skirting the deep flood meres and the sour
bogs that surrounded them. In the end, it led her to a high
valley, a sort of bay wedged among the tall cliffs, where a
chapel had been built, looking like something that had grown
of itself from the lichened stones.

The chapel was filthy. It had clearly served as a stable, and
its altar had been further defiled by all the gross usages of
which drunken and violent men were capable when they grew
bored. Starhawk was used to this kind of thing and had moreover been raised to believe that the worship of the Triple God

was an intellectualized heresy; nevertheless, she was angered that men would treat holy things so, simply because they were holy.

Still, the roof was intact, and the single doorway narrow enough to forbid the entrance of wild beasts, if a fire were kindled there. She cleared a place among the mess to lay Anyog down and set about gathering damp brushwood, then barked her knuckles with flint and steel lighting it.

It snowed in the night, with bitter wind keening around the open chapel door. By dawn, it was obvious to Starhawk that Uncle Anyog would never recover.

Yet he was too tough to die quickly. He lingered on the cloudy borderlands of death, sometimes in a cold sleep that she would have mistaken for death, had it not been for the painful wheezing of his breath, other times weeping and raving feebly of Altiokis, of the nuuwa, of his sister, or singing snatches of poems and songs in a cracked little voice like the grating of a rusty hinge. Occasionally he was lucid enough to recognize her cropped hair and brass-studded doublet as the marks of a trooper and struggled with feeble determination against the gruel she fed him or the water she washed him with.

On the third night of this, it crossed her mind that the sensible thing to do would be to kill him and go on with her quest. There was no hope of his recovery—even if what remained of the little wizardry he had been taught was strong enough to pull him back from death, it would be long before he could embark on another journey by travois. One way or the other, she would have to free Sun Wolf from the Citadel of the Wizard King alone, without the aid of a wizard—without the hope now of ever finding one.

It was better that she got on with it and did not delay further.

Yet she stayed. The cold deepened over the high peaks, and the snow locked its grip on the valley tighter. Daily the Hawk trudged to the few tufts of birch and aspen at the lower end of the little valley by the spring to cut firewood. She saw in the snow the marks where deer had pawed at the crust to feed on the dead grasses underneath; she hunted, and the calm absorption of it eased her heart. During the night she meditated, contemplating in the stillness of the Invisible Circle the truths of her own violent soul. In spite of her own faith in the Mother, she tended the altar of the Triple God, ridding the chapel of its pollutions and cleansing the stone with ritual fire; and in that, too, she found comfort.

Night after night she sat listening to Anyog's quiet murmuring and staring out into the still darkness of the silent valley and the flooded lands beyond.

What had happened to her, she wondered, those weeks in Pel Farstep's tall stone house? She did not want to become like them, like the busy, bustling Pel or the placid Gillie. So why did her mind keep returning to that peaceful place and the small beauties of everyday things?

Would she even love the Wolf when she met him again, or would she find that he was like the men she had killed, brutish, dirty, and crass?

The Mother knew, she'd seen him perform worse outrages than that when they'd sacked cities.

But her own experience with the wild, careless arrogance of victory prevented her from thinking that what one did during a sack was what one would do in cold blood.

Would it be better if she found that she did not love him, for that matter? Had Fawnie had the right idea, to marry a well-off man who would cherish her?

If the Wolf was a mercenary like the others, why did she still love him enough to seek him? And if she still loved him with that same determination, why did she not kill Anyog, who was dying anyway, bury him, and leave?

From there she would settle herself into meditation; but the answers that she found within its stillness were not the answers that she sought.

One night the wind changed, squalling down over the mountains in a fury of driving, intermittent rain. Droplets hissed loudly in the little fire; Starhawk could hear its fitful beating against the stone walls of the chapel, but within the hollow darkness at the far end of the holy place, the altar lights burned with a steady, hypnotic glow. Her mind focused upon them, drawing them into herself, and the light and darkness merged and clarified into one entity—rain and earth, wind and silence, that which was known and that which was yet to be—the single Circle of Is.

She found herself in another wind-sounding darkness, hearing the far-off beating of the sea. She knew the place well—the Mother's chapel on the cliffs, part of the Convent of St. Cherybi, which she had left to follow Sun Wolf to learn the ways of war. She had heard of other nuns doing this, for each point of the Invisible Circle was each point, everywhere, and it was possible, she had heard, to step from one to another.

Moonlight shone down through the sky-hole, the only illumination in that dark place, a blinding sliver on the edge of her drawn sword. Peace filled her, as it had always done here. She wondered if this were a dream of her past, but knew, even as she formulated the thought, that it was not so. There were small changes from what she had known—weather stains on the floor and the walls, slight shifts in the way the vessels stood upon the bare stone of the shadow-obscured altar—which told her that she was truly there, and this did not surprise her.

When she saw Sun Wolf, standing in the darkness near the door, she knew that he, too, was truly there—that he had come there to find her...

She had never cried as an adult. But when she returned to the barren darkness of the chapel in the Stren Water Valley, tears were icy on her face, and exultation and bitter grief warred in her heart.

I'm sorry I did not know it in time, he had said. And yet, when he lay dying in Mandrigyn, he had contrived to come to her.

So near, she thought. *Had I not stayed in Pergemis with Fawn...*

But she knew she could not have deserted the girl.

Grief and defeat and exhaustion weakened her; long after her sobbing had ceased, the tears ran down from her open eyes. She had followed him for years to war, and they had saved each other's life a dozen times, almost casually. She must have known, she told herself, that he was going to die sometime.

Was this grief because she had always expected to be at his side when it happened? Or because of this stupid, cursed, miserable condition that people called love, which had broken her warrior's strength and given her nothing in return?

She wondered what she would do, now that he was dead.

The gray house in Pergemis came to her mind, with the booming of the sea and the mewing of the wheeling gulls. Pel Farstep had said that Starhawk would always have a home with them. Yet it would be shabby treatment of so good a man as Ram to make him forever her second choice; and shabbier still to live in that house, but not as his wife. Though the peace that she had felt there called to her, she knew in her heart that their way—to count money, and raise children, and wait for ships to come in—was not her way.

Wrynde? It was peace of another sort, the rainy quiet of the winters and the mindless violence and glory of campaign. Her friends among the mercenaries returned to her mind, along with the bright joys of battle and war. But what was known could never be unknown. One day, she thought, she might become a warrior again. But having lived among her victims, she knew that she could never ride to the sacking of a town.

The altar lights flickered. As she walked through the darkness of the chapel to trim them, she automatically made the sign of respect, although it was a holy place of the Three, not of the One—the worship of the Triple God had always struck her as rather sterile and businesslike; and in any case, she knew that ritual was for the benefit of the worshipper and not from any need of the God's.

As she stood in the deep silence beside the altar stone, it came to her that she could remain here.

The chapel's guardian had been chased away or killed by the mercenaries who had camped here, but the building had been recently inhabited. Even in the depths of the holy place, the crying of the wind came to her, and the sporadic flurries of rain; it was close to dawn, the valley around the chapel an empty darkness, inhabited only by winds, wolves, and deer. To have this life, this peace . . . this place of meditation and solitude . . . a place to find her own road . . .

She stepped down from the altar and crossed the darkness once again, to the wall niche where Anyog slept, like a corpse already awaiting burial.

He, too, had loved her, she thought. It seemed that Sun Wolf's father had been right, after all; love brought nothing but grief and death, as magic brought nothing but isolation.

But as Anyog had found—and as she, to her grief, was finding—the lack of them brought something infinitely worse.

Why Mandrigyn? she wondered suddenly.

He had said Mandrigyn, not Grimscarp . . . What was the Wolf doing in Mandrigyn?

Distantly, the woman's face returned to her—the dark-haired woman she had seen so briefly in Sun Wolf's tent the night he had shown her the letter. *Sheera Galernas of Mandrigyn . . . a matter of interest to you . . .*

She stopped still in the darkness of the chapel, her mind suddenly leaping ahead. *Sweet Mother, he didn't change his mind and accept her proposal, after all, did he?*

Why wouldn't he have told anyone? Why the illusion of Ari? He'd never have left the troop to find its own way home . . .

How the illusion of Ari, for that matter?

Was there another wizard in it, after all? Or a partial wizard, like Anyog—one who had never passed through the Great Trial?

What the hell was the Wolf doing in Mandrigyn?

From the darkness, she heard Anyog whisper, "My dove . . ."

The chapel was tiny; a step brought her to his side, and she bent down to take his cold hands in hers. Anyog seemed in the last few days to have shrunk to a tiny skeleton, wrapped in a suit of withered skin. His features were the features of a skull; from dark hollows, black eyes stared up at her, clouded with fever and fear. She whispered, "I'm here, Uncle," and the thin lips blew out a pettish sigh.

"Leave you . . ." he murmured, ". . . face him alone."

She stroked his clammy forehead. "It's all right," she assured him quietly.

Outside, a rainy morning was struggling with the wind-torn rags of the sky. Through the door, she saw that much of the snow had melted; the long stretch of the valley below the chapel looked dirty and sodden, like the earth in the first forewhispers of spring.

Skeletal little fingers tightened weakly over hers. "Never the courage," he breathed, "to grasp . . ."

Her love? she wondered. *Or the Great Trial, the fearsome gate to power?*

"What was it?" she asked him and brushed his sunken cheek gently with her scarred hand.

"Secret . . . from master to pupil . . . So few know now . . . No one remembers. Not Altiokis . . . no one."

"But you must know it, if you feared it," she said, wondering, in the back of her mind, if the knowledge could be used. If there were an untried wizard in Mandrigyn who had had something to do with the Wolf's death . . .

He shook his head feebly. "Only the mageborn survive it," he murmured. "Others die . . . and even for those who survive . . ."

"But what was it?" she asked him.

His breath leaked out in a little gasp, and the dark eyes closed.

Then he whispered, "Anzid."

CHAPTER

——— 16 ———

"ALTIOKIS IS COMING."

"To Mandrigyn?"

Sheera nodded. "Wilarne had it from Stirk the harbor master's wife this morning." Above the frame of her starched lace collar, her jaw muscles were settled into a hard line.

Sun Wolf rested his shoulders against the cedar upright that supported the roof of the potting room and asked, "Why? To replace Derroug?"

"Partly," she assented. "And partly to make a show of force against the rumors of insurrection in the city. Wilarne said he was supposedly bringing troops." She leaned against the doorpost and looked down at her hands, clasped in the wine-colored folds of her skirts. Like most of the women, she had abandoned wearing rings—a warrior's habit. In a quieter voice, she began, "If I hadn't killed Derroug . . ."

"He'd have had every guard in the palace down on us," Sun Wolf finished for her. Still she did not meet his eyes. "Does Drypettis know?"

Sheera shook her head, then glanced up, weary hardness in those brown eyes. "No," she said. "In fact, I had the impression that his death really didn't concern her one way or the other. It—it was almost as if she didn't know about it."

The Wolf frowned. "You think that might be the case?"

"No," Sheera said. She moved her shoulder against the doorframe; the light glimmered on the swirls of opal and garnet that armored her bodice and festooned her extravagant sleeves. "I went to see her the day after it happened, and she did mention

221

it. But—in passing. Almost for form's sake. The rest of our talk that day was about—other things." Her mouth tightened a little at the memory. "And I'm inclined to think you were right about her, after all."

He was silent for a moment, studying her face. Her eyelids were stained with weariness and, he saw now, had begun to acquire those sharp, small creases that spoke of character and responsibility, which men claimed ruined a woman's looks. "What did she say?"

"Not much to the point." She shrugged. "Why did I take your part over hers? Why did I let you poison my mind against her? Were you my lover?"

"What did you tell her?"

She looked down again. "That it wasn't her affair."

"She'll take that for a 'Yes.'"

"I know." Sheera shook her head tiredly. "But she'd have taken 'No' for a 'Yes.'"

"Very likely," he agreed.

Sheera occupied herself for a long moment in rearranging the folds of the lace that cascaded from her cuffs over her hands. Sun Wolf noticed what Gilden had pointed out to him only yesterday—that Sheera, along with most of the women in the troop and scores of women who were unaware of its existence, had gone over to what they called the "new mode" of dressing, without the stiff boning and lacing-in and padded panniers. Though as elaborate and ostentatious as the old style had been, it allowed for more comfort and quicker movement. Privately, the Wolf thought it was more seductive as well.

She raised her eyes to his again. "What do you think of her?" she asked.

He considered the question for a moment before replying. "What do *you* think of her?"

"I don't know." She began to pace, her restless movement somehow feral, like that of a caged lioness. "I've known her from the time we were girls in school together. She said I was the only person who was ever good to her. Good to her! All I ever did was extend her common courtesy and keep the other girls from teasing her because she was proud and solitary and talked to herself."

He smiled. "In other words, you were her champion."

"I suppose. One goes through a stage of being someone's champion—or at least, I did. And I know one goes through a stage of being in love with another girl—oh, perfectly innocently! It's more a—a domination of the personality. A 'pash,' we called it—a 'rave.' And it seldom goes beyond that. But—I suppose you could say Dru never outgrew her 'pash' for me." She shrugged again. "Dru was such a precocious child, but socially she was so backward."

"She still is a precocious child," the Wolf pointed out, "at the age of twenty-five."

Sheera's eyes flashed suddenly, and he saw in her again the head girl of the school, beautiful and imperious at the age of ten, taking under her wing the wealthiest, proudest, and most miserable child in her class. She had always, he thought, been a champion, even as she was now. "It doesn't mean Dru would betray us," she said defiantly.

"No," he agreed. "But what it does mean is that there's no knowing which way she'll go if she's pushed. With most things—men or women, horses, demons, dogs—you know at least to some degree what they'll do if you push them—get angry, break down, stab you in the back. Drypettis..." He shook his head. "The bad thing is that we've given her a certain amount of power."

"You wouldn't have," Sheera said glumly.

The Wolf shrugged. "I wouldn't have given you power, either," he returned. "I've been wrong before."

Absurdly, color flushed up under that thin, browned skin. "Do you really mean that?"

"Am I in the habit of saying things I don't mean?" he inquired. The yellow fox eyes glinted curiously in the gloom of the potting room. "You're a fine warrior, Sheera, in spite of the fact that you're crazy; and if it weren't for the sake of another warrior who's both finer and also crazier than you, I might just be tempted to fall in love with you. Though the thought makes me shudder," he added.

"Good grief, I should hope so!" she said, genuinely appalled at the idea.

Sun Wolf laughed. It was a horrible sound, like the scraping of rusty iron, and he stopped, coughing. Sheera had the grace to look unhappy. The loss of his voice was her doing, and she knew it.

"Listen, Sheera," he said after a moment. "How long would it take the mining superintendents' comfort brigade to find out how many men Altiokis is bringing with him?"

Sheera frowned. "I think Amber Eyes can get a report within a day. Why?"

"Because it occurs to me that this may be our time to strike, while Altiokis and a lot of his troops aren't in the Citadel at all. Yirth says that the tunnels from the mines up to the Citadel are guarded with illusion and magic—but if Yirth is going to be the one to try and break the illusions, it would probably be better if she did it when Altiokis was gone."

Sheera was staring at him, her dark eyes blazing with sudden fire. "You mean—strike now? Free the men now?"

"When Altiokis comes to Mandrigyn, yes. Can you?"

She took a deep breath. "I—I don't know. Yes. Yes, we can. Eo's made copies of the keys to most of the weapons stores and gates in the mines . . . Amber Eyes can get word to Tarrin to be ready . . ." She was shivering all over with suppressed excitement, her hands clenched in the velvet of her skirts. "Lady Wrinshardin can get word to the other Thanes," she continued after a moment. "They can be ready to strike once we've freed the men."

"No," the Wolf said. "The Thanes are always ready to fight, anyway—we won't give Altiokis the warning of a rumor. He's here to investigate the rumors Gilden and Wilarne started the night they burned the Records Office. How soon will they arrive?"

A meeting was called that evening in the orangery, the heads of the conspiracy arriving secretly, slipping across the canals and through the tunnels to assemble in the vast cavern of the dim room. Amber Eyes came in with Denga Rey, their constant company in the last few days since Amber Eyes had parted from the Wolf explaining a lot of things about the gladiator's commitment to the cause. Gilden and Wilarne arrived by separate routes—a different sort of friendship, the Wolf thought; probably closer, for all its lack of a physical or romantic element. Having waded through the morass of their jokes, verbal and otherwise, he had developed a hearty sympathy for his half-pints' respective husbands.

After a few minutes of the swift crossfire conversation among those four, Sun Wolf saw Yirth arrive, fading soundlessly from the shadows of the door and moving like a cat to take her place in the darkness beyond the single candle's flicker. She'd been there almost ten minutes before any of the others noticed her, listening, her crooked mouth smiling; Denga Rey's expression when she finally did see her was almost comical. But when they heard the sound of the door closing again, and all eyes turned—as they always did—to watch Sheera stride into the circle of the candle's light, Sun Wolf felt the witch's gaze, brief and speculative, touch him.

Sheera sat down among them, and her look traveled from face to face. "Well?"

"Eo says the keys are ready," Gilden reported.

"Yirth?"

"I have read and studied," the witch said softly, "everything that my master left me on the subject of Altiokis and upon illusion. I am as prepared as any can be who has not crossed through the Great Trial."

Sheera smiled and reached across the table to clasp the long, heavy-knuckled hands. "It's all we ask of you," she said. "Amber Eyes?"

"Cobra just got back from the mines," the girl reported in her low, sweet voice. "She says they expect a force of about fifteen hundred with Altiokis, leaving about that many in the Citadel. Cobra says Fat Maali was going to see if she could find Tarrin himself. She'll come to us directly here."

Sheera's face was half in shadow, half edged in the primrose softness of the dim light. Sun Wolf, watching her, saw the change in her eyes at the mention of Tarrin's name, saw the champion, the war leader, the woman who would be Queen of Mandrigyn, change suddenly for a fleeting second to a girl who heard her lover's name. In spite of all she had done to him, his heart went out to her. Like Starhawk, she was seeking, with single-minded brutality, to find and free the man she loved.

Then she was all business again. "Captain Sun Wolf?" she asked. "Would you say the women are ready?"

"I'd rather have another two weeks," he said, the harsh scrape of his voice startling in the gloom. "But I think Altiokis' absence and fewer troops make up for the lack. I have only one request of you, Sheera."

She nodded. "I know," she said. "Yirth, I was going to ask you—"

"No," Sun Wolf said. "It isn't that. I want to lead the troops myself."

The silence was as echoing as the silence that followed thunder. The women were staring at him, openmouthed with astonishment. In that silence, his eyes met Sheera's, defying her to refuse to let him shove his nose in her right to command.

"You may be a decent commander," he said after a moment, "and you may even be good, in about another five years. But I've trained these women and forged them into a weapon; and

I don't want that weapon being broken by inexperience. If you're taking on Altiokis, you'll need a seasoned leader."

Sheera's eyes were wide and dark in the candlelight; surprise and relief at having a seasoned general and fighter like the Wolf struggled with resentment at being supplanted and relegated to second place. After a moment of silence, she breathed, "Would you? I mean—I thought—" The resentment faded and vanished, and the Wolf smiled to himself.

"Well, we both thought a lot of different things," he growled. "And if I'm going to mess around with magic, anyway, I want to make sure the job gets done right."

It was a momentary stalemate whether the leadership of the resistance forces of Mandrigyn would behave like grim and serious conspirators or like thrilled schoolgirls; and regrettably, instinct won out. Wilarne flung her arms around Sun Wolf's neck and planted an enthusiastic kiss on his mouth, followed in quick succession by Gilden, Sheera, Amber Eyes, and a bone-crushing hug from Denga Rey. Sun Wolf fought them off with a show of disgust. "I knew this would happen when I went to work for a bunch of skirts," he snarled.

Gilden retorted, "You hoped, you mean."

He was conscious again of Yirth's watching him from the shadows, of the puzzlement in the sea-green eyes. He glowered at her. "What's the matter? You never seen a man change his mind before?"

"No," the witch admitted. "Men pride themselves on their inflexibility."

"I'll get you for that," he promised and saw, for the first time, an answering sparkle in the sardonic depths of her eyes.

Then the sparkle vanished, like a candle doused by water; she swung around, even as he raised his head, hearing the sound of footfalls on the wet gravel of the garden path. A moment later the orangery's outer door opened, and the woman they called Fat Maali came in.

Fat Maali was clearly one of Amber Eyes' skags, the lowest type of camp follower, of the class of women whom mercenaries referred to by a name as descriptive as it was unrepeatable. She could have been thirty-five, but looked fifty, immense, blowsy, and strong, with a hard face that had never been beautiful and was now ravaged by poverty and debasement. Her eyes were limpid blue and cheerful. Sun Wolf wouldn't have wanted to be drunk in her company, if she knew he had any money on him.

She was dressed in a filthy green gown with clearly nothing underneath. Brass-colored curls tumbled down over her shoulders like a young girl's. The effect was almost as horrible as the stench of her perfume.

She said, "I've seen Tarrin."

Sheera was on her feet, her face alive with eagerness. "And?"

"He says don't do it."

Sheera sagged back as if struck, shock and disbelief parting her lips without words.

It was Amber Eyes who spoke. "Did he say why?" she asked quietly.

Fat Maali nodded, and her eyes were downcast. "Yes," she said softly. "He says—and I—I agree with him—that if we attacked the Citadel while Altiokis and his men were in the town, he's afraid of what would happen to the people here. The ones who didn't have anything to do with any of it, who just want to be let alone. He says the old bastard would massacre 'em, sure." She looked up, her eyes troubled but unwavering. "And he would, Amber. Y'know he would."

There was silence, the fat woman's gaze going worriedly from Amber Eyes to Sheera, and to the faces of the others in turn—Denga Rey, Gilden, Wilarne, Yirth, Sun Wolf. It was Sun Wolf who broke the silence. "He's right," he said.

"M'lord Tarrin—" Maali said hesitantly. "M'lord Tarrin said he wouldn't buy his freedom or the city's at that cost. He said he'd die a slave first."

Two days later, on orders from Acting Governor Stirk, the larger portion of the population of Mandrigyn turned out along the Golden Street, which led into the town from the tall land gate, to welcome Altiokis of Grimscarp, Wizard King of the Tchard Mountains. Though the crowds that lined the way were thick—troopers of the governor were going from house to house to make sure of it—they were silent. Even those who had welcomed the soldiers who had put an end to the succession troubles in the city ten months before in Altiokis' name no longer cheered.

In the thick of the crowd, dressed in his patched brown gardening things, with Gilden and Wilarne brightly veiled and giggling on either arm, Sun Wolf watched the Wizard King ride in.

"He never came after Iron Pass," Gilden whispered, her calmly businesslike tone belying the caressing way she rubbed her cheek on his arm. "The captain of his mercenaries—the Dark Eagle, his name is—led his troops into the city, with Derroug and Stirk and some of the other chiefs of the council who'd been exiled by Tarrin. Amber Eyes tells me . . ."

A harsh blare of trumpets rose over the deeper drone of the battle horns, cutting off her words. The Wolf raised his head, the sounds prickling his spine. Rolling like thunder down the wide, tree-lined street, the deep boom of the kettledrums was picked up and flung from wall to marble-fronted wall. Sun Wolf and the girls had taken their positions in the last straight reach of the Golden Street, where it ran down to the Great Landing; beyond the crowds, the gilding of the ceremonial barge flashed in the wan sunlight. Across the way, on a balcony draped with pennons, one of Amber Eyes' girls sat combing her hair, preparing to tally the number of troops as they passed.

"There," Wilarne whispered.

Around the corner of the lane they appeared, a mass of black-mailed bodies, their measured tread lost in the sonorous crash of the drums. Antlike heads, faceless behind slit-eyed helmets, stared out straight ahead. Sun Wolf wondered, with a prickle of loathing, whether the eye slits were functional or merely to keep the populace from suspecting. Like the nuuwa in the palace gardens, these soldiers marched unarmed.

"Altiokis' private troops," Wilarne breathed, under cover of the Wolf's drawing her closer to him as if to protect her. *Though his ancestors help the man who thought this sloe-eyed scrap of primordial mayhem needed protection!* "That's Gilgath at their head, riding the black horse. He's the Captain of Grimscarp, Commander of Altiokis' Citadel."

The Wolf considered the inhuman, mailed bulk with narrowed eyes. Like his men, Gilgath was masked and hidden by his armor. Men at his sides led beasts on chains—huge, strange beasts, like slumped dog-apes with chisel teeth and mad, stupid eyes—ugies, Lady Wrinshardin had called them.

More of them walked with the black-mailed guards around the Wizard King's ebony litter. The people in the street had fallen utterly silent; the only sounds now were the blows of the drums, steady and inescapable as doom.

At the sight of the litter, the Wolf felt his flesh crawl. It was borne by two black horses, their eyes masked with silver, led by the black-armored guards. Pillars of twisted ebony, whose capitals flashed with opal and nacre, supported dead-black curtains; where the curtains had been drawn back, the interior of the litter was masked by heavy lattices of carven blackwood. Sun Wolf, who stood taller than anyone around him in that chiefly female crowd, craned his neck, but could see nothing of the wizard within, except for a still, dark shadow, unmoving against the blackness of the cushions.

And yet, at the sight of it, something stirred in Sun Wolf, anger and an emotion deeper than anger; revulsion and an implacable hate. The impact of his feelings startled him, with the awareness that he looked upon pollution. And behind that came the horrible and revolting certainty that he had sometimes felt in the haunts of the marsh demons of the North—the certainty that he looked upon that which was not entirely human.

This was not a demon, he knew, edging his way forward through the crowd to follow the litter with his eyes. But something . . .

He pushed ahead to the front edge of the packed throng as the litter descended to the landing stage and the waiting barge. No snake, no spider, no foul and creeping thing had ever affected him with such cold loathing, and he struggled for a glimpse of the thing that would emerge. Distance and the angle confused his line of sight; Gilgath, the Commander of the Citadel, was deploying his soldiers across the covered tunnel of the Spired Bridge, to line the canal route toward the governor's palace. Behind him, other marching footsteps echoed in the narrow street as the rest of Altiokis' force approached.

Then the Wolf heard a single deep voice call out, "Arrest that man." Turning, he found himself staring up into the face of the Dark Eagle, captain of Altiokis' mercenary forces.

The Eagle hadn't changed since they'd campaigned together in the East. The sardonic blue eyes still held their expression of bitter amusement as Sun Wolf turned to flee.

He found himself hemmed in by the civilians at his back and the City Troops that were running toward him from all sides. Gilden and Wilarne had melted away into the crowd, already heading in opposite directions to get the news to Sheera. The Eagle spurred his black mount forward toward him, bowmen clustering around his stirrups—if the Wolf remembered the Dark Eagle's specialties, there wasn't much chance they'd miss. Civilians were crowding away from him, panic-stricken. Someone grabbed his arm from behind and shoved a sword blade against his ribs; he ducked and feinted. An arrow shaft

burned his shoulder as it buried itself in the body of the man
behind him.

The Wolf grabbed the sword from the slacking grip and
spun to meet his would-be captors, throwing another one of
them into the path of the second arrow and darting for the
mouth of the nearest alley. A man in his way cut at him with
a halbred; he parried, slashed along the shaft, and jumped over
the falling weapon. The crowd milled and scattered before him.
The Eagle's mercenaries and the City Troops broke ranks to
pursue.

He was closed in, he saw. He cut another man's face open
and turned to strike a third. Though battle concentrated his
mind, he was somehow peripherally aware of movement near
the landing, of a stirring in the black curtains . . .

Something, he did not know what, like a smoky and con-
fusing cloud, struck at his face, and he turned to slash at it.
His sword cleaved it like air, haloed in a splattering of red
lightning. In the last second in which he realized that it was
merely an illusion sent to break his concentration, something
hit him on the back of the head, and darkness closed around
him.

CHAPTER
—— 17 ——

"C*APTAIN SUN WOLF.*"

The voice that penetrated the blackness of his mind seemed to come from a great distance away. It was the Dark Eagle's, he recognized, obscured by the buzzing roar that filled his skull.

"And in such clothes, too. Open your eyes, you barbarian; I know you can hear me."

The Wolf pried one grit-filled eye open and squinted against the burning glare of yellow light.

"They say when you hire out your sword, you meet acquaintances in all corners of the world," the Eagle went on, "but I hardly expected to see an old friend here."

Sun Wolf blinked painfully. The light that had blinded him a moment ago resolved itself into the smoldering fireball at the end of a torch stuck in a greasy iron wall sconce, just behind the Dark Eagle's shoulder. He became slowly aware of the burning ache in his arms; when he tried to move them, he found that they were, in fact, supporting the weight of his limp body. The short chain that joined his wrists had been thrown over a hook a few feet above his head. He was hanging with his back to the stone wall of a room which he guessed was underground—under what was left of the Records Office, presumably—and the memory of another small underground room and the drifting sparkle of unknown fire on the air brought sweat to his stubbled face. He got his feet under him and stood, glaring at the mercenary chief, who was, for the moment, the only other man in the room.

"The least you could have done was keep your flapping mouth shut," he growled hoarsely.

The Dark Eagle frowned. He was a stocky man of medium height, his black hair falling forward over his bright eyes. "Lost your tongue?"

"A lady poisoned me, and I lost my voice over it," the Wolf answered quite truthfully, hearing, as he said the words, the metallic rasp of the sound.

The flicker of concern that had glimmered behind the blue eyes fled. The mercenary chief laughed. "I hope you had your revenge. The reason I took you in is that I'm paid to keep order in Altiokis' domains. Why ever you've decided to winter in this lovely town, I'd have to clean up the mess sooner or later. Where are your men?"

"At Wrynde."

"I didn't mean your troops, I mean the men you're leading. And believe me, Wolf, I'm not going to accept that you're in this town to no purpose. What men are you at the head of?"

Sun Wolf sighed, leaning his head back against the rough rock of the wall behind him. "None," he said. "No one."

"You put up one hell of a fight for a man with a clear conscience."

"You wouldn't know a clear conscience if you found one in your bed. What in the name of all your sniveling ancestors are you doing serving that demon?"

The Dark Eagle frowned. "Demon?"

"Whatever was in that litter, it wasn't human. I'll take oath on that."

The blue eyes narrowed to slits. "You always could spot them, couldn't you? But Altiokis is no demon. I've seen him summon demons and I've seen him handle the things they dread to protect himself against them."

"He's no demon, but—I don't know what he is."

A white grin split the swarthy countenance, and the uneasy look vanished. "He's the greatest wizard of the world—and a man of uncommon appetites to boot." The smile faded. "Why do you say he isn't human?"

"Because he isn't, dammit! Can't you tell it? Can't you feel it?"

The blue eyes hardened. "I think we hit you harder than we intended, my friend," the Eagle said. "Or maybe your light-skirts' poison addled your never-very-stout brains. Altiokis is a man—and a man who can afford to pay damned well to keep trouble out of his lands. As you shall see."

He moved toward the cell door, then paused, his hand on the handle. In a quieter voice, he said, "I'd advise you to tell him whatever you're in, Wolf."

He opened the door and stepped aside.

Altiokis entered.

Two impressions, spiritual and physical, seemed to overlap for a second in Sun Wolf's brain.

The spiritual was the impression of a half-rotted tree, leprous with age, its cancered bark still standing but enclosing another entity, a black and lucid fire that showed through the cracks.

The physical was the sight of a man of medium height, impossibly obese from eating rich foods, with bad skin, the suspicion of a shadow of stubble on his pouchy jaw, and too many rings embedded in the flesh of his fat fingers. Contact with merchants' wives had sharpened Sun Wolf's appreciation of the value of cloth; the black velvet that formed the under-pinning of the jewel-beaded embroidery of the immense doublet sold for fifty silver crowns a yard. The jeweled belts that supported the overhanging rolls of fat would have purchased cities.

In the back of his mind, the Wolf heard Lady Wrinshardin's acid voice saying, "He is vulgar."

And he knew, watching the Dark Eagle's face and the faces of the gaunt harbor master, Stirk, and of Drypettis, who stood in the shadows of the corridor behind him, that the physical being was all anyone ever saw.

He wanted to scream at them, "Don't you see it? Don't you understand what he is?" But he did not understand himself.

Sunk in their pouches of fat, the cold little eyes gleamed with smug amusement. The Wizard King stepped forward, raising his staff. Like the pillars of his litter, it was carved of ebony in twisting patterns, its ornate tip flickering with the ghostly gleam of opal and abalone. The touch of it on Sun Wolf's neck was like ice and fire, a searing dart of pain, and he flinched from it with a stifled cry.

A satisfied little smile decorated the puffy lips.

"So you're the man who thought he could go against me?"

Sun Wolf said nothing. After the ordeal of the anzid, pain had changed its meaning for him, but the shock of being touched by that staff had taken his breath away. He was aware of Drypettis, standing in the doorway, like some monstrous orchid in her orange gown and veils; he could see her huge brown eyes watching him with an unreadable mixture of coldness and hatred and spite. He wondered if she had thought to tell Sheera where he was being held and what good it would do anyone if she had.

Or was she waiting to see if he broke, to slip away and warn the others when he did?

Altiokis' voice went on. "Who hired you, Captain?"

The Wolf swallowed and shook his head. "He never told me his name," he whispered. "He said he'd pay me to spy out the city, the gates, and the canals and to lay out a siege plan . . ."

"Probably one of the Thanes." Altiokis yawned. "They're always stirring up trouble—and it's time they were put down."

"Where did he meet you, this man?" the Dark Eagle asked.

In a stifled voice, the Wolf replied, "In the Peninsula, after the siege of Melplith. He arranged a meeting with me, three weeks from now, in East Shore. I was to come here, which I did, overland, and lay out my plans . . ."

"Yes, yes," Altiokis said in a bored voice. "But who was he?"

"I tell you, I don't know." The Wolf glanced from the Eagle to Altiokis and back again, sensing that the Wizard King didn't really much care who had hired him. Was he that confident of his own powers and of the magic that protected the Citadel? Or had he, as a result of his endless life, merely reached the point of bored carelessness with everything?

"The man chose an expensive spy," the Dark Eagle commented thoughtfully. "The world abounds in cheaper ones."

The Wolf flashed him what he hoped was an angry dagger of a glance. "Would you hire a cheap one?"

Then he flinched in agony from the glowing tip of the Wizard King's staff.

"Remember to whom you're talking, barbarian," Altiokis said, with a kind of quiet relish. He brought the staff toward Sun Wolf's face, the white metal of its tip seeming to glow with an unholy luminescence. The Wolf drew back from it, feeling the sweat that poured down his cheeks, staring as if hypnotized at the star-flash of the opals and at the twined jaws of the inlaid serpents that held them. Something that was not heat seemed to smoke from the jeweled tip, like a cold promise of unbearable pain.

"I am Altiokis," the Wizard King said softly. "No one has the temerity to speak thus to my servants."

The burning jewels were within a half inch of the Wolf's eyes when he whispered, "I'm sorry, my lord."

Past the opals, he saw the little smirk appear and wrenched his head aside as the staff touched him again. A cry of pain escaped him, and he felt the flesh along his cheekbone sear and curl, the shock of it piercing his whole body like a sword.

Savoringly, Altiokis said, "I could chip you away, piece by piece, until you begged for the chance to tell what you know and the mercy of a cut throat. I may do it yet, merely to amuse myself."

Sun Wolf made no reply to this. For a time, speech was beyond him. Sickened with the pain, he hung from the chain above his head, trying to regather his thoughts, telling himself that, no matter how bad it was, the anzid had been far worse. But beyond that, he was conscious of both anger and outrage that a man with powers of the Wizard King should use them so, like a cruel child pulling the wings from a fly. He had met enough men in his time who were amused by pain. He had not expected a man who had mastered the hard disciplines of wizardry to be one of them.

"Governor Stirk . . ." Altiokis said, and Stirk looked up, the surprised gratification on his face reminding Sun Wolf of a dog that hoped for a pat. The tall harbor master came forward, almost wagging his tail. In the doorway, Drypettis stiffened with outraged indignation. Stirk actually went down on his knees and kissed the Wizard King's jewel-crusted shoe. Altiokis almost purred.

"Did the interrogation chamber survive the fire?" the wizard asked.

The new governor's face fell. "Alas, no, my lord," he said, rising and unobtrusively dusting his knees. "The upper level of the prisons was gutted by the fire the night Governor Derroug was murdered."

My ancestors, the Wolf thought, through the raw anguish that seemed to be pouring into his flesh from the open burn on his face, *are looking out for me, after all.*

There was a pout in the fruity voice. "Then he shall go with me to the Citadel in the morning. When I depart, Governor Stirk, I shall leave a force of men here under the command of General Dark Eagle, to be billeted in the houses of citizens as you choose. Do not think that in the event of these disruptions, the annual tribute from this city will be excused. Moreover, I feel sure that you are moved to make some suitable show of gratitude for your elevation to your new position."

Stirk almost fell over himself agreeing; Sun Wolf wondered what Altiokis could possibly want with more wealth.

"As for this—arrogant barbarian . . ." The butt end of the staff licked out and cracked sharply on the side of Sun Wolf's knee. Beside the agony of his seared face, he hardly noticed. "I scarcely feel that he is telling us all the truth; but in time, we shall learn from him the names of the men ill-intentioned enough to hire such a person to spy out my city. From my Citadel, I can see all. No army can approach without my knowledge. But it will save trouble to know whom to punish."

The words were rhetorical, and Sun Wolf knew it. Altiokis didn't much care whom he punished or why; to a man a hundred and fifty years old and of no great mental resources to begin with, the infliction of pain was one of few amusements left. Sun Wolf's eyes followed the fat wizard as he waddled toward the door, with Stirk bowing along at his heels. The Dark Eagle, his face a smooth and cynical blank, brought up the rear.

Did others wonder about this, too? the Wolf asked himself, watching them mount the few steps to the hall. *How could something that trivial, that spiteful and vicious, have acquired this kind of power?*

Didn't any of them see?

"One more thing."

Altiokis turned back, the torchlight from the hall outside streaming over his jewels like a spent wave over a barnacle-encrusted hull. He snapped his fingers. Past him, the Wolf saw the guards in the hallway startle, heard Drypettis give a sharp squeak of alarm.

Two nuuwa entered the cell.

Sun Wolf felt his heart stop, then pound to life with a surge of terror that momentarily drowned out all things else. He cast one quick glance at the hook that held his chained hands helpless above his head, calculating whether he could get free before they began ripping at his flesh, then stared back at them, knowing he was trapped. Altiokis' smile broadened with delight.

"You like my friends, eh?" he asked.

Both waggling heads turned toward Sun Wolf, as if they could see him or smell the blood in his veins. Drool glistened on the misshapen chins, and they champed their impossibly grown teeth and fidgeted as the wizard laid companionable hands on the sloped backs. Their uniforms—foul, torn, and crawling with lice—were so filthy the Wolf wondered how anyone could bring himself to touch even those, let alone the mindless, unclean flesh beneath.

"You'll be quite safe." Altiokis smiled. "As long as you make no attempt to get away, they shall curb their appetites and be content with—ah—contemplation. But believe me, should you try to get away, I'm sure they could chew off quite large portions of you before your screams brought the guards— if any guards would be willing to try to separate them from their victim."

That pleased smile widened still more at the thought, and the most powerful wizard in the world paused thoughtfully to excavate a nostril with his jeweled finger. He wiped it fastidiously on Stirk's sleeve. Stirk gave a fatuous smile.

"I hope I shall see you in the morning."

The door shut behind him.

For a long time Sun Wolf stood, his twisted shoulders racked and aching from the drag of his body against the chain, his mind chasing itself blindly from thought to thought.

The most powerful wizard in the world! His stomach turned at the thought of that power and that waste.

But the power came from nothing within Altiokis himself. He was a man half rotted from the inside by something else; the power was not of his own finding. That first, fleeting impression was all the Wolf had to go on; afterward, he had seen the wizard only as others saw him—obese, omnipotent, and terrifying. Sun Wolf felt as he had in his childhood, frantically insisting to his father and to the other men of the tribe that he could see the demons whose voices taunted them from the marsh mists and being sharply told to shut up and follow. He had been right then, he knew. And he knew now that there was something in Altiokis that was neither human nor clean nor sane.

Tomorrow he would be taken up to the Citadel. He'd seen enough torture to harbor no illusions about his own abilities to withstand it for any protracted period of time. Altiokis was right—the threat of being given anzid again, or of being put into a room with whatever it was that could transform a man into a nuuwa, would have him selling off all these women he had come to be so fond of without a moment's hesitation.

Except, he thought, that it probably would not save him, anyway. Even upon short acquaintance, he knew Altiokis too well for that.

His eyes returned to the nuuwa. Altiokis had left a torch, burning in its bracket on the other side of the room. The nuuwa wore the uniforms of Altiokis' troops, but they were already ragged and fouled, for the creatures were too brainless to change them or even unsnag them if they caught on something. It occurred obliquely to the Wolf, in the one corner of his mind not occupied by horror, that what undoubtedly became of nuuwa, if they weren't killed, was that they simply rotted away from self-neglect. One of these already had what looked like a badly festered gash on its leg, visible through the torn and soiled breeches.

Now that he had seen them made from men, the Wolf could tell that one of these was more recent than the other—the one eye seared out and scarred over, the other rotted out from within and already scarring. The second nuuwa was older, the bones of the face changed and deformed, the shoulders more slumped. It was impossible to tell through which eye the flame-creature had bored.

They stood unmoving, watching him from eyeless holes, their reek filling the cell. Sometimes one of them would shift from foot to foot, but neither stirred itself to brush away the roaches that crawled over its feet in the straw. Once Sun Wolf looked cautiously over his head at the chain and hook again, and they grew restless, snuffling and fidgeting.

He gave up the attempt.

His mind returned to that windowed cell in the burned-out wing of the prison. The flake of flame, the young slave screaming as he clutched his bleeding eye . . . Altogether it had taken nearly a minute, the Wolf calculated, between the time the thing had got the boy and the time it had bored through to the brain. Had he known what would happen to him in those endless, racking seconds? Or had the pain been too great?

The Wolf shuddered with the memory of it. In his heart, he already knew what was intended for him, whether he revealed any plans or not.

The anzid had changed his tolerance for pain, which was already higher than most men's, but it had given him a hearty appreciation of how bad pain could get. And even with the blessing of ignorance, without the knowledge that one's scooped-out husk would be ruled by Altiokis' foul will, the sixty seconds or so that it took for the thing—fire, insect, or whatever—to bore its way inward would be like the distilled essence of the deepest Hells.

He glanced at the nuuwa and then back up at the chains.

It would be possible, he saw now, to stretch his body and arms enough to lift the manacles up over the top of the hook that held them. The hook was positioned for a slightly shorter man—few of the men of Mandrigyn topped six feet—and he thought that he could manage with a struggle. But it would take a short while; in the meantime, his body would hang exposed and helpless before those mindless things drooling in their corner.

He wondered how far his own abilities of nonvisibility went.

He'd experimented with them since the night he'd first called them into use on the roof of the palace kitchens, the night he and the women had rescued Tisa. With a little practice, he had found that he could, within certain limits, avoid the eyes of someone entering a fairly small and well-lighted room, provided he did nothing to call attention to himself. The nuuwa had no eyes—it stood to reason that they saw with their minds. But if that were the case, his nonvisibility should work better on them, since it was, in fact, avoidance of the attention.

It might be worth a try.

In any case, he was aware that, objectively, in the long run, he would not be worse off. Being devoured alive by them would be a messy and hideous way to die, but he wondered whether it would be worse than becoming a nuuwa himself.

It was a choice he had no desire to put to the test.

Hesitantly, he groped his mind out toward theirs, shifting their attention past him, toward the stones of the wall and the crawling straw at his feet, letting them look through him, around him, turning that intentness toward trivial things, and making them forget that he was there. He found himself sweating with the effort of it, trickles of moisture running down his aching arms and down his face and his body. He made himself relax into the effort, becoming less and less important in their minds against their general awareness of the cell and occupying their attention, their senses, with the crackle of insect feet in the straw, the smell of the torch smoke . . .

He braced his body, then began to reach upward, rising on his toes and stretching his stiff back and shoulders toward the iron hook.

The nuuwa stared stolidly at the walls to either side of him.

Delicately, he hooked the tips of his half-numbed fingers under the short links that joined the metal bracelets. He strained to lift them toward the tip of the hook, loosening his back muscles against the shooting fire of cramps that raced down them from their long inactivity. The sweat burned in the raw flesh of his opened cheek, and his arms trembled at the effort of movement. The tip of the hook seemed impossibly high. One of the nuuwa belched, the sound sharp as an explosion in the silent room; half hypnotized by the effort of concentration, the Wolf never took his mind from the illusion of nonvisibility that he held with his whole attention, despite the physical strain that occupied his limbs. He had been trapped once by having his concentration broken. Even if they tore him to pieces, he would not do so again.

The metal slipped over metal. The slacking of the hook's support was abrupt, as the links slid over it. The Wolf felt as if all the weight of his body had dropped suddenly upon his exhausted muscles. He could have collapsed in a thankful heap on the fetid straw, but he forced himself to remain upright, lowering his arms slowly to his sides, shaking all over with the effort. The separate agonies of the day were swallowed in an all-encompassing wave of anguishing cramps in arms and back.

The nuuwa continued to look at the wall.

As soon as he was satisfied that his legs would support him, Sun Wolf took a cautious step forward.

There was no reaction.

His mind held their attention at bay, but the concentration required most of his strength, and he knew he could not keep it up for long. He took another step and another, without either of them appearing to notice... *No mean feat*, he thought in that clear cynical corner of his mind, *to keep a nuuwa from going after ambulatory food.*

The door was bolted with an iron dead bolt, not merely a wooden drop that could be lifted with a card. He glanced over his shoulder at the nuuwa, the nearest of which stood, a stinking lump of flesh, less than six feet from him.

He decided to risk it.

"Dark Eagle!" he yelled, lifting his raw voice to as carrying a pitch as he could manage. "Stirk! I'll tell you what you want to know! Just keep them off me!"

His concentration pressed against the nuuwa, a sheer physical effort, like that of trying to hold up a falling wall. The nuuwa shifted, scuffling around the cell, arms swinging, lolling heads wagging, as if seeking for what they could not find. *Rot your eyes, you poxy corridor guard*, he thought, *don't you want to be the first with the news that your prisoner's broken?*

He yelled again. "I'll tell you anything! Just get me out of here! I'll tell you what you want!"

Running footsteps sounded in the corridor. One man, he guessed from the sound, hesitating outside the door. *Open it, you cowardly bastard!* the Wolf demanded silently. *Don't call your chief...*

The bolt shot back.

Sun Wolf came slamming out of the cell, throwing his full weight on the door, heedless of any weapon the man might have had. The guard's drawn short sword jammed in the wood of the door and stuck; the man had his mouth open, too startled to scream, showing a wide expanse of dirty teeth. Sun Wolf grabbed him by the neck and hurled him bodily into the arms of the advancing nuuwa.

He sent the door crashing shut and shot the bolt against the man's screams, pulled the sword free, and ran up the empty corridor as if heading for the half-closed doors of Hell.

CHAPTER

—— 18 ——

"*AND YOU TURNED THEIR MINDS ASIDE?*"

Sun Wolf nodded. Yirth's drugs could ease pain without dulling the mind, but the release of concentration acted almost like a drug in itself. Lying in the fading light of her tiny whitewashed attic room, he felt as exhausted as he did after battle. The smell of the place, of the drying herbs that festooned the low rafters in strings, filled him with a curious sense of peace, and he watched her moving around, gaunt and powerful, and wondered how he had ever thought of her as ugly. Stern and strong in her power, yes. But the marring birthmark no longer drew his eyes from the rest of her face, and he saw her now as a harsh-faced woman a few years older than he, whose life had been, in its way, as strenuous as his own.

As if she felt his thoughts, she turned back to him. "How did you do this thing?" she asked.

"I don't know," he replied wearily. "It was the anzid, I think." He saw her sudden frown and realized it wasn't much of an explanation.

"I think the anzid did something to me—besides half killing me, that is. Since I was brought back, I've been able to see in the dark, and I've had this—this ability to avoid people's sight. I've always been good at it, but now it's—it's uncanny. I used it the first time when we rescued Tisa, and I've been practicing since then. I used to—"

She held up her hand against his words. "No," she said. "Let me think."

She turned from him, pacing to the narrow window that

looked out over the wet, red roofs of Mandrigyn. For a long moment she stood, her dark head bent, the gray light gleaming in the pewter streaks that frosted her hair. Outside, the plop and splash of a gondola's pole could be heard in the canal, and the light tapping of hooves over the bridge nearby. Yirth's cat, curled at the foot of Sun Wolf's narrow cot, woke, stretched, and sprang soundlessly to the floor.

Then Yirth whispered, "Dear Mother." She looked back at him. "Tell me about the night you spent in the pit," she said.

He returned her gaze in silence, unwilling to share the extent of grief and pain and humiliation. Only one person knew the whole and, if she were even still alive, he did not know where she was now. At length he said, "Sheera had her victory over me. Isn't that enough?"

"Don't be a fool," the witch said coldly. "There was no anzid left in your system when she led us back to you."

He stared at her, not comprehending.

"Did you have visions?"

He nodded mutely, his body shaken with a fit of shivering at the memory of those dreams of power and despair.

She put her hands to her temples, the thick, streaky hair springing over and through her fingers, like water through a sieve of bone. "Dear Mother," she murmured again.

Her voice sounded hollow, half stunned. "I found it among her things when she was killed," she said, as if to herself. "Chilisirdin—my master. I didn't think . . . In our business there are always poisons. We deal in them—poisons, philters, abortifacients. Sometimes a death is the only answer. I never thought anything else of it."

"What are you talking about?" he whispered, though it was coming to him, in a kind of unveiling of horror, what she meant.

Her face, in the deepening shadows, seemed suddenly very young, its stony self-possession stripped away by fear and hope. "Tell me, Captain—why did you become a warrior and not a shaman among your people?"

Sun Wolf stared at her for as long as it would take to count to a hundred, stunned at the truth of her question, struck as he had been during the tortured visions in the pit, with the memory of his black and icy childhood and of all those things of beauty and power that he had set aside in the face of his father's bleak mockery. In a voice very unlike his own, he stammered, "The old shaman died—long before I was born. The one we had was a charlatan, a fake. My father..." He was silent, unable to go on.

For a time neither spoke.

Then he said, "No." He made a movement, as if thrusting from him the thought that he could have what he had known from his earliest childhood was his birthright. "I'm no wizard."

"What are you, then?" she demanded harshly. "If you hadn't been born with the Power, the anzid would have killed you. I was surprised that it didn't, but I thought it was because you were tough, were strong. It never crossed my mind otherwise, even though my master had told me that the Great Trial would kill any who were not mageborn to begin with."

Cold and irrational terror rose in him. His mouth dry, he whispered, "I'm no wizard. I'm a warrior. My business is war. I stay out of that stuff. My life is war. Starhawk..." He paused, uncertain what he had meant to say about Starhawk. "I can't change at my age."

"You *are* changed," Yirth said bitterly. "Like it or not."

"But I don't know any magic!" he protested.

"Then you had best learn," she rasped, an edge of impatience stinging into her voice. "For believe me, Altiokis will come to know that there is another proven wizard in the world, another who has passed through the Great Trial. Most of us undergo the training first, and the Trial when we have the strength to endure it. You had the strength—either from your training as a warrior or because the magic you were born with is strong, stronger than any I have heard tell of. But without training in the ways of it, you are helpless to fight the Wizard King."

Sun Wolf lay back on the cot. The smart of his arms and shoulders and the raw places on his wrists where the spancel had been removed bitterly reinforced his memory of the Wizard King. "He'll follow me wherever I go, won't he?" he asked quietly.

"Probably," Yirth answered. "As he hounded my master Chilisirdin to her death."

The Wolf turned his eyes toward her in the dark. The daylight had faded from the attic, but among themselves, wizards had no need of light. "I'm sorry," he said. "I was just given for free what you would have sold everything you owned to possess; and here I am complaining because I don't want it. But I was raised to steer very clear of magic, and I—I'm afraid of the Power."

"You should be," she snapped. In a quieter voice, she went on. "It is unheard of for an untrained mage to pass through the Great Trial. You must leave Altiokis' domains, and quickly; but if you take my advice, you must seek out another wizard as fast as you can. You do not know the extent of your powers; without the teaching and the discipline of wizardry, you are as dangerous as a mad dog."

Sun Wolf chuckled softly in the darkness. "I know. I've seen it a thousand times in my own business. When a boy comes to me to be trained in arms, he's the most dangerous between the fourth month and the twelfth. That's when he's learned the physical power, but not the spiritual control—and he hasn't quite grasped the fact that there's anyone alive who can beat him. That's the age when someone—myself or Starhawk or Ari—has to trounce the daylights out of him, to keep him from picking fights with everyone else in the troop. If a boy survives the first year, he has the discipline and the brains to be a soldier."

He heard her small, faint sniff, which he rightly interpreted as laughter. "And to think I once despised you for being a soldier," she said. "I will teach you what I can while you are hidden here, until we can get you out of the city. But you must find a true wizard—one who has had the fullness of his power for many years and who understands in truth what I know only in theory."

"I would do that in any case," Sun Wolf said quietly. "I know that my days as a warrior are done."

Clear and sharp, the vision returned to him of his own hands seared to the bone from grasping the molten fire of his dreams. It hurt to let the old life go, to release what he had striven for and taken pride in since he was a boy old enough to wield a child's sword. It left him with a stricken feeling of emptiness, as if with the sword he had given up an arm as well. Ari would take the troop and the school at Wrynde. Starhawk...

He looked up. "There'll be a woman coming here," he said, knowing that with the Hawk's stubbornness, even his vision manifesting itself to her in a dream and telling her to give up the search would not be sufficient to turn her aside. *Stubborn female!* he added to himself. "She's looking for me. Tell her..."

Tell her what? That he'd gone on, searching for a wizard in a world long bereft of such things? That she should follow him once again?

"Tell her to meet me in Wrynde, before the summer's end.

Tell her I swear that I will come to her there." He paused, picturing her with sharp and painful clarity in the quiet of the stone garden below the school. He had not walked its paths in summer for nearly twenty years. "Tell her what became of me," he added quietly.

The deformed mouth quirked suddenly into a wry smile, showing teeth white as snow in the gloom. "A long way to travel," she remarked. "Shall I teach you how to find this woman yourself?"

He saw what must have been his own expression reflected in the one of deepening amusement in her eyes and grinned ruefully. "If I'm going to go back to being a schoolboy at my age," he said, "I'm certainly developing the reactions of one."

"That, Captain, is only because you have never before this particularly cared where anyone else was, or if that person lived or died," Yirth replied calmly. "The relationships of the body are the business of women like Amber Eyes—the relationships of the heart are mine. I have made as many love philters as I have made poisons and abortifacients. They all tell me why. They are driven to tell; I do not ask. There is nothing that I have not heard.

"And do you know, Captain, that I have heard men sneer at—what do they call? A respectable man of full age—suddenly discovering what it is to love another person. Doubtless you yourself know what they say."

Sun Wolf had the grace to blush.

"But if a man who has been crippled from childhood is healed at the age of forty, will he not jump and dance and turn cartwheels like a young boy, scorning the dignity of his years? The mockers are those who themselves are still crippled. Think nothing of it." She shook back the thick mane of hair from her shoulders, her face framed in it like the white blur of an asymmetrical skull in the gloom. "Will you sleep?"

He hesitated. "If you're tired, yes," he said. "If you're willing, I'd rather spend the night learning whatever you have to teach me about my new trade."

And Yirth laughed, a faint, dry, little sound that Sun Wolf reflected he was probably the first member of the male sex to have heard. "What I have to teach is meager enough," she said. "I have the learning, but my powers are very small."

"Will they increase when you yourself pass through the Trial?"

She hesitated, the indecision in her green eyes, the fear

robbing her of her years of experience, making her look again like a thin, bitter, ugly young girl—like the duckling in that rather comforting fable, who knew that she would never grow into a swan. "They should," she said at length. "And I will read and learn all that I can about it before I take the anzid myself, so that I may meet Altiokis as a proven wizard when Sheera and Tarrin agree that it is time to attack. And that must be soon. Altiokis has long suspected there is another person born with the powers of wizardry here in Mandrigyn; after the Trial, it will be harder to hide."

In the darkness, he heard her move, stepping to the narrow window that overlooked the slimy alley outside, the reflected light from the other houses that crowded the Little Island touching the hooked aquiline profile and the spider threads of silver in the dark masses of her hair as she turned back to face him once more. "As for the Trial itself, I think that my strength is sufficient to carry me through it alive," she went on. "For thirty years, since I came to my powers as a child, I have felt them in me, chafing and twisting at the walls that flesh and mind set against their exercise. I know they are strong—there have been times when I have felt like a woman in travail with a dragon's child, unable to give it birth."

She was silent again, only the ragged draw of her breath audible in the cool, herb-smelling darkness of the bare attic room. Seeing her clearly in the darkness, the Wolf could see also the girl that she had been, like a young tree girdled with steel as a sapling, warping a little more each day as it strove despairingly toward a destiny not permitted it—*And ugly*, he thought, *to boot*. He knew now that the limitations that beauty set upon a woman were far pleasanter, at least at the time, than the ones ugliness placed—and he knew from bitter personal memory how cruel the world could be to women who were not pleasing to men's eyes.

But he only said, "At least you knew why you were in pain. I never did."

"Knowing why only made it worse," she whispered.

"Maybe," the Wolf said, sitting up a little in the narrow bed and bracing his shoulders against the dry, smooth wood of the wall. "I'm not sure whether it would have been better to know I'd been robbed or to grow up trying to hide from everyone— particularly my father—the fact that I suspected that I was mad."

Against the reflected window lights, he saw her head turn

sharply and felt the touch of her green eyes on him. He wondered suddenly how long it had been between the time she had realized her own powers and the time she had found someone who understood what they were.

When she spoke again, her voice was quieter, and the edge of bitter mockery was gone from it, leaving it sweet in the darkness, like the sweetness of the smell of drying rosemary. "I should look to the Trial as a gate to freedom—freedom from all that I have been—even if it is only freedom to challenge Altiokis and die. But—I saw you when we brought you up out of the pit, Captain."

Then she turned away, covering her fear of pain with brusqueness, as the Wolf had seen warriors curse rather than weep when their bones were set. "Come. If you intend to learn tonight, we had best start."

Twenty-five years of hard soldiering had not given Sun Wolf much background in wizardry or love, but they had taught him discipline and the concentration to set aside physical weariness and apply himself to what must be done. As he worked under Yirth's guidance through the dark hours, he was constantly aware that it might be months or years before he found another teacher. *I will sleep*, he told himself, *when I get on the road*.

One of the first things that she taught him were the spells to hold back the need for sleep and rest and the drugs to reinforce them. He'd been familiar already with the drugs—most mercenaries were.

But this was only a beginning.

As with the body, there were exercises of the mind and spirit, without which large portions of wizardry would be impossible to comprehend, even for those born with its seeds within them. Those exercises she also taught him, in the shadowy dimness of that long workroom with its arcane charts, its age-worn books, and its phials of poisons and philters—things that in a year, or two years, or five years would come to fruition, if he meditated daily and practiced and learned the complexities of mathematics and music which were as much a part of wizardry as drugs and illusion. At one point, she stopped in her teaching and regarded him across the cluttered table, her long hands resting tranquilly among the diagrams that strewed its waxed surface.

"You are certainly the most cooperative student I have ever heard of," she commented. "At this point, I was in tears, arguing with my master. I hated the mathematics part."

He grinned ruefully and pushed the lank, sweat-damp strands of his hair back from his stubbled face. "Mathematics has always been a closed book to me," he admitted. "I know enough about trajectories to get a rock over a wall with a catapult, but this . . ." He gestured in amazement at the abstruse figures that covered the yellowed parchments. "I'm going to have to take a couple of hours and memorize it by rote, in the hopes that one day it will make sense to me. By the spirits of all my drunken ancestors, it sure doesn't now!"

She sat back, a wry expression on her craggy face. "For a warrior, you're certainly peaceable about accepting things on faith."

"I accept that you know more about it than I do," he told her. "In fact, that's exactly what made teaching those wildcats of Sheera's so easy. To teach men, I have to prove to them that I'm capable of whipping the daylights out of them—and I have to go on proving it. Women don't care." He shrugged. "That was the most surprising thing about it. Women are a pleasure to teach the arts of war."

Her white teeth glimmered again in a smile. "For the sake of your self-esteem I shall not pass that along to Sheera. But I tell you this also—it is a pleasure to teach this . . ." The spare movement of her hand took in not only the charts but the whole of the long room, the gold gleam of the book bindings in the brown shadows, the jungles of hanging plants, and the skeletal shapes of the instruments that read the stars. ". . . to a mind that has already grasped the concept of discipline. That is what I myself found hardest to learn."

It was the discipline of a warrior that carried him through that night. Toward morning, he snatched an hour or so of sleep, abovestairs, in the little whitewashed attic where Yirth had cared for so many exhausted mothers, but rest eluded him. When the witch descended the stairs to her workroom at dawn, she found him already up and dressed in the shabby, brown smock of Sheera's gardener, as still as stone over the mathematical exercises, memorizing their incomprehensible patterns.

Sheera came after sundown that evening. He could tell by the way she spoke to him that she had heard what had happened to him; when she thought he was not looking, he caught the glimpse of something in her eyes that was almost fear.

"Altiokis left for the Citadel this morning," she reported, settling wearily onto the carved X of a folding chair in Yirth's long study. She rubbed her eyes in a way that told the Wolf

that she had had hardly more sleep than he. He himself had
dozed a little in the afternoon, but always the pressure was
nagging at his mind—that he must learn, must absorb all that
he could, before he left this stern and clear-hearted teacher.
Yirth had spoken to him of what her own master Chilisirdin
had told her many years ago, and he knew that it might take
years of searching before he could find another wizard with
even Yirth's limited education to continue his training. And in
those years, Altiokis would be searching for him.

"According to Drypettis, the Dark Eagle has orders to remain with the troops here in Mandrigyn and hunt for you. The
gates of the city are double-guarded. There are far too many
for a couple of girls and a phial of laudanum to account for."

"I'll get out," Sun Wolf said.

Yirth raised one of her straight brows. "Illusion is a thing
that comes only with long study," she said. "This nonvisibility
I cannot do—I must look like someone, not no one. You can
elude the guards, if you move quietly and keep from drawing
attention to yourself. Once men see you, you cannot vanish.
But get through locked gates you cannot, without calling down
their eyes upon you."

"I'll leave at dawn, when they unlock the land gates."

"There'll be a horse waiting for you in the first woods,"
Sheera said. "There will be gold in the saddlebags . . ."

"Ten thousand pieces?" Sun Wolf inquired, with mild curiosity, and saw Sheera flush. "I'll let you owe me," he tem-
porized with a smile.

She hesitated, then rose from her chair and went around the
end of the table to lay her hands on his broad shoulders. "Captain, I want to say thank you—and, I'm sorry."

He grinned up at her. "Sheera, it has been far from plea-
surable to know you; but, like dying in the pit, it's something
I think I'm glad I did. Take care of my ladies for me."

"I will." Behind the graveness in those brown eyes, he could
read the same grim purpose that he had seen four months ago
in his tent below the walls of Melplith. But the wildness in
them had been tempered by experience and by the knowledge
of her own limitations. She bent gravely, to touch her lips to
his.

"Makes me sorry I never bothered to seduce you," he murmured and was pleased to see her bristle with her old rage.
"When are you going to hit the mines?"

"Two weeks," she replied, swallowing her angry words at

him with difficulty. "We'll send word to Lady Wrinshardin to start an insurrection in the Thanelands, and draw Altiokis out of his Citadel that way. By then, Yirth will have had time to go through the Great Trial herself and to recover from it. Tarrin . . ."

"You know, I'll always be sorry I never met Tarrin," Sun Wolf mused.

Sheera was touched. "He would have been honored . . ." she began.

"It isn't that. It's just that I've heard so much about his perfection, I'm curious to see if he really is seven feet tall and glows in the dark."

"You—" she flared, and he caught her drawn-back fist, laughing, and kissed her once again.

"I wish the poor bastard joy with you." He grinned. "Be careful, Sheera."

There was fog the next morning. It had begun to creep in from the sea during the night; the Wolf had seen Yirth sitting alone in the shadows of her study, surrounded by her herbs and her charts of the sky, stirring at the surface of the water in her ancient pottery bowl, watching as the liquid within grew gray and clouded. He had not bidden her good-by, not wanting to break her concentration and knowing that she would understand.

The Golden Gate loomed before him through the slaty darkness, like the bristling back of a sleeping dragon. Sun Wolf moved quietly from shadow to shadow, hearing and feeling around him the faint noises of the awakening city, wary as an animal going down to drink. Distantly, the lapping of the canals came to his ears and the far-off mewing of the gulls in the harbor.

He wondered if he would ever see any of these people again.

It was not something that had ever troubled him before; in twenty years, he had left so many cities behind! He wondered whether this was an effect of Starhawk's influence on him or simply that he was forty now instead of twenty; or because he was a solitary fugitive, with no idea of where he would go. Three days ago, from this street, he'd been able to look beyond the walls to the dark crags of the Tchard Mountains; they were hidden now in fog, and the Wizard King was within them. If Sheera's plan succeeded, he would be able to return to Mandrigyn eventually. If it did not—if she and her Tarrin met defeat and death—he would be hounded by Altiokis to the ends of the earth.

They would need a wizard on their side to emerge victorious.

Yirth's face returned to him, and the fear in her eyes as she'd said, "I saw you when they brought you up out of the pit." She had to want her power very badly, if she proved willing to seek it in the racking of her body and the lightless pits of her mind. He did not doubt that she would do it, but he understood her fears.

Would I go through that voluntarily, if I knew?

He didn't know.

Like a ghost, he drifted into the looming shadows of the turreted gates.

There were soldiers everywhere, and the gold of the torch-light within the passage under the overspanning gatehouse flashed on polished mail and leather. The great gates were still shut, barred, bolted, and studded with iron. A group of the Dark Eagle's mercenaries loitered around the winch that would raise the portcullis; others were dicing in an archway opposite, their gleaming steel breastplates catching the red firelight, sil-houetting them against the impenetrable dark beyond.

Sun Wolf melted himself back into the shadows of another of the numerous arches that supported the gatehouse overhead and waited. It wouldn't be long. Already he could hear the market carts assembling on the other side of the gates, bringing in produce from the countryside. It would be easy enough to drift out in the confusion.

And yet . . . The memory returned to him of the fight in the street, when the Dark Eagle had taken him, and of the illusion that had broken his concentration. In the heat of battle it took very little to break a defensive line; and once an army began to flee in panic, there was little hope of its rallying. Was that how Altiokis had defeated them, up at Iron Pass?

Would Sheera be able to handle that, even with Yirth at her side? She had the courage of a lioness, but she was inexpe-rienced—as inexperienced as Yirth would be against Altiokis' greater magic.

The red-haired slave boy in the prison came back to his thoughts, and the obscene thing that had raped the boy's mind. What of that?

It was Altiokis' doing that Sun Wolf would have to search the earth for someone to teach him to handle the powers he

had. If the women met defeat in the mines and the Citadel, it
was Altiokis who would pursue him.

Beside their bonfire, one of the soldiers cracked a rude joke
and got a general laugh. Outside the gates, farmers' voices
could be heard. The gray mists in the wide street behind were
paling. He thought of Starhawk, hunting for him somewhere,
thought of telling her that he was a warrior and her captain no
longer, but that he was a fugitive, neither wizard nor warrior,
doomed to wander.

He thought again of Altiokis.

Very softly, he turned and started back toward the streets
of the town.

Like the flare of a far-off explosion, amber light sprang into
view in the darkness of a pillared arch. Curiously hard-edged,
a glint of light fell like a round hand from there onto his
shoulder, and the Dark Eagle's voice said, "Good morning,
my barbarian."

The chief of Altiokis' mercenaries materialized from the
shadows. In one hand he held a sword; in the other, a mirror.

A faint, steely rattle sounded and men stepped from behind
pillars, from around the turrets and gargoyles, and from the
black pockets of shadow behind the columns of the gatehouse
stair. Flattened back into a niche, Sun Wolf found himself
facing a battery of arrows, the bows straining at full draw. He
let his sword hand fall empty to his side.

"No, no, by all means, draw your weapon," the Eagle chided.
"You can throw it here at my feet." When Sun Wolf did not
move, he added, "When you've lost enough blood to pass out,
we can always take it from you, I suppose. My lord Altiokis
will not be pleased to receive you in a damaged condition—
but believe me, my barbarian, he will receive you alive."

The blade clattered on the stone pavement. The Dark Eagle
snapped his fingers, and a man ran warily out to fetch it.

The mercenary captain flashed the mirror in the torchlight,
his eyes glinting pale and bright under the dark metal of his
helmet. "We were warned you'd grown trickier. You can fool
the eyes of a man, my friend, but not a piece of glass. Hold
your arms out to the sides, shoulder-high. If you touch the men
who are going to put the bracelets on you, you may find yourself
conducting your interview with my lord Altiokis from a stretcher
on the floor. So."

"Who told you I'd be here?" Sun Wolf asked quietly as the
irons were locked to his wrists. He shivered at their touch—

there were spells forged into the metal of the bracelets and into the five feet of chain that joined them.

The Dark Eagle laughed. "My dear Wolf—your secret is how you've acquired your wizard tricks, mine is how we learned where and when you would make your break. Ask your precious ancestors about it. You'll be seeing them soon, but not, I daresay, soon enough."

CHAPTER
— 19 —

STARHAWK HEARD THE HOOFBEATS OF THE CAVALCADE LONG before they emerged from the gray mists. She was in the open country of stubble fields, not far from the walls of Mandrigyn; there was but little cover beyond the fog itself. Still, they sounded to be in a hurry.

She scrambled down the dead and matted vines of the roadside ditch and curled herself half under a tangle of gray and web-spun ivy just above the brim of the ice-cold water. Yesterday the water in the ditches had been scummed with ice and every leaf rimmed with a white powder of frost, but the weather seemed to have turned. In a few more weeks it would be spring.

Pebbles thrown from the hooves of the horses clattered around her. She heard the brisk jingling of mail and the rattle of weapons and trappings. She estimated the force to be a largish squadron, between fifteen and twenty riders. Yesterday at the crossroads, where the wide trade road from the Bight Coast joined the Mandrigyn Road up to the Iron Pass, she'd found the unmistakable spoor of a huge force going from the Citadel to the city and the marks, not many hours old, of a smaller force returning. Yet this road was also marked with cart traffic, farmers taking vegetables to town, so at least the place wasn't under siege.

Starhawk lay with her head down under the wiry thicket of the vines, listening to the riders pass, and wondered what she would do when she reached Mandrigyn.

Seek out Sun Wolf? He had said he was dying.
Seek out Sheera Galernas?

May his ancestors help the poor bastard, Sun Wolf had said, *who falls afoul of her*.

The memory of the vision came back, the aching confusion of misery and despair and a weird, deep-seated peace. She had been right in her love for him, right to seek him, as, at the end, dying, he had sought her. But she had been too late— after months of journeying, she had missed him by less than a week.

And now he was dead.

She remembered his face, pain-ravaged and exhausted, and how warm the blood on his hands had been in contrast with the coldness of his flesh. What had happened to him in Mandrigyn?

Had Altiokis done that to him?

He said that he loved me.

She had tried to hate Fawnie for delaying her, but it had not been Fawn's fault. All she had done was what the Hawk herself had done—sought for the man she loved. That she had been injured doing so was only due to the difference in their training; that she had found another sort of happiness altogether was something that the Hawk could not pretend couldn't just as easily have happened to herself.

None of it changed the fact that she had been too late.

Anyog had lived for three days after the night of her vision, sinking gradually into deeper and deeper delirium. At first he had raved about the Hole, about Altiokis, about the spirit that dwelt in that sunless gap between worlds. Between tending him and hunting in the woods, she had had little time for other thought, or to wonder why she wanted to make this final conclusion to her quest.

When Anyog had died, she had buried him in the birch grove at the bottom of the valley, with tools she had found in the cell of the chapel's former guardian. Whether because of the old man's love for her, or because Sun Wolf's death had broken some last wall of resistance within her soul—or simply because, she thought without bitterness, she had, after all, grown soft—she had wept over Anyog's grave and had been unashamed of her tears. Tears might be a waste of time, she had thought, but she now had time; and the tears had been a medicine to her chilled soul.

The hoofbeats faded into the distance. Starhawk got to her feet, brushing the damp ivy from her buckskin breeches and from the quilted sleeves of her much-stained black coat. It only

remained for her to make her way to Mandrigyn and seek out
Sheera Galernas, to ask her why and particularly how she had
been able to carry off a full-grown and presumably protesting
captain of mercenaries—and what had become of him.

The woman in the marketplace from whom she asked directions looked askance at Starhawk's sword belt and brass-
buckled doublet, but directed her without comment to the house
of Sheera Galernas. It stood upon its own island, like so many
of the great townhouses of that checkerboard city; from the
mouth of the narrow street that debouched into the canal just
opposite it, Starhawk studied its inlaid marble facade. Carved
lattices of interlocking stone quatrefoils shaded the canalfront
arcades; red and purple silk banners, their bullion embroidery
gleaming wanly with the lifting of the morning's white mist,
made stripes of brilliant color against the black and white starkness of the stone. Two gondolas were already moored at the
foot of the black marble steps—a curious thing, the Hawk
thought, at so early an hour.
She followed the narrow wooden catwalk that formed a
footpath for a few dozen yards above the waters at the edge
of the canal, crossing eventually by a miniature camelback
bridge that led into the maze of alleys on the next islet. It was
difficult to maintain any kind of sense of direction here, for
the high walls of that crowded district cut her off from any
glimpse of the roofline of Sheera's house; but by dint of much
backtracking over tiny bridges and through the twisting streets,
she was eventually able to circle the grounds. From the catwalk
along the wall of the nearby church-owned public laundry, she
could look down into the grounds themselves and guessed that,
with so much waste space, Sheera Galernas must be rich indeed. Behind the house stretched elaborately laid-out gardens,
fallow and waiting for the rains to end, a big, boarded-up
orangery and a string of new, glass-roofed succession houses,
and a stable court and what looked like a pleasure pavilion or
a bathhouse, brave with pillars of colored porphyry.
It occurred to Starhawk that there were an unnatural number
of entrances to those grounds.
She glimpsed movement in an alleyway on an adjacent island and pressed herself back against the uneven brick of the
laundry's high wall. A stealthy figure descended the few steps
that led from the alley's mouth to the opaque green waters of
the canal and glanced quickly to the right and left. From where

she stood on the catwalk above, Starhawk could see the
woman—for it was a woman, wrapped in a dark cloak—go
to the cellar door of the last house on the alley and from it
produce a plank, which she laid across the canal to a disused-
looking postern door in Sheera's back wall. In spite of the
postern's dilapidated appearance, it did not seem to be locked,
nor, the Hawk noticed, did the hinges creak. The woman crossed,
pulled the plank after her, and shut the door.

Curious, Starhawk swung down the rickety flight of steps
and wound her way through the alleys to where the woman
had been. The cellar door wasn't locked; in the muddy-floored
room lay quite a few planks.

Intrigued, Starhawk returned to the mouth of the alley. It
led straight down into the dirty canal water, about two feet
below. The stones of the alley were uneven, slimy and offensive
with moss; she guessed this was the neighborhood dumping
ground for chamber pots. Leaning around the corner of the tall
house beside her, she could see the backs of all the houses
along the curve of the canal; women were laying out bedding
over the rails of makeshift balconies to air, and someone was
dumping a pan of dishwater from a kitchen doorstep directly
into the murk a few feet below. A couple of the houses had
little turrets, with long green smears of moss on the walls below
them to announce their function.

A quiet place, altogether, she thought, glancing back at the
deep-set little door in the wall. It wasn't the regular kitchen
entrance—that was visible down at the far end of the wall, a
double door and a kind of little step for deliverymen unloading
from gondolas.

The Hawk had another careful look around, then fetched a
plank from the cellar, as she had seen the furtive woman do.
It just reached from the pavement to the doorsill; Starhawk
realized that all these planks had been cut to the same length.
She drew her sword, took a final look around, and slipped
across.

The postern was unlocked. It opened directly onto a thicket
of laurel bushes, which masked it from the main house. There
was no one in sight.

Starhawk pulled in her plank and added it to the three that
already lay concealed under the laurels. The ground here was
trampled and grassless. As Ari would say, somebody had more
up the sleeve than the arm.

Well, of course Sheera was involved in a cause—meaning

a conspiracy. But whether she'd been able to involve Sun Wolf in it . . .

The Hawk moved soundlessly around the edge of the laurel thicket and stopped, startled by what she saw.

The gardens were empty, the brown, formal hedges marching in elaborate patterns away toward the distant terrace of the main house. But here someone had quite recently half built, half excavated, a pocket-sized wilderness in one corner of those formal beds, the rocks settled like the bones of the sleeping earth, waiting for their attendant vegetation.

Sun Wolf had laid out those rocks.

She knew it, recognized his style in the shaping of them, the lie of the colored fissure in the granite, and the latent tension between large shapes and small. How she knew it she was not sure—the aesthetics of rock gardening was a subject she knew only through him—but she was as certain of it as those who could look upon a painting or hear a tune and say "This was created by that person."

The warrior in her remarked, *He was here, then*, while some other part of her throbbed with a deep and unexpected ache, as if she had found his glove or his dagger.

And then, an instant later, an absurd throught crossed her mind: *I knew good gardeners were hard to find, but this . . . !*

She knew from working with him on the one at Wrynde that rock gardens like this were the work of days, sometimes weeks.

Steam billowed from the laundry quarters at the back of the house, drifting across the brown beds of the gardens. Voices came to her, like distant bird song.

A high, twittering voice insisted, "I've told you, he's learned all he wants to know! There's no danger! He's looking for men, and looking in the Thanelands . . ."

Among the bare white stems of the ornamental birch, Starhawk saw two people descending the terrace steps—a black-haired woman in purple and sables, with amethysts snagged in the dark curls that lay scattered across her shoulders, and a small, curiously childish shape pattering at her side, rattling with incongruous masses of heavy, jingling jewels, a king's ransom in bad taste.

The dark-haired woman she recognized at once as Sheera Galernas.

"We don't know that," Sheera said.

The smaller woman said, "We do! I do! I heard them talk

of it. Altiokis has no interest in questioning him. And Tarrin
says—"

"Tarrin doesn't know the situation here."

The little woman looked shocked. "But he does! You've
kept him informed . . ."

"For God's sake, Dru, that isn't the same as being here!"

The women passed through the door of the orangery. As it
shut behind them, Starhawk glimpsed other forms moving about
inside.

Who, she wondered, had Altiokis taken for questioning—
or not for questioning, as the case might be? The hoofbeats of
the passing cavalcade returned to her with new meaning. Greatly
interested, she slipped cautiously across the open space that
separated her from the orangery and glided along its wall until
she found an open window that let into a sort of potting shed
built out of one wall. It was empty. She found it a simple matter
to force the catch with her dagger and climb in unheard. The
women in the main, boarded-up section of the building were
talking far too intently to hear the small sounds of her feet.

Sun Wolf had been here. Looking about her in the gloom,
she was virtually certain of it. He had been here and had worked
here. She knew the way he habitually laid out things at his
workshop back in Wrynde too well to think that another could
have his same order of putting up those mysterious little medicines to succor ailing plants.

But—it made absolutely no sense. Holy Mother, had Sheera
really kidnapped him to do her gardening? And why—and
how, for that matter?—had he appeared to Starhawk in a dream,
and how and why had he died? Her hand tightened over the
worn hilt of her dagger. *That, at least, Sheera Galernas will
tell me. And if it was her doing . . .*

Starhawk stopped. She had far too much experience with
the motivations of sudden death to make an unequivocal threat,
even in the privacy of her mind. It was perfectly possible that
Sun Wolf had asked for the fate he got—and in fact, knowing
the Wolf as she did, more than likely.

She pressed her ear to the door.

A confusion of voices came to her, the high, strident twitter
of the little woman called Dru, insisting over and over again
that they were safe. Starhawk found a knothole in the door just
as a tiny, golden-haired lady snapped impatiently, "Oh, button
it, Dru!"

Dru swung around, blazing with self-righteous wrath. "You

dare speak that way to me—" she began furiously. Then she caught Sheera's disapproving eye and relapsed into red-faced and stifled silence.

Sheera said to another woman, "What about it, Amber Eyes?"

Starhawk had noticed her before, a slender girl of about Fawn's age, standing almost shyly in the circle of her big, dark-eyed friend's arm. But the moment she spoke, the Hawk realized that the helpless shyness was only an illusion—she was clearly the stronger of the partners.

She said, "It's true we don't know where Tarrin and the other leaders are working today. But Cobra and Crazyred have both been all over the mines, as I have, and we've all made maps. We can get you to the armories, to the passages up to the Outer Citadel, and to the storerooms where they keep the blasting powder. There's enough blasting powder to destroy half the Citadel, if it could be placed. It doesn't need magic to be ignited, just a slow match."

"What if he's talked already?" her friend demanded worriedly. "Altiokis might question him up at the Citadel—from what Dru told us, it's in the wizard's power to put him to what no man could stand. They could be lying in wait for us when we get there."

"I tell you—" Dru began in her high, hissing voice.

Then from the dark doorway of the potting room, Starhawk spoke. "If that's the case, you'd better chance it and strike now."

All eyes swiveled to her. The women were shocked into silence as she stepped forth from the shadows. To do them credit, they weren't frozen with astonishment—three of them were already moving to flank her as she emerged. Sheera Galernas was frowning at her, trying to place her, knowing they had met before.

Starhawk went on. "Waiting won't buy you anything if your friend breaks."

"We could get out of the city—" someone began.

A thin little woman in the dark robes of a nun asked, "Do you really believe Altiokis would not hound us over the face of the earth, once he knew who we were?"

Starhawk rested her hands on the buckle of her sword belt and surveyed the group quietly. "It isn't any of my affair, of course," she said, surprised at how easily she fell back into her habit of command, then accepting the way they listened to her, somehow knowing her for a commander. "I'm only here to speak to Sheera Galernas." From the tail of her eye, she saw Sheera startle as the memory returned. "But if your friend was the one who passed me under escort this morning, I'd say strike, if you think he has any kind of strength to hold out against questioning."

The little blonde murmured, "He has the strength."

"They won't reach the Citadel until after noon," the Hawk continued. "That gives you maybe an hour or two hours to gamble on whatever you plan to do. It all depends on how tough you think your friend is."

She saw their eyes, exchanging glances, questioning. As a rule, she had found that women vastly overestimated a man's stamina against torture, as men underestimated women's. That seemed to be the case here—none of them appeared to be in much doubt, except Sheera herself. To her, Starhawk said, "I won't trouble you now, if you're going into battle. But there's something you owe me to speak of when you're done."

Sheera's eyes met hers, and she nodded, understanding. But a taller woman, harsh-faced and ugly, who had stood in the shadows, spoke up. "He said there would be a woman coming to seek him." The voice was as low and soft as a rosewood flute, the green eyes like sea-light in the dimness. "You are she?"

There was no need to ask who "he" was. Starhawk said, "I am."

"And your name?"

"Starhawk."

There was a pause. "He has spoken of you," the beautiful voice said. "You are welcome. I am Yirth." She came forward and held out long slender hands. "He told me to tell you what became of him."

"I know what became of him," Starhawk replied grimly. On all sides of them, the women watched silently, amazed both at her presence and at the fact that this dark, lanky woman seemed to have expected her. To them, the exchange between Yirth and Starhawk must be cryptic, half intelligible; but none asked for an explanation. The tension in the room was too electric; they feared to break it.

Starhawk said, "I know that he died. What I want to know is how and why."

"No," Yirth said quietly. "He did not die. He is a wizard now."

Shock left Starhawk speechless. She could only stare at

Yirth in blank astonishment, scarcely aware that her surprise
was shared by all but a very few of the other women in the
room.

Yirth added, "And he is Altiokis' prisoner."

"And I don't think there is any question," Sheera put in,
her voice suddenly hard and cutting as a sword blade, "that
Altiokis' mercenaries knew where to look for him."

She swung around, her eyes going from face to face—
browned faces, darkened from exposure, some of them with
the bruises of training hidden under carefully applied cosmetics.
There were pretty faces, faces plain or homely, but none of
them weak, none of them afraid. "Starhawk is right," she said
quietly. "We must strike and strike now."

Drypettis caught her petaled sleeve. "Don't be a fool!" she
cried. "Do you know how many men there are in Grimscarp
now?"

"Fifteen hundred less," purred a red-haired woman in a
prostitute's thin, gaudy silks, "than there were a week ago."

"And Altiokis!" the little woman squeaked.

"And Altiokis," Sheera echoed. She turned back to Yirth,
who still stood at Starhawk's side. "Can you do it, Yirth? Can
you fight him?"

Yirth shook her head. "I can lead you through illusion,"
she said, "and to some degree protect you from the traps of
magic that are set to guard the ways to the Citadel from the
mines. But my wizardry is knowledge without the Great Power,
even as the captain's is Power without the knowledge of how
to use it. We are equally helpless before Altiokis' might, though
he is stronger than I. But as I see it, neither I nor any of us
has a choice. It is now or never, prepared or unprepared."

"Don't be fools!" Drypettis cried hysterically. "And you *are*
fools, if you let yourselves be stampeded this way! Altiokis
doesn't care about information. All he wants is Sun Wolf's
death! I know—I overheard Stirk and the mercenary captain
speak of it! If we rush in now, before Yirth has a chance to
gain the power she needs, before we can coordinate with Tarrin,
we will cast away everything!"

"And if we wait," Gilden lashed, "Sun Wolf is going to
die."

"He would have let the lot of us die!" Drypettis retorted,
her face suddenly mottled with red blotches of rage. "Even
those of you he made his sluts!"

Gilden's hand came up to strike her; but with a curiously

practiced neatness, an equally tiny lady standing behind Gilden caught her wrist before she could deliver the blow. Drypettis stood before her trembling, her face white now but for the spots of color that stood out like rouge on her delicate cheekbones.

In a cold voice, Sheera said, "He was brought here against his will, Dru. And as for the rest, that is hardly your affair."

The little woman whirled on her in a hurricane of jangling metal and tangled veils. "It *is* my affair!" she cried, her brown eyes blazing with shame and rage. "It is exactly my affair! How is the good and the decent in this city to triumph, if it debases itself to the level of its enemies to defeat them? How are we to face the men whom we wish to free, if we make trollops of ourselves to free them? That is precisely what this captain of ours has done. He has debased us all. Debased us? Seduced us into debasing ourselves, rather, with this lure of success at any cost! We should have suffered the evils that befell us and learned to work around them, before we turned ourselves into coarse and dirty soldiers like this—this—" Her jerking hand waved violently toward the startled and silent Starhawk. "—this camp follower of his!"

Her tone changed, became wheedling. "You are worthy of the Prince, Sheera, worthy to wed the King of Mandrigyn and to be its Queen. And I would have supported you in this, given everything to you for it—my wealth and the honor of the most ancient House in the city! I would have given you my life, gladly. But to have given these, only to see you turn them and the cause itself over to such a man as that—to transform an ideal of decency and self-sacrifice into a base, athletic exercise in brute muscle and sneakiness—"

Sheera strode forward, caught the hysterical woman's shoulders in powerful hands, and shook her with terrible violence. All the ridiculous jewelry jangled and rattled, catching in the sudden tumble of unraveled brown hair. She shook her until they were both breathless, her eyes burning with fury; then she said, "You told them."

"I did it for your sake!" Drypettis screeched. "I have seen what one man's influence can do—how far one man's influence can defile everything that he touches! You are worthy—"

"Be quiet," Sheera said softly. "And sit down."

Drypettis obeyed, staring up at her in silence, tears of fury pouring down her round, red-stained cheeks. Watching their faces, Starhawk was conscious of that curiously concentrated quality to Drypettis' gaze, as if Sheera and Sheera alone had any reality for her, as if she were literally unaware that she had enacted a lovers' quarrel in the presence of some fifty other people. For her, they did not exist. Only Sheera existed— perhaps only Sheera ever had.

Very slowly and quietly, Sheera said, "Drypettis, I don't know whether or not you ever wanted yourself to be queen of Mandrigyn, rather than me, as the ancient lineage of your House might qualify you to be. I never questioned your loyalty to me, or your loyalty to my cause."

"I was never disloyal to you," Drypettis whispered in a thin voice, like the sound of a crack running through glass. "It was all for you—to purge the cause of the evil in it that could destroy it and you. To make it pure again, as it was before that barbarian came."

"Or to get rid of a man of whom you were jealous?" Sheera's hands tightened over the slender shoulders. "A man who took it away from being your cause, operated by your money and your influence, and threw it open to all who were willing to fight for it, no matter how rough their origins, how crass their motives, or how inelegant and dirty their methods might be? A man who changed the whole game from something that was bought to something that was done? A man who put commoners on the same level with yourself? Who treated you like a potential soldier instead of a lady? Is that why?" she asked, her voice low and harsh. "Or do you even know?"

Drypettis' face seemed to soften and melt like wax with grief, the exquisite brown eyes growing huge in the puckering flesh. Then she crumpled forward, her face buried in her hands, sobbing bitterly. The faint, silvery light from the high windows danced like expensive glitter over the incongruous riot of ornaments strewn through her hair. "He has done this to you," she keened. "He has made you like him, thinking only of victory, no matter how dishonorable you become in the process."

Sheera straightened up, her mouth and nostrils white, as if with sickness. "Defeat will only make us dead," she said, "not honorable. I will never say anything to anyone about what has happened here, and no one else in this room ever will, either; not even to one another. That's not an order," she added, looking about her at the stunned, silent circle of women. "That's a request, from a friend, that I hope you will honor." She turned back to the bowed form of Drypettis, now rocking back and forth in the straight-backed chair where she herself had sat, during that first meeting in the orangery, the night Sun Wolf had come to Mandrigyn. "I will never speak of this," she repeated, "but I do not ever want to see you again."

Her face still hidden in her hands, Drypettis got slowly to her feet. The women made way for her as she stumbled from the room; through the orangery door, they could see the colors of her clothes, a gaudy fluttering of whalebone and panniers, veils and jewels, against the liver-colored earth of the garden, until she vanished into the shadows of the house.

Sheera watched, her face white and tears glittering like beads of glass upon her wind-burned cheeks; the grief in her eyes was like that on the face of Drypettis, the grief of one who had lost a close friend. At her sides, her sword-bruised hands were clenched, the knuckles white under the brown of the skin.

Not what she needed, Starhawk thought dryly, *with her first battle before her*; and if for nothing else, she cursed the woman for that selfishness.

That was first; and then the anger came—anger at the petty jealousy of Drypettis, at her own slow realization that the man whose capabilities to resist torture they had been speaking of was, in fact, the Wolf himself, still alive—but in horrible danger. She had missed him by hours. He had passed within a dozen feet of her as she lay hiding in the roadside ditch, the stones of his horse's hooves showering her with pebbles . . .

He was alive! Whatever else had happened to him, would happen to him, he was alive now, and that knowledge went through her like a living heat, kindling both blood and spirit.

But, with her customary calm, she turned to the woman beside her, the woman who still gazed, with her jaw set, out into the now-empty garden, grief and the bitterness of betrayal marked onto her face like a careless thumbprint on cooling bronze. A sister in the fellowship of arms.

The women around them were silent, not knowing what to say or how to speak of that betrayal.

It was Starhawk who broke the silence, her natural habit of command laying the course for all the others to follow. Sheera's grief was her own; Starhawk understood, and was the first of them not to speak of it. She laid a hand on the woman's shoulder and asked in her most businesslike voice, "How soon can your ladies be ready to march?"

CHAPTER
—— 20 ——

*I*F WHAT LADY WRINSHARDIN HAD SAID WAS TRUE—AND SUN Wolf could think of no reason for her to have lied—the fortress of the Thanes of Grimscarp had once stood at the base of that rocky and forbidding knee of stone which thrust out of the mountain above the Iron Pass. The siegecraft that had been bred into his bones picked out the place, even as the Dark Eagle and his men took him past it—a weed-grown rubble of stones, just past where the road divided. There was no signpost at the fork, but Amber Eyes and her girls had told him that the right-hand way went up to the southward entrances of the mines below the Citadel, then wound around the base of the mountain to the main, western entrances above Altiokis' administrative center at Racken Scrag; the left-hand way twisted up the rock face, toward the Citadel itself.

Weary from two days with little sleep and from half a day's hard ride up the rocky Iron Pass, his wrists chafed and raw from the weight of some thirty pounds of iron chain, Sun Wolf looked up through the murk of low-lying cloud at the Citadel, where the Wizard King awaited him, and wondered why anyone in his right mind would have made the place the center of his realm.

There was the legend Lady Wrinshardin had quoted about the stone hut that Altiokis had raised in a single night—the stone hut that was supposed to be still standing, the buried nucleus of the Citadel's inner core. But why Altiokis had chosen to do so made no sense to the Wolf, unless, as he had begun to suspect, the Wizard King were mad. Perhaps he had built the Citadel in such an impossible, inaccessible place simply to show that he could. Perhaps he had put it here so that no city could grow up around his walls; Racken Scrag perforce lay on the other side of the mountain.

The Gods knew, the place was defensible enough. The impossible road was overlooked at every turning by overhanging cliffs; if Yirth were right about Altiokis' powers of far-seeing, he would be able to detect any force coming up that road, long before it got within sight of the Citadel, and bury it under avalanches of stone or landslides of burning wood. But when they reached the narrow, rocky valley before the Citadel's main gate, Sun Wolf understood why it was cheaper and simpler to haul the food for the legions up through the mines, for here Altiokis' fears had excelled themselves.

Most of the works in the valley were new, Sun Wolf judged; with the expansion of his empire, the Wizard King had evidently grown more and more uneasy. The Citadel of Grimscarp had originally been built between the cliff edge that looked northward over the wastes of the Tchard Mountains and a great spur or rock that cut it off from the rest of the Scarp on which it stood; its main entrance had tunneled straight through this unscalable knee of rock. Now the floor of the valley below the gate had been cut with giant pits, like a series of dry moats; slave gangs were still at work carving out the nearer ones as the Dark Eagle and his party emerged from between the dark watchtowers that overhung the little pass into the vale. While they paused to breathe the horses after the climb, Sun Wolf could see that the rock and earth within these long moats were charred. If an enemy managed to bridge them—if any enemy could get bridges up that winding road—the ditches could be floored with some flammable substance and ignited at a distance by the magic of the Wizard King.

They were bridged now by drawbridges of wood and stone, things that could easily be torn down or destroyed. The bridges did not lie in a direct line with the gate, which was cut directly into the cliff face at the other side, without turrets or outworks. The Wolf knew instinctively that it was the kind of gate that could be concealed with illusion; if Altiokis willed it, travelers to that Citadel would see nothing but the stark and treeless gray rock of the Scarp as they reached the head of the road.

He was coming to understand how a man such as the Wizard King had built his empire, between unlimited wealth and animal cunning, between hired strength and the dark webs of his power.

The men who held the reins of Sun Wolf's horse led him on, down the slope toward the bridges and the iron-toothed, forbidding gate. The hooves of the horses echoed weirdly in the smooth stone of the tunnel walls. Guards in black armor held up smoky torches to look at them. The Dark Eagle repeated passwords with a faint air of impatience and led them onward. The tunnel itself reeked with evil; its stone walls seemed to drip horror. The air there was fraught with latent magic that could be turned into illusions of unspeakable fear. Great gates led into wide, downward-sloping ways, the lines of torches along the walls fading into blackness at the end. The warm breath that rose from these tunnels stank of muddy rock, of illusion, and of the glittering, nameless magic of utter dread. It was as if Altiokis' power had been spread throughout his Citadel, as if his mind permeated the tunnels, the darkness, and the stone.

Sun Wolf whispered, almost unaware that he spoke aloud, "How can he spread himself so thin?"

The Dark Eagle's head snapped around. "What?"

There were no words to express it to someone not mageborn; it was a concept impossible to describe. The closest the Wolf could come to it was to say, "His spirit is everywhere here."

White teeth flashed in the gloom. "Ah. You've felt that, have you?"

The Wolf could see that the mercenary captain thought that he spoke in admiration, or in awe. He shook his head impatiently. "It's everywhere, but it isn't in himself. He's put part of his power in the rocks, in the air, in the illusions at the bottom of the mine shafts—but he has to keep it all up. He has to hold it together somehow, and—how can there be anything left back at the center of him, the key of his being, to hold it with?"

The Dark Eagle's smile faded; that round, swarthy countenance grew thoughtful; in the darkness, the blue eyes seemed very bright. "Gilgath, Altiokis' Commander of the Citadel, has said that my lord has been slipping—he's been with Altiokis far longer than I." His voice was low, excluding even the men who rode about them. "I never believed it until about two years ago—and what you say makes sense." He shrugged, and that wary look left his face. "But even so, my barbarian," he continued, as slaves came to take their horses, and they passed through the courtyards of the heavily defended Outer Citadel, "he has power enough to crush his enemies to dust—and money enough to pay his friends."

Other guards surrounded them, men and a few women in the bright panoplies of the mercenary troops. They were escorted through the courts and gateways of the Outer Citadel, up to the massive gatehouse that loomed against the sky, guarding the way into the Inner Citadel. The Dark Eagle strode now at Sun Wolf's side, the chain mail of his shirt jingling, the gilded spike that protruded through the dark, fluttering veils of his helmet crests flashing in the wan daylight.

"Wait until you come into the Inner Citadel, if you think his power has thinned."

They entered the darkness of the gatehouse, two men holding the chain that joined Sun Wolf's wrists, the rest of the troop walking with drawn swords behind him. All the while the Wolf was concentrating, his mind calm and alert as in battle, waiting for his chance to escape and reviewing the way down the mountain.

Daylight blazed ahead. Like a huge mouth, a gate opened around them. As they stepped from the dense shadows, Sun Wolf saw that it led onto a kind of causeway that spanned the long, stone-walled ditch separating the Outer Citadel from the Inner. At the center, the causeway was broken by a railless drawbridge. The pit itself crawled with nuuwa.

In spite of the day's cold, the carrion stink of them rose in a suffocating wave. Halfway across the drawbridge itself, the Wolf stopped. Turning, he saw that the Dark Eagle had his hand on his sword hilt. "Don't try it," the mercenary said quietly. "Believe me, if I went over, I guarantee that you'd go, too."

"Would it make that much difference?"

The Dark Eagle cocked a sardonic eyebrow. "That depends on what you think your chances of escaping from the Inner Citadel are."

Below them, the nuuwa had begun to gather, their grunting ululations shattering the air. Sun Wolf glanced at the men holding his chain, then back at the Eagle. He could see that the sheer wall of the Inner Citadel was broken by two gates, one fairly close and one several hundred feet away, with steps leading down into the pit of the nuuwa, plus the heavily guarded gate on their own level that let onto the causeway. There were gates into the pit from the Outer Citadel as well. It was a good bet that those were all heavily barred.

It was a gamble—to die horribly now, or to risk an uglier fate against an almost nonexistent chance of escape.

Compared with this, he thought bitterly as he moved off again toward the looming maw of the Inner Citadel's gates, the choice Sheera had given him on the ship appeared monumental in its opportunities. But he would not give up when the chance remained to play for time.

The nuuwa's screams followed them, like derisive jeers.

"You'll be down there soon enough," the Dark Eagle remarked at his elbow. "It's a pity, for no one knows as well as I how fine a soldier you are, my barbarian. But I know that's what my lord Wizard does with those who go against him. And after that thing gets through gnawing your brains out, you won't much care about the accommodations."

Sun Wolf glanced back at him. "What is it?" he asked. "What are those—those flame-things? Does he create them?"

The mercenary captain frowned, as if gauging the reasons for the question and how much he would give away in his answer. Then he shook his head. "I don't know. There's a— a darkness in the room at the bottom of the Citadel, a cold. They come out of that darkness; usually one or two, but sometimes in flocks. Other times there'll be days, weeks, with nothing. He himself won't go into the room—I think he fears them as much as anyone else does. He can't command them as he does the nuuwa."

"Can he command the darkness they come from?"

The Dark Eagle paused in his stride, those swooping black brows drawing together beneath the crested helmet rim. But all he said was, "You have changed, my barbarian, since we rode together in the East."

The black doors of the Inner Citadel opened. Its shadows swallowed them.

The dread of the place, the eerie terror that permeated the very air, struck Sun Wolf like a blow in the face as he crossed the threshold. Like a dog that would not pass the door of a haunted room, he stopped, his breath catching in his lungs; the men dragged him through by the chain on his wrists, but he could see that their faces, too, were wet with sweat. Fear filled the shadowy maze of tunnels and guardrooms on the lower level of the Citadel, as if a species of gas had been spread upon the air; the men who surrounded him with a hedge of drawn swords looked nervously about them, as if they were not certain in which direction the danger lay. Even the Dark Eagle's eyes darted from shadow to shadow, the only restlessness in his still face.

But more than the fear, Sun Wolf could feel the power there, cold and almost visible, like an iridescent fog. It seemed to cling to the very walls, as it had pervaded the tunnel of the gate—a strength greater than that of Altiokis, all-pervasive and yet tangible. He felt that, if he only knew how, he could have gathered it together in his hands.

They ascended a stair and passed through a guarded door. It shut behind them, and Sun Wolf looked around him in sudden, utter amazement at the upper levels of the tower, the inner heart of the Citadel of Altiokis, the dwelling place of the greatest wizard on the face of the earth.

Quite factually, Sun Wolf said, "I've seen better taste in whorehouses."

The Dark Eagle laughed, his teeth and eyes bright in his swarthy face. "But not more expensive materials, I daresay," he commented and flicked with a fingernail the gold that sheathed the inner side of the great doors. "A house, as my lord Wizard is fond of saying, fit for a man to live in."

Sun Wolf's eyes traveled slowly from the jeweled garlands that embroidered the ivory panels of the ceiling, down slender columns of pink porphyry and polished green malachite twined with golden serpents, to the tastelessly pornographic statues in ebony, alabaster, and agate that stood between them. Gilding was spread like butter over everything; the air was larded with the scent of patchouli and roses.

"A man, maybe," he said slowly, realizing it was only a gross exaggeration of the kind of opulence he would have gone in for himself, not too many months ago. Then he understood what had shocked him in his soul about the place and about all the fortress of the Wizard King. "But not the greatest of the wizards; not the only wizard left on the face of the earth, damn it." He looked back at the Dark Eagle, wondering why the man did not understand. "This is obscene."

The captain chuckled. "Oh, come now, Wolf." He gestured at the shamelessly posturing statues. "You're getting squeamish in your old age. You've seen worse than this in the cathouses in Kwest Mralwe—the most expensive ones, that is."

"I don't mean that," the Wolf said. He looked around him again, at the gilded archways, the embroidered hangings, and the bronze lampstands on which burned not flames, but round, glowing bubbles of pure light. In his mind, he was comparing the garish waste with Yirth's shadowy workroom, with its worn and well-cared-for books, its delicate instruments of brass and crystal, and its dry, muted scent of medicinal herbs. "He is deathless, he is powerful; he has command over magic that I would trade my soul for. He can have anything he wants. And he chooses this—trash."

The Dark Eagle cocked an amused eyebrow up at the Wolf and signaled his men. They jerked on the chain and rattled their swords, leading Sun Wolf on through the wide, softly lighted halls of the upper levels, their feet scuffing over silken rugs or whispering over carved jade tiles. "I remember you almost cut my throat fighting over trash very much like this when we looted the palace at Thardin," he reminded the Wolf with a grin.

Sun Wolf remembered it. He could not explain that that had been before the pit and the ordeal of the anzid; he could not explain, could not make the Eagle understand, the monstrousness of what Altiokis was. He only said, "How could a mind that trivial achieve this kind of power?"

The Dark Eagle laughed. "Whoa! Teach him a few tricks and he knows all about wizardry and power, does he?"

Sun Wolf was silent. He could not say how he knew what he knew, or why it seemed inconceivable to him that a man with a mind whose greatest ambitions rose no higher than dirty statues and silk rugs could have gained the power to become deathless, could have made himself the last, most powerful wizard on the earth. He understood, then, Yirth's anger at his frightened rejection of his power; he felt it reflected in his own outrage at a man who would not only so waste his own vast potential but destroy everyone else's as well.

Doors of white jade and crystal swung open. The room beyond them was black—black marble floor and walls, pillars of black marble supporting a vaulted ceiling of shadow. A ball of pale bluish light hung over the head of the man who overflowed the huge chair of carved ebony between the columns at the far end of the room, and the light picked out the details of the sculpted dragons and gargoyles, of the writhing sea life and shining insects, that covered the chair, the pillars, and the wall. The incense-reeking darkness seemed filled with magic; but with a curious clarity of the senses, Sun Wolf saw how flawed it was, like a prostitute's makeup seen in the light of day. Whatever Altiokis had been, as the Dark Eagle had said, he was slipping now. Having destroyed everyone else's power, he was letting his own run to seed as well.

Looking at him as he squatted, obscenely gross, in his ebony chair, for a moment the Wolf felt, not fear, but angry disgust. Not even unlimited evil could give this man dignity. Sun Wolf's captors pushed him forward until he stood alone before the Wizard King, his shoulders dragged down by the weight of his chains.

Altiokis belched and scratched his jewel-encrusted belly. "So," he said, in a voice thick with brandy, "you think the palace of Altiokis, the greatest prince this world has known, looks like a whorehouse?"

His wizard's senses had spread throughout that tawdry palace; he had heard every word that they had said. The Dark Eagle looked frightened, but Sun Wolf knew how it was done, though he himself could not do it. He only looked at the Wizard King, trying to understand what unlimited life, unlimited power, and unlimited boredom had done to this man, this last and most powerful wizard.

"You poor ass, did you really think you could get away from me that easily?" Altiokis asked. "Did you really have any idea of what you'd be up against when you accepted the commission of that fool, whatever his name was—the man who hired you? One of the Thanes, I think we said. Not that it matters, of course. I know who my enemies are. We'll have them gathered in . . ."

The Dark Eagle's bright blue eyes widened with alarm. "My lord, we don't know—"

"Oh, be silent," Altiokis snapped pettishly. "Cowards—I am surrounded by cowards."

"My lord," the Dark Eagle grated, "if you arrest without proof, there'll be trouble among the Thanes . . ."

"Oh, there's always trouble among the Thanes," the Wizard King retorted angrily. "And there always has been—we needed only the excuse to put them down. Let them come against me—if they dare. I will crush them . . ." The dark, little eyes glittered unnaturally bright in the gloom. ". . . as I will crush this slave."

He had risen from his chair, his eyes holding Sun Wolf's, and the Wolf saw in the wizard what had struck him before. There was very little that was human left of the man. The fire within was eating it away, his soul literally rotting, like the minds of the nuuwa. Like them, the Wolf realized, Altiokis existed almost solely to devour.

Sun Wolf fell back a step as the Wizard King raised the staff with its evil, gleaming head. At a distance of several feet, he could already feel the searing pain that radiated like waves of heat from the metal. Altiokis raised it, and the Wolf retreated until he felt the sword points of the guards press his back.

"Are you stupid," the Wizard King whispered, "or only a nerveless animal? Or don't you believe what could happen to you here?"

"I believe you," Sun Wolf said, keeping a wary eye on the staff, which hovered a foot or so in front of his throat. His voice was a dry rasp, the only sound in that hushed darkness of perfume and sweat. "I just don't believe that anything I can say will stop you from doing what you choose."

It was as polite a way as any he could think of to say that he made it a policy never to argue with a crazy man.

A sneer contorted the greasy face. "So it has wisdom, after all," the wizard said. "Pity you did not exercise it sooner. I have lived longer than you know. I am versed in the art of crushing the soul from the body, while leaving the brain time for—reflection. I could put the blood worms on you, until a month from now you would be nothing but a crawling mass of maggots, begging me for the mercy of death. Or I could blind and cripple you with drugs and find a job for you hauling bath water for my mercenaries—eh? Or I could wall you into a stone room, with only a cup of water, and that water filled with anzid, and leave you to choose between slow death from poison and slower from thirst."

Sun Wolf fought to keep his expression impassive, knowing full well that the fat man had both the power and the inclination to mete out any one of those fates, merely for the entertainment of seeing him die. But, sickened as he was by horror, two things remained very clear in the back of his brain.

The first was that Altiokis had never passed the Great Trial. He clearly had no idea that anzid was anything other than a particularly loathsome poison. And that meant that he had derived his power from some other source.

It would explain some things, the Wolf thought, his mind struggling to grasp that awareness. The power that pervaded the lower level of the tower and that filled the mines was then not entirely from Altiokis' attenuated personality. It was something else, something foul and filthy, not like Yirth's academic

sorcery, nor what the Wolf felt of the wild magic that seemed
to fill his own soul. Was the power only channeled through
the Wizard King from the darkness that the Eagle had spoken
of, the darkness that dwelt in the innermost room of the tower?
A power that had no ambitions, but that Altiokis had seized
upon to fulfill his own?

The second thing Sun Wolf realized was that, like a cruel
child, Altiokis was simply telling him this, not to learn any
information, but in order to see him break. He knew from his
own experience that a screaming victim was more satisfactory
to watch. He did not doubt for a moment that they would get
down to the screaming sooner or later, but he was damned to
the Cold Hells if he'd give the Wizard King that pleasure now.

Altiokis' face changed. "Or I could give you worse," he
snarled. He snapped his fingers for the Dark Eagle and his
men. "Downstairs," he ordered. "With me."

The mercenaries closed in around Sun Wolf, dragging at
his wrist chains, thrusting from behind with their swords. A
door opened in the wall, where no door had been; the blue
brimfire that floated over Altiokis' head illuminated the first
steps of a stair that curved down into darkness. The Wolf balked
in sudden terror at the power, the evil, that rose like a nauseating
stench from the pit below. The blackness seemed filled with
an alien, hideous chill, like that from the demons he had seen
in the marshes of his childhood—a sensation of seeing something that had risen from unknowable gulfs of nothingness, a
sensing of something that was not of this earth.

Someone shoved a blade against his ribs, pushing him through
the door. The soldiers seemed unaware of what lay below; they
could not know what he knew and still be willing to go that
way themselves. He almost turned to fight them in the doorway,
but Altiokis reached forward with his staff and used the glowing
head of it to drive the Wolf forward down the stairs. The men
surrounded him again, and the eldritch cold rose about them
as they descended.

The descent was less far than he had thought. The stair
made one circle, then leveled out; the floor, he saw, was rock
and dirt. They must be at ground level, at what had been the
top of the crag, close to the cliff's edge. At the end of the
short, lightless vault of the hallway was a small door. Even as
his soul shrank from it, he thought, *I have done this before.*

The room beyond was like the one Derroug Dru had shown
him in the prison below the Records Office in Mandrigyn. It

was small and dank, furnished with a huge, carved chair whose black velvet cushions boasted bullion tassels. The white glow of the witchlight gleamed oilily on the wall of glass before the chair. The only difference from that other chamber was that there was a door beside the wide window that looked into darkness.

Something like a restless flake of fire moved in that dark beyond the glass.

Sun Wolf had known this was coming to him, all the long road up the mountain. In a way, he had known it since Derroug Dru had first shown the abominations that Altiokis had given him, in the cell beneath the Records Offices. Horror went through the Wolf like a sword of ice; horror and despair and the terrified consciousness that in that room, not in the fat man chuckling throatily beside him, lay the centerpoint of the evil power that pervaded the Citadel. Whatever was in there, it was the source, not only of the creatures that turned men into nuuwa, but of the power that had let Altiokis become the swollen and abominable thing that he was.

Behind the glass, the bright flake of fire zagged idly in the air, leaving a thin fire trail in the stygian dark. It was waiting for him, waiting to devour his brain, to make him one of the mewing, slobbering things that were filled, like the dead stones of the Citadel, with Altiokis' perverted will.

Swords pressed into Sun Wolf's back, forcing him toward the narrow door. All of his senses seemed to have dulled and concentrated; he was conscious of no sound but the frantic hammering of his own heart and of no sensation but the cold of sweat pouring down his face and breast and arms. The sharpness of the steel was driving him forward. His vision had shrunk to that idle flake of fire, to the dark door, triple-barred with iron, and to the hands of the men unbarring it.

Cold and evil seemed to flow forth from the black slot of the opening. With curious, instantaneous clarity, he saw the round stone walls of Altiokis' original hut, the weeds that lay dead and tangled about the edges, and the scuffed, fouled dirt within. But all that was peripheral to the awareness of that black pit at the center, a boundaryless, anomalous, and utterly hideous vortex of absolute darkness that seemed to open in the air of the room's center. It was a Hole, a gap of nothingness that led into a universe beyond the ken of humankind. Through it flowed the power that filled the Citadel, filled the nuuwa, and filled Altiokis' corrupted, deathless flesh and rotting, brain.

But worse than the awareness of the power was the knowledge of the mind of the Entity that lived within the Hole, of the Thing that was trapped there, its thoughts reaching out to him, as shocking as ice water flowing over his naked brain.

Not human, nor demon . . . demons were of this world, and quite ordinary and comforting compared with that ice-cold, streaming black fire. Yet it was alive, and it reached to fill him.

Hands thrust him, unresisting, forward to the threshold of that tiny room. Unaware that he spoke aloud, he said, "It's alive . . ." And in the last second, as the guards shoved him in, he turned his head, meeting Altiokis' startled, dilating eyes with a sudden knowledge of where he had seen that Thing before. He said, "It gave you your power."

The Wizard King was on his feet, shrieking. "Bring him out of there! Shut the door!" His voice was frenzied, almost in panic.

The guards wavered, uncertain whether they had heard aright. The Dark Eagle grabbed Sun Wolf by the arm and pulled him backward, slamming the door to with a kick; Sun Wolf staggered, as if he had been released from a chain that held him upright, and found there was no strength left in him. He clutched the door bolts for support.

Altiokis was screaming, "Get him out of here! Get him away from here! He sees it! He's a wizard! Get him away!"

"Him?" the Eagle said, rather unwisely. "He's no wizard, my lord . . ."

Altiokis strode forward, swinging his staff to knock Sun Wolf's hands from the door bolts, as if he feared the Wolf would throw the door open and fling himself inside. Ignoring his captain of mercenaries, Altiokis clutched with his fat, jeweled hands at the grubby rags of what remained of Sun Wolf's tunic, his face white with hatred and fear.

"Did you see it?" he demanded in a stinking blast of liquor and rich food.

Exhausted, leaning against the stone wall at his back for support, Sun Wolf whispered, "Yes, I did. I see it now, in your eyes."

"It might choose to call another wizard," the fat man gasped hoarsely, as if he had not heard. "It could give him its power, if he were lucky, as I was lucky . . ."

"I wouldn't touch that power!" the Wolf cried, the thought

more sickening to him than the horror of that flake of fire boring steadily through his eye.

Again the Wizard King appeared not to have heard him. "It could even give him immortality." The black, lifeless eyes stared at Sun Wolf, desperate with jealousy and terror. Then Altiokis whirled back to his guards, screaming, "Get him out of here! Throw him to the nuuwa! Get him out!"

Like the tug of a fine wire embedded in his flesh, Sun Wolf felt the touch of that black Entity in the Hole, whispering to his brain.

Furiously, he thrust it aside, more frightened of it than of anything he had yet seen, in the Citadel of Altiokis or out of it. He fought like a tiger as they half dragged, half carried him along the maze of corridors to where a shallow flight of steps led downward to a broad double door. Altiokis strode at their heels, screaming incoherently, reviling the Eagle for bringing this upon him, and cursing his own means of divination that had not shown him this new threat. One of the guards ran ahead to peer through the judas in the door, and the faint yellow bar of light from the westering sun picked out the scars on his face as he looked. He called, "There are few of them out there now, me lord. They're mostly gone in their dens."

"Open their dens, then!" the Wizard King shrieked in a paroxysm of rage. "And do it quickly, before I throw you out to keep him company!"

The man darted off, his footfalls ringing on the stone of the passageway. Sun Wolf twisted against the hands that gripped him, but far too many men were holding him to give him purchase to fight. The doors at the bottom of the steps were flung open, and sunlight struck him as the Dark Eagle shouted a command. He was flung bodily down the steps, the harsh granite of them tearing at and bruising his flesh as he rolled.

The filthy reek of the nuuwa was all around him. As he heard the doors clang shut above him, the shrill howls began to echo from all sides. He saw that he was in the long ditch between the inner and outer walls. From various points in the shade of the looming wall, a dozen nuuwa and two or three of the apelike ugie-beasts were lolloping toward him, heads lolling, dripping mouths gaping to slash.

Sun Wolf knew already that there was no further hope of escape. The walls of the ditch were too steep to climb. It was only a matter of time before he would be overpowered, torn apart, and eaten alive. He flung himself back up the few steps to where the embrasure of the door made a kind of hollow in the bald face of the wall, taking advantage of the only cover in sight. He put his back to the massive, brass-bound wood, gathered the five feet of chain that joined his manacled hands, and swung at the first of the things that hurled itself upon him. Brains and blood splattered from the burst skull. He swung again, slashing, the heavy chain whining through the screaming, stinking air. Anything to buy time—minutes, seconds even.

The chain, close to thirty pounds of swinging iron, connected again, flinging the creature that it hit back against two of its fellows. He brained one of them while they were fighting each other; the remaining monstrosities turned on him, spitting mouthfuls of rotted flesh, and he slashed, swinging desperately, keeping them off him as long as he could, praying to his ancestors to do something, anything . . .

You can control them, that black slip of fire whispered in his brain. *Turn them aside. Make them do your bidding*.

Chain connected with flesh. His wrists were scraped raw from the iron, and the smell of the blood was driving the nuuwa to madness. He could feel himself tiring, instant by instant, and knew to within a moment how long his strength would last. All the while, the thought of the Entity he had seen, that black intelligence glimpsed in the Hole and in the Wizard King's possessed eyes, whispered to him the promise of the life that it could give him.

The world had narrowed, containing nothing but blood-mouthed, eyeless faces, ripping hands, pain and sweat and the foul reek of the air, screaming cries and that terrible, nagging whisper of uncertainty in his brain. He was aware of other sounds somewhere, distant noises in the Outer Citadel, a far-off howling like the din of a faraway battle.

An explosion jarred the ground. Then another, heavier, louder, nearer, and he thought he heard, through the shrieking of the mindless things all around him, the triumphal yells of men and the higher, wilder keening of women.

He was aware that no new attackers were running toward him. He swung grimly at those that remained, half conscious of things happening elsewhere in the long ditch—of fighting somewhere—*on the causeway?*—of fire . . .

Teeth slashed at his leg and he stomped, breaking the neck of the ugie that had crawled up below the arc of the swinging chain. Whatever else was happening was only a distraction, a break in his concentration that could cost him his life.

Another explosion sounded, this time very near, and it took all his will not to look. The chain crushed a final skull, the last nuuwa fell, wriggling and snapping at its own flesh, and he stood gasping in the doorway, looking up to see the causeway drawbridge fall in flames.

The top of the outer wall was a friezework of struggling men. A rear guard of black-armored soldiers was being cut to pieces on the causeway itself. What looked like an army of black and filthy gnomes was pouring through the causeway gate and down makeshift ladders into the ditch, brandishing picks, adzes, and weapons stolen, from the armories in the mines. The blood of their wounds gleamed bright through the rock dust, and their screams of triumph and anger shook the air.

Then he heard a voice pitched as only a warrior's could be to carry over the roar of battle—the one voice that, of all others, he would have given anything he had ever possessed to hear again.

"DUCK, YOU OAF!"

He ducked as an axe splintered into the wood of the door where his head had been. He saw the advancing forces of the Dark Eagle's mercenaries pouring down from the other side of the causeway to meet the miners in battle in the ditch. With a great scraping of bolts, the doors behind him were thrown open, and reinforcements poured through in a mixed tide of mercenaries, regulars, and nuuwa. The battle was joined on the corpse-strewn steps around him.

Somehow, Starhawk was there, where he knew she always should be, fighting like a demon at his side.

"I thought I told you to go back!" he yelled at her over the general chaos. His chain smashed the helmet and skull of a mercenary before him.

"Rot that!" she yelled back. "I've quit the troops and I'll look for you as long as I bloody well please! Here . . ." She stooped to wrench a sword free from the dead fingers that still grasped it and thrust the bloody hilt at him. "This will get you farther than that silly chain."

"Cheap, rotten, general-armory issue," he grumbled, testing the edge on the neck of an advancing nuuwa. "If you were going to get me a sword, you might at least have made it a decent one."

"Gripe, gripe, gripe, all you ever do is gripe," she retorted, and he laughed, teeth gleaming white through the filthy stubble of his beard, joyful only to be with her again.

They were silent then, except for the wordless yelling of battle, merging with the dirty mob of the advancing forces. But he was conscious of her at his side, battle-cold and bright, filled with concentrated fire, and he wondered how he had ever thought her plain.

The men now around him were gaunt as wolves but rock-muscled from hard labor, their dusty hides striped with the scars of beatings. He knew they were the husbands, the lovers, or the brothers of those crazy and intrepid wildcats he'd spent the winter training. There were more of them than he'd thought; the long ditch was rapidly filling with men. The gate at the top of the steps was disgorging more and more of Altiokis' troops. The mêlée was deafening. A momentary sortie drove the miners down the blood-slick steps, and he heard a woman's voice—Sheera's voice—raised in a piercing rallying cry.

Someone came running up behind him, and he swung around, sword ready, heavy chain rattling. A dusty little man yelled, "Are you Sun Wolf?"

"Yes." Under the grime, he saw that the man's hair was flame-gold, the mark of the royal House of Her, and he asked, "Are you Tarrin?"

"Yes."

"Does one of your people have the key to this mother-loving chain?"

"No, but we've got an axe to cut the links free. We'll get rid of the bracelets later."

"Fine," the Wolf said. Eo loomed up out of the confusion of the fight, half a head taller than Tarrin and brandishing an enormous axe. Tarrin positioned the chain over a corner of the stone steps; they all winced as the axe blade slammed down.

"You girls make it in all right?" the Wolf asked, after Eo had whacked the chain free of the bracelet on his other wrist.

Her reply was drowned in the renewed din of the fighting, the sounds of the struggle rising like a voiceless howling, elemental as a storm. More men were pouring from the doors, impossible numbers of them—the Wolf had not thought there were that many in the fortress. He caught up his sword and plowed back into the fray on the steps at Tarrin's heels. Eo followed with her axe. Battle separated them. Sun Wolf pressed upward, fighting his way to the shadow of the gate, where the line of defenders was weakening. Freed of the chain's weight, he felt he could fight forever.

He slashed and cut, until the sword embedded in flesh and bone. He looked down to pull it loose and froze in nauseated horror at what he saw. The flesh of his àrms was white with leprosy.

He didn't see the enemy sword that slashed at his neck until Starhawk's blade deflected it, so frozen was he by sickened despair. She yelled at him, "It's an illusion! Wolf! Stop it! It isn't real!"

He looked up at her, his face gray with shock. She, too, had momentarily stopped fighting, though the battle raged on all sides of them.

"It's an illusion, rot your eyes! Do you think leprosy takes hold that fast? That's how he won at Iron Pass. We've already been through six things like this coming out of the mines!"

Her own face was blotched with it, like lichen on stone. But as he blinked at her, his mind coming back into focus, he saw that what she said was true. As with the seeing of demons, he became aware that by changing his perceptions slightly, he could see the whole flesh under the superimposed illusion of rot. Blood and anger slammed, raging, back into his veins. The men and women struggling all around him didn't have his power to see through, or Yirth's power to combat, illusions— but they had seen the Wizard King's illusions before. And now they were too angry to care.

Cursing like a bullwhacker, the Wolf threw himself back into the fray. He could see through the gate to the corridors beyond, clogged with Altiokis' troops; and, as if the realization that the leprosy was an illusion had somehow cleared a block from his eyes, he saw that three-quarters of these new warriors were illusion as well. By the way they cut at them, the others could not tell the difference, and he knew himself to be fighting as a wizard would fight, and seeing as a wizard would see. Starhawk, at his side, slashed at one of the insubstantial figures as a real warrior cut at her with a halbred. Sun Wolf hacked the man's head off before the blow landed and wondered how many others would fall to just such a fraud.

Behind him, he heard a man cry out in terror.

He whirled, looking into the darkness of the Citadel gate. There was something there, visible behind the backs of the retreating sortie, a shapeless shape of luminous horror, a coldness that ate at the bones. Altiokis' men were retreating through the doors. Tarrin and his miners were unwilling to follow, frozen by the coming of that horrible fog and what was within it. They fell back toward the sunlight of the ditch, and the doors began to swing shut, as if of themselves.

Sun Wolf, left momentarily alone with Starhawk by the ebbing forces, scanned the darkness, searching it with his mind rather than with his eyes . . . and finding nothing but the shape of Altiokis, far back among those glowing wraiths, his hands weaving the illusion from the air.

He bellowed, "It's an illusion, dammit! Don't let them close the gate!" He plunged forward, hearing Starhawk's footfalls at his heels. He heard her voice somewhere in back of him, calling out to the others, and heard them follow. Then he heard the gate slam behind him.

The luminous fog vanished. His arms, as he glimpsed them, swinging his sword at the men who crowded toward him, were clean again. There were few of Altiokis' men still around the gate, the rest having gone to the fighting on the walls, and those few he dispatched or drove away. Then he plunged after the retreating shape of the Wizard King.

The darkness beneath the Citadel seemed thicker than it had before, defeating even his abilities to pierce it. He tore a torch from its holder, and the smoke of it streamed like a banner in his wake. Altiokis' fruity laugh taunted him from the black hole of a corridor arch; Sun Wolf sensed a trap and advanced cautiously, the curious perception that detected reality from illusion showing him the ghostly outlines of the spiked pit in the floor beneath the illusion of damp flagstones. He edged past it on the narrow walkway that the Wizard King had used; but by then his quarry was out of sight.

He seemed to be caught in a maze of twisting rooms and corridors, of doors that opened to nowhere, and of traps in the walls and floor. Once nuuwa attacked him in a room that had seemed empty—purposefully, controlled by another mind, as the nuuwa had fought in the battle. He cut at them with sword and fire, wedging himself into a niche in the wall. As he split skulls and burned the dirty hair and rotted flesh, he felt again that eerie little whisper at the back of his consciousness.

You can control them yourself. You only have to give a little part of your mind to that cold, black fire, and you can control them . . . and other things as well.

Turn away, and what can you offer this woman you want

except a battered and poverty-stricken wanderer? Do you really think Ari will give up the troop to you?

He remembered the sightless blaze burning in the rotted remains of Altiokis' failing brains and fought grimly, humanly, bloodily, exhaustedly. He killed two of the nuuwa, and the rest of them drew back, retreating into the stone mazes away from his torchlight, dodging through the stone walls like bats.

Altiokis, he reflected, *must be running out of nuuwa if he's started conserving them.*

Grimly, he pursued.

There was a trap of some kind in one guardroom. His hypersensitive sense of direction let him pick out a way around it, seeking the source of the fat man's wheezing breath. He saw Altiokis then, fleeing up a dark corridor. The torchlight bounced crazily over the rough stone of the walls as the Wolf ran. It glittered on the blood that smeared his arms and on the far-off glint of the jewels on the Wizard King's doublet. He heard the gasping of Altiokis and the stumbling, clumsy footsteps. Ahead, he saw a narrow door, bound and bolted with steel. A darkness, a last illusion, confused his sight, but he heard the door open and shut.

He flung himself at it, tore it open, and plunged through, holding the torch aloft to see. As he passed through the door, he realized that the wall in which it was set was the same as the wall of that tiny, windowed chamber—the rough stone wall of the original hut that Altiokis had built in a night.

And he knew that Altiokis had never come through that door.

It crashed shut behind him, and he heard the bolts slam home. He turned, gasping, his lungs stifling with terror. Black and empty, the Hole of darkness lay before him, absorbing and drowning the light of the flames. On the far side of the Hole, he could make out the window to the observation room and the narrow door beside it—the door, as he recalled, that Altiokis had not bolted when he'd ordered Sun Wolf out of the room.

But the width of the room lay between it and the Wolf, and the ugly, evil, screaming depths of that silent blackness lay between. The sword dropped from his nerveless fingers at the thought of having to walk past it; he could see the light of the torch wavering over the shadowy walls with the shaking of his hand. He stood paralyzed, conscious of the Entity that he would have to pass and of the mindless intelligence of fire and cold trapped these hundreds of years between this universe and whatever arcane depths of unreason it called its home.

Something bright flickered in the corner of his vision, like a spark floating on the air. Too late, he remembered the other danger, the horror that even the Entity that wanted his mind could not prevent. As he wrenched his face away, fire exploded in his left eye, a numbing, searing blast followed by the horrible wash of pain. From his eye, it seemed to be spreading throughout every muscle of his body. He could hear himself screaming, and his knees were buckling with agony. With a curiously clear sliver of the remains of rational thought, he knew exactly how many seconds of consciousness he had left, and the single thing that he must do.

CHAPTER
—— 21 ——

*T*HE DOOR OF THE WINDOWED OBSERVATION ROOM WAS PUSHED carefully open. Altiokis, Wizard King of the greatest empire since the last rulers of Gwenth had retired in a huff to their respective monasteries, peeked cautiously around the door-jamb.

The big mercenary lay face-down on the floor a few feet away. He must, Altiokis thought, have gotten through the door somehow—a glance showed that it wasn't bolted—in his final agony. A trickle of blood ran out from beneath his head.

Altiokis relaxed and smiled with relief. His earlier panic had been absurd. *Drink is making me foolish*, he thought with a self-indulgent sigh. *I really should take less*. He had always suspected that the Entity in the Hole had no real control over the gaums, and it was for that reason that he had never gone near it unprotected. But there was always the risk that some other wizard would know the secret of destroying them—if there was a secret.

He frowned. There was so much that his own master—whatever the old puff-guts' name had been—had never told him. And so much that he had been told had not made sense.

He padded into the little room, two nuuwa shuffling at his heels. Really, it had only been sheerest luck that he hadn't become a nuuwa himself, he thought, looking down at that huge, tawny body at his feet. All those years ago . . . How many had it been? There seemed to be so many periods of time that he couldn't quite recall. It was only by sheerest chance that the men he'd been out with that night—the old Thane's men, silly old bastard!—had their eyes burned out and their brains destroyed, while he hid in the brush and watched. Oh, he'd heard of the Holes, but he'd never thought to see one. And he'd never realized that Something lived in them.

Something, that is, other than gaums.

That was another thing old—old—whatever his name was—had never bothered to tell him.

Altiokis bent down. *A wizard!* After all these years, he'd hardly expected that any dared to oppose him still. But there were those he hadn't accounted for, over the years, and perhaps they'd had students. That was the big advantage, he'd found about living forever, as the Entity in the Hole had promised him he might do.

Well, not promised, exactly. He couldn't recall. Nevertheless, he had won again, and he gave a delighted little giggle at the thought as he bent down to examine his newest recruit to the ranks of the mindless.

A hand closed around his throat like a vise of iron. With bulging eyes, Altiokis found himself staring down into a face that was scarcely human; the one eye socket was empty and charred with fire, but the other eye was alive, sane, and filled with livid pain and berserker rage.

The fat wizard let out one gasping squeak of terror. Then Sun Wolf found himself holding, not a man, but a leopard by the throat.

Claws raked his back. His hands dug through the soft, loose flesh of the white-ruffed throat. Even shape-changed, Altiokis was a fat, old animal. The Wolf rolled to his feet, dragging the twisting, snarling thing toward the narrow door of the room where the Hole waited. Peripherally, his single eye caught the bright movement of more of the fire-flecks beyond the glass, and the smoldering yellow glow of the torch where it lay, burning itself out on the stone floor. The leopard must have known, too; for its struggles redoubled, then suddenly changed, and Sun Wolf found himself with nine feet of cobra between his hands.

It was only for a moment. The tail lashed at his legs, but the poisonous head was prisoned helplessly in his grip.

The next thing was horrible, something he had never seen before, bloated and chitinous, with clawed legs and tentacles raking at him like whips. He yanked open the door.

The nuuwa stirred uneasily, held still by the tangle of forces in the room. The Wolf could feel Altiokis' mind drawing them, and blocked it with his own. With the door open, the whispering in the thoughts was overwhelming. Past the shrieking mouths and flailing antennae of that horrible head between his hands, he could see the movement in the darkness, surrounded by the mindlessly devouring motes of flame. The thing in his hands twisted and lashed, and the blood ran fresh from his clawed shoulders and from the ruined socket of his eye. The monster was hideously strong; he felt the muscle and sinew of his arm cracking under the weight of it, but he refused to release his strangling grip.

As they struggled on the threshold of that vile room, Altiokis became once again a fat man, crazy and sweating with fear. Sun Wolf slung the man inside and crashed the door shut with all his strength. It heaved under the weight thrown against it. He shot the bolts and stood hanging onto them, as he had done before, feeling them jerk and pull under his hands with desperate spells of opening. The two nuuwa jiggled from foot to foot, and he threw the barriers of his mind against them, keeping them from understanding, wondering if it would be worth it, just this once, to yield to the drag in his mind and order them away.

Then the screaming started. The fight to free the door bolts ceased; he heard Altiokis blundering around the room, shrieking with agony, hitting the wall, and falling. Sun Wolf leaned against the door, sickened by the sound, remembering those endless seconds and counting them down.

He had been in enough dirty fighting to know how to gouge out an eye. He doubted that Altiokis had the knowledge and the resolution to do it or the determination needed to sear the bleeding socket with fire. The brutal action had saved him, but he was sure that he would never—could never—erase from his mind the long seconds that it had taken him to nerve himself to do it.

He knew by the screaming and by the change in the behaviour of the nuuwa when what remained of Altiokis' mind was gone. He turned the nuuwa's attention to the opposite walls and walked nonvisible, between them and out into the Citadel.

The black flames tittered in his mind.

Hearing the yelling confusion that came to him from every corner, he guessed that the nuuwa, released from control, had become as they were outside Altiokis' domains—randomly rampaging, turning on the troops beside whom they had fought.

He plunged down the corridors, finding his way back to the entrance into the ditch from whence he had come.

The doors were barred. He could hear the slam of a battering rams against them and, faintly, Tarrin's ringing voice. But the defenders, clutched in a corner, fighting the small swarm of nuuwa that had suddenly turned upon them, were in no shape to prevent him from dragging back the bars.

Two of the nuuwa broke away from the main group and shambled toward him, groaning and slavering, as the first blazing crack of daylight opened through the doors. He started to order them away and stopped himself. His brain seemed to be swimming in dark, murmuring liquid, his thoughts struggling against insistent, alien urges.

Men poured through the gate around him. He found himself clutching the doorposts for support. Then hands were gripping his arms. A voice called him back to himself.

"Chief! What in the name of the Mother happened to you?"

He clutched Starhawk's shoulders, holding to her as if to the last spar of sanity in the sea in which he felt himself sinking. "That Thing—the Thing in the room..."

"The Hole?"

His eye focused. He noted distantly, automatically, that his depth perception was gone and that he'd have to retrain to compensate. The slanted light of late afternoon that streamed through the gate showed him Starhawk's face, grimy, bloody, and unsurprised. Her gray eyes were clear, looking into his. Though there was no reflection of it in her face, he realized that he himself must have been a choice sight. *Trust the Hawk*, he thought, *not to ask stupid questions until there's time to answer them.*

"How did you know?"

"The wizard Anyog told me," she said. He realized he hadn't seen her in four months; it only seemed like yesterday. "Where is it?"

"Back there. Don't go near it. Don't go in that room with it..."

His hands left patches of bloody dirt where they rested on her shoulders. She shook her head. "Is there any room near it? Around it—to put blasting powder from the mines? We were bringing some up to take care of the gate."

"Blasting powder?" The draw on his mind was growing stronger. He wasn't sure he had heard.

"To blow out the walls," she explained. "Daylight will destroy it." She put a hand to his face, slimy with the scum of battle, gentle as a lover's. "Wolf, are you all right?"

She wasn't asking about his eye or the claw marks and sword cuts that covered his body as if he had rolled in broken glass. She knew his physical toughness. Her fears for him went deeper than that.

"Daylight," he said thickly. "Then . . . The hut was built at night."

"Yes, I know," she said.

He didn't bother to ask her how she knew. A darkness seemed to be edging its way into his thoughts, and he shook his head, as if to clear it. "Altiokis' forces are still holding that part of the Citadel," he said. "You'll have to fight your way in."

"Is the room itself guarded?"

He shook his head.

"Then we'll make it. We can leave a long fuse . . ."

Others had come up to them. The battle was raging past into the corridors. Sheera's voice gasped, "Chief! Your eye!" Amber Eyes' hand on his arm was suddenly motherly in spite of the fact that her arms were smeared with blood to the shoulders. A viselike grip that he recognized as Denga Rey's closed over his elbow, offering support.

Starhawk gave them a rapid précis of what needed to be done. The women nodded, evidently on terms of great friendliness with her. Sun Wolf wondered suddenly how Starhawk happened to be there in the first place, then discarded the thought as irrelevant. It was true that in the crisis of battle, the most appalling coincidences were commonplace.

Amber Eyes said, "We can't leave a long fuse, though. It would have to be long enough to let us get clear of the Citadel. In that time, someone would find it."

"You're right," the Hawk agreed.

"Could we wait until the battle's over?" Sheera asked. "By nightfall we should have the place. Altiokis' forces are holed up in the upper part of the tower—once they got clear of their own nuuwa, that is. Then we could—"

"No," Sun Wolf said hoarsely. The Thing—the voice, the urge, whatever it was—he could feel it tearing at the fraying edges of his mind, growing stronger as final exhaustion took its toll on his body. Sunrise tomorrow seemed hideously far away. "It has to be before sunset tonight."

Amber Eyes and Denga Rey looked at him, deeply troubled,

but Starhawk nodded. "He's right," she said. "If there's some kind of living thing, some kind of intelligence in the Hole, we can't give it the night to work in."

"We've only got about an hour and a half until sunset," Denga Rey observed doubtfully.

"So we have to work fast. We can stack powder around it. Damned good thing Tarrin had it brought up from the mines to blow the gate or we'd be forever getting it."

"Yirth could light it from a distance," Amber Eyes said suddenly. "I've seen her light torches and candles just by looking at them. If we could get her out here, then she could light the powder . . ."

"Get her," Sheera said.

The lovers vanished in opposite directions. He leaned back against the wall behind him, suddenly weak, his mind drifting. The roar of battle seemed to sink to an unreal whispering.

"Chief!"

He blinked into Starhawk's frightened face. Somehow, Amber Eyes and Denga Rey were back, and Yirth was with them, standing with Sheera, grouped around him as they had been on the ship. He thought for a moment that he had fainted, but found he was still on his feet, leaning against the stone arch of the gate, the long fosse with its carpet of trampled dead stretching away to both sides.

He shook his head, with a sensation of having lost time. "What happened?"

"I don't know," Starhawk said. By the pale light that came through the gateway beside him, her scarred, fine-boned face looked as calm and cold-blooded as ever, but he could hear the fear in her voice. "You were—you were gone. I talked to you, but it was as if you were listening to something else."

"I was," he said grimly, suddenly understanding. "Yirth, can you set fire to something at a distance without having seen it first?"

The witch's dark brows plunged in a startled frown. She alone of them, though she wore a man's doublet and breeches for convenience, bore no marks of physical fighting. But under the crown of her tight-braided hair, her harsh face was set with fatigue, the ugly smear of the birthmark appearing almost black against her pallor. She looked older, the Wolf thought, than she had before she'd led the women through the traps into the Citadel. All her scars would be upon the fabric of her mind.

"I cannot set fire to anything at a distance," she said. "I must see it to bring fire."

The others stared at her, shocked at the limitation; the Wolf was puzzled. "You can't—can't bring fire to a place that you know in your mind?" he asked. "Can't form it in your mind?" The act of bringing fire seemed so easy to him, though he had never done it—like turning away the minds of those who sought him, or changing the way he saw things, to pierce another wizard's illusions.

She shook her head, clearly not understanding what he meant. "You can, perhaps," she said. "But it lies beyond my power."

So it was Sun Wolf, after all, who had to lead the small crew through the winding mazes, toward the Hole once again. Yirth followed them, though he had warned her against entering the observation room of the Hole itself; two or three of the freed miners helped carry the sacks of blasting powder. To Sun Wolf's ears, the fighting was far off in the upper part of the tower and, by the sound of it, it was turning into the grim, messy business of mopping up, fighting in pockets here and there—the bloody scrag ends of battle.

Closer and more real in his own mind was the buzzing darkness that ate at the corners of his consciousness, demanding, insistent as a scarcely bearable tickling. He rested his hand on Starhawk's shoulder for support and saw, almost disinterestedly, that his fingers were trembling. He was conscious in a half-detached way of the sun sliding down the outside walls of the Citadel, changing colors as it approached the ragged horizon; though, when he mentioned to Yirth this awareness of things he could not actually see, she shook her head and looked at him strangely with her jade-colored eyes. The Entity whispering in his mind was more real to him than his own body, more real than the stone halls through which he stumbled like a mechanical thing—more real than anything except the sharp bones of the shoulder beneath his hand and the cold, pale silk of hair that brushed the backs of his fingers when Starhawk turned her head.

Through the little window of the observation room, they could see that Altiokis was still moving. Rolling, flopping grotesquely, he would occasionally stagger to his feet or mouth at the window glass. The jewels of his clothing had caught on the rough walls and ripped as he'd moved, and fat, white flesh bulged through the rents. One eye was gone, the other already being eaten away from within; his face was starting to change, as the faces of nuuwas did. Sheera made a gagging noise in her throat and looked away.

Sun Wolf scarcely saw. He remained by the door while the sacks of powder were stacked in the room and in the hall beyond, where Yirth waited. There was enough powder to blow out the whole western wall of the Citadel. His gaze went past the window, past the darkness, to deeper darkness, where he could see the Thing moving.

The giggling, scratching sensation in his brain was almost unendurable. It knew him. Threads of it permeated every fiber of his consciousness; he had a momentary, disturbed vision of himself, visible in the shadows through the thick, black glass of the window, his half-naked body clawed and filthy, his wrists still weighted with the iron bracelets, the blood from the ripped flesh of them slowly dripping down his fingers; his left eye was a charred and gory pit in a face white with shock and strain. The other people in this vision were mere puppets, grotesque, jerking, and unreal as they stumbled about their meaningless tasks. The Entity—whatever it was—could no more see them than they could see it. They were only half-guessed shapes, more like monkeys than human beings.

He watched as one of the shapes shambled up to him and reached a fiddling, picking hand out to touch him.

He closed his eyes, and the vision dissolved. When he opened them, Starhawk was looking worriedly into his face. "Chief?"

He nodded. "I'm all right." His voice sounded like the faint rasp of a fingernail scraping metal. He looked around him, fixing the room in his mind—the stone walls, the shadows, the grayish-white cotton of the sacks that he knew the flames would lick over when he called them, and the carved ebony chair, shoved unceremoniously into a corner.

Starhawk and Denga Rey supported him between them as they led him from the room.

"You sure this is going to work?" Sheera asked nervously.

"No," the Wolf said.

"Could Yirth . . ."

"No," Starhawk said. "We have enough problems without its getting its claws into another wizard."

They turned a corner and followed a narrow passage toward the gate. With the smoothness of a door closing before them, the way was suddenly filled with armed men in black mail. The Dark Eagle stood at their head.

"I thought," he said, smiling, "that we would still find you wandering around here. And Starhawk, too . . . You did bring your men, after all." The Eagle's swarthy face was grimed with blood and dirt in the torchlight, the swirling, petal-edged crests of his helmet torn and hacked with battle, their dark blue edges black in places and dripping; but through it all, his grin was no less bright.

"Let us out of here," Sun Wolf said in a voice that shook. "This is no time for fighting."

"No?" One black brow lifted. "The nuuwa seem all to have gone crazy, but we should be able to drive them off the walls without much trouble. Altiokis should be pleased to hear—"

"Altiokis is dead," the Wolf whispered, fighting to keep his thoughts clear and to keep the words that he spoke his own and not those that crowded, unbidden and unknown, to his throat. His harsh voice had turned slow and stammering, picking at his words. "His power is broken for good—there's no need to fight—just let us out . . ."

The mercenary captain smiled slowly; one of his men laughed. Sheera made a move to draw her sword, and Starhawk caught her wrist, knowing it would do no good.

"Quite a convincing tale," the Dark Eagle said. "But considering that I have here my lord Tarrin's lady—no uncommon general, I might add, my lady—not to mention the witch who led the miners through the traps and into the Citadel—*if* my lord is dead, which I have yet to believe, the power he wielded will be up for the taking. We can—"

"If you can touch the power he had, it will snuff your brains out like a candle flame," the Wolf said harshly. "Go down the corridor and through the door. Look through that pox-rotten glass of his—look at what you see. Then come back, and we'll talk about power!" His voice was trembling with strain and rage, his brain blinded with the effort of holding itself together against those tearing, muttering, black roots that were thrusting it apart. "Now let us the hell out of here, unless you want that Thing in there to take root in my brain as it did in his!"

The Dark Eagle stood for a moment, staring up into Sun Wolf's face, into the hagridden, half-mad, yellow eye that stared from the mass of clotted cuts, stubble, and filth. The captain's own face, under the soot and grime of battle, was smooth, an unreadable blank. Then without a word, he signed to his men to let Sun Wolf and the women pass. The Dark

Eagle turned and walked down the corridor toward Altiokis'
observation room.

Sun Wolf had no recollection of passing the gate of the Inner
Citadel or crossing the causeway over the fosse that was littered
with the bodies of the slain. The men the Dark Eagle had sent
to guard them halted at the far end of the causeway, and the
Wolf slumped down in the shadows of the turreted gates, with
his back against the raw, powder-burned stone. Looking back,
he could see the towers of the Inner Citadel alive with men
and nuuwa, fighting in the corridors or looting the gilded halls.
The shrieking came to him in a vast, chaotic din, and the
shivering air was rank with the smoke of burning. The sinking
sunlight gilded huge, billowing clouds of smoke that poured,
black or white, from the tower windows. Heat danced above
the walls, and now and then a man or a nuuwa would come
running in flames from some inner hall, to fall screaming over
the parapet, gleaming against the sunset like a brand. In the
direction of the distant sea, torn rags of cloud covered the sky.
It would be a night of storm.

Wind touched his face, the breath of the mountains, polluted
by the stinks of battle. Everything seemed remote to him, like
something viewed through a heavy layer of black glass. He
wondered idly if that had been how things appeared to Altiokis—unreal, a little meaningless. No wonder he had sought
the grossest and most immediate sensations; they were all he
could feel. Or had his perceptions changed after he had given
up?

Darkness seemed to be closing in on Sun Wolf. He reached
out blindly, not wholly certain what it was that he sought, and
a long, bony hand gripped his. The pressure of Starhawk's
strong fingers helped clear his mind. His remaining eye met
hers; her face appeared calm under the mask of filth and cuts;
the sunset light was like brimstone on her colorless hair. Against
the grime, her eyes appeared colorless, too, clear as water.

Beyond her, around them, the women stood like a bodyguard, their own blood and that of their enemies vivid on their
limbs against the rock dust of the mines. He was aware of
Yirth watching him, arms folded, those sea-colored eyes intent
upon his face; he wondered if, when his mind gave up and was
drowned in blackness, she would kill him.

He hoped so. His hand tightened over Starhawk's.

There was a brief struggle on the far end of the causeway.
A sword flashed in the sinking light; one of the soldiers at that

end, in the armor of Altiokis' private troops, went staggering over the edge into the ditch.

The Dark Eagle came striding back, sheathing his sword as he picked his way carefully across the makeshift of rope and pole that had been thrown up to replace the burned drawbridge. Under the tattered wrack of his torn helmet crests, his face was green-white and gray about the mouth, as if he had just got done heaving up his farthest guts. The dying sunlight caught on the gilded helmet spike as on a spear.

When he came near, he asked, "How do you mean to destroy it?"

"Light the powder," Sheera said. "Tarrin and the men are clear of the place now."

"There are nuuwa all over the corridors," the Eagle informed her, speaking as he might speak to any other captain. And so she looked, Sun Wolf thought, with her half-unraveled braids and black leather breast guards, her perilous beauty all splattered with blood. "By God and God's Mother, I've never seen such a hell! You'll never get back to put a fuse to it. And even if you did . . ."

"The Wolf can light it," Starhawk said quietly. "From here."

The Dark Eagle looked down curiously at the slumped figure propped among the women against the wall. His blue eyes narrowed. "His Nibs was right, then," he said.

Sun Wolf nodded. Fire and cold were consuming his flesh; voices echoed to him, piping and far away. The shadow of the tower already lay long over the fosse and touched him like a finger of the coming darkness.

Fumblingly, as if in a drugged nightmare, he began to put together the picture of the observation room in his mind.

He could not see it clearly—there were nuuwa there, shambling over everything, blundering into walls, shrieking at their mindless brother and maker, who clawed and screamed through the black glass. He formed the shadows in his mind, the shapes of the powder sacks, the harsh lines of the broken chair . . .

The images blurred.

Suddenly sharp, he saw them from the other side of the window.

He pushed the image away with an almost physical violence. It intruded itself into his mind again, like a weapon pushed into his hands. But he knew if he grasped that weapon, he would never be able to light the flame.

Both images died. He found himself huddled, shaking and

dripping with sweat, in the blue shadow of the tower, the cold wind licking at his chilled flesh. He whispered, "I can't."

Starhawk was holding his hands. Trembling as if with fever, he raised his head and looked at the setting sun, which seemed to lie straight over the mountain horizon now, glaring at him like a baleful eye. He tried to piece together the image of the room and had it unravel in his hands into darkness. He shook his head. "I can't."

"All right," the Hawk said quietly. "There's time for me to go in with a fuse."

It would have to be a short fuse, he thought . . . There were nuuwa everywhere . . . If she didn't get out by the time it went off . . .

There would be no time for her to get out before the sun set. And it was quite possible that she knew it.

"No," he whispered as she turned to go. He heard her steps pause. "No," he said in a stronger voice. He closed his eyes, calling nothing yet, losing himself in a chill, sounding darkness. He heard her come back, but she did not touch him, would not distract him.

Small, single, and precise he called it, not in pieces but all at once—room, shadows, chair, powder, window, nuuwa, darkness. He summoned the reality in his mind, distant and glittering as an image seen in fire, and touched the gray cotton of the sacks with a licking breath of fire. The nuuwa, startled by the sudden heat, drew back.

The thunderous roar of the explosion jerked the ground beneath him. The noise of it slammed into his skull. Through his closed eyes, he could see stones leaping outward, sunlight smashing into the centuries of darkness . . . light ripping where that darkness had taken hold of his brain.

He remembered screaming, but nothing after that.

CHAPTER

—— 22 ——

"*THERE ISN'T THAT MUCH MORE TO TELL.*" STARHAWK CROSSED her long legs and tucked her bare feet up under the tumble of sheets and flowered silk quilts at the end of the bed. Against the dark embroidery of her shirt and the gaily inlaid bedpost at her back, she looked bleached, clean as crystal, remote as the winter sky, with her long, bony hands folded around her knees. "Amber Eyes had a picked squad of the prettiest girls— Gilden and Wilarne were two of them—and they tarted themselves up and went in first, to slit the throats of the gate guards before they knew what was happening. The alarm was out after that, but it was too late to keep the troop out of the mines; once we'd made it to the first of the armories and Tarrin got his men rallied, it was easy."

Sun Wolf nodded. From long professional association, he understood what Starhawk meant by easy. The women all bore wounds of hard fighting. Twelve of the fifty had died in the darkness of the mines, never knowing whether their cause would succeed or not. But the fight had been straightforward, with a clear goal. He doubted whether either Starhawk or Sheera had ever questioned their eventual victory.

He leaned back against the silken bolsters and blinked sleepily at the primrose sunlight that sparkled so heatlessly on the diamond-paned windows. Waking in this room, he had not been certain of his surroundings. It turned out that this was Sheera's best guest room, and that amused him. Never in his stay in Sheera's household had he been permitted inside the main house. He had half expected to wake up in the loft over the orangery again.

Sheera had not yet come.

"She'll be at the coronation," Starhawk said. "It killed me to miss it, but Yirth said she'd rather not have you left alone. Yirth stayed with you yesterday when I went to the wedding— Sheera and Tarrin's, I mean. There was a hell of a dust kicked up over it with the parliament, because Tarrin and Sheera insisted that they be married first and then crowned as joint rulers, rather than have Tarrin crowned King and then take Sheera as Queen Consort." She shrugged. "Parliament's meeting this afternoon, and there'll be a town-wide gorge on free food and wine all night to celebrate. Tomorrow, if you're up to it, you'll be received by Tarrin and Sheera in the Cathedral Square."

He nodded, identifying at last the faint wisps of noise that had formed a background to the room. It was music and cheers, coming from the direction of the Grand Canal. If the town had found time to reorganize itself for celebrations, he realized, he must have been unconscious for longer than he had thought.

He smiled, picturing to himself the jewel-box vaults of the Cathedral of the Three and Sheera in a gown of gold. Drypettis had been more right than she knew. Sheera was worthy to be Queen—but Queen on her own terms and not on any man's. He was glad she'd achieved it, no matter what the hapless Tarrin had felt on the subject.

"What do you think of her?" he asked. "Sheera, I mean."

Starhawk laughed. "I love her," she said. "She's the damnedest woman I've ever met. She's a good general, too, you know, easily better than Tarrin. She always had her forces at her fingertips—always knew what was going on. Even in the worst of it, getting through the traps that guarded the ways up to the Citadel, she never batted an eye. Yirth showed her the true way, and she followed, through illusion and fire and all hell else. The rest had no choice but to do the same."

Sun Wolf grinned and reached up to touch the bandage over his eye that would soon be replaced by the patch that he would wear for life. "Even a man's deepest fear of magic," he said in his hoarse voice, "isn't strong enough to make him admit that he's afraid to follow where a woman leads."

One of those dark, strong eyebrows moved up. "You think I haven't capitalized on that ever since you made me a squad captain? One memory I'll always cherish is the look on the face of Wilarne M'Tree's husband when they met in the battle in the tunnels. It was a toss-up whether he'd die of a stroke induced by outrage or I'd die laughing. She all but hacked the arm off a mine guard who had him cornered—she's wicked with that halbred of hers—and he looked as indignant, when he finally recognized her, as if she'd made a grab at him in the street."

Sun Wolf laughed. "I suspected Sheera would be a good fighting general," he said. "But sending her green into her first battle—and an underground one involving magic at that—in charge of fifty other people, would be one hell of an expensive way to find out I was wrong."

"You know," Starhawk said thoughtfully, "I always did suspect you were a fraud." The gray eyes met his, wryly amused. "The hardest-headed mercenary in the business . . ."

"Well, I was," he said defensively.

"Really?" Her voice was cool. "Then why didn't you sneak off to Altiokis first thing and offer to trade information about the whole organization for the antidote? It would have got you out."

Sun Wolf colored strangely in the pale, butter-colored sunlight. In a small voice, he answered her. "I couldn't have done that."

She extended her foot like a hand and patted the lump of his knee under the covers. "I know." She smiled, got to her feet, and walked to the window. The shadows of the lattice crisscrossed her face and her short, sulfurous hair. Over her shoulder, she said to him, "The Dark Eagle says there's going to be years' worth of pickings, with Altiokis' empire broken up. Tarrin told me this morning they'd gotten news of a revolt in Kilpithie. You know they lynched Governor Stirk—the man Altiokis appointed here in Derroug Dru's place. There's already war in the North between Altiokis' appointees in Racken Scrag and the mountain Thanes. With the fortune Altiokis amassed in a hundred and fifty years, the money will be incredible."

Her back was to him, only a part of her face visible, edged in the colors of the window; her quiet voice was neutral.

Sun Wolf said, "You know I can't go back, Hawk."

She turned to face him. "Where will you go?"

He shook his head. "I don't know. To Wrynde, at first. To let Ari know I'm alive and to turn the troop over to him. To give Fawn money."

"To pay her off, you mean?"

There was a time when he would have lashed back at those words, no matter who had said them, let alone Starhawk, who had never criticized his dealings with women before. Now he only looked down at his hands and said quietly, "Yes." After a moment, he raised his head and met her eyes again. "I didn't treat her badly, you know."

"No," the Hawk said. "You never treated any of them badly."

It was the first time he had heard bitterness—or any other emotion, for that matter—in her voice. It both stung him and relieved him, to let him know where she stood.

"Do you blame me for it?" he asked.

"Yes," Starhawk said promptly. "Completely illogically, since I was the one who never told you that I loved you—but yes."

Sun Wolf was silent, trying to choose his words carefully. With any of his other women, he would have fallen back on the easier ploys of charm, or excused himself on the grounds of his own philandering nature. But this woman he knew too well to believe that her love for him would keep her by his side if he was anything other than straightforward with her. With any of his other women, he realized that it had not much mattered to him whether they stayed by him or not. The last several months had taught him that he did not want to live without Starhawk in his life.

At last, finding no adequate way to excuse himself, he only said, "I'm sorry I hurt you. I wouldn't have done it knowingly." He hesitated, fumbling for words. "I don't want to have to do this to Fawn, because I know she is fond of me—"

"Fawn," Starhawk said quietly, "loved you enough to leave the troop and come with me to look for you. She traveled with me as far as Pergemis. She loved you very much, Wolf."

He heard her use the past tense and felt both sadness for that gentle girl and shame. Shame because he had, in fact, loved Fawn no more than a kitten, no more than he had loved the others—Gilden, Wilarne, Amber Eyes, or any of his concubines before. "What happened in Pergemis?" he asked.

"She married a merchant," Starhawk replied calmly.

Sun Wolf looked up at her, the expression of hurt vanity on his face almost comical.

Starhawk continued. "Farstep and Sons, spices, furs, and onyx. She said she would rather marry into a firm of merchants than be the mistress of the richest mercenary in creation, and to tell you the truth, I can't say that I blame her. I was asked to stay there myself," the Hawk went on in a softer voice. "I thought about it. We had lost so much time, I don't think she ever thought you'd come out of this alive."

"She wasn't alone in that opinion," the Wolf growled. "Will he be good to her?"

"Yes." Starhawk thought of that tall stone house near the Pergemis quays, of Pel Farstep in her tall hood and elaborately wrought widow's coif, and of Ram and Imber and Orris, smoking and arguing in front of the hearth, amid a great brangle of children and dogs. *Anyog should never have left there*, she thought, and then wondered whether he would have been any happier living among them constantly than she would have been, had she given up her quest and accepted Ram's love.

She realized she had been too long silent. Sun Wolf was watching her, curious and concerned at the change that had come over her face. She said to him, "They are good people, Wolf. They're the kind of people whose homes we've looted and whose throats we've slit for years. I can't go back to our old life in Wrynde any more than you can."

She walked back to the bed and leaned her shoulder against the gay carvings of the inlaid pillar, her long fingers lying among the curved patterns of ivory and gold, like something wrought there of alabaster, the strong knuckles and wrinkled, pink war scars like the work of a master craftsman against the alternation of abalone and ebony. "So here we are," she said ironically. "Your father was right, Wolf. We've been spoiled for our trade by love and magic."

He shrugged, leaning back against the shadowy silk of the many pillows. "Looks as if we'll have to seek a new trade. Or I will, anyway."

He reached up and touched the eye bandage again. As he suspected, his depth perception was completely gone. He'd have to retrain himself with weapons to compensate, if he ever wanted to fight again. "Sheera told you what happened to me that night in the pit?" he asked.

Starhawk nodded, without comment.

"Yirth was right. I need to find a teacher, Hawk. I feel the Power within me; there are things that I know I can do, but I dare not. I don't want to become like Altiokis. I need to find someone to teach me to use my powers without destroying everyone and everything I touch. And the damned thing is, I don't know where to look. Yirth was cut off from the line of her master's masters—Altiokis managed to wipe out most of the lines. I'll have to search—and I have no idea where that search will take me."

He paused, studying that calm, unexpressive face that

watched him in the shadows of the bed canopy. He scanned the strength of its bone structure under the straight reddish mark of a war scar, where once her cheek and jaw had been laid open to the bone, fighting to get him off a battlefield when he'd been wounded, and the cool, smoke-gray eyes that seemed to look at all things—including his soul and hers—with such lucid calm.

Then he gathered all his courage into his hands and asked, "Will you come with me? It will be a long search. It could take years, but . . ."

"Wolf," she said softly, "years with you is all I've ever wanted."

She came quietly around the end of the bed and into his arms.

He was received by Tarrin and Sheera in a public ceremonial in the Cathedral Square the following day.

The cold and rains of winter had changed, seemingly over-night, into the first breath of spring. The windless balminess of the morning had a frost-edge sparkle to it, but the crowds that filled the square before the Cathedral of the Three all seemed to be wearing flowers on their shoulders, bosoms, and hatbands, like the pledge of beauty to come. Sun Wolf saw that most of the women wore what had come to be called the new mode, the flowing and easy-moving lines introduced by the fighting women. The men, laced into whaleboned and pad-ded doublets, looked as if they were far thinner than they had been when they had worn that finery last. The faces of the men were pale; those of the women, brown.

The thirty-odd surviving members of Sheera's corps, he saw, were standing in a body at the foot of the Cathedral steps, about where Drypettis had gotten him arrested the morning he had gone to ask Yirth to give him his freedom. Drypettis was not among them, though Starhawk had told him last night that the woman who had betrayed him had come to make her bow to Tarrin at the new King's official reception into the city. She was, after all, the last representative of the most ancient and honorable House in Mandrigyn.

"I was half afraid she would kill herself," he had said when Starhawk had told him, remembering the numerous, ugly scenes he had witnessed and heard of between Dru and Sheera. "Not that she didn't deserve thrashing—but it wouldn't have done Sheera any good. She was fond of the little snirp."

Starhawk had shaken her head with a wry grin. "Drypettis

is far too vain to kill herself," she'd said. "In fact, I'm not entirely certain she's even conscious that she did wrong. She still looked upon war as something that gentlefolk—particularly women—hired the ruder classes to do for them, not go out and do themselves. She honestly thought that Sheera had sullied herself and prostituted her soul by becoming a soldier. No, Drypettis will go to her grave believing herself ill-done-by, walling herself tighter and tighter into her own world of the past glories of her House, and exulting in her reputation as one of the original conspirators to the end."

On the way to the square, the gondola in which Sun Wolf and Starhawk were riding had passed the House of Dru, the only one of those marble-fronted palaces of the old merchant nobility to be undecorated and without a hundred watchers on every one of its tiered, trellised balconies. As Sheera's servants had poled the graceful boat past, they had heard music played in one of the rooms above; a single harpsichord, pure, lilting, and disinterested.

The other women were there, massed together as they had been that first night in the orangery, their eyes bright as they followed Sun Wolf's movements. He saw Wilarne M'Tree with Gilden, Eo, and Tisa. Across the square, he saw a man whom he vaguely recognized as Wilarne's husband with their stiff-necked, twelve-year-old son, looking haughty and uncomfortable. He thought Wilarne looked worn, her eyes stained with the blue smudges of fatigue. Here was one, at least, whose reunion had been less than peaceful. But she still stood with the women rather than with her family, and her menfolk did not look happy about this in the least.

There were others of the women who looked the same. But Amber Eyes and Denga Rey were like newlyweds in black velvet. Denga Rey glittered in her new panoply as Captain of the City Guards.

Yirth was there, too, standing a little to one side, her bony hands tucked into the star-stitched sleeves of her night-blue gown, her dark hair braided back, her face showing fully in daylight for the first time since the Wolf had known her—perhaps for the first time in her life. Even at a distance, before he realized what had changed about her, he knew she had passed through the Great Trial, sometime while he had been ill, and had grasped the wider understanding of such magic as she had been taught. The change was clear in her carriage and in her sea-colored eyes. Sun Wolf was quite close to her before he realized that the birthmark which had marred her face was gone, leaving only a faint shadow of a scar. It was, he thought, probably the first thing that she had done when she had the Power.

Near the women were the Thanes, and he glimpsed Lady Wrinshardin among them, haughty as an empress in her barbaric splendor, with marigolds in her white hair. Her gaze crossed his, and she winked at him, to the evident scandal of a podgy young man at her side who was obviously her son.

On the other side of the Cathedral steps, the dark-robed members of the parliament were banked, most of them still with the pale complexions and calloused hands of their former trade of deep-rock gold miners. Between the women and the parliament, Tarrin and Sheera stood like snow and flame, blazing with the pride of their love and triumph.

Clothed in the white silk majesty of his office, Tarrin of the House of Her, King of Mandrigyn, was no longer a dusty, quick-moving little man in a grimy loincloth, but a very elegant prince indeed. Against the miner's pallor of his face, his hair was a golden mane, a shade darker than Amber Eyes'; but of very much the same texture, rough and springing; his eyes were vivid blue. The festoons of lace that fell from his sleeves covered the shackle galls on his wrists. Beside him, Sheera was an idol in bullion-stitched gold, her high, close-fitting lace collar not quite concealing the bandages underneath. Sun Wolf remembered seeing the sword cut on her shoulder and breast when they'd been together in the Citadel and thinking that she would carry the scar to her grave.

Most of the women who had been at the storming of the mines would bear such scars.

Sun Wolf and Starhawk came forward to the foot of the steps. Carpets of eastern work had been laid down on the pavement and on the steps above, crimson and royal blue, scattered with roses and daffodils. The roaring of voices silenced as the rulers of Mandrigyn descended the steps; a hush fell over the square.

Tarrin's face was set and expressionless as he held out his hands to Sun Wolf. In his right hand was a parchment scroll, the seals of the city dangling from it by purple ribbons; he made no other gesture of welcome.

Sun Wolf took the scroll doubtfully, then glanced at Tarrin, puzzled.

"Read it," the King said, then swallowed.

Sun Wolf unrolled it and read. Then he looked up from the parchment, too incredulous even to be shocked.

"You *what*?" he demanded.

Starhawk looked around his shoulder quickly. "What is it?"

Sun Wolf held it out to her. "It's an order of banishment."

"It's *what*?" She took it, scanned it over, then looked up disbelievingly at the Wolf, at Tarrin, and at Sheera, who stood looking off into the distance, her face an expressionless blank.

Sun Wolf's single eye glittered, yellow and dangerous; his raw voice was like metal scraping. "I did not ask to come here," he said quietly to Tarrin, "and in the course of this winter I have lost my eye, I have lost my voice, and I have damned near lost my life five times over." His voice was rising to an angry roar. "All for the sake of saving your lousy city. And you have the unmitigated and brass-faced nerve to banish me?"

To do him credit, Tarrin did not flinch in front of what ended as a harsh vulture scream of outrage; when he spoke, his voice was quiet. "It was voted upon yesterday in parliament," he said. "I'm afraid the—the original measure was much more punitive."

The paper read:

By Order and Fiat of the Parliament of Mandrigyn, Month of Gebnion, First Year of the Reign of Tarrin II of the House of Her and Sheera, his wife:

Be it herein proclaimed that the bounds and gates of Mandrigyn are closed to one Sun Wolf, wizard and formerly captain of mercenaries, residing at one time in Wrynde in the North; that as from this day he is banished from the City of Mandrigyn and all the lands appertaining to that City, and all the lands that hereinafter will become sway of that City, in perpetuity.

This by reason of his flagrant violation of the laws of the City of Mandrigyn, and for his wanton corruption of the morals of the ladies of Mandrigyn.

Be it known that hereafter from this day, if he sets foot upon the lands of the City of Mandrigyn, he will become liable for the full penalties for these his crimes.

TARRIN II, KING
SHEERA, HIS WIFE

"It means," Starhawk said, with quiet amusement, into Sun

Wolf's dumbfounded silence, "that you taught the ladies of Mandrigyn to bear arms."

The Wolf glanced at her and back at the King. Tarrin was looking deeply embarrassed.

"If I hadn't taught your ladies to bear arms," the Wolf said in a tight, deadly voice, "you and all the members of your pox-rotted parliament would still be tapping great big rocks into wee small rocks in the dark at the bottom of Altiokis' mines, without hope of seeing the sunlight again."

"Captain Sun Wolf," Tarrin said in his light voice, "believe me, your deeds toward the City of Mandrigyn have earned the gratitude of our citizens, down through many generations. I am sure that once the present social disruptions arrange themselves, the order will be rescinded, and I will be able to welcome you as befits—"

"Social disruptions?" the Wolf demanded.

Behind him, he heard Starhawk give a very unwarriorlike chuckle. "He means," she said, "that the ladies won't turn back control of the city, or of the businesses, or go back to wearing veils, and the men aren't pleased about that at all."

Tarrin went on. "The social order of Mandrigyn is built upon generations of traditions." There was a thread of desperation in his voice. "The—repercussions—of your action, laudable and necessary though it was, have brought nothing but chaos and confusion to every household in the city."

Starhawk's voice was amused. "I think the men are out for your blood, Chief. And I can't really say that I blame them."

"That's ridiculous!" the Wolf said angrily. "There weren't above fifty women in the poxy troop! And the women had started to take over running the businesses of the city from the minute the men marched off to fight their witless war! Hell, most of the crew of the ship that brought me here were skirts! And anyway, it wasn't my idea . . ."

"The fact remains," Tarrin said, "that it was you who schooled the women in these—" He glanced at the glowering members of his parliament. "—unseemly arts; and you who encouraged them to consort with gladiators and prostitutes."

Sun Wolf's voice was a croaking roar of rage, *"And I'm being banished for that?"*

"Not only for that," Sheera said quietly. Under the rose and gold of her painted lids, her eyes were touched with something that was not quite sadness, but not quite cynicism either. "And it isn't only the men who want to see you go, Captain. Do you have any concept of what has happened in this city? We were all of us raised to participate in a dance—the men to cherish, the women to be cherished in return, the men to rule and work, the women to be protected and sheltered. We knew what we were—we had harmony in those times, Captain.

"We have all passed through a hell of terror and pain, of toil and despair. We—Tarrin and I, and every man and every woman—fought not only for our city but for the dream of that way of life, that dance. We thought that with victory, all that old comfort of being what we were raised to be would be restored. But the men have returned to find the dream that sustained them in the mines forever broken. The women—" She paused, then went on, her voice level and cool. "Most of those women who did not fight did not even want what has happened. They wanted to be free of Altiokis, but not at the price that we have forced them to pay. We have pushed chaos and struggle into their lives without their consent. You yourself, Captain, and your lady, know that you cannot unknow what you know. And even those who fought find victory an ambiguous fruit to the taste."

As if against his will, the Wolf's eyes went to where Wilarne's husband and son stood without her, their eyes both sullen and confused. How many others of the troop, he wondered, would meet with that mingling of outrage and incomprehending hurt? Not only from those close to them, he now saw—not only from the men. Most of the women in the crowd were silent and looked across at him and at the ladies he had trained with wariness and disapproval, with the anger of those who had something taken from them without their consent and who did not want what was offered in return. The seeds of bitterness were sown and could not be picked out of the soil again.

And, logically, he saw that he was the only one they could banish. He was not the disrupter of the dance, but he was the only one of those new and uneasy things that they could dispose of without tearing still further the already riven fabric of their lives.

He looked back at the young man before him, clothed in the stiff white ceremonial garb of the ruler of the city, and felt an unexpected stab of pity for the poor devil who would have to sort out the ungodly mess. At least he and Starhawk could get on their horses and ride away from it—and there was a good deal to be said simply for that. He grinned and held out his hand. Tarrin, who had been watching his face with some trepidation visible beneath his own calm expression relaxed and returned the smile and the handclasp with broken-knuckled, pick-calloused fingers.

"Along with the curses of parliament," Tarrin said quietly, "I give you my personal thanks."

"Of the two, that's what matters." The Wolf glanced over his shoulder at the sound of hooves clicking on the pavement behind them. The crowd opened in a long aisle, from the steps where they stood to the flower-twined stone lacework of the Spired Bridge, which led toward the Golden Gate of the city and to the countryside beyond. Down it, a couple of pages in the livery of the city were leading two horses, with saddlebags already packed and the Wolf's and Starhawk's weapons strapped to the cantles. One of the pages, it amused him to see, was Sheera's daughter, Trella.

With a mercenary's typical preoccupation, Starhawk gave one of the saddlebags an experimental prod. It clinked faintly, and Sun Wolf asked, "All ten thousand there?" That was a patent impossibility; no horse in creation could have carried the unwieldy bulk of that much gold.

"The rest of the money will be forwarded to you at Wrynde, Captain," Sheera said, "as soon as it can be raised by parliament. Have no fear of that."

Looking from her calmly enigmatic face to the disgruntled countenances of the members of parliament, the Wolf only muttered to Starhawk, "Where have we heard that before?"

She swung lightly into the saddle, her fair hair catching the sunlight like pale silk. "What the hell does it matter?" she asked. "We're not going back there, anyway."

The Wolf thought about that and realized that she was right. He had sold his sword for the last time—like the women, like Starhawk, he was no longer what he had been. "No," he said quietly. "No, I don't suppose we are." Then he grinned to himself, mounting, and reined back to where Tarrin and Sheera still stood at the foot of the steps. Sun Wolf held out his hand. "My lady Sheera?"

Sheera of Mandrigyn came forward and raised her lace-gloved hand for his formal kiss. In former days he would have asked the permission of Tarrin, but the King said no word, and the glance Sheera cast them silenced the parliament, like a spell of dumbness. For the first time since he had seen them together, Sun Wolf noticed that Sheera stood an inch or so taller than Tarrin.

He bent from the saddle and touched her knuckles to his lips. Their eyes met—but if she had any regrets, or wished for things between them to be or to have been other than they were, he could find no trace of it in that serene and haughty gaze. She was Sheera of Mandrigyn, and no one would ever see her with mud and rain and sweat on her face again.

He said softly, "Don't let the men get your ladies down, Commander."

She elevated a contemptuous eyebrow. "What makes you think they could?"

The Wolf laughed. He found that he could take a great deal of pleasure in seeing those he loved behave exactly like themselves. "Nothing," he said. "May your ancestors bless you, as you will bless those who follow you with blood and spirit."

He reined his horse away; but as he did so, Starhawk rode forward and leaned to take Sheera's hand. A few words were exchanged; then, in a very unqueenly gesture, Sheera slapped Starhawk's knee, and Starhawk laughed. She rode back to him at a decorous walk; the crowd moved aside again to let them ride from the city.

As they moved under the flamboyant turrets of the Spired Bridge, Sun Wolf whispered, "What did she say to you?"

Starhawk glanced at him in the shadows, her wide, square shoulders and pale hair silhouetted against the rainbow colors of the throng they had just left. Past her, the Wolf could still see Tarrin and Sheera, two glittering dolls beneath the scintillating bulk of the Cathedral of Mandrigyn.

"She told me to look after you," the Hawk said.

Sun Wolf's spine stiffened with indignation. "She told *you* to look after *me* . . . ?"

Her grin was white in the gloom of the covered bridge. "Race you to the city gates."

To those standing in the great square of the Cathedral, all that could be heard of the departure of Sun Wolf and Starhawk from the town was the sudden thunder of galloping hooves in the tunnel of the enclosed bridge and, like an echo, a drift of unseemly laughter.

ABOUT THE AUTHOR

At various times in her life, Barbara Hambly has been a high-school teacher, a model, a waitress, a technical editor, a professional graduate student, an all-night clerk at a liquor store, and a karate instructor. Born in San Diego, she grew up in Southern California, with the exception of one high-school semester spent in New South Wales, Australia. Her interest in fantasy began with reading *The Wizard of Oz* at an early age and has continued ever since.

She attended the University of California, Riverside, specializing in medieval history. In connection with this, she spent a year at the University of Bordeaux in the south of France and worked as a teaching and research assistant at UC Riverside, eventually earning a Master's Degree in the subject. At the university, she also became involved in karate, making Black Belt in 1978 and competing in several national-level tournaments.

Her books include the Darwath Trilogy: *Time of the Dark*, *The Walls of Air*, and *The Armies of Daylight*, and a historical whodunit, *The Quirinal Hill Affair*, set in ancient Rome.